# WHISPERS ON A

*By the same author*

Blind Date

# WHISPERS ON A PILLOW

Philippa Todd

Hodder & Stoughton

Copyright ©1998 by Philippa Todd

First published in Great Britain in 1998 by Hodder and Stoughton
A division of Hodder Headline PLC

The right of Philippa Todd to be identified as the Author of the Work has been asserted by her in accordance with the Copyright, Designs and Patents Act 1988.

10 9 8 7 6 5 4 3 2 1

All rights reserved. No part of this publication may be reproduced, stored in a retrieval system, or transmitted, in any form or by any means without the prior written permission of the publisher, nor be otherwise circulated in any form of binding or cover other than that in which it is published and without a similar condition being imposed on the subsequent purchaser.

All characters in this publication are fictitious and any resemblance to real persons, living or dead, is purely coincidental.

British Library Cataloguing in Publication Data
Todd, Philippa
Whispers on a pillow
1. Love stories
I. Title
823.9'14 [F]

ISBN 0 340 68024 5

Typeset by Palimpsest Book Production Limited,
Polmont, Stirlingshire
Printed and bound in Great Britain by
Mackays of Chatham PLC, Chatham, Kent

Hodder and Stoughton
A division of Hodder Headline PLC
338 Euston Road
London NW1 3BH

To Craig, for his love

Grateful thanks for their help to Edward Orton M.D., Janet Shields B.Sc.(Hons.) D.C.R., and C.V.Randall, Master Army Aviator, USA, Ret.

# ONE

'Two sugars,' I thought I heard him call from somewhere within his luxury apartment.

Lord, how I wished that I had not agreed to share his bed.

I was only taking the route through his kitchen now, on my way out, as swiftly as I decently could, to swill under the tap and leave to drain our water glasses from the night before.

Nor was I in the best of moods, having waited while he took for ever over his ablutions in the bathroom. Even though I'd explained to him that, owing to pressure of work, it was important I made an early start.

Maybe I could use his son's bathroom, I ventured, since the lad was breaking horses in Australia, post Eton College and pre Cambridge University? Regretfully, no, came the answer; it was locked.

Locked, for heaven's sake. What could he be hiding in there; or did I perhaps know?

Didn't Hugo have a spare key? His deafness came in handy then; I let it pass.

Anyway, thanks to those unforeseen hold ups, I would now be late for a vital meeting with the builders at my new premises. Due to be ready for their launch in two days' time, such items as the completion of the black and gold sign writing, the painting of the interior walls, and dare I mention getting rid of the electricians was of paramount importance. Only the expectation of my arrival, I was well aware, would keep things moving at even the steadiest pace.

I moved enquiringly to the doorway that led from kitchen to dining-room and thence from dining-room to sitting-room in his open-plan apartment, but could not tell where the voice was coming from.

'Excuse me, Hugo, I didn't quite hear,' I called in reply, projecting my voice and trying to keep the agitation I was feeling out of it, as I noted the time on the kitchen clock.

'Two sugars, old thing,' his voice came back. 'For me . . . in my tea, darling.'

I walked through the dining-room and across the sitting-room towards his voice, which seemed to be coming from within a large bay window that had been designed to show a waterside spectacular of the Thames below.

Sure enough, there he was, elfin-like, hidden from my view by the wings of a high-backed leather armchair which was placed with its back to the room and facing the window, thereby allowing the occupant to appreciate the glories of a summer morning and the activity on the river. Which I'm sure would have given him pleasure, had he not been holding the *Financial Times* wide open in front of his face.

The face, I might add, that did not turn one iota towards me as he spoke, but remained staring at the stock market columns through half-moon reading glasses, as though he'd been paralysed by the plummeting market prices of his no doubt substantial investments.

His tailored silk maroon paisley dressing-gown was neatly tied by a sash at the waist. His racehorse thin white ankles and slightly wrinkled calves showed above his tiny feet. These were thrust into wine-coloured velvet, gold-monogrammed slippers which are, as you know, the hallmark of the aristocrat. I've often found myself wondering, do the entwined embroidered initials face outwards for the onlooker, or towards the wearer to remind him who he is? But I've never felt I could stare for long enough to find out, and the morning in question was no exception.

'Sorry, Hugo, I don't have time,' I answered as I reached him. 'How about if I put the kettle on for you and drop a teabag into a mug?'

He looked up at me as though I had let loose in Taiwanese, gave a 'humphing' type of snort, and pouted. 'Bad show, Catherine, old girl. Now I suppose I'll have to wait till my secretary shows up?'

Or make it yourself, perhaps, I longed to suggest, as the urge to slap him on the top of his bald sun-spotted head very nearly overcame me.

He usually winters in Jamaica, and obviously forgets to wear a protective sun-bonnet or he wouldn't have the rather unsightly problem. But to show that I was a nice lady really, despite my lack of early morning humour, I planted a kiss between the motley discolourations, and wished him a fond goodbye. Then I quickly battled with the six locks on his front door before guilt and pity overcame me and I found myself involved in preparing rice crispies and toast on a tray; and escaped via the lift to the basement garage six floors below.

I hadn't wanted to stay the night with Hugo one bit, but he'd been begging me to do so for the whole of the six months I'd been dating him.

Believe me, I wouldn't stay again. I shall draw a veil over the night's activity, save to say that it wasn't very active. Which suited me fine.

We'd met at a dinner party during what I have since come to call my Old Fart period. Every man I met who looked my way was over sixty-five, it seemed. And however many years they admitted to, I swear some were nearer eighty.

It didn't do much for my confidence, this age thing, and my confidence threshold had been battered enough as it was through the years.

How old did they think I was, for God's sake, these people who so cheerfully paired me off with OFs? Didn't they know any middle-aged men, or, dare I suggest, even slightly younger ones than that? I'm not yet fifty, but not far off, and I intend to stay on the right side of that half-century for as long as possible.

My daughter, Abigail, said that I was not to worry, and tried to persuade me that those sort of distinguished OFs didn't like brainless dolly-birds (it was news to me, however). To them, she said, I was a sophisticated younger woman, and that should make me feel good. It doesn't. I much prefer the idea of being a sophisticated *older* woman dated by besotted young men. Well, a girl can dream, can't she?

If I have to settle for older men as dates, then so be it. But from now on it will have to be platonic. I cannot cope with being an old man's darling, or face staying the night with one of them ever again.

Not even a man of distinction like Hugo, an old soldier of merit, a retired SAS major with enough medals for wartime bravery to fill a whole cabinet in his country house and make it impossible to wear them all at once on parade, I would think, without assistance.

It was the state in which he'd left the bathroom that made me disinclined to linger even long enough to do my teeth, let alone shower and make myself presentable.

Apart from the toothpaste in the washbasin there was the question of the lavatory. I mean, was the man blind? Couldn't he see that he'd left a brown floating island there, looking forlornly like a miniature South Pacific atoll when the French had finished with it? And what a way to treat a so-called girlfriend. Didn't I even mean enough to this Lord of the Manor to rate a double flush?

My desire to decamp as quickly as possible now meant that I had to go home through early morning rush-hour London traffic before beginning a day's work that was in danger of lasting till midnight at best.

Never mind that the night before I had carefully taken to Hugo's place a clean white shirt and a beige summer suit in a plastic cover to avoid that very journey, and enable me to go on to do an important fitting in a stately home after I had talked to the builders.

I have a dress-designing business, you see, and I'm in the throes of moving to larger premises: a three-storeyed building that used to be a town house in Georgian times, and now has a pretty shop frontage.

My accountant had a fit about my affording it when I told him I wanted to make the move. But I'd managed to bring him round with flattering words about appreciating his concern.

For the first time in my dressmaking career there'll be room for a really large cutting area, and space for the right-sized table on which to work. I do all the pattern-making myself, you see, and the hand cutting of the garments.

Much time has been wasted in the past having lady outworkers, and needing to deliver and collect the work has been quite a drag. Now, I shall have the room to house us all under one roof, and to stock a few accessories as well; I've already made one trip to Italy for luxury items such as belts, scarves, and bags.

I couldn't quite overcome the feeling, as I drove out of the front area of Hugo's apartment block and into the heavy morning traffic that was more crawling than flowing, that my annoyance was not all Hugo's fault.

I was consumed by guilt over going off to stay the night with a man whose bed I didn't relish sharing. What *had* I been thinking of? Especially at my age. It seemed positively immoral, and it didn't sit well on my middle-class conscience.

But then again, I asked myself, how far was I supposed to go just because we'd been to the theatre and had a nice supper? Had he, do you suppose, forgotten that we'd shared the expenses? Or that afterwards I'd honoured him with a quicky in his bed before he'd downed a large Scotch without offering me one, turned his back, and instantly gone to sleep?

Pressure of work and frequent headaches in the last few weeks have made me easily irritated, I admit, and it came into play, to prove my point, as I sat in the traffic in the middle of Battersea Bridge, trying hard not to sound my horn at the chap in front of me, who went on reading his morning paper when he could have moved a few inches and so helped my tension.

Add that to my annoyance that it was too early, in most cases, for me to make calls from my car, and that the builder, who should have been available, was not answering his mobile phone, which meant that he was not, as yet, on site, and you will get the picture.

But all of that's by the way. If I was unable to cope with OFs, I shouldn't go out with them. I should settle down to a life without men, and concentrate only on my work.

**Philippa Todd**

The trouble is though, you see, and the fact gets me nowhere at all, I prefer younger men. As we women all know, there's no future in that, because men, in general, prefer women younger than themselves.

I fantasize sometimes of meeting my dream man and living happily with him, sharing sorrows and joys, sharing a bed; in fact, just sharing.

But I've already been married to two men whom everyone thought were dreamy, and I've lived *sans mariage* for a spell with a handsomely rugged man, mainly because he made me laugh and had an inner-city sense of humour that was new to me, whom my children called my bit of rough. That was, until he got himself rehoused at Her Majesty's pleasure for bank fraud, while never actually letting on how he'd laid his hands on some of my hard-earned money, never mind about the bank people, without me even feeling the pain until it was too late.

Hallelujah! Home at last.

I collected my dog from a neighbour, let myself in through the front door of my tiny terrace house and headed up the stairs, tearing off last night's clothing and heading for the bathroom.

With a start like that one, I could hardly expect it to be a normal sort of day. And it wasn't.

But going home unexpectedly had its upside. It meant that I could tell Sacha, my Alsatian bitch, that never again would I dump her in favour of an Old Fart. And I could drink a large cup of much-needed coffee and swallow the working girl's substitute for the hearty English breakfast, a well-buttered, toasted muffin.

I checked my telephone messages and to my delight there was a message from the man who'd brought my three children into the world a long time ago: family friend Richard Crossley.

Richard is a nice man, handsome, young-looking too, and definitely not on my OF list. He's retired now and lives alone, his wife having run off a long time ago with an Argentinian breeder of polo ponies and a fortune in a Swiss bank. I'm fond of him, and I know that he likes me a lot too.

I returned his call there and then and we made a date to meet. He often takes me out, and I look forward to it.

'Congratulations, Cathy,' he said, after a pause.

I didn't get the point. Was he making some sort of a joke? Did he mean about the opening of the new premises? He didn't know what I'd been doing last night, did he?

'Haven't you looked in your morning paper?'

'No, not yet. Should I?' (At least it wasn't about last night.)

'Page fifteen, must rush. I'll pick you up for lunch on Sunday.'

I hurriedly spread open the paper on the kitchen table and there it was, making me flush and feel rather nervous now that I was faced with it. A week sooner than I'd expected: a half-page spread on me and the business. And what is more, surprisingly for once, it didn't mention that I was the ex-wife of the notable Clive Anthony.

Looking down at my own head-and-shoulders photograph made me blush as though I were being watched. It was a flattering picture too, and I don't get many of those, the camera not being too keen on small insignificant noses and wide eyes topped off with short thick dark hair that only looks good if I keep it well washed and blow dry it upside down.

Still, I suppose I should be thankful for one thing: I have not yet gone grey.

The telephone rang. I looked at my watch; God, I really had to get to the new premises. Should I pick it up, or let it go on to the machine? I snatched it up.

'I'm so happy about the article, Cathy,' she said, all breathy and caring.

It was my favourite client, the golden-haired princess with the largest pair of blue eyes God ever created.

'You're very kind,' I answered humbly, touched that she had taken the trouble to telephone.

'You must be thrilled,' she continued. 'And what about that great picture?'

I could scarcely speak for smiling. 'Flattering, isn't it?' was all I could think of to say in response.

She then wanted to know, all laughter and good humour, now that I was going to be renowned, would I like to make her fitting later in the day than arranged, or even tomorrow, perhaps?

'Not at all, I have heaps of time,' I lied to her. Well, what else could I have said to a princess with enough gumption to treat a commoner nicely.

'Are you sure?' she asked, with concern in her voice. 'You do sound the tiniest bit fraught.'

'Well, an hour later perhaps, if it will not cause a major inconvenience for you?'

'Not even a small one.' She laughed. 'Shall we say four o'clock?'

The dog was first into the car. She doesn't seem to care much where she's going, as long as she's not left behind.

The traffic was appalling, I was anxious about the time, and I needed petrol. London buses by their dozens were being rerouted ahead of me. No one was moving and side exits were blocked. Whole streets were closed. The newsreader on the car radio told me that yet another bomb scare was in operation, and my anxiety seemed to climax in my head as my adrenalin flow doubled.

The driver of a cab, behind and one vehicle to the left of me, sounded his horn at the car in front for no apparent reason in the stationary traffic. He appeared to be going ape behind the wheel, putting himself in danger of having a seizure, I thought.

I looked at the car driver in question, who was looking at me. He shook his head, shrugged his shoulders and smiled. It was the friendly smile of a man for a female driver, stuck and bored, like he was.

But it was enough to make me wish that I had a male partner to telephone, to whinge to about the traffic, to ask what he fancied for dinner later; anything.

Some of my clients have the right idea, those rich enough to afford it, or whose husbands are not inclined to mind. They find unattached and upwardly mobile toy boys, and either move them into their homes, or install them in separate apartments. Then provide them with a financial allowance, a sophisticated wardrobe, and promises of exotic travel. They tell them what they like to have happen in bed, and which nights each week they will be expected to escort them socially, then give them a free rein to have a life of their own if they want it.

Sounds all right to me, but there's not a hope of my achieving it. From what I hear in the fitting-room when my mouth is full of pins, you need serious money for that way of life.

I have some lovely clients, I'm happy to say. Most of them rich, a few of them well known and some of them titled. And, can you believe, two princesses. One of them you already know about; to my mind at least, she's the most beautiful princess in the world. What with that figure and those long legs, she's a dream to design clothes for.

She doesn't give us her most important clothes to make, not her evening dresses for grand balls, or her high-profile suits. But she lets me design some of her day dresses, and most of her casual trousers and blazers. Meantime, I dream that one day she will think us good enough to extend her range in our direction.

The other princess is from the Emirates, and is a very nice person. She buys me embarrassingly expensive presents, and gives me lots of orders for clothes, I'm happy to say. Her money seems to flow like water; or should I say like oil.

Making clothes for the sort of ladies who can afford to come to me is taxing work. But give or take the conflict of working while bringing up children, or battling with the occasional heartbreak, I've enjoyed it.

I don't take on problem figures (that's dressmaker-speak for fat), because their owners don't like what they see in the mirror no matter how hard you try. And it causes frustration all round.

Some of my present clients I knew when I was married to Clive Anthony, the well-known and much-loved (by many a lady) plastic surgeon. They are usually the ones who ask me to their parties, and that's how I get to meet so many OFs.

I enjoy my work, tough as it is, and I'm happy again at last. That is, apart from not liking living alone, and loathing the weekends, unless I'm asked into the country or manage to see friends.

If not, I usually go and potter in my workrooms, and take my dog along for company. But when I look through the windows and see everyone strolling along in pairs, drat it, especially on a Sunday afternoon, it doesn't do much to perk me up, or make me feel needed. I'm a woman who *wants* to be with a man, you see, no matter what I say.

Let's face it, I'm seeing and dealing with women all day long, and while I like the idea of driving into the country with a girlfriend for Sunday lunch, or happily queueing for brunch in Knightsbridge on a Saturday at the Fifth Floor Café, and shop gazing in Sloane Street, having lots of laughs together as only women can, for going to the cinema on a Saturday afternoon or watching sport on TV with the feet up, well, I prefer a man's company for that.

My panic became total when there was yet another traffic hold-up, as a mounted battalion of soldiers in full dress uniform, astride shining black horses sporting perfect leather and dazzling brass, attracting hundreds of tourists with cameras akimbo, were leaving Buckingham Palace after changing the guard.

If only there could be a stampede, I thought; of horses, not tourists, at least it might create a passage for my motor through the mêlée. However, progress was finally made, if slowly, and when at last I could see my new premises coming into view, and the sign-writer working away over the Georgian-paned window, it was a happy moment.

I long to dress that window myself, and work front-of-house sometimes. To have the opportunity to change out of my work clothes of jeans and tee-shirt under my workroom white coat into something more dressy for welcoming clients.

We're a small team, more like a family than a firm. We often all have lunch together, and usually our coffee breaks, and use these times to sound off and swap opinions.

I double-parked, put my hazard lights on, and hoped for the best. It was just a case of my seeing the builders briefly, checking that the carpenters were working to instructions, and having a few words with Fran, my American secretary, who was overseeing till I arrived in the interests of speed.

Fran is a great girl, very bright, attractive, loyal, and a good friend.

We both agreed right off when she came to work for me not to subscribe to the mania of the title 'secretary' going out and 'personal assistant' coming in. My person doesn't particularly need assisting, but my secretarial abilities certainly do.

She told me at her interview that she had made the decision to move to England from the States because she felt like a change of scenery. She also wanted a total change of occupation, she said, somewhat cagily I thought, and I gathered from her curriculum vitae that she'd previously worked with the National Security Agency at Fort Meade in Maryland. All that derring-do, I thought, how exciting . . .

'I'm gay,' she'd said, positively and of a sudden, as I finished reading her CV, as though anxious to get it out.

It hung in the air for a moment, until I lifted my eyes.

'I came to that conclusion after two unsuccessful romances, and since homosexuals aren't allowed to work in the NSA I resigned. I'm not quite out of the closet yet, though. Is there a problem with any of that?'

'No,' I answered, rather too quickly, unable to withhold a mental picture of the gay rights movement banging on my door and accusing me of prejudice if I didn't take her on. I derided myself for being a bigot.

'Normally I don't say anything over here,' she continued in a measured, slightly Southern accent, looking me right in the eye. 'But, well, you do deal with women, and I feel duty bound to mention it. You look like a person who would say so if you felt threatened.'

She looked so feminine, so fresh and beautiful, that the first emotion I felt was one of sorrow that she would never experience the joy of having sex with a man she loved, and never know the fulfilment of childbearing. And had she thought enough about lesbian life, I wondered, quite overlooking the fact that it would be something out of her control.

'I'm not altogether comfortable with it myself,' she added, as though reading my mind. 'I prefer to be among heterosexual people, and I get on extremely well with them. In my last job I worked almost exclusively with men, and one of them is still a very good buddy. It's just that from now on I only want to be involved emotionally and sexually with a woman, and the thought of a man violating my body makes me cringe.'

She smiled gently at me as she spoke, as though she could see that I was naïve on the subject and she wanted to help me over the hurdle.

'You've taken me aback,' I said. 'I have this dreadful urge to say something motherly and trite, to ask if you'll be happy when you're old and you don't have a man to protect you, and you might be terribly lonely if you don't find the right woman. And then again, it's none of my business.' I knew that I was digging a hole for myself.

She had a way, and has it still, of looking right into my soul. 'You don't have a man to protect you, I suspect,' she answered. Adding quickly, 'Not that you're old. And I think that you might be terribly lonely too. Right? How do any of us know what's in store? We should live our lives one day at a time and grab what happiness we can. Sexual preference has nothing to do with that.'

It was quite a speech. But she was right. I told her that I hadn't meant to pry.

'No problem,' she said.

We shook hands on her coming for a trial period and we'd see how it all worked out. And that was a year ago.

The sign-writer came down his ladder, stepped aside, and watched my face for the expression of approval and, hopefully, pleasure. He'd made an excellent job of inscribing my name on the fascia-board; and I told him so.

Fran, watching us, opened the door while telling the dog and me to mind not to brush against the wet pristine white paint. Sacha wagged her tail in anticipation of Fran giving her a fondle as she usually did.

'Great stuff in the paper,' she said, smiling broadly. 'Nice picture too. The girls are thrilled, and lots of people have left messages for you. I have them with me.'

'Thanks, Fran,' I answered, brushing past her carefully. 'I haven't read the article properly yet. Do you fancy coming round to my house tonight? I'll send out for something, and we can run through a few vital last-minute things regarding the launch?'

'Sure,' she answered.

'So, let's hear about problems. There surely have to be some,' I said, listening to the distant blare of the workmen's radio from a room upstairs.

'Okay. There's been a water leak in your new office from a radiator above. No real damage, and mended now. The carpenters got their measurements a touch wrong on the corner shelving here in reception. I've sent them back to their workshop to put it right. That's about it.'

'And the electricians?'

'Ah, well, I'd hoped you wouldn't ask. A slight problem there. The recessed lights in the front fitting-room don't recess properly. I told them you'd go ballistic. But I suggest you don't, and let them put it right after the launch. No one will actually notice after one glass of champagne.'

Into the car again, and over to my old workrooms. Where, apart from the serious business of packing up ready for the move, I hoped that someone, anyone, was seeing to the serious business of finishing my dress for the big night.

The trouble was, a lot of our clients wanted new dresses for the launch, knowing that in all probability they would be photographed for the fashion mags, and I've had a tough time slotting my own garment in for making up.

I sketched it sitting up in my bed over a mug of hot milk, and cut it out in the workroom late one night. Then Suzie, my head sewing lady, and the one in charge, who's been with me since the earliest days when we worked from the kitchen table, the days when my elder son Charles was still a baby, took over the responsibility of making it up.

I'd found some pimento red silk among my stock, and I'll be wearing a daringly backless long-sleeved slinky number before I'm too old for such a style, or have too many wrinkles. I've cut it on the bias, so that it moves with the body and kicks out correctly when I walk. Suzie is hand-stitching all the seams, even though I suggested she cheat a little and machine-stitch at least a few of them.

I read my messages, swallowed a coffee on the hoof, then kept quiet while Freda, the fitter, helped me into my almost-finished dress. Apart from a nip and tuck here and there I was more than pleased with it and told a beaming Suzie so as she hovered in the fitting-room doorway, and looked me up and down like a headteacher. I felt the need to tell her that, apart from my muffin that morning, I had eaten very little for a week, to ensure that I am flat where I'm supposed to be.

After that I bundled Freda into the back seat of my car to cradle

# Philippa Todd

the princess's dress, which was carefully encased in calico, across her knees, and we were off to Kensington.

'Nice jacket,' the princess said to me as we were shown into her private sitting-room; all chintzy, and bright and not at all starchy, making one think of cucumber sandwiches for Sunday tea, morning papers scattered on the floor and happy, smiling young people. A world away from the swathed silk-velvet rooms of the rich where I usually sat to await my clients' pleasure. Which sometimes took ages.

I'd hoped she'd notice the jacket; it was the very reason I was wearing it: an understated, well-tailored casual jacket that I'd been endeavouring to perfect for almost a year.

'Thank you,' I answered modestly, while Freda, looking on, beamed delightedly at the comment.

'It would look a treat in light navy, would it not?'

It would indeed. I made a mental note to have a pattern on hand, in case she should ask me to make her one.

'You look great, Cathy.'

I smiled as fittingly for a compliment from a princess as I knew how.

She meant the jacket of course, but that was okay. It was music to my ears.

I was tired, bushed, exhausted. But I forced myself to change into sweat-pants and tee-shirt when I returned to the workrooms and jogged for a spell around Hyde Park with the dog at my heels. Well, we girls have to stay healthy, don't we?

By the time I reached home it was gone seven o'clock and Fran was due round in an hour. I tugged off my Reeboks in the hall, fed the starving dog in the kitchen, changed her water bowl, took two aspirin for my continuing headache, showered, and stretched myself out on my bed to relax, and, at last, to digest the newspaper article.

Fran and I always have so much to talk about. It was a necessary release of tension for me to talk about things other than work. And Fran is a good listener.

Running a business takes its toll and causes anxieties, and there are times, as I've said, now that I don't have a mate, when I desperately miss being able to unload personal neuroses.

'The problem is for people like you, Cathy,' Richard Crossley had once said to me, at a time when I was feeling particularly vulnerable, 'you appear to be so put together, so able to cope with everything, it can work against you.' How right he had been.

'A dollar for your thoughts,' Fran said, as we finished off the Chinese takeaway at the kitchen table, drained the last of the *vin du pays* into our glasses, and I had fallen silent.

I took another sip of wine. 'Just navel-gazing. And thinking about my father. You'll meet him at the launch.'

'You're close, aren't you?'

'Yes, I think we are,' I answered thoughtfully. 'He wanted me to be a boy, you know, brought me up like one; always called me Charlie.'

'That must have been quite a burden. But perhaps it explains why you're the kind of diverse person you are.'

I contemplated opening another bottle of wine, and leaned back on my kitchen chair. 'I remember once when I was about ten, I fell out of a tree. He told me that it was best not to cry.

'"Little girls cry, Charlie," he said.

'"But I am a girl, Daddy," I answered, somewhat distressed.

'He patted my head and said, as if to himself, "Yes, of course you are."

'But it started me wondering; caused me a lot of confusion.'

'If parents only stopped to think more about how they influenced their children wouldn't it be a help? And that influence lasts the whole of our lives,' Fran said thoughtfully.

I crossed the kitchen and selected another bottle of red wine from the rack on a far wall. 'I longed for my mother to be more positive,' I said as I went. 'To give me direction. But she simply couldn't help me through the things that bothered me most: like the pubes experience, and menstruating.'

Fran drained her glass. 'Wasn't that time just too awful? I hated it.'

'I wouldn't go through that time again for anything,' I reminisced, as I pulled the cork. 'A girl at school, I remember, asked me if I'd "started". Not knowing about periods because I hadn't been told, I thought she meant had I begun a special essay we'd been given to write, and I answered, "Yes, ages ago." It was years before I solved the mystery of why I was turned into a minor class celebrity overnight.'

'And what about figuring out where babies came from?' Fran asked, laughing, collecting up food cartons.

I poured more wine into both our glasses, and we sat down again.

'Don't start me off,' I begged her. 'When I asked my mother that one, she told me that a man planted a seed under a bush. She wasn't too far wrong really. And then that seed magically found another seed, she said, and together they slowly grew into a baby. I worried myself sick wondering what happened to those babies-in-the-making if the nights turned cold.

'Of course when I was invited to discuss the subject *sotto voce* with the rest of my classmates, on account of I'd "started" and that made me special, in knowledgeable fashion I recounted my mother's story.'

'Oh, my God, you didn't,' Fran said, leaning back and slapping her thighs. 'What happened then?'

'They knew quite a bit more than I did, so they fell about laughing. I was the class joke; and I had trouble forgiving my mother for that inaccurate pearl of wisdom.'

'Was she nice, your mother?'

'Yes,' I told her. 'She was lovely. Quiet, rather fearful of the unknown. She knew the Latin name for every flower, I remember. I have always thought that she was born out of her time though. She'd have made a really wonderful Edwardian writer of genteel stories. Or been the perfect diarist, perhaps.'

'I must go,' Fran said, suddenly looking at her watch. 'I'm unbelievably tired.'

I stood up, wishing that Fran had not mentioned the tired word.

'I'll call a cab from the rank down the road.'

'Thank you, Cathy. By the way, would you mind if I bring Scott Peters to the launch?'

'Scott Peters?'

'Yes. You know, my American buddy from the agency. He'll be over here.'

She stood, and gathered up her things. We went slowly down the hall towards the front door.

'Of course you can. We could do with the odd extra man.'

'That's what I thought.'

The cab driver rang the doorbell.

'Is he nice, this Scott Peters?'

'Good steady type. You'll like him.'

I opened the door. We kissed cheeks.

I reckoned I'd just about manage to lock up, put the lights out and make it to bed before I fell asleep.

God, it was great to be under the counterpane. And joy of joys, my cleaning lady Madge had changed the sheets. How I did love the feel of fresh newly laundered bed-linen. Heaven, sheer heaven.

My eyes closed without any help from me.

Scott, did Fran say his name was? Scott was a nice enough name; the surname was Petro, or Petrill, something like that.

But a good steady type? Yuck, how boring. He probably wore apple green trousers, like Yanks do, and had a short-back-and-sides haircut. I should have asked her where he came from. Mid-West Bible belt, most likely; Jesus, I hoped not. And I hoped I hadn't done the wrong thing saying that she could bring him to the launch. Supposing he wore his apple green trousers?

And he just might. Apart from mythical characters like James Bond, spies never seem to dress well, do they? I mean, take some of those scruffy chaps one sees on the television news being nabbed in Russia for exchanging secrets. They often don't even look clean. Something to do with blending in with the rest of the world, I suppose.

Well, it was too late now. God, I hoped he didn't chew gum, as well. If he did I just might lose my cool.

# TWO

Why is it that you feel you've done the humping and the hauling and the dragging and shifting all by yourself when you spend time with removal men?

Now, dammit, thanks to that tiring experience yesterday, I've overslept this morning on our very important day.

Oh, for the invention of a magic pill one could swallow to lessen the bags of fatigue and the crow's feet that seem to settle under the eyes just when you least want to suffer them.

The late start would entail my rushing like mad to get to the new premises at the same time as the rest of the team, and would mean all systems going at the greatest of speed for most of the day if we were to be ready in time for the Big Launch.

Only my third morning of trying to get to the new premises on time, and already I was having nagging doubts about the distance.

Any previous ideas I had entertained of returning home before the party, in time for a rest, a facial and ice packs on the eyes, had flown out through the window; it would be wiser, it seemed, to take everything I needed with me, plan to put my feet up for a spell if I could on my new office desk, and forget the rest.

The builders had all but finished, thank the Lord, give or take a couple of door handles still to be fixed, a few patches of paint to be touched up, and the usual rush at the end for the electricians. What is it with electricians, do you suppose? Why can they never get to the end of the job until they've experienced the pleasure of you begging on bended knees for them to finish, and leave?

Later than intended, therefore, I finally bundled Madge into the front seat of my car, the dog into the back, and everything else that was needed into the boot: such diverse items, that is, as double rations of dog food, an extra pair of sheer tights, along with headache pills, anaesthetising foot spray, and the all-important make-up.

Madge is a lovely Cockney woman who 'does' for me three times a week. Today is her idea of a special treat. Joining the team to prepare for the evening's entertainment was something she'd looked forward to for weeks.

'I loves company. An' I loves to 'ave a laugh,' she said to me. 'An' my old man, 'e don't understand that, miserable bugger.'

I'd wanted her to come as a guest, like the rest of the team. After all, we were close. She knew as much about me, and the ups and downs of my life as anyone did, and she'd been a loyal friend.

'No, I couldn't do that,' she'd said. 'I can't talk to those sort of people. Give me a tray to carry, or some of them ashtrays to empty and I'll be 'appy as Larry.'

'But you have a nice new dress, Madge.'

'Oh, yes, an' you was good enough to give it to me. I'm gonna wear it, an' all. Don't you worry, Mrs A., I won't let you down.'

It had occurred to me earlier that week, if all the people who had accepted our invitation to join us for the evening turned up, and those who had not replied came too, guests would be spilling out on to the road outside. I hoped that my new neighbours in King William Street would be understanding about the inconvenience.

To avoid any grief, Fran, when I told her of my concern, had a brilliant idea. She quickly designed little notes on her computer telling everyone within close proximity that we would be delighted if they called in for a glass of champagne during festivities, for us to have the honour of meeting them.

God help us, too, if *they* all turned up, I thought. Together with the professional gatecrashers who were the bane of all 'open door' parties in London, it could mean we'd run out of refreshment before the evening came to an end.

Things were shaping up nicely come midday.

Three ridiculously young female chefs had turned up to deliver an array of canapé miracles you simply would not believe possible. They worked for my daughter Abigail's catering company, which I'm pleased to say has become most successful.

'I want to cook, Mummy, not wear a stethoscope,' was all Abigail ever used to say, as she poured scorn on my plans to turn her into a doctor. This was after I'd abandoned any hope of her taking over my business eventually. Her artistic talents simply did not lie in that direction. Even trying to sew on a button that had come adrift, I noticed, gave her the hump.

What a cook she became though, that girl. I was proud of her.

The large ground-floor area of the new premises was to remain relatively unfurnished until after the party. So I had used some of my off-cuts of silks from the East to drape into odd corners for light relief and to give extra colour where I felt it was needed.

Large blow-ups of model girls wearing my creations from our prêt-à-porter range lined the French mustard walls of the reception area; and just for fun I'd slipped in two blow-ups of myself and my two special friends Rose and Charlotte from the wild sixties when we ourselves were modelling. All black-rimmed doe eyes we were, bloodless-looking lips and thin legs sticking out of very short dresses. Most weird and way out, but so 'in' at the time.

I'd hired a few narrow tables to go along the walls to provide a surface for ashtrays and to serve as a dumping ground for party detritus in general. A large floral display would stand in the middle of each table, but apart from that the area was empty, and the newly laid carpets had been professionally covered for the evening.

On the first floor, my spanking new office was to be locked when the party began, and the main fitting-room left open to receive coats. Though as the night was warm and lovely I did not anticipate many people needing that facility.

**Philippa Todd**

On the second floor, my as yet unused cutting- and sewing-rooms were to be left open for the overflow of guests.

The newly installed lift was out of bounds to everyone except butlers, chefs and the infirm, if any, and a security man was posted on it at ground-floor level. I did not want merry party guests overloading it and getting stuck between floors.

Besides, the staircase had been magnificently designed in Georgian times to weave strategically between floors. It was a joy to walk up, and, to my mind, it was the most attractive feature of the building.

When finally the flower displays were in position, and the last of the workmen had been shooed out through the front door, grabbing mislaid hammers, screwdrivers and half-empty paint pots as they went, we all sat around on the floor over sandwiches and pots of tea and discussed our outfits for the evening. The fun part had begun.

My dress was better even than I had anticipated, and the end result, with the hidden cross-seaming and hand-rolled hem being painstakingly finished off by a trainee seamstress at that very moment, was superb.

Fran, too, was to sport a new dress for the evening. It was a gift from the firm as was everyone else's: but in her case on the understanding that it could be copied, and was an opportunity for us to try out a new soft, flimsy, see-through, dropped-at-the-waist feminine style that I'd been working on for some time.

'What does this buddy of yours actually do?' I asked as I pinned up her dress an extra inch, and a seamstress stood by to make the changes quickly.

Fran waited until she had departed, then closed the door.

'He's on loan to the National Security Agency, for specialized surveillance from the air.'

'On loan from whom, exactly?' I removed the pin-holder from my wrist.

'Well, you know . . . a government department.'

'Over foreign countries, you mean?'

Fran busied herself getting back into her shirt and her trousers. 'Yes,' she answered.

'But isn't that spying? And dangerous?'

She looked right at me. 'Something like that. But that's between the two of us. And please don't mention to him that I've told you, should you find the time to speak with him.'

'So what do I say that he does if anyone asks me? I can hardly say meet my secretary's buddy what's-his-name, he eavesdrops on other people's lives from the air.'

'He would say that he's a corporate pilot, and leave it at that.'

We were parting company when I remembered to say, 'Tell me his name once more; you know what I'm like on names.'

'It's Scott Peters.'

'Ah, yes, Scott Peters. Even I should be able to remember a name like that.'

I was wary of moving my head too much when I returned from the hair magician, which caused the staff to tease me. Michael had managed, the Lord knows how, to put my hair up; and to help him in this near impossible direction he'd used a few 'extensions', and I'd not had my bob cut for a month in anticipation of him achieving success.

Now it looked so glamorous, with tiny tendrils falling casually around my neck and ears, I simply couldn't recognize myself.

I showered in the cubicle fitted into the corner of the prettily tiled ladies room after returning from taking the dog for a hurried run, and prepared to put on my make-up.

Two days previously I had invested in a whole new range of make-up to assist my confidence, and, indeed, the magic of 'honey beige' foundation and 'dark rose' blusher had done a lot for my self-esteem. Crow's feet and laughter lines disappeared under a creamy application of the 'honey beige', just as the beautician in the cosmetic department of Harvey Nichols had said they would.

Forgive me if I say it myself: my dress, when the time came for me to put it on, looked fantastic (well anyway, judging from what I saw in the mirror). And for a few hours at least I felt, if not a raving beauty, then as close to it as I was ever likely to get.

We all oohed and aahed over each other's dresses.

## Philippa Todd

Fran looked so pretty, Suzie looked so smart. Madge looked, well, like Madge in a party dress, with her hair newly permed, back-combed and immobilized with lacquer, and her lips a rather startling shade of magenta that clashed with the colour of her dress.

'You look great, Madge,' I heard one of the girls say to her.

'Sod off, flatterer,' the answer came back; in a fond fashion though, and accompanied by her friendly rasping laugh.

I greeted every guest at the door for almost an hour, feeling more nervous than I cared to admit, this being my first attempt at such a grand party.

I'd made several visits to the Tanning Shop with my launch night specifically in mind, and the best music to my ears was a constant comment on how well the red dress set off my Mediterranean suntan.

How did I ever find the time for holidays? guests wanted to know.

I just kept smiling.

Some of my clients came alone, the ones who did not have or did not want toy boys, or whose millionaire husbands were currently abroad doing big business deals in Argentina or the Philippines. Or at least pretending that they were in those sort of places while romping in king-sized beds in St John's Wood with their current mistresses.

Either way, I had asked a few of my OFs to come along to even out the numbers, and I'd invited Richard Crossley too, because he was so good-looking. I knew also that he would respond patiently to the ladies' medical questions on HRT treatment, how to cope if they'd gone off sex after the birth of their third child, and personal stuff like that.

I'd tried to limit the OFs to the reasonably interesting ones, or at least to the ones who were not hopelessly deaf. Or, if they were, then not so vain as to refuse to be seen wearing a hearing-aid.

I would have asked Hugo, only he'd had a major heart attack a few hours after the 'two sugars' incident and managed to land himself in hospital. He was, in fact, in intensive care; though I'm happy and relieved to say, off the danger list.

I wasn't going to mention it, because, well, I feel the tiniest bit guilty. Only, hell, how was I to know that he had a dicky heart and had sported a pacemaker for the last five years at least.

It wasn't my idea that we should attempt sex that fateful night, and I would have been more than happy not to have done so. Especially after I'd witnessed the size of the dinner he'd eaten, on the hottest May night in London for forty years; and him in a vest, and not yet having cast a clout, not even for bedtime.

The local member of parliament gallantly called in to honour his obligatory invitation, and fortunately I had Fran standing by to remind me of his name.

I say gallantly, because that very morning his picture loomed large in all the newspapers as the story broke that his ex-secretary had announced, rightly or wrongly, that she was pregnant by him. His equally gallant wife came too, smiling as only a politician's wife can, holding her husband's hand, and looking lovingly into his troubled eyes, hoping to show the world that there was nothing amiss in their family nest; the way we women tend to do, when husbands are in trouble.

What a launch that was in my new premises that night. What a great party. No drunks, no bad tempers, very few gatecrashers; and those who did crash all behaved so well, as far as I could see, that I had the hired security guards allow them to stay.

I doubt that too many deep and meaningful conversations took place because it was difficult to hear even your own voice in those crowded rooms, never mind other people's. But it didn't seem to matter; the whole building was full of beautiful people, who, in the main, only wanted to see and be seen. And I spied a few notebooks being scribbled in as the boys and girls of the press sorted out the wheat from the chaff.

We ran out of food long before people left, but that was because they wouldn't go home so I didn't feel too badly about it.

My clients looked divine to the last and plainest lady, and I felt proud that the dresses they wore, every single one, were designed by yours truly, and made by the team.

**Philippa Todd**

The unattached men, gays and heteros alike, and a few OFs, circulated well with the young and the lovely, and even with the dowager duchesses, of which there was a sprinkling. My two handsome sons also, under sufferance, did the rounds, and ardent toy boys too, when allowed to by their 'bosses'.

That lovely Princess of Hearts was very sweet; she called in on us for twenty minutes en route to making an unscheduled visit to the ballet. She charmed everyone in sight, looked lovely as always with her azure eyes shining and her tanned skin glowing, and she put my pa in a daze for a week on a mere introduction.

And, wait while I tell you: she wore the prototype of my short, sleeveless, body-skimming dress, that, as she knew, was to be the leader in my new prêt-à-porter range.

How about that for a helping hand from a woman of such classical distinction!

I couldn't help noticing, as I began to circulate, a gaggle of well-dressed women grouped around a stranger in a far corner of the reception area. I sneaked my distance specs from my small clutch bag and surreptitiously put them on, all the better to see him.

He was a total stranger, but a handsome one; and, as far as I was concerned, with looks like that he could stay as long as he wanted to. But security had to be observed with so many well-heeled women wearing so many rich pickings; and I could not allow gatecrashers to get away with it unchallenged. Or so I told myself.

Not able to see a security guard in sight, or even Fran for moral support, I made my way towards that far corner.

God, he's a handsome devil, I thought as I slowly made my oft-interrupted way through the room; and got close enough to see that he sported a dark suit, a dark shirt that set off his tan, and, dammit to hell, I don't know why, but whenever I see a young man who is prematurely greying at the temples it always sets my heart racing.

There really is no justice. Here was a man, at my very own party, who was undoubtedly too young to notice the hostess even if she rode into the room side-saddle with ruby-studded reins threaded through her fingers, on the back of a tall black stallion that was foaming at the mouth.

He was taking his admirers in his stride all right, in a casual, laid-back sort of way. And just before I reached him, as I began to hear his deeply toned American voice, he saw me coming, and he smiled at me.

'Do I know you?' I asked, removing my glasses with decorum and a smile, as he fixed me with his intense blue eyes.

'He's Scott Peters. From Washington,' one of the female guests said. 'He knows a friend of mine who lives in Georgetown.'

Well, he would, wouldn't he? I thought. And how come Fran had only told me that he was a good steady type and not mentioned the greying temples or the knee-trembling voice?

'How do you do, Scott Paters? I'm Catherine Anthony,' I said, swapping hands with my champagne flute in order to extend the right one in greeting if it looked as though I would be needing it.

He lifted my hovering hand and held it.

'Actually, it's Peters. And I do know who you are; it was extremely kind of you to ask me here tonight. I appreciate that.'

He wasn't exactly flirting, I felt, but I might have liked it if he had been.

'You look lovely,' he added, for all the world as though I were the only woman in the room.

I mentally shook myself and stopped drooling. Naturally he would treat me with grace and charm and say I looked lovely. I was his hostess, for God's sake.

An extremely tall female guest, whose name escapes me, hovered close and bent her head to my ear. 'He's gorgeous,' she whispered, as the man with her possessively took her arm and eased her away. 'Where *did* you find him?'

I flushed a bit, took a sip of my champagne for courage and looked down at the glass of clear liquid he was holding in his hand. Ah, so he was a vodka and tonic man, I thought.

'I see you prefer hard liquor,' I said, desperately searching for something reasonably intelligent to say. 'Don't you like champagne?'

He looked down at his glass as though surprised. 'Oh, this. No, actually this is Perrier water. I seldom drink alcohol; and I have a busy day tomorrow.'

I took another sip. Maybe he didn't need alcohol; but standing next to him, I can tell you, I certainly did.

'Have you seen Fran?' I asked.

'Oh, yes. You were busy with your guests when I arrived. She warned me that you'd most probably think I was a gatecrasher when she left me to go upstairs.'

'Oh, really, I can't imagine why.' I'm going to kill that girl one of these days.

'You're not too good on names, I understand?'

Fran and her big mouth. No kidding, I really am going to kill her. 'I'm not brilliant, but you're not supposed to know that. I shall try hard to remember yours though from now on. Paters, not Peters, is that right?' (And I'll sure as hell remember what you look like.)

He laughed. 'I think you're putting me on. But when I have the opportunity to return your hospitality, I'll wear a sticker on my lapel.'

He patted the left side of his chest as he spoke and I noticed that all four fingers on his right hand were slightly misshapen, as though they may have been broken and not set properly.

Eventually we eased the last of the guests out through the doors and discreetly locked and bolted them. Then we, the hard-core specials who remained, retired to my office for prearranged sandwiches and a post-prandial gossip. We sat on the floor, or wherever we could, my pa commandeering the only armchair yet delivered.

The champagne having made me bold, I patted the floor beside me as Scott came through the door.

'You don't mind if I take my shoes off, do you?' I asked as he lowered himself down rather awkwardly.

I felt as though I shouldn't watch, and I looked down at my drink.

When I looked at him again, he was smiling broadly.

'I'm sorry, I've forgotten your name,' he said.

As I took a breath, that second before I told him what it was, it occurred to me that he was teasing. Of course he knew my name. 'Mary Whitehouse,' I said, looking at him unblinkingly and trying to keep a straight face as I returned the proverbial ball to his court.

He laughed. 'It is not.'

'It is so.'

'No, it is not, you're teasing me. You're Catherine Anthony, the lady whose party this is and with whom I have the privilege to be sitting on this floor.'

'Cathy to my friends,' I said, not taking my eyes from his rugged face because it fascinated me.

'So, may I call you Cathy?' he said, and this time it was *he* who had to look away.

But you'll never *guess* what I said then. It was so awful I'm ashamed even to think about it, let alone put it into words, and it sent me rushing off in search of Fran to plead with her to put things right.

'You can call me whenever you want to,' I said, and the minute it was out I realized my mistake. He had said, 'May I call you *Cathy*?' meaning could he use the shortened version of my first name, and I had heard, 'May I call you, Cathy?' as in could he telephone me.

How absolutely awful, how gross. Oh, my God, he would think that I was flirting with him. And I've always been so critical of that sort of thing; older women getting skittish with younger men and making fools of themselves.

I excused myself so quickly, almost calling out Fran's name the way a child does in a crisis for its mother, that I plunged my heel through the hem of my dress in my haste.

Fran refused to see the seriousness of what I had done as I resolutely started to hit the bottle.

'You worry too much,' she said. 'Scott'll just think it's English-type humour, and will be sitting there relishing it right now.'

'No, he won't,' I moaned. 'He'll think I'm the worst type of older woman he's ever met. Trying hard to give him the come-on like mutton done up as lamb.'

'Bullshit. You're not that old,' she answered, as she irritatingly continued to cut up sandwiches into fancy shapes, and refrained from looking at me. 'Go back in and face him, tell him you could die of shame, make a joke of it. He'll just laugh anyway.'

'Not on your life, I'll never face him again,' I said, grabbing another half-empty discarded warm bottle and refilling my glass. 'I'm going home,' I added, desperate to get her undivided attention.

She was working on another batch of sandwiches. How dare she not give me the attention I merited as her boss, I thought, as I hiccupped; on the most important night of my career too.

The night that I had now effectively ruined.

As usual, she got the message. But Fran was smart and she didn't look up as she said clearly, 'You may not have noticed but the kitchen staff have long departed. And this lot look as though they're set up for the night.'

'I really am going home,' I answered, hiccupping a second time, and ignoring what she'd said.

She looked up at last, pointing towards me with the bread knife as she did so. 'You can't do that, Cathy. Your father's staying with you and he's still having a great time. You can't take him away yet, it would be unkind. So get your arse back into that room pronto.'

I wanted to throttle her; what right did she have to think that she could speak to me like that? But she was right, I was behaving badly. Not to mention stupidly.

'If you insist,' I said bravely. 'I'll get those bottles that I hid at the back of the fridge before the main party started.' (And merely nursing them as I go might give me comfort, which is more than you are doing right now.)

'Great,' she answered, holding aloft a large platter of sandwiches. 'Take those in first, and don't chicken out.'

I stared at her. 'They don't look like chicken.'

'What the hell are you talking about, Catherine? Are you drunk?'

I looked at her in panic. 'You're not coming in too?'

She gave a long-suffering sigh. 'Of course I am, you dummy. Now get going.'

I found myself wondering if she had been hitting the bottle also. 'Just one more thing,' I ventured as I took the platter from her grasp.

She sighed, patiently. 'What is it now?'
'How old is he? Say it quietly so no one hears.'
'Thirty-five, I think.'
Jesus Christ, a baby! I hiccupped again, and tried to concentrate on walking through the door in a straight line.

'Your back hurting?' I heard Fran ask him as she approached.
'Yeah,' he answered, getting up off the floor painfully. 'I guess I should take a pill and walk around for a spell.'
I went from one person's glass to another as a hostess should, refilling them from a new cold bottle of champagne. When I poured some for Fran I asked her, 'Is Scott in pain?'
'A little. He broke his back a year or so ago and it still bothers him now and then.'
I wanted to look across at him and show concern, but I couldn't bring myself to do it. 'How did he do that?' I asked her.
'Helicopter crash,' she answered casually.
'Oh, my God. How come?'
'No idea, no information leaked. But he was laid up for ages. Now let's go and sit by your dad; it's time you paid him some attention. I reckon he's feeling lonely.'
I turned to look at him, my pa I mean, and he smiled at me.
'Well, you know how it is,' I said to Fran. 'My mother died only last year, and he misses her.'
'They had a good marriage?' a man's voice asked, close to my ear.
It was Scott, having returned from his walkabout, who was now standing at my elbow.
'Apart from having her, I reckon they did,' Fran said, nodding in my direction as she moved away.
I laughed. 'They didn't mind me so much, but I was destined to be an only child, and I was supposed to be a boy.'
Scott looked at me with an unflinching gaze, and smiled. 'Did that bother you?'
'When I was little I used to wonder if I might be a boy, and everyone had made a mistake.'
'Did that worry you for long?'
I laughed again. 'Not too long. I invented a lying-down game

with the boy next door and looked up the leg of his short trousers. That was the day I found out what a willie was.'

'Charlie, you're not listening,' my father was saying as I came back from the ladies room. He eased me on to an arm of his chair, and I noticed that Fran was already seated on the other.

'Scott wants to know how you learned to be a dressmaker. I only remember you taking something called fashion design at art school. And then I seem to remember that I bought you a sewing machine in your teens. Isn't that right, Charlie?'

'Yes,' I said, turning towards Scott. 'And I practised the art by making clothes for myself.'

'But she turned her life around with her talent when she had to,' my father persisted. 'Tell him, Charlie.'

'Oh, Pa, not now.'

Scott waited in gentlemanly fashion. Then he smiled at me. 'So what did you do?'

I shrugged. 'Well, Fran may have told you, I worked as a model during the sixties, but I woke one morning a few years later to find my back to the wall, when Charles over there was a baby, and models were getting younger with the advent of Twiggy. So I changed my profession, transformed my flat into a couple of workrooms and tried my luck at dress designing. My baby had to bunk in with me to make room for the sewing machines, didn't you, Charles?'

'My father had died suddenly, you see,' my son Charles explained for Scott's benefit. 'From a stroke, on the steps of the law courts. He was a barrister.'

My first husband, Charles's father, had been much older than myself. A sort of substitute for my own father, I suppose.

Fran filled my glass and I continued to sip, knowing full well that I'd already consumed far too much champagne.

I think my father also had drunk too much whisky. Two pink patches had appeared on his cheeks, and he was in danger of becoming maudlin.

'She ran away to London when she was eighteen, didn't you, Charlie?' he said to everyone in general.

I stroked the top of his head from my perch on the arm of his chair.

'Well, I hardly ran, Pa. I seem to remember that I hid my suitcase and my sewing machine behind the hedge at the top of the drive the night before, and had to stagger two miles to the station at six o'clock in the morning. It was raining too.'

My father patted my knee. 'Tell them where you went to live in London when you arrived.'

I groaned. 'Pa, please.'

'No, go on,' he persisted, looking around the room. 'Tell them, they won't believe it.'

'It isn't all that interesting.'

'I'd like to hear it,' Scott said, smiling at me.

I felt sure that I must be slurring my words. 'I shared a flat with two other girls, over a pub in Shepherd Market. It was such a pretty spot, but I didn't know at the time that it was in the middle of a well-known red-light district. My father nearly had a stroke when he found out where I was living. I've often meant to ask him how he knew so much about the area . . .'

'You must show it to me some time,' Scott said, gazing into my face intently and causing me to look away while I thought of how best to change the subject.

'So what were you doing, Scott, when you were eighteen?' my father asked, as though reading my mind.

Scott perched on a corner of my desk, stretched his back, and looked thoughtful. 'Oh, at eighteen? I guess I was getting out my surfboard and making it to the beach whenever possible. It's all California kids ever do.'

'It sounds all right to me,' I said.

'Well, pretty unreal, actually,' he answered, still looking thoughtful. 'But I didn't know that at the time. We all thought that California was the only place to live on the planet Earth.'

I was in no state to drive my car. Scott offered to drive us home in my car if I showed him the way. I took him up on the offer, feeling rather embarrassed at being more than a touch tipsy.

But he put me at my ease in no time, glancing across at me as I sat beside him, struggling to keep my eyes open.

'I don't envy you the state your head will be in tomorrow. I simply hated hangovers. It was one of the reasons I signed the pledge.'

'What were the other reasons?' I asked, trying to be conversational.

'Oh, needing to stay sharp. It's difficult keeping your wits about you if there's alcohol in your veins.'

'Tell me about it,' I said, trying not to hiccup. 'Go right at the next lights, then second left.' My father grunted from the back seat.

Later, when the old boy was safely indoors and Scott was about to get into a cab to return to Fran's place, he kissed my cheek.

'Thank you, Cathy, for including me in your party celebrations,' he said.

'It was lovely having you, Scott,' I answered.

'I'll be back next Thursday. May I buy you dinner?'

I swayed a bit on my unsteady legs. 'If you would like to.'

'I'll call you.'

'That would be nice.'

It was only when I noticed the dog staring at me in silent accusation as I struggled out of my dress that I realized it was prime stretching the legs and emptying the bladder time in her book.

Hadn't I been a fool, I thought. I'm sure that Scott would have accompanied me, if only I'd thought to ask him.

Like it or not it was into a track suit and out into the night again. I gathered up my personal alarm, my torch and my antiquated police truncheon and wove my way on foot to a nearby patch of grass that Sacha considers her own.

I don't remember too much about walking back, and I don't remember at all taking aspirin tablets in the night. But the open packet beside my bed next morning proved that I had done so, and if the empty jug meant anything, a considerable amount of water went down to accompany them.

It had been a great party though, more successful even than I had hoped for, I thought. And in my wildest dreams I hadn't expected to meet a man like Scott Peters. Or was it Paters? One of the two . . .

No way could it come to anything, of course.

At that very moment, in the cold light of day, he could be

remembering how he saw a few wrinkles on my face, and start wondering how old I was. That was if Fran the Mouth had not already informed him.

I'd be lucky anyway if he even remembered that he'd asked me out to eat next Thursday.

Still, it had been nice while it lasted; and women of my age had to be grateful for small mercies.

# THREE

Luckily, I didn't have to go to work.
I'd given everyone the day off to show my appreciation for their monumental efforts, and to make it a long weekend in celebration of a successful launch.

Arrangements had been made for the new building to be cleaned up by a team of professionals, and the redoubtable Fran had volunteered to watch over that operation.

Goodness knows what her head must have felt like. But why was I worrying about the state of Fran's head? Mine beat relentlessly like a ship's engine battling with a storm.

However, it was an opportunity for me to go 'through the books', and I had brought the relevant computer print-outs home with that task in mind.

My accountant, being the man he is, prefers to deliver bad news to me first-hand, and to forget to mention the good (you probably know him). And doing a little checking myself makes me feel better.

Despite my post-party headache, after several black coffees and a round of toast, I made a stab at the accounts.

There's no doubt that the new place has cost me an arm and a leg, and I'll need to tighten my belt and work at breakneck

## Philippa Todd

speed to recoup the expenditure. Luckily the bank was quite happy to lend me money to expand, which was good news indeed, since we all know that banks only want to press you to accept a loan when they are sure (though not in my case) that you don't actually need it.

I was delighted to discover I was still solvent and decided to celebrate by getting out the business cheque book and paying myself some well-deserved and long-overdue wages.

But never again shall I allow myself to be overstretched in the way that I was last recession time. My cash-flow problems kept me awake night after night, worrying that I could not pay the bills, and knowing that any one of my creditors, at any time, could put me into liquidation. I reached the stage where anything delivered by hand, no matter what the size, looked to me suspiciously like a liquidator's warrant, or whatever it is that gets laid into your unsuspecting palm at such a time.

I even contemplated, during one fretful night, asking Clive for a loan. Though I never did find out if he would have obliged, because an obstinate streak of pride stopped me from asking, and I staggered on until I was unexpectedly rewarded by the Arabian Princess of Oil who, wanting her pound of flesh at such an opportune time, and who can blame her, gave me an order for twenty-four day and evening dresses, provided that I was prepared to give her cut-rate prices.

And you bet your life I was.

I had been forced into letting all but one of my seamstresses go, and naturally the one to stay was the ever loyal Suzie. Together and apart we worked all day, and almost every night, until we had completed the order.

Long before then I visited all my creditors, dazzling them with figures that were inflated, and enthusiasm I wasn't feeling. I persuaded each and every one of them, with a hollow feeling in the pit of my stomach like a prisoner awaiting the verdict of a jury, to allow me to pay off my debt to them by instalment. Or through never-never land, as I came to call it.

The happiest day of my life, excluding those when I gave birth to my children, was when I wrote the last cheque to the last creditor secure in the knowledge that it wouldn't bounce and come back bearing the dreaded stamp of 'return to sender'.

I had survived. I was one of the lucky ones.

A disturbing incident happened to me that afternoon, which rates a mention only because the young man in question reappeared later in my life in a most bizarre coincidence.

My pa had declined the offer to go for a stroll, and had fallen asleep in an armchair. So to clear my head of taxing paperwork I took the remains of my hangover and my alsatian dog on to Hampstead Heath for some seriously overdue exercise for us both.

I parked my car by the wooded area of the heath, because that was where we liked it best. Very few people go to our secret spot, and in no time at all the dog was clocking up mileage in and out of the trees, chasing leaves, and running after squirrels she hadn't a hope in the world of catching.

I was chewing on an apple for the benefit of my fragile stomach as I strolled along, already lost in thoughts about the launch, and about Scott Peters, when a twig cracked nearby.

Though I couldn't see anyone around, and certainly Sacha was not in the vicinity to be disturbing the undergrowth, it happened again. More quietly this time, as though someone was desperately trying to prevent it happening at all.

Then I saw him, the image we all dread, and the incident all we women hope will not happen to us. I knew that I should ignore him and walk on, but this was tricky because the natural path between trees and foliage was narrow. Furthermore, if the dog had come trotting innocently back she would sense danger and may react.

Both he and I moved at the same time, he to open his threadbare overcoat and reveal his milk-white nakedness, me to stuff two fingers in my mouth and give a shrill whistle for the dog.

Never was I more thankful for having been brought up to do boysie things than at that moment. I can remember the very day that I mastered the art of the two-fingered whistle, sitting on the cross-bar of a bicycle ridden by a male school friend; and luckily, I hadn't lost it.

I could hear Sacha crashing through the undergrowth in response, and so could the flasher. But he stood stock still,

## Philippa Todd

even keeping his coat open, as though in shock. That was all right by me, however; as long as he was holding his coat, I knew what both his hands were doing. Though it is said, if we are to believe it, that flashers are harmless, and do not carry weapons.

All this had crossed my mind with the speed of light by the time Sacha came into view and I screamed at her to 'stay'. Headlines in the *Ham and High Gazette* that a dangerous dog had helped herself to male genitals for her tea was not something I particularly wanted to read about.

Bless her canine heart, she stopped dead, snarled in the flasher's direction, then sidled over to me and sat leaning against my leg and resuming the ominous growl. I took hold of her collar, but only for effect. She would not have dreamed of attacking without the command unless he had rushed at me.

We had a good relationship, she and I; we were a team; she was no ordinary dog, and certainly not likely to forget that I had rescued her from Battersea Dogs Home after she had been found in the most appalling condition chained to a fence so tightly that her front legs barely touched the ground.

'Is she going to attack me?' the flasher asked, in a surprisingly mellow and pleasant-sounding voice.

'Only if I tell her to,' I answered, not so mellow.

'What's her name?'

'None of your business.'

My heart was beating ninety to the dozen but I wasn't going to fall for that one, so that he could use the dog's name and confuse her into thinking that he was a friend.

I made myself look him in the eye as fearlessly as I was able, knowing that I had the advantage as long as I was in control of the dog, and it was he who had to find a way of escape, not me.

At least, that is what I told myself.

He was, in physique, a puny young man, with pale ginger body hair, no eyebrows, or so it seemed, and matted ginger hair on his head made darker with dirt.

His blue-white genitals were extremely large, and hung down heavily between his thin legs. Clive once told me that flashers were always well hung like that, and in their poor maladjusted minds they saw themselves as overlooked in life because, being of a weedy build, everyone would assume that they were small and under-formed in their most important department.

I knew I had to make the first move. The flasher seemed reluctant to turn his back and stride off, and talking to him seemed a reasonable way to begin.

'Why don't you button up your overcoat?' I suggested.

He smiled, for all the world as though we were passing the time of day. 'That's the title of a song. Fred Astaire sang it,' he said.

'Do up your coat before I lose my temper,' I replied with emphasis, and the dog took up my mood, letting rip with a louder growl.

'Bet you've never seen a bigger one than this,' he said, looking down at himself and I noticed that he was getting an erection. Suddenly the wood, even with Sacha beside me, seemed an extremely lonely place, and I just wanted to be out of there, at home where it was safe, having tea with my pa, and eating biscuits or some other sort of comfort food.

Without actually speaking I nudged gently at the dog's side, and she stood erect suddenly and rolled back her lips in a hideous way. I took all my fingers except one slowly from around her collar, knowing that he was watching my every move.

'I'll give you twenty seconds to get going,' I said, not feeling as brave as I hoped I looked. 'After that, my friend, I won't care what my dog does to you.'

He buttoned his coat carefully. 'I only wanted to show you my parts,' he said, in a most pathetic way.

'Well, you've taken a terrible risk,' I said, trying at least to be kind because the chap was obviously sick. 'I think that you should try to be more sensible in future. Now go. I can't hold this dog much longer.'

I noticed tears forming in his eyes.

'You going to set it on me the minute I turn my back?' he asked in the voice of a frightened youngster.

'Not if you go right away,' I answered. 'You should know better than to go scaring people in public places like this.'

He put his hands in his pockets and hung his head. 'That's what my mum says.'

**41**

The dog's hair rose in a long ridge along her quarters, and she rolled back her lips once again.

Dear God, I just wished that he would go away. My knees were beginning to tremble, my throat was dry and Sacha was getting restive.

'And try to stop worrying your mother, will you?'

'Yes, I shall,' he said, still standing there, uncertainly.

'Then do it. Go home,' I almost screamed, feeling a bit out of control. In my wildest dreams I had never expected to find myself having a conversation on Hampstead Heath with a young man wearing nothing but a soiled and threadbare mackintosh.

He turned then and started to run. 'Thank you,' he called over his shoulder. 'Promise to hold on to that dog.'

I waited until I could no longer see him and couldn't hear the cracking of twigs or crunching of undergrowth, then I let go of Sacha's collar, but called her to heel swiftly as I turned in the direction from whence we had come. Thankfully for me, though not for the dog, who'd missed out on exercise, the car was reasonably nearby.

I sat behind the wheel without moving, tears flowing, and my fingers trembling as though I had a palsy; wondering why it is that women shed tears when they are frightened. After all, men don't, do they?

Suddenly a police car, approaching from the opposite direction, came into view. I flashed (pardon the pun) my lights twice, opened the driver's window and waved my hand at them. The driver returned my signal, crossed the road and pulled up in front of me.

I quickly wiped my tears and blew my nose as the two young men of the law came purposefully towards me.

'Please don't ask me to get out,' I said wearily through my open window to the one chap bending down at it. 'I've just encountered a flasher and my knees are a bit weak from the experience.' I told them what had happened.

They explained that they'd had a complaint an hour previously from the other side of the wood and were en route to investigate when I'd called them over.

I told them that the flasher seemed harmless enough, but none the less it had been a frightening experience. They said they thought they knew who it might be, and if they were right his mother was a retired local councillor.

After I'd made my statement I asked them, as an afterthought, not to be too tough on the flasher. They said goodbye, glancing at me strangely, as if wondering whether I had a few cells missing.

I stretched out on the sitting-room sofa when I got home, feeling lonely, wishing there was someone I could talk to. I couldn't burden my children on the telephone with such a small item, or even Fran, and my pa would become much too upset if I told him of the incident.

The event in the wood wasn't all that traumatic, let's face it, and certainly not the worst thing that could have happened to me. But it left me unnerved, and troubled about the young man in question. He needed treatment and sympathy, and I'm sure he could be cured if someone out there was prepared to try.

I very nearly telephoned Clive, and then thought better of it. I didn't think that I could cope if he was in one of his pompous moods.

I must have fallen asleep then, because the next thing I knew I was startled by the telephone ringing, and I had trouble remembering where I was.

'Feeling frail, are we?' Richard Crossley said as I picked up the receiver. 'No wonder, all the work you put into that very successful party.'

'Richard,' I said, trying to get my head together. 'I didn't see you leave last night. But I hope you had a reasonable time.'

'That's because you were busy charming a particularly good-looking guest. I didn't want to interrupt you, so I slipped away.'

'Well, you know how it is. But as long as you did enjoy it.'

'Immensely,' he answered. 'And you looked absolutely lovely. You should wear red more often.'

I laughed to cover my embarrassment at the rash compliment. 'Thank you, Richard. I'll remember that.'

'Cathy, are you doing anything tonight?'

'Not apart from going to bed early; after I've put my pa safely on a train at seven o'clock.'

## Philippa Todd

'Oh, well, it doesn't sound as though you'd be interested in coming out to dinner.'

He was confusing me. I thought it was supposed to be Sunday, at lunchtime, that we were meeting.

'I know that we made a date for Sunday,' he said. 'But there's nothing to stop us seeing each other tonight, is there?'

My first reaction was to say that I couldn't possibly; and then I wondered why not. It would beat the hell out of beans on toast on a tray, all alone.

'I'd love to,' I answered.

On the way to the station my pa became a little sentimental. 'You're doing a good job, Charlie,' he said, patting my knee with one hand, wiping away a tear with the other.

'I try,' I answered, not quite knowing how to deal with him.

'It was a good thing I sent you to London when you were young.'

This was strange news to me. Pa hadn't intended me to have any sort of serious career, and it had become obvious quite early on that I would only be allowed to bide my time doing courses, and the like, while he put into practice his desire to marry me off to the 'right' young man at an early age. It was this realization that helped propel me into action and gave me the courage to leave home.

Aren't parents strange how they forget facts from the past?

I must remember to try to be different, I decided.

I deposited him into a forward-facing seat on the train opposite a nice-looking, smartly dressed elderly lady, knowing it would not be long before he was regaling her across the table with exaggerated stories of his dress-designing daughter and her burgeoning career.

I knew it had been a smart move on my part, when I reminded him in a clear voice that it was a fast train with only one stop before his, and she volunteered that she was getting off at the same stop, and they could disembark together.

He surprised me by handing over two letters as I was about to alight from the train. One was addressed to the blue-eyed princess, and the other was addressed to me.

When I read them later, never intending that the princess would receive hers, I found that mine was thanking me formally for inviting him to such a nice party.

The one addressed to the princess was to tell her how beautiful she was, and to say, PS, shouldn't she be giving his daughter lots more of her wardrobe to design.

I think the old boy is getting a touch wobbly in the head.

Richard took me to the Savoy for dinner; and I was in the mood for that. Whenever I am in his company I feel comfortable and relaxed, and I must say it was nice to be with a man again (I say 'again' as in after Clive) who knows his wines and is a gourmet. Richard lives for good food.

I found myself watching him as he selected a red wine from the list, and wishing, rather unfairly, that he were younger. Not quite as young as Scott, perhaps, but anyway not a day older than me.

Then my eyes fixed on his lovely hands (doctors usually have nice hands, don't they?) and they reminded me of the night I became engaged to Clive. He had taken me to Maxim's for dinner while spoiling me with a weekend in Paris for the special event. I remember watching every sophisticated move he made as he organized our food, his beautiful hands moving so magnificently over the menu and hovering sensuously on the wine list. I had found it all positively sexual.

Richard touched my hand as though he knew what I was thinking. 'How long now since we first met, Cathy?' he asked.

I smiled at him. 'I make it a rule never to go back more than thirty years.'

'Is it as long as that?'

The waiter gave him the wine to taste.

'Afraid so.'

'And you look so young.'

The waiter poured the wine.

That's the up-side of being out with older men; they always find you young.

'You look young too, Richard,' I answered. 'Shall we raise our glasses and thank the good Lord for that particular mercy?'

As we returned our glasses to the table he startled me by saying, quite suddenly, 'Will you marry me, Cathy?'

I was saved for a moment by the arrival of the first course, and the hovering of two waiters over our plates.

'Have I embarrassed you?' Richard asked as they left.

I smiled at him. 'How could I be embarrassed with you over anything? We have no secrets. You delivered my children, and we've had countless other intimate medical encounters since then. You know more about my anatomy than anyone else does, and quite a lot about my mind.'

'Are you blushing then because I've been so bold?' he asked.

'A little. You've taken me by surprise.'

'Why is that, Cathy? You must know that I care for you?'

I looked down at my plate. 'Why on earth would you want to marry again at your time of life? Oops, sorry, I didn't mean that the way it sounded.'

He laughed. A really wonderful deep chuckle, rather like Scott's, only slightly huskier. 'I know that I'm quite a few years older than you are, but do I really appear to have one foot in the grave?'

I touched the back of his hand. 'Of course not. And you already know I'm extremely fond of you.'

We started our delicious main course of baby lamb chops on a purée of sweet, minted peas, and ate for a time in silence.

I found myself wishing that I *was* in love with him. He would make a lovely companion: he was intelligent, he was good-looking, comfortably off, and he had a great sense of humour. He had, in fact, all the attributes of a sophisticated, understanding, eloquent man. And if my stomach had churned just once in physical longing as I told myself all that, I would have weakened; and to hell with younger men.

'Does that mean the answer's no?' he said at last. 'Or are you going to say that you'll think about it? Which usually means the same thing, I suspect.'

I took a sip of wine. 'Not if you promise you won't say that you love me enough for both of us. I've never been able to take that remark to heart.'

He laughed. 'Perhaps not that, Cathy. But I do love you.'

Oh, God. What was I to say next? Everything would sound like a put-down.

'Tell you what' – it came out clumsily – 'let's enjoy our wonderful meal, and then I'll explain how foolhardy I think you are. Supposing I accept, then you could really be in trouble.'

He laughed again. 'That's what I like about you, you're always teasing. And you make me feel as young as you are when I'm in your company.'

'I'm glad, Richard,' I answered, not knowing, at that point in my life, how wonderful it is when that happens between two people of differing ages.

The following morning I took the long-overdue opportunity to get up late, linger over the morning papers, stay in the bath as long as possible with face pack and eye drops, and savour the luxury of idleness.

I spent the afternoon more profitably doing some rough sketching for next summer's fashion craze that is currently giving credence to the well-worn adage that there is nothing new under the sun, and predicting a return to the long-skirted short-topped gypsy look of the early seventies.

Only this time it's threatening to be see-through.

Not that my clients are going to wear that kind of thing, but I'll need to adapt the look to couture standard for the few ladies who are dedicated followers of fashion; tame it down a bit, improve on cut. And I'll certainly need to include the see-through variety in my prêt-à-porter range.

My clients, unless they are cruising on their yachts, or staying on remote islands, or holing up in their beach-front houses, will want smart cotton or linen suits, as usual, or sleek straight sleeveless dresses, just like this year.

But I'm going to try a few changes that I shall suggest to them. Changes with the pockets, the shoulders maybe, and the buttons. There's no end to what can be done if you set your mind to it.

I'll sketch a few swimsuits too. I haven't told anyone yet but I fancy trying my hand at swimwear next summer. And soon I think I'll take a quick trip to Italy to see if I can have the right type of stretch cotton and silk woven for me. I've not been too impressed with anyone's swimsuits this year.

I've just had a killingly busy week; what with moving, and all, it has been positively chaotic. And that's without mentioning the setbacks.

We seem to have 'lost' some of my basic but important patterns, in as much as they left the old workrooms, but don't appear to have arrived at the new.

Having hired a removal van at great expense to move the more expensive materials from the old premises, wouldn't you know, the driver discovered that he needed petrol, and, if he is to be believed, he left his vehicle unlocked when he went to pay for it after filling up. When he came out on to the concourse four youths, most likely high on drugs, had grabbed a few items (the best, of course, such as my special electric irons) and were making off in a car that it took the police just fifteen minutes to discover had false number plates. Is it surprising that I'm getting headaches?

Anyway, enough of that; nice things have happened too. Imagine my surprise when Scott telephoned me from the States to confirm that he was expecting to take me out on Thursday.

He would pick me up at eight to go to an ethnic restaurant he hoped I would like, which he'd book in advance, he said.

'Ethnic?' I'd repeated. But he didn't seem to hear me.

Later on, when I asked a po-faced Fran if she could throw light on which kind of ethnic, she just shrugged.

My God, I thought, suppose he meant Scottish ethnic? I knew that he was of Scottish descent; and being American he was no doubt into hamburgers. A table at McDonalds would be all I'd need . . .

In the middle of this chaos, I managed to acquire two new clients; and that's not including Hugo's daughter, Sophie. I say not including her because it seems that Hugo is paying; and we all know what that means. But more about that later.

The new client I'm best pleased with is a well-known fashion magazine editor. She'll demand special rates of course. But I understand that in return she'll give me a spread in her monthly women's magazine, featuring outfits designed by me and made in the Catherine Anthony workrooms; and that will be the best publicity I could ever hope to get.

My other new client, whom I find a most unusual challenge, is a housewife from Essex by the name of Clara Holiday who has just won five million pounds on the lottery. You may have seen her picture in the paper.

She came in bearing an extensive shopping list like a trophy, and already weighed down with several Bond Street shopping bags. She wants me to make her a wardrobe for a cruise she is taking herself on; one of those 'singles' shindigs that are all the rage in America.

I asked Fran to pour us a glass of champagne each to celebrate Clara's winnings, and to drink to our new relationship.

'Blimey,' she said as Fran handed her the glass, 'I've never been given champagne in a shop before.'

'Cheers, Clara,' I said. 'Good health.'

She lifted her glass. 'Here's to you, dear. I read about you in the paper the day my winnings came through, and I liked the look of you. I knew I had to invest in some new clothes, or I wouldn't get nowhere. Proper ones that fit well, not my usual crap. But I felt shy, till I saw your picture, and made a note of your name.'

I have to tell you, Clara made my day. She was the most refreshing person I'd met in my long career.

Her husband, she told me, is an ambitionless motor mechanic called Fred, who has treated her with indifference for years, and only comes home to eat on his way to a football match or after the pubs close.

She made no secret of the fact that she is looking for another man now that she has money. Someone to show her respect was how she put it. And I hope she finds him.

So what I would like to say to the unknown Fred is, best to mind your Ps and Qs in future, and look up in the dictionary what the word respectful means. Or you might find that your wife and her winnings have moved to Marbella, and you are left with only the mortgage and your rusty old car for company.

She left eventually for Harrods, where she wants to buy

some expensive make-up, and to organize an appointment to go blonde, shedding the premature grey.

'But proper like,' she said. 'Not that brassy peroxide look which is all they know about in my neck of the woods. And then you can't get your comb through it for love nor money. I'm fed up to the back teeth with all of that.'

I told her what 'honey beige' had done for me, and wrote down the names of various perfumes that she should ask to try at the counter.

She's lovely, is Clara; nice figure, great boobs, curves where they ought to be, and the most divine laugh. I shall enjoy making clothes for her; and not just because she liked my picture in the press.

She's already chosen materials; and didn't mind one bit my changing her mind for her on one of her choices which would not have suited her. Next week she's coming in again to see some sketches, and she asked me if I would do her the honour of letting her take me out to lunch.

She did something so rare on leaving that has almost never happened to me before. She insisted that I allowed her to pay a fifty per cent deposit in advance.

She looked so proud too as she opened her lovely new cheque book; and then checked the date on the dial of her new Rolex watch.

On Thursday evening, with an eye on the clock and a hot feeling around my cheeks, I selected from my closet a slim black dress that ended just above the knee (not too far up, in keeping with my years), in the hope that it would be suitable for wherever Scott was taking me.

I couldn't overcome the excitement of having a date without knowing where I was going, in the company of a man who was not only young and extremely handsome, but vital, and brainy; a man of action.

I had just doused myself with the Givenchy eau de toilette atomizer, licked my palms, smoothed them up my tights, and squeezed my feet into my favourite shoes when the doorbell rang.

The dog reached down to the depths of her lungs to find her

killer-dog bark, and propelled herself towards the front door. I'd more or less trained her to do this as we are the only two occupants of the house.

But this time though, she stopped short, sniffed at the base of the door and began to wag her tail. Scott seemed to have the same effect on her as he did on me, I mused.

We smiled at each other across the threshold. God, he looked handsome. I held the door open wide.

'I'm ten minutes late, I'm sorry,' he said, coming in.

'You should try running my kind of business,' I answered. 'Ten minutes late definitely wouldn't even rate a comment, let alone an apology.'

We kissed each other warmly on both cheeks.

'How are you, Cathy?' he asked.

I stared at him enthralled. The depth of his voice, that interesting drawl, his lovely blue eyes; was I ever lucky for once, or what?

'I'm fine, Scott, thank you,' I answered, even though I was in danger of fluffing my lines, and still unsure of my next move. 'Are we going straight out, or would you like a drink first?' (And then I can keep you company, it'll help me to get myself together.)

'It would have to be water for me; I need a clear head. So why don't we go straight out, if that's all right with you?'

I asked him into the sitting-room while I gathered my things.

'Nice house you have here, Cathy,' he said, looking round.

'Thank you. I like it too.'

'D'you know something interesting? My town house is very like this one. D'you know Washington at all?'

'I've only been there once,' I answered, as I grabbed my jacket from a chair. 'I thought that it was a wonderful place.'

He took my jacket from me, held it open. 'I like London better. I want to purchase an apartment here. I'm positively in love with England.'

I slipped my arms into my jacket.

The dog drooled beside him, presenting her head within his reach. He pulled affectionately on her ears.

'I've booked at Harry's Bar,' he said.

'What, no ethnic fare?' I asked.

He laughed. 'That was just a small wind-up. Is Harry's Bar all right with you?'

Was it ever all right, I loved Harry's Bar. It was always buzzing, and the food was good. I didn't get taken there nearly often enough.

My hand hovered over my car keys on the hall table. 'Do you have a car or shall we take mine?'

'I don't keep a car in London yet, and this trip I haven't hired one. But let's get a cab, and then we can both relax.'

I simply could not believe how much we talked in that place; you'd have thought we'd been friends for many a year.

We even gave each other advice on how to treat the opposite sex; as in, for example, achieving a successful marriage; which I had to admit to him I hadn't been too good at.

'I'm sure Fran has told you that I'm totally unattached now,' he said.

'I didn't ask her about your marital status,' I answered, truthfully, wishing now that I had.

'How about you?' he asked. 'I know that you've been married twice, the same as me. Your first husband died, and the second time you had a divorce. Why was that?'

'It's simple. My husband had too many other women,' I said, sipping on my water because he had omitted to ask me if I wanted wine. 'He found it impossible to be faithful. It was all so hurtful, and degrading somehow.'

'Sonofabitch,' he muttered.

'It sapped my confidence,' I added, 'knowing that he'd been to bed with most of the women who were supposed to be my friends.'

'Didn't you talk to him about it?'

'Of course, but he simply couldn't understand my complaint. "You're the one who has me," he'd say. "And a casual roll in the sack with a woman who has the hots for me isn't important." I tried to tell him that it was important to me. I was usually crying at the time, which didn't help.'

We were sitting beside each other on a banquette, backs to the wall.

Scott placed his hand lightly on my arm; I was startled at the sudden jolt of electricity which shot through me at his touch.

'It sounds as though you adored the man and he hadn't the sense to recognize that.'

'I was crazy about him, and he didn't think that I'd ever leave him.'

I couldn't say so to Scott but Clive didn't think I'd ever leave him on account of the fact he knew that I found him irresistible in bed. He had literally taught me the joys of sex, never mind that I already had one child. I was so in love with him, for a long time there was no room for moral standards on my part.

'He was a fool,' Scott said. 'Do you have someone else now? You look like the kind of woman who would have a secret lover: a member of parliament perhaps, or an earl with an invalid wife.'

'I wish,' I answered, laughing. 'I'm still trying to come to terms with being unattached. Truth is, I don't really like it though.'

He fixed me with his blue eyes. 'You never know what's around the corner, Cathy.'

'So I'm told. Which is a pity. I'd love to know what's around *my* corner. Meantime, I keep telling myself how lucky I am really.'

'I don't think that luck comes into anything,' he said, looking serious.

'Well, you know what I mean; I have nice children, plenty of acquaintances, a reasonably successful business, that sort of lucky.'

'Oh, that, sure.'

He looked serious for quite a time. I began to see sadness there too.

'My second wife died the most awful death,' he said at last. 'The big C got her, and she was so young. The trouble was we'd been estranged before it happened and we were living apart. That made me feel worse, because I had no love left. Only sorrow, and a feeling of having failed.'

I touched his arm briefly. 'Sad memories are hard to overcome, I know. I've learned that there are no short cuts to grief.'

I wanted to hug him, hold him, kiss him.

'Were you born in Washington?' I asked, by way of changing the subject.

'No, I was born in Berkeley, California. My dad was an attorney. We had a second home in Oregon in the Cascade Mountains; it's where my forebears settled after crossing overland after their ship docked on the east coast.'

'Is that where you learned to fly?'

He laughed. 'No, that was in San Francisco. I had my first ride in an airplane with my uncle when I was very small. Then, when I was old enough, I hung around the local airport, Buchanan Field, and washed airplanes to trade for rides and instruction. But I messed my life up unbelievably. My father wanted me to go to law school and join him in his practice. But no, not me. I was the pony-tailed whizz kid who had to go out and get married for no godamm reason. Except to annoy my dad.'

'And of course you were much too young for marriage, just like I was, I suppose?' I ventured.

'Oh, sure. It was right after I'd graduated from San Francisco State University. The girl was only seventeen, but did she ever know her way around. I tell you, she was one bad experience for me. My father was so mad, and so convinced she was after our money he struck me out of his pretty extensive will for a time, stopped my allowance too. I was broke. Needless to say my bride didn't hang around when she found that out.'

'So what did you do?'

'I played guitar with an up-and-coming band for a while, wrote a few songs, raced motorcycles professionally; cars too. Pretty soon I was able to take flying lessons again.'

'It seems to me that you only really ever wanted to fly?'

He looked thoughtful. 'It's a fact. But my life was in a mess. My choices were either to drop out or get out and start a career. So without telling anyone I went to the military recruiting office and signed up for the Warrant Officer Flight Programme at Fort Rucker in Alabama.'

He called for the bill quite abruptly after coffee for me, tea for him, and looked for the tenth time at his watch.

'I notice that you keep looking at your watch,' I commented. 'Do you have to go on somewhere?'

He checked the bill, not seeming to have heard me.

'Can we do this again, Cathy?' he asked, as he handed a credit card to the waiter.

'I'd love to. Then I can drive you round Shepherd Market and show you where I used to live. Would you like to come in for some more tea when we get home?'

'I can't tonight, I'm afraid. But let's repeat this, very soon.'

Was he trying to be rid of me? I wondered. Was he disappointed in my company? Was this a hasty retreat?

'I'll call you for a date,' he added, much to my relief; but I hoped it wasn't because I'd looked dejected.

'A little warning helps,' I replied. No point in letting him think I would be sitting around waiting for his call. 'Sometimes I make evening appointments to see my working clients; and then of course I can't break them.'

He looked at his watch yet again. 'I understand. I'm fairly sure I'll be this way again in about a week, so I'll call you then.'

We stood up; he took my hand.

He thanked the waiters for their attention, and squeezed my fingers gently.

We were walking out of the restaurant when he casually flung an arm around my shoulders and whispered in my ear, 'I find you a most unusual woman, Cathy. I do hope I can get to know you better . . .'

He turned from me to hail a distant cab, then he added, as though reflecting, 'I haven't been seriously interested in many women. Somehow there wasn't time, and young girls always bored me.'

There was no answer to that. Maybe he was trying to make me feel better about my advancing years.

The cab pulled up to the kerb; he opened the passenger door.

'The nearest subway station for me, driver. Then I'd like you to take the lady safely home,' he said through the driver's open window.

When seated beside me, he took my hand in his.

I said, feeling puzzled about the subway station, 'You already know what I do for a living, but I don't know what you do, other than you fly aeroplanes and helicopters all over the place.'

He squeezed my hand and laughed. 'I promise I'll explain a bit more next time we meet. Most of it's very boring anyhow.'

He was smiling at me, but not looking into my eyes as I was already learning he was prone to do when preoccupied. I could see that his mind was elsewhere. Again he looked at his watch as the driver pulled up outside Piccadilly tube station.

He kissed my hand and looked at me, properly this time. Then, suddenly, he kissed my lips. It was brief, and as he pulled away he pushed a lock of my hair from out of my eyes.

'Take care of yourself, Cathy,' he said.

'You too, Scott,' I answered. 'And thank you for dinner. It was lovely; much better than ethnic.'

From the kerb he gave the driver a ten pound note, and my address. 'I'm relying on you to take her home safely,' I heard him say.

The driver, a man of few words, nodded his head.

We pulled out into the traffic. I looked out of the side windows, then turned quickly to peer through the back. I wanted to see him going into the tube station, or standing on the kerb, or hurrying off down the road. Anything at all to assuage my curiosity.

But he was gone, vanished, swallowed up by the London night.

I thought about him as I was driven home. I thought about him as I played my telephone messages (listening for the one from him that I knew it would be impossible for me to get).

Then I thought of him again when I took the dog for her late-night stroll, then again while doing my teeth; and with a glass of wine in bed.

There was definitely something about him that excited the hell out of me. It made his face stay in my mind; along with his hands, his voice, his thick but prematurely receding hair. And the way he spoke.

It was ridiculous. I wasn't young enough for him; he was

just being kind taking me out, returning my hospitality. And he was lonely perhaps; hadn't the time in his sort of job to forge friendships in strange cities.

I was safe for him as a date; I was cosy, unattached, available. To read more into it than that would be forging a path to disaster. Get yourself together, Catherine, I told myself. This is foolish stuff.

A plane flew overhead as I sipped my wine. Nothing unusual about that, I was on the flight path for Heathrow. But wasn't it too late for a scheduled aircraft to be taking off? Might it be him? I wondered. Hadn't he said something about flying out before dawn? Perhaps not, but I wished that I could remember.

For all the knowledge I had he could be on a train right now, or on a bus, in a car, or walking along a footpath somewhere.

# FOUR

I'll call you up for a date, I clearly remember him saying. But he hadn't, and that was, oh, I can't remember when, but we're now into July.

Who am I kidding, it was five weeks ago.

God, how I wished that I could see him again. I find I'm either restless or introspective; either inward-looking, or showing false gaiety.

I try to sound casual when I mention his name; as I did to Fran the other day. But she went closed-face on me, so I've had to swallow my pride and come right out with it.

'Any news of Scott yet?' I ventured.

'None,' she said, not looking at me.

'So you've no idea where he is?'

'He must be in another part of the world.'

I tried to fix her with my eyes. 'I rather gathered that, but where?'

'Well, there's trouble everywhere, and America is very committed.'

I tried to make her look up from the computer screen. 'No telephone number?'

'Nothing.'

'I thought I'd remembered him saying that you had his number in the States.'

'I don't. And who says he's in the States?'

'Is he not?'

She sighed. 'I don't know, Cathy.'

I didn't believe her. Either she was still connected to the NSA and I'd been sold a bum steer with her CV, or she was close to someone who was giving her information.

'Oh, I wouldn't mind betting you do know,' I said, hoping to shame her into telling me.

But I had nothing with which to back up the challenge, so I tried another tack. 'I would have liked to invite him to this birthday party I'm giving for the twins. Both Todd and Abigail met him at the launch, if you remember. I'm sure they'd like to see him again.'

She refrained from answering, and, lucky for her, the telephone rang.

I threw myself into my work and my family, and decided that Scott was a thing of the past. But, I have to admit, I'd been quite unhinged by the Peters experience. I'd even contemplated telling Richard that I would marry him, to settle me back down, and to hell with no lurching stomach when I put myself through the mental sex test. I had never felt more lonely in my life.

Things that I should have taken in my stride began to get me down. Like the day I had a funny sensation in my left arm, which seemed to force my hand to go where I didn't guide it. But I didn't allow myself to worry unduly. It was all to do with stress and pressure of work, of course. But somehow my crayons wouldn't fly over the sketching paper as they usually did.

It was at the exact time that Freda, the fitter, had to have a hysterectomy, and was out of action for a few months.

Charles split up with his girlfriend, and took his mother out to dinner twice in one week in desperation to talk about it. We commiserated both times. At least it gave me someone to talk to about Scott, and it gave him the opportunity to go on a bit about his emotional problems with his ex. Well, isn't that what mothers and sons are for?

But nothing terrible, or even mildly irritating goes on for ever, as we all know, and yesterday morning, just as I was draping a skein of silk around a dressmaker's dummy in the forlorn hope of inspiration, Hugo came in to see me. With the object, it seems, of doing me a good turn.

Not knowing his reasons for paying me a surprise visit I immediately put my foot in it. And how his dear old face did fall when I told him that the silk material alone that his daughter Sophie had chosen for her evening dress for the Red Cross Ball had come to a thousand pounds.

It was to be her birthday gift from Daddy, with special thanks for her tenderness during his recent illness. All very noble and wonderful, since she was motherless, and cared for him dearly.

Then there was the labour cost on top, which I couldn't forgo, I had to explain to him, feeling bad as he seemed to crumple visibly. But he could relax, I said, to cheer him a little; I would refrain from adding my usual profit margin.

I could see he was thinking wasn't it a pity that 'darling girl' Cathy was not prepared to shave more off the labour cost for old times' sake.

However, gent as he undoubtedly is, he thanked me kindly for discarding the profit margin and went on to tell me how we could both gain from it.

I was rooted to my chair waiting to hear what he had to say, and as it was very nearly midday I offered him a whisky and soda; and watched his face light up like a beacon as I poured.

The young daughter of a titled friend of his was preparing for her wedding, he said; or rather her mama the duchess was. And the young daughter, whose name was Clementine, had as yet not chosen a designer for her gown.

Personal recommendation being the best advertisement in the world, or so I'm told, Hugo had, with the help of my press profile, gently persuaded her to meet me, with a view to my making her wedding dress and those of her four bridesmaids.

'How about it, old thing,' he said to me enthusiastically. 'I suggested we meet her tomorrow in Bucks Club. Lunch is on me. If darling Clemmie takes you on, I'd like ten per cent. What say you?'

The daughter of a duke? Think of all that important publicity.

**Philippa Todd**

'Done, Hugo,' I said. 'I'd love to come to lunch and meet the lovely Lady Clementine.'

Bucks is a gentlemen's club in Mayfair and there simply cannot be many institutions left around the world to rival the sheer gall and arrogance of the place.

The club is unique for being on that ever-shortening list of establishments that only let women (with male escort, naturally, otherwise not at all) into the main dining- and drawing-rooms in the evening, and never letting them into any other public rooms, other than for a private function; and not as much as through the front door to gain access if they're not accompanied by a club member. Who, by definition, will be male.

Therefore, mixed invitations to lunch in that handsome old town house mean assigning a separate entrance for the skirts: around the corner into the next street, along the side of the building quite a distance and in through a door made for dwarfs, when the staff have deigned to open it, thereby gaining lonely access, because your male escort went in through the handsome front door to sign you in at a dusty register presented by a mole-like aged bursar. Then on into a separate dining-room well away from everything. Which, I must mention, the man entertaining the said skirt uses under sufferance, because it's more fun for him (if fun is the word) in the men-only dining-room in the main part of the house.

Hugo, however, with his percentage in mind, I suspect, was perfectly charming about it all; and not knowing anything of my OFs list or what my thoughts were on that fateful morning just prior to his heart attack, bought me a Buck's fizz to drink while I waited for Clementine to arrive.

He knew everyone there, of course, because Hugo's that kind of a man, and most people knew him. Some of them came over to our table to enquire after his health, and being the perfect host he introduced them to me. Most of the clothes adorning the women I met looked as though they could do with a total sartorial going-over; and that made me wish I could discreetly leave a few cards around.

Maybe I should make Hugo an agent for such places, I thought. But that was before the Elspeth incident.

\* \* \*

### Whispers On A Pillow

Clemmie was a lovely girl, pretty as a picture, with shining shoulder-length fair hair, fresh peaches and cream complexion, a sweetly fetching figure and huge blue eyes.

We talked about the wedding most of the time. I confided to her that I had in safe keeping some antique lace that would look divine for a bride's gown worn over duchesse satin; long flowing skirt, tight classic bodice and sleeves. I could see it all so clearly in my mind.

'It sounds truly wonderful,' she said breathily, her beautiful eyes shining.

I promised to deliver sketches and swatches to the family town quarters in St James's Palace within a week.

She asked me right off about the cost. I quoted a figure that should have made her toes curl; and surely would the duke's. But not a hair turned on her pretty blonde head.

Hugo looked delighted as he quickly did a sum in his head, and I knew he'd reached the noughts that followed the main figure when his eyes sparkled and he couldn't hold back a smile.

I'm not complaining either, because His Highness the Duke will be paying for Hugo's percentage; or I don't deserve to be running a business.

A waiter was delivering our puddings when my happiness changed; and caused me to wonder why God, or whoever it is up there pulling our strings, puts us down sometimes for no apparent reason. Can it possibly be when we are too pleased with ourselves, do you think? Or when we're sure we have it all?

Two large and extremely ugly women, both dressed in country tweeds that only the seriously upper class would have the nerve to wear in a large city, were eating with two old men whose clothes needed dusting off, and who were so blatantly suffering while entertaining them to lunch, that they simply had to be their marital partners.

They hammered away, those women, in overly loud voices about inconsequential things, until suddenly one ugly wife turned to the other ugly wife and said in an aristocratic screech that could have been heard south of the river, 'Elspeth, do tell, is dear Hugo over there in better health now? It must have been grief that caused his ghastly heart attack.'

**Philippa Todd**

'Yes, dear, quite so. It must have been,' Elspeth screeched back.

'Such a pity that his darling Caroline died so young.'

I sat there viewing Hugo in a fresh light. I didn't know that he'd had a young wife.

Elspeth noticed just in time that a dollop of white sauce, which should have been blanqueting her smoked haddock, was running down her hairy chin and answered while mopping it up with her large damask napkin. 'Tragic, dear,' she said. 'What a beautiful woman she was too; pity about her being so much taller than Hugo. It must be ten years now since she died, surely?'

Ah, so she wouldn't have been so young if she'd still been alive today, I thought.

Her friend stared at me with open hostility, then turned back to the Elspeth person and said, 'Might you know, Elspeth, who that woman is, the one having luncheon with old Hugo and darling Clemmie?'

Elspeth didn't need to look, she had sized me up earlier. 'Oh, she's no one who matters, dear,' she answered, her voice reaching, if that were possible, even higher octaves and certainly increasing in volume.

I cast a glance in Hugo's direction wondering how he was going to deal with their veracious rudeness if he had heard it, and certainly it was delivered loudly enough to be heard by even the very deaf. But he was tucking into his vanilla ice-cream and hot butterscotch sauce without even waiting for his guests to lift their spoons, and was totally unaware of what was happening around him.

I spent the next two minutes feeling mightily put down, scowling to myself, and hoping that Clementine hadn't heard, while thinking up an equally cutting remark that I could deliver on leaving as I passed the table *chez Elspeth et cie*.

Something said very clearly, I thought, would be in order. But uttered in a tone more subtle than those two old harridans were capable of using. Something such as, 'Listen you ugly old bats, I certainly am someone who matters. I'm me, and I'm proud of it.'

But just then, the duke's lovely daughter caught my eye from across the table, smiled at me, and winked.

# Whispers On A Pillow

I felt better after that, knowing that she too had found their behaviour unacceptable; and my dented confidence was somewhat restored.

'I shall enjoy having you make my wedding clothes,' she said, tenderly. 'Such a weight off our shoulders. Mummy will be pleased, too. When you come round with the sketches and things, do have lunch with me; maybe I can arrange for you to meet my fiancé, if he can get away from the City.'

The last few days have been rather fraught, and packed with the sort of hysteria that I wouldn't wish on an arch enemy. (Not even Elspeth, though she does spring to mind.)

Every client on my books, it seems, has her own idea of a closet emergency; and the telephoned demands to speak to me in person go on all day.

The interesting thing about rich women, I've discovered, is that despite the fact that their wardrobes are crammed with outfits enough to leave the rest of us convinced we wouldn't need to shop ever again, they never seem to have anything to wear. They simply must have a brand-new outfit for every single engagement, and not doing so would be nothing short of an irreversible tragedy. Not for them the delving among the coathangers until they find the item that 'will do'.

Still, by making rash promises down the telephone I managed to placate those on the other end, and I shall worry about being able to live up to those promises at a later date.

Today has been slightly better, and I cheered up immensely when I was invited by Fran to join her and a group of her American friends to attend a charity indoor tennis event at the Albert Hall, with top players from both sides of the Atlantic performing, and champagne and cold supper served in the ringside boxes.

Fran thinks that I may be able to win over some of the female guests, as they love to shop expensively around the world, and so I'm laying on drinks in my new salon before the show.

'How do you know them?' I asked her during a much-needed coffee break.

'One of the women is the ex-wife of my boss at the National

Security Agency,' she answered. 'We've always been good friends.'

My heart gave an extra beat as she mentioned the NSA name, and I could not help thinking of Scott.

I was a little apprehensive about revisiting the Albert Hall: it brought back uncomfortable memories.

I remember one fateful night when Clive took me to a concert there, and as we were looking for our correct entrance he was tapped on the shoulder from behind, and then lovingly embraced by a gorgeous female he reluctantly introduced to me as a patient.

But she never was; she behaved in much too sexual a way around him for that. My suspicion enveloped me and spoiled everything. Of course, I questioned him later and the exchange became very heated. Guilt made him attack and I became the stupid little wife. Couldn't I see from her ample unsupported cleavage that she was a cosmetic patient? he wanted to know.

'She's in love with you,' I cried, wringing my hands.

'They all are,' he answered smoothly. 'Stop being a silly girl, and come to bed.'

Apprehensive or not about the Albert Hall, it felt really good to be going out for an evening. Of course, I'd wished that Fran was about to tell me that Scott would be there too. But one date didn't make a life-long commitment; even if the man you really liked showed all the signs of really liking you in return.

I hadn't been out socially for some time, and I relished the chance to dress up, choose an outfit I couldn't wear too often, splash out on my favourite perfume. I enjoyed going to pains with the way I looked that night, rifling through my closet to select a blue silk shirt, narrow black velvet pants, flat black shoes and some gold jewellery that didn't often see the light of day.

I calmed my nerves with a glass of wine before I left home and took a cab to my salon, in the interests of not drinking and driving. I was sure that I was not late, but Fran and her guests had arrived ahead of me.

And so had Scott Peters.

He came forward as the others turned to stare. He was smiling, looking directly into my eyes as he walked towards me. When he reached me he squeezed my arms in greeting, kissed me on one cheek warmly enough to affect my stomach, then murmured into my ear. 'Hello, Cathy. I love that perfume.'

After Fran had introduced me to her other guests, she took me aside. 'Sorry about the shock,' she said, looking guilty.

'You should have warned me.'

'I only knew yesterday that he was coming over this way. I had the devil's own job getting another ticket.'

'And you kept it to yourself. How could you?'

'He asked me not to tell you; he wanted it to be a surprise.'

'Well, it certainly is.'

'He says that you excite the hell out of him.'

I smiled to myself. That was nice of him to say so; and he certainly excited the hell out of me . . .

We were seated in good time in our ringside box; the Americans as a race seem to enjoy being early for functions.

The women had previously raided my hanging rails; and all had expressed a desire to come and see me next day to talk about clothes. 'I want you to make me two of those blazers, Cathy,' one of them had said to me as we left. Fran's promise to produce an American connection for me seemed to be coming true.

She sat me down in a chair next to Scott in our box.

'This is wonderful,' he exclaimed, looking all around him as we made ourselves comfortable. 'I've always wanted to come to the Albert Hall.' He touched the back of my hand, and added, 'I feel sure you must come here often.'

'No. I've only been here three times since my teens,' I answered quietly. 'I was brought here once by a young man called Serge to see the Kirov Ballet. He was a dancer himself. It turned out to be quite an evening.'

He placed a hand on my arm and to my surprise said, 'Let's swap seats with each other, shall we?'

When we were reseated he leaned over and explained, 'I had a blow to my left ear a while back, and I don't hear too well with it now.'

Then he smiled broadly as I looked at him enquiringly.

'But I make up for it on my right side. You can whisper all

you want into that ear. So tell me more about him, Serge. Were you in love with each other?'

'We thought that we were. But I became pregnant the first time we had sex. It happened the night he brought me here. I never saw him again after that.'

The tennis players walked on then to tremendous applause.

Scott placed a hand over mine and left it there. The first set had reached three love before he squeezed it gently, and brought me back from the past.

'So what did you do then, about being pregnant?' he asked me later during the interval, while we were eating supper on our knees.

I smiled sadly. 'Serge shrugged when I first told him of my fears, and said in his black-eyed Slavic way that I should let him make love to me again, preferably standing up, then everything would be all right. I might have believed him, but he'd terrified me that first time around.'

'Nice try,' Scott answered.

'Then he sulked when I declined his offer, and walked away. When I knew for certain that I was pregnant I went to find him, only to discover that the ballet company had moved on and Serge had left it and gone to America in search of a new dance company that would take him on.'

We ate in silence for a time. I knew that Fran was watching me.

Then Scott said quietly, 'How old were you at the time? Did you tell your parents about being pregnant?'

I shook my head. 'I was just eighteen. I couldn't tell my father, it would have broken his heart. I tried to tell my mother on the telephone. I even told her I'd been raped to shock her. But it was no use, she couldn't handle it, and never once did she mention it again. The only course left open to me was to tell my flatmates.'

'A much better idea,' Scott said. 'The only person I told when I got a girl pregnant was my best friend on campus.'

I turned to stare at him. 'You made someone pregnant too? It's a great life being a man.'

'Well, it can happen. But I agree with you, it's tougher on the girls.'

'Then what did you do about the girl?'

'I was lucky, I guess. She had a miscarriage at eight weeks, or so she told me. I never set eyes on her again after we graduated.'

Well, it hadn't been like that for me, worse luck, I told him.

I'd bought cheap white wine and a large box of cigarettes – everyone smoked in those days – as a ploy to arrest my flatmates' attention and keep them in one place long enough for me to ask them for advice. Neither of them went on as many modelling assignments as I did, and played around much more. I think it had something to do with both of them having a whacking financial allowance, and upper-class parents who were happy to leave them alone.

'Well, first of all,' Rose had said, looking at my tear-stained face and drawing heavily on her cigarette, 'you simply must not think that the world has come to an end. Must she, Charlotte?'

Charlotte took a long swig of wine.

Secretly, Rose called her Charlotte the Harlot, on account of her being so wild, and happy to be passed around the Hooray Henrys like the hot potato she was.

'Hell, no. She'll have an abortion,' Charlotte answered in her fruity upper-class drawl, as though I were not in the room.

'Oh, no, I couldn't possibly,' I cried out, tears welling up in my eyes once more.

'Do you have a better alternative?' Rose asked. 'D'you want to have a baby?'

'No, not like this.' I blew my nose into my already wet handkerchief.

'Well,' Charlotte said, 'it's like this: Serge the Russian shit isn't going to appear out of a clear blue sky offering to marry you.'

'Use your brain, Cathy,' Rose said.

'Have you ever done it? Had an abortion, I mean,' I asked them, not looking up.

'Once,' Rose replied.

'Same here,' Charlotte said. 'Don't worry, Cathy, we'll see you through.'

'He said that he loved me,' I moaned.

'Don't they always,' Rose answered.

Charlotte stood up. 'Now, I'm going round the corner to get

fish and chips for three. It's time to eat. I don't know about you two, but I'm bloody well starving.'

I didn't want to tell Scott, or anyone else for that matter, but without doubt that abortion was the most horrible thing that has ever happened to me. I would rather draw a veil over the whole terrible episode. I wouldn't have gone through another if my life had depended on it.

Scott took my arm as we walked out into the night with the rest of the Albert Hall crowds. Of course, the American players beat the Brits at tennis, and I was seriously teased by Fran and the guests.

'I'm going to bring you back here at least once a year,' Scott whispered in my ear. 'We can't have these skeletons spoiling things for you.'

'Oh, I'm over it all now. But you know how it is, now and again . . .'

He turned me around and held me towards him. 'When can I take you out, just the two of us?'

I looked up at him. 'I'm always here, you're the one who makes promises he doesn't keep.'

'Ouch, that was a low blow,' he said. 'Maybe I'd better deliver you home to show that I care.'

'It isn't necessary,' I replied, wishing that I meant it. 'I heard you say earlier that you were flying off at five in the morning.'

'That's true. I wouldn't come in, I'd just see you home safely.'

'Is that instead of taking me out, just the two of us?' I joked.

'No,' he replied, sliding an arm around my waist loosely, and smiling as we strolled on along Kensington Gore, dodging people.

'My next mission this way is in five days' time. How about Wednesday? That's the day I fly in.'

'I'd love that, but won't you be tired?'

'No, not if we don't have a terribly late night.'

'It sounds very demanding, this job of yours.'

He tightened his grip. 'You better believe it. So, how about it, Ms Cathy. Can I have the pleasure?'

'Of course,' I replied. 'I try not to have very late nights myself during the week. I'm not young enough any more to burn the candle at both ends.'

He squeezed my waist. 'Oh, come on, Cathy, you're positively youthful.'

I laughed, even though the age difference was something I'd been thinking about. 'If only that were true. You can't have forgotten that I'm older than you are.'

'You're thirteen years older than I am.'

I stopped, and looked at him. 'How d'you know that?'

He was smiling. 'Fran told me.'

'I'll kill her. Actually you look older than thirty-six if you don't mind me saying so. With your thoughtful expression and your greying temples. It's because of your job, I suppose?'

'I shall have my sideburns dyed immediately,' he answered, ignoring my question.

'Oh, no, you can't do that. Greying temples are so sexy on younger men. Look, there's a taxi. Attract the cabbie's attention and I'll ask him to drive me home.'

'Now I definitely am going to deliver you home after a remark like that,' he said as the cab did a U-turn in the road and stopped abruptly beside us.

He bundled me into the back seat and jumped in beside me after giving my address to the driver.

'You didn't need to do this, really,' I said, as he played with my fingers. 'And what was the remark I made?'

He gave me an amused sideways look. 'Make sure you never tell a man in the States that he can drive you home.'

'Why ever not?'

'Because in the Deep South it's a saying meaning that he can have sex with you.'

We both laughed.

'I must remember that,' I replied.

He came with me to take the dog for her nightly stroll, and to lecture me on staying aware of danger.

'Do you know how to protect yourself against an attacker?' he asked.

'Well, up to now I've relied on my dog. But I reckon I could give a mean kick to the groin if I had to. At least, I'd try.'

**Philippa Todd**

He turned me towards him. 'The dog isn't looking this way, is she?'

'Not at the moment.'

'Okay, I'm an attacker. Kick me.'

'I can't,' I said. 'I might hurt you.'

'Kick me, Cathy,' he said sternly.

I raised my leg full stretch and kicked out. But he wasn't there. He was behind me, arm round my throat.

He released me. The dog came up and, can you believe it, she wagged her tail at him.

'Are you a karate expert, or something?' I asked him.

'Black belt,' he said, taking my arm and smiling at me. 'But do you see what I mean? I'm going to give you some lessons in self-protection some time soon.'

'I hope so,' I said, turning towards him, and making it difficult for him not to kiss me.

Back at the house he said that it was best he didn't come in, when I offered him a noggin of hot tea for his trouble.

'I'm now seriously worried about getting enough sleep,' he said, looking at his watch.

I wanted to offer him the guest bed, but it would have sounded like a come-on.

'Let me call a cab for you.'

'There's no need, I'll find one on the corner.'

He walked me up the four steps to my front door. The dog lay down, as if she knew something I didn't.

Scott folded his arms around my waist. I placed mine around his neck. We kissed, withdrew, and kissed again more lingeringly.

He eased away and looked into my face. God, how I wanted him! He looked as though he wanted me, too. I took my arms from around his neck to help me keep my senses.

'I'd better go,' he said.

'Yes, I agree.'

He took my hands in his and looked into my face. 'I'll try to telephone you, if I possibly can.'

'I'll expect you on Wednesday.'

'I'll be here,' he said. 'Same hour. This time you can choose where you would like to go to eat.'

'I'll do that,' I answered, as he walked back down the steps. He turned at the bottom. 'Go in before I leave.'

I turned towards the door, put the key in the lock. The dog sighed, hauled herself up.

'Oh, just one thing,' he called.

I turned to face him.

'I'd like to see that place where you lived called Shepherds Market next time we go out.'

'It's Shepherd; no s.'

'Okay. Would you do that for an American in London?'

'Of course. Especially if you agree to drive me home afterwards.' How bold could a girl get?

He laughed, and threw me a kiss. 'You drive a hard bargain, Ms Cathy,' he called, assuming a Deep Southern drawl.

# FIVE

Today has been full of surprises.
I walked into my office early, rather bleary-eyed and not seeing too well on account of last night. I'd sketched until I fell asleep around one in the morning. Luckily, in the cold light of day I'm not too unhappy with the results of my work; let's hope that Lady Clementine is happy with them too.

Tomorrow I have to deliver the drawings to her home; and as I've been informed that I won't have a parking problem at St James's Palace, I shall take the whole huge piece of beautiful old lace with me in the car, so that she can see the subtlety of the intricate design. I'll also be taking a fair-sized pattern of very fine flesh-coloured duchesse satin, and samples of tiny seed pearls, which will look divine sewn on to the train; I want this to be a very special dress.

A new member of staff has joined us, and this is her first day; a young girl by the name of Annabel whom I'm taking on to assist me in the cutting-room. She's newly out of art school, and comes highly recommended. So I have high hopes; and certainly, I need help.

The time has come for me to design and cut the clothes for our

### Philippa Todd

modest contribution to next summer's London Fashion Week and I'll need assistance from plenty of personnel if I am to keep abreast of the expansion I have longed for.

With more clients coming in through the door than ever before, I need to be front-of-house more, and yet still have free time to hunt down the special materials and accessories that are so important to a fashion house.

And then there is the prêt-à-porter range, the off-the-peg label for the young and successful business women. Those young ladies in the professions, the high-flying personal assistants, the up-and-coming managers, the PR girls, all earning high salaries and wanting to wear good clothes. They all want business suits, slit skirts, leggy narrow trousers, skimpy sleeveless tops, backless dresses for nightclubs. Long coats, short coats, big coats; but make no mistake, only bang-up-to-the-minute or avant-garde styling will do; and I had better believe it, they are the new power dressers, the ones in the fast lane of fashion.

They treat as a religion what the fashion shows of Milan decree and the High Street boutiques then copy. They note the slightest change in width of shoulder line, length of splits in skirts, plunge of necklines; and designer labels or not, the designer who makes the clothes will only succeed if she gets it right first time.

Which reminds me, next week I must pay another visit to the factory in Wales which makes up our prêt-à-porter clothes, and take a new batch of patterns. The weeks all slip by so quickly, I have trouble keeping abreast.

I had intended to spend far more time in the cutting-room with Annabel that morning but it simply wasn't possible; though I've high hopes that she will be a great help to me. I'm working on the art of delegation. It isn't easy, though, when you so long to do it all yourself.

Though these small mystifying sensations I'm getting in my arm are enough to make me realize that I need to delegate more cloth-cutting than I am doing at the moment, and save myself for the making of patterns. Suppose I'm getting arthritis? What if my arm is suffering from what is now fashionably called repetitive strain injury? What would I do then without adequate help?

Imagine my delight when I was interrupted by a telephone call from the personal assistant to the princess, who, after exchanging pleasantries, went on to say that a school friend of her boss, someone she was particularly fond of, was getting married in September. An affair without fuss it was to be, not a white wedding.

The princess would like the bride's outfit to be a secret present from her, but absolutely no one must know. We both knew what that meant: any leak at all and I could kiss my blue-eyed royal client goodbye. She was ruthless on that front.

Would I like to design and make the bride's ensemble? the personal assistant wanted to know. And the princess had said to be sure to tell me that the lady was dark-haired, lean-limbed, androgynous and fashion-conscious.

It sounded too good to be true.

'I would like that very much,' I said, in what I hoped was a business-like voice. 'Please thank the princess for thinking of me.'

She laughed then, so I think my enthusiasm must have been more obvious than I realized.

It made a nice stimulant to the day. Save that it enveloped my thoughts, and I was still mentally designing a wedding dress for the mystery young lady long after the telephone call, while endeavouring to explain the importance of the bias cut, and the trick of the unseen dart to my new assistant.

The lean look came to my mind for the lovely-sounding creature who was about to be my latest client. A straight, body-skimming, sleeveless, longish sheath perhaps. Slit up one side to mid-thigh if her legs were good. Matching jacket cut long, or a coat, maybe, as it would be knocking on autumn by then; with high revers, a slight flare at the back, and maybe an eye-catching small feature at the cuffs. Single-breasted of course . . .

I then gave my new assistant a roll of calico and some patterns to experiment with, and beat a retreat from the cutting-room, my mind caught up with finding a pattern of silk grosgrain. I'd found it in Italy, I remember; and it was the most incredible colour. If it was of the correct weight it could be wonderful for a smart yet informal wedding.

I remember we all fell in love with the colour some time back, when it was chosen for a ballgown by a particularly popular client of mine, a dark-haired beauty from Brazil. I always thought of it as 'crushed-up raspberries mixed with cream', and if the princess's friend has anything like the Brazilian client's dark and mysterious sort of colouring, she would look eye-catchingly exotic in such a rich colour.

Clara from Essex called in unexpectedly to talk about clothes in good time for a new winter wardrobe. It's just as well; she's ordered ten outfits and two overcoats for delivery before Christmas.

She'd enjoyed her last cruise, she told me on arrival, and wants to go on another.

'I met this Greek bloke on the last one,' she said cagily, as I handed her a coffee. 'But, well, he had his old mum with him; she was in a wheelchair. So he's coming to London to see me, next week.'

'Nice work, Clara,' I told her. 'Be careful though, won't you? What's the latest on feckless Fred?'

'Don't ask, it would ruin my day to tell you,' she answered, giggling. 'Hey, I heard you being interviewed on Radio 4's *Woman's Hour* the other day.'

'Oh, that,' I groaned, not wanting to be reminded. 'I was terrible, I was so nervous.'

'I had a right laugh the way you said about one of them whores from Shepherd Market babysitting for you when you was left widowed and alone and had to work.'

'Oh, you mean Myrtle,' I said. 'Yes, she was a great girl, kindness itself. My son Charles says he wishes he could remember her. He reckons he has to have been the youngest male ever to have been sponged down and lain on a bed by a whore.'

Clara gave her lovely laugh and rocked in her chair as she tended to do when amused. 'Oh, that's a good one; and what about you having been married to that famous plastic surgeon what's-his-name. Was he nice?'

'Well, everyone thought so. Yes, of course he was nice.'

'Oh, what a life you've had. How did you meet a man like that?'

I refilled our coffee cups from the pot I kept hot in my office. Clara looked as though she was settled for the day, and we hadn't even talked about her winter wardrobe yet.

'We met at a wedding,' I told her. 'I was lucky enough through my friend Charlotte to have been commissioned to make the bride's dress. It was a glamorous affair too; they called it the wedding of the year in the gossip columns, and luckily I got a mention.'

'Oh, go on, tell me about your hubby.' Clara was clasping her hands together.

'He'd come into the church late, and seated himself in a back pew on the opposite side from me. I was there to make sure the bride's dress did as it was told for the photographs.'

'So then what?'

'He thought I was a guest. I just couldn't resist turning to peek at him because he looked so handsome in his grey morning suit, and when I did so he gave me a most fetching smile, and winked.'

'Oh, how wonderful,' Clara cried.

'I very nearly winked back,' I said. 'But I thought it might dislodge my mascara.'

'It all sounds so romantic. I bet you fell for him really quick.'

'Instantaneously, for my sins,' I answered.

Oh, yes, and it happened exactly as I told her it did.

When I slipped outside to be ready to give the bride's dress the once-over as she posed in the church doorway, he followed me; and I was hooked.

'I didn't see you singing?' he'd said, amusement lighting up his twinkling dark eyes and his handsome face.

I blushed, I remember. 'I'm no vocal diva. I knew those choirboys would do it better.'

He held out his large hand with its long tapering fingers and nicely manicured nails. 'I'm Clive Anthony.'

I shook it. 'I'm Catherine. My friends call me Cathy. My father always calls me Charlie. How do you do.'

'Well, Catherine, Cathy, Charlie, you must be a friend of the bride's. Can't really say I know her. The groom's the reason I'm here. We meet up in the theatre a lot.'

Funny, I thought. I would never have guessed he was an actor.

'Actually, I made her gown. I'm a dressmaker, you see.'

He gave a most wonderful slow smile, and looked me up and down.

'You clever little thing; and such a beautiful dress it is too. I hope you're not going to run away before the fun starts. I'd like to get to know you better . . .'

Clara looked at me dreamily. 'Imagine going to bed with a man like that. And you had his twins, didn't you?'

I pointed to the photograph of Abi and Todd on my desk. 'They're all grown up now of course,' I said.

'I had a baby once,' she said quietly, looking down into her lap. 'But he died.'

'Oh, Clara, I am so sorry. How awful for you.' I didn't know what else to say.

She stared up at the ceiling. 'Yes, it was terrible. I found him dead in his cot. And Fred weren't no help. He's not a very nice man really, but I try not to tell anyone.'

'Better luck next time,' was all I could think of to say.

'That's if I ever find the courage to take the plunge,' she said ruefully.

'You will, Clara, I'm sure.' I hoped that I was right.

She looked into my face. 'D'you think you'll ever fall for anyone else; I mean, after an exciting man like you had?'

I thought for a moment. 'Yes, I think I might,' I said at length.

We had some very good news that afternoon.

Fran and I had just downed a quick sandwich in the office when a call came through from a PR agent. It seems that we have been recommended, and a sponsor has been acquired by the board of two charities, for a fashion show to be staged next summer, for which the tickets will be at a premium.

After expenses, the funds are to be divided between cancer research and a heart foundation. The sponsor in question is a BIG name in jewellery.

My staff, all nine of them, are over the moon about it, and every one of them has pledged undying devotion to the cause, loyalty to the very limits, and to put in as many extra hours as it takes to obtain perfection. And it's going to take quite a few, I can tell you.

I couldn't wait to telephone Abigail to tell her the good news about the charity thing, and to demand, mother-fashion, that she put in a quote for the catering at the fashion show. Not too big a quote, I said, as it was all in a good cause and would be good publicity for her; but not so low as to lose money.

'Yes, Mother, I'm quite good at pricing,' she said patiently.

'A small selection of special canapés, I think.'

'Yes, Mum,' delivered less patiently. As though she obtained such big orders every day of the week, for goodness sake.

'And little petit fours after.'

'Okay, Mum, I heard you. Now pin back your ears. I have something important to tell you.'

More important, I thought, than having your name linked to a charity fashion show in St James's?

My God, she must be pregnant.

'You still there, Mum?'

'You're pregnant,' I said, waiting to be deflated.

'No, you idiot. Tim wants to make an honest woman out of me. He's proposed.'

'Wonderful,' I answered, a trifle tardily, as it sank in. 'And not because you're pregnant.'

'Mum, what's this fixation with being pregnant?'

'It does happen, you know. Have you told anyone yet?'

'Well, I thought you might like to tell the family so I'll leave that to you. You always said that if I managed to persuade a man into marriage, you would make my wedding gown.'

There was a pregnant pause; no pun intended.

'Did I say that? There goes my mouth again.'

'This is a real old-fashioned wedding dress I'm talking about, like you promised,' she said.

I realized that I'd been standing all this time, and I lowered myself into a chair. 'My God, you don't mean a church affair?'

'Why not? Just because you've never had one.'

'All the more reason why you should, of course,' I said quickly, feeling rather guilty at my lack of maternal enthusiasm. 'But can it be an off-white dress? Only virgins are supposed to wear pure white. It's something to do with showing the world you are not as yet deflowered.'

'That's cobblers.'

I peeked at my next year's calendar. 'Some time in June perhaps? It's looking like an impossibly busy year for me.'

'June nothing. April the first,' she said, laughing.

'Oh, Abi . . .'

'Bye, Mum, must rush, can't natter any longer.'

It was time for me to leave. It looked as though it was about to rain and the dog had to be exercised. I also wanted time for a quick rest before getting ready for my date with Scott.

To my delight when I entered the house there was a message from him on the answerphone.

'Hello, Cathy,' he said. 'This is Scott. I hope you're expecting me, because I've landed and I'll arrive on time. Can't wait to see you again . . .'

God, he had such a sexy voice, it quite turned my stomach to jelly.

From my prone position on the bed I blindly made a few telephone calls to the family about Abi's wedding plans. Miraculously, both Charles and Todd received the wedding news with genuine pleasure.

'Tim's a good bloke,' Todd said defensively, as though I might say otherwise.

Clive was not at home, his housekeeper informed me. He had an emergency in the theatre, she said, lowering her voice in deference; a child whose arm had to be sewn back on. I asked her to tell him that I had some news that would give him pleasure, when he felt like telephoning me.

He probably would forget to return my call, and I'd need to telephone again, but for now, I had done my duty. He would just have to wait for the good news about his daughter.

\* \* \*

The hour was late, but still we talked.

Back home, after dinner, I made a pot of herbal tea, and we drank it sitting opposite each other at the kitchen table.

'I have to find an apartment,' Scott said, spooning sugar into his tea. 'Where do you think I should look? London's so enormous.'

'Something overlooking the river would be nice. I know an agent or two, if you need some help.'

'It would be great if you can find the time.'

'Of course I can,' I answered. 'Will you be living over in England permanently?'

'I have reason to believe I'll be assigned to operate from Europe exclusively quite soon. All subject to change, of course.'

'As a pilot, you mean?'

He took my hand and placed it under his on the table. 'Flying is what I do, Cathy. In the main.'

'But for what reason? I mean, if you can tell me.'

He touched my face with his fingers. 'I go on covert Anglo-American government missions. Anti-terrorist, drug work, stuff like that. The details are pretty secret. So it's mighty difficult for me to talk too much about it.'

'All on your own?' I asked, aghast.

He laughed. 'Not always. It does involve others. Now let's change the subject.'

'It sounds dangerous.'

He smiled at me and gently pushed aside a lock of my hair from my forehead. 'Crossing the road is dangerous too.'

I was pleased that he had at least told me something.

Before we'd left the house I'd overheard him making a telephone call that was a total puzzle.

'I must just make a call, Cathy,' he'd said.

'Oh, please, help yourself.' I gestured to the phone in the corner of the sitting-room and prepared to leave him in peace.

'I'll use this one I carry with me,' he said.

'There's no need,' I persisted.

'It's best,' he said. And the unflinching expression in his blue eyes told me to leave him alone.

I confess to staying within earshot.

He gave a series of numbers that seemed like codes. Then

several names that seemed like passwords. I heard him say a word that could have been 'Bingo'. Then, 'Anyone gone down there?' This was followed after a pause with, 'All the way down, or halfway?'

There was a long listening period, then, 'No, that'll be me.' Then words out of context like soonest, and reinforcements, and I'll be watching . . .

'I like the idea of an apartment on the river,' he said, across the kitchen table. 'Especially if there's garaging. Then I can buy myself a car.'

'Yes, being near water is nice.' I sipped my scalding tea.

He placed a hand on mine. 'That was fun tonight, Cathy. Thank you for showing me places.'

I smiled at him. 'It was fun for me too.'

And so it had been. I'd chosen The Ivy Restaurant for dinner. Always good value; plenty of interesting faces to see and such nice staff.

We talked non-stop at the corner table, and never seemed to be lost for words.

I told him about Abigail's news. He told me that he'd been listening in on drug barons somewhere in France.

'From a jet?'

'No, from a helicopter. I've been in Europe for two days.'

'But you flew into London by jet?'

'Yes.'

'It's all so confusing.'

He smiled at me. 'I'm pleased to hear it.'

I'd taken him on a serious tour of Soho, and other interesting night spots; not just the tourist routes. Eventually we ended up walking through Shepherd Market and I showed him where I used to live, and the pretty houses where the prostitutes hung out.

He put his arm around me as we strolled.

'I was scared to death that day I moved in,' I said, remembering how I'd felt when I found my friends were not yet there. 'But those street girls were so nice to me. I must have appeared unbelievably green to them.'

Scott stopped, and turned me towards him. 'You've come a long way since then, Cathy,' he said.

Then he placed both arms around my waist, drew me gently to him, and kissed me.

'Let's go back to my place now,' I said breathlessly as he released me. I had not been kissed like that, standing in the street, since senior school.

Now, I watched him as he spooned sugar into a fresh cup of mint tea, and thoughtfully stirred. Then suddenly he took my hand, palm upwards, and turned my fingers slowly inwards, one at a time, while staring down at them.

He looked up; we caught each other's glance. The expression in his eyes, the warmth of his hand around mine filled me with a sudden longing.

'You're just the greatest person I know, Cathy.'

We leaned towards each other. 'That's what I think about you,' I answered.

We kissed. Drew away. Opened our mouths. Kissed again.

'I don't want to leave you tonight,' he said, holding me away from him.

I stroked his thick hair. 'Do you have to?'

'I have to fly out on a short mission in the morning. Just to northern France.'

'Then stay with me.'

We stood up. The dog stood up too, hopefully, and whined.

Scott tilted my chin and kissed me. 'Tell you what. You go up, and I'll take the dog out. If she'll come with me, that is.'

'Just watch her,' I said. 'Take the door keys with you. They're on the hall table.'

I lay in bed with the covers pulled up, wondering how I'd feel if he left the bedside light on. Would those thirteen years' age difference prove too much for him? Had he really thought about it? Despite all that, I felt sexual, I wanted him.

He came into the room, a towel around his waist. His skin was tanned, his chest veiled in dark hair. I noticed a scar to one side, another on his arm. He saw me looking.

He touched the one at the side of his chest. 'This one was the result of an injured spleen when I was a motor-cycle racer. I skidded on a particularly bad bend and other motorcycles went over me. I was lucky not to be killed. The one on the arm was caused by a knife attack some time later.'

'You've led a rough life, Scott Peters,' I said as I sat up, drew my knees up towards me, modestly holding the covers across my breasts.

He sat down on the edge of the bed and placed a hand on my knees. 'The dog's in the kitchen. I've put all the lights out.'

A boldness born of desire took hold of me. I reached forward, stroked his face. 'I think it's time you came to bed, Mr Scott and stopped being so domestic,' I said, letting my hand drift slowly across his shoulders and down one arm.

Then I reached over, turned back the covers beside me, and patted the bed.

It seemed to be morning before we were sated.

Scott woke first. I awakened to find I was encased in his arms, and he was kissing me long and tenderly, twining my hair between his fingers, and whispering into my ear that it was time for him to leave.

I returned his kisses, reluctant to relinquish my place in his arms.

'We could have something good beginning, Cathy,' he said quietly, his face close to mine.

'I think so too. If you don't mind my being so much older than you.'

'I prefer it. The only other woman I've truly cared for was older than me.'

'What happened?'

'She was married to a friend. It had to end.'

'Let's give it a try then,' I whispered from my pillow. 'Can you stay here with me tonight?'

'I'd love to.'

I ran my hand lightly through his chest hair. 'If I know what time you're returning, I'll prepare supper for us.'

'I'd like that,' he answered softly. 'The weather forecast isn't brilliant for northern France, but I'll return before dark. I'm happy to take you out to dinner, though.'

'No, I want to cook for you,' I said quickly. 'Is it safe for you to fly helicopters in bad weather?'

'Would six thousand hours' experience in all winds and weathers make you feel better?' He traced a finger, one that was slightly misshapen, across my forehead. 'You don't need to worry about me, ever, Cathy. If the job was too much for me, I'd give it up.'

I took hold of the hand that was damaged and caressed the fingers. 'What happened to you here?'

'I was shot down in Iraq and captured before I could escape. Like the other POWs, I was tortured by bastards who enjoyed it. The fingers couldn't be repaired any better than this.'

Without warning, he slid from beside me, leaped out of bed and drew back the curtains. I hid my face against the morning light.

He knelt over me, kissed my lips once more and traced the outline of my breasts with a finger. I hoped they would meet with his approval.

I opened my eyes, wallowed in his fine physique, his lovely nakedness.

'How did you manage to get such a fine tan?' I asked him, to take my mind off him looking at my body.

He laughed. 'I love the subtle way you have of checking up on me. I was working in a great climate for a few weeks. They do give me some time off, you know, now and then.'

I watched him as he crossed the room and disappeared into the bathroom. Then I stretched, closed my eyes. I was a woman engulfed in post-coital joy. A woman not accepting at that special moment that her happiness might be fleeting . . .

I woke with a start, a moment before he kissed me.

He was ready to leave. Beside the bed stood a mug of steaming hot tea. 'I hope I'm right in thinking that you don't take sugar,' he said, moving a tendril of damp hair from my forehead.

'Oh, Scott, you shouldn't.'

'I took the dog out quickly to give you a break. Now I must fly, literally.'

I reached up, put my arms around his neck and pulled his head down towards me. I kissed his lips.

'Goodbye, Scott.'

He straightened up. 'Bye, Cathy. See you later. I'll try to make contact.'

\* \* \*

**Philippa Todd**

I arrived, not surprisingly, rather later than usual at the salon, feeling re-energized in the very best of ways. Even I could see how happy and bright I looked in every reflection. So what hope was there of hiding it from others?

There was a spring in my step as I strode around positively in my loafers and jeans, I sang softly to myself, and smiled into the faces of everyone I met.

I planned to spend the morning pattern-making for the prêt-à-porter collection until I had to leave for St James's Palace, and Clementine.

I instructed my staff to let me work undisturbed, taking no telephone calls, and leaving everything out front to Fran, but it was no time at all before she was upon me, before I even had a chance to reach the workroom.

She smiled into my face. 'No need to ask if it was you Scott stayed with last night.'

I blushed like a teenager and moved over towards the safety of my desk, smiling politely.

'Don't worry, I'm not going to ask for details,' she said. 'He looked every bit as sheepish as you do when he blew in this morning.'

'I didn't mean to arrive so late,' I said, not looking at her.

'You can make up for lost time,' she said, smiling at her own *double entendre*. 'It so happens that I'm extremely happy for you. You should both go for it, I say.'

I leaned against the edge of my desk and looked at her. 'I like him a lot,' I answered. 'Of course, I'd like it still more if he were around ten years older.'

She put her head on one side. 'What the hell difference does age make if you're right for each other?'

'Thank you for your support, Fran. I appreciate it.'

'No problem. You can count on me. Of course I'm jealous as all hell.'

I stood up straight, her words bothering me. 'I didn't think you'd mind. I didn't realize. Did you and Scott once have an affair?'

'Not Scott, silly. Not a man. I just want to belong to someone, the way you seem to, now.'

Annabel, my new assistant, knocked at that moment and

came in to say that everything was ready for me. Our girlie conversation was at an end.

The business telephone board flashed; Fran rushed to take control. The fax machine spewed out paper. My private line began to ring. I literally ran towards the cutting-room.

Beginning is always the most difficult part at the pattern-making table, but soon I fell into the swing of things.

Annabel had prepared the room well: large heavy sheets of paper conveniently stacked, drawings placed on easels where they were easy to see at a glance; chalk, scissors, tape measures, rulers. Everything was where it should be, and the table was cleared ready for action.

She asked me many questions, and we worked well together.

She would only be as good a pupil as I was a teacher, I knew that. And as from today, I wanted her to be especially good. I was bold enough to be thinking that if my affair with Scott had any kind of a future, I might need a little more free time to be with him . . .

I managed to check my thoughts in that direction. I had to remember that I was going through a vulnerable patch. Only the other week I'd been contemplating marrying Richard.

If I stupidly allowed the excitement of one night in the sack with Scott to envelop my mind to the point of seeing a future in our relationship I could be riding for a heavy fall. Wasn't it a fact that I could not afford to let that happen? If anything at all affected my business, just when it was peaking nicely, I would be in real trouble. I'd wasted enough time over trivialities through the years as it was. Now, it was essential to surge ahead in an unblinkered fashion.

I was explaining the intricacies of sizing to Annabel – the simplest way of going up in centimetres from size eight to size fourteen – when my left arm gave the usual trouble. Nothing terrible, but twice it gave little involuntary seizures, and those, I assure you, I didn't much like. But I really didn't have the time to worry about it.

I looked at my watch and found it was time to change and

leave, not time to fuss about an arm. I gave Annabel some practice work to do, asked her if she would help me carry the antique lace and sketches to the car, and went off to have lunch with the delightful Lady Clemmie.

# SIX

He rang the bell twice. I rushed to open the door, pausing only to regain my breath in the hope of appearing calm. I'd expected him to arrive sooner, but I was grateful for the extra time.

The lunch in St James's Palace had gone on for quite a while, but I was glad to be introduced to the duchess, and the handsome fiancé who came over from his banking establishment to join us for dessert and coffee.

It had been quite a rush for me to get away from the workplace later, with enough time to take the dog around the park, and call at the supermarket for lamb chops, new potatoes, out of season tropical fresh fruit and vanilla ice-cream.

But here I stood now, behind the front door, showered, perfumed, groomed to high heaven, and wearing my only pair of expensive silk lounging pyjamas; with everything prepared for supper, the dining-table set for two, candles in place, tiny flowers as a centrepiece, my special Crown Derby china standing by, and the best of my cutlery collection.

I took one last deep breath, threw open the door, smiling happily; and there he stood, the blast from the past, Leon the Lawless, the usual grin on his wide mouth that I remembered well. The one that was so easy for him to produce when events necessitated it.

His dark curly hair reached down to his shoulders and was going grey. Gone was the flamboyant Italian sartorial splendour. His insignificant grey suit was creased and shapeless, the collar of his blue shirt was dirty and the top button was open under his stringy blue tie. He was a sorry state to behold, looking every inch the ex-convict that he was from head down to dusty-shod toe.

The ragged hold-all at his feet and the large brown paper parcel tied up with gardener's twine said it all; and I confess to wishing that he had landed anywhere but on my doorstep. It had been over between us long before he walked into trouble.

'You didn't need to climb into silk pyjamas for my arrival, Dolly,' he said, still grinning, not taking his hands out of his trouser pockets.

My emotions ranged from fear I couldn't explain because I had no reason to regard him a violent man, through anger at his audacity, to pity at his thinness and unkempt appearance; and in my confusion I merely stood there, silently.

'You could ask me in, I don't bite,' he said, looking me up and down with those heavily lashed dark eyes of his that gave nothing away. 'Or were you expecting someone else?'

I began to shiver; either from the chilly night air blowing on my scantily clad warm body, or from a nervous reaction.

'Why are you here, Leon?' I asked, ignoring his question.

He lifted his hands theatrically in the old familiar gesture. 'Ah, things are looking up, the lady remembers my name. I've been in gaol, funnily enough, or had you forgotten?'

He picked up his hold-all and parcel. 'Am I supposed to be coming in, or what?'

I stood aside reluctantly and he stepped over the threshold.

My dog, who had never met him, gave a low bark from the kitchen where I had shut her, not wanting her to leap all over Scott when he arrived.

'Surely, departing inmates are sent off before lunch, rather like hotel guests?' I said, not without sarcasm, and not particularly liking myself because of it.

'Nice one, Dolly. Keep it in the script,' he answered, looking around him, trying to ascertain what might be happening further down the hall.

'The name's Cathy.'

'Yeah, that's what you always used to say. You posh birds never have a sense of humour.'

I stood where I was, looking past him.

'Pretty place you've got here, too. Did you get a good price for the flat where we lived?'

I ignored the question. 'I suppose you've been tramping around all day hoping to find someone willing to put you up?'

It would not have been easy for him, I was sure of that; the Lord only knows how many people he has done over in his time.

He looked down at me. 'Something like that. I didn't imagine you'd be overjoyed to see me, but a fella can hope. Could we go somewhere so I can put these things down?'

I led the way through the hall and towards the kitchen, calling a command to the dog as I went.

'You told me in the only letter you ever wrote to me that you'd bought a dog. I wondered if you were trying to tell me something.'

'What would you like to drink?' I asked, ignoring his remark. 'I don't have much time to give you.'

I wished I felt as calm as I hoped I sounded. Scott was already late. He really had to arrive at any moment.

Leon pulled out a chair from under the table, sat down heavily, stretched out his legs, and laid a hand tentatively on the dog's head as she sniffed at him.

'A beer would go down a treat. Who are you expecting?'

'A house guest.'

The telephone rang. I hurried across the kitchen and snatched it up; please, God, let it not be Scott phoning to cancel, I said to myself.

'Hello, Cathy,' he said. 'Scott here. I'm sorry, I've been held up. I'll be another half an hour.'

'Anything wrong?' I asked anxiously, thankful that he couldn't hear the thumping of my heart.

'No. I've just landed.'

'You do still want supper?'

'You bet, I'm ravenous, Cathy. I've been listening in on crooks choosing great lunches in restaurants without a hope of getting food myself.'

'Where are you?' I asked, aware that I was sounding anxious.

'Fairly close by. Are you all right, Cathy?'

'Yes, perfectly. A friend has just called in for a few moments.'

'Oh. Well, I won't be long.'

'I hope not.' But please be long enough for me to get rid of Leon, I prayed.

He bent forward to untie a shoelace as I placed a can and a glass in front of him.

'No, don't do that, Leon,' I said quickly. 'You can't stay here. We're through, you know that.'

True to form, he raised his hands in a pacifying gesture, denoting that he was merely trying it on. Nothing had changed. As I had suspected, it would take more than a spell in gaol to change Leon.

'Okay, okay,' he said quickly. 'I suppose I was hoping – well, never mind.'

He looked down at his hands. My gaze followed. I noticed they were dirty. It was not like him; at least he had been fastidious when I knew him.

I was miserable for him; but in truth I wished that he would leave before Scott arrived. I couldn't even remember if I'd mentioned anything at all about him to Scott. My brain was in turmoil.

'Have you told your mother that you're out?' I asked, in desperation.

'My old girl? No,' he answered. 'I've given her nothing but grief really, why would she care?'

'But mothers always forgive, you know that. Ring her up, tell her you've nowhere to stay. Be honest with her. She won't turn you down.'

He continued to avoid my gaze. 'She never came to see me in the nick. Not once. Said seeing me behind bars would upset her. Pretty lame excuse.'

'Well, now's the time for you to forgive each other.'

He looked into my face for the first time. 'You reckon?'

'I'm sure. Ring her now.'

**Whispers On A Pillow**

I brought the telephone to the table, watched while he reluctantly dialled the number, and then quickly replaced the receiver.

The line was busy, he said. Could he have another beer?

As I put the second can down in front of him, he grabbed my hand. 'I was going to ask you. Could you lend me something?'

I freed my hand from his. 'I don't keep money in the house,' I said, knowing that if I gave him anything, no matter how small, he would see it as weakness, and be back for more.

'Anything at all. A small amount. I'm borasic lint . . . skint.'

'I'm sure that your mother will help you,' I said firmly. 'Try the number again.'

This time I heard it ringing, heard his mother pick up the receiver.

I turned away, and as I did so the doorbell rang.

I told the dog to stay in the kitchen with Leon, and hurried down the hall to let Scott in.

'Sorry about this,' he said as he stepped inside, looking great but rather work-weary in a black leather flying jacket over a dark polo-necked sweater and black jeans, putting down his black leather bag in order to place his hands on my shoulders and kiss me.

I noticed as he pulled away that there was a scratch on his left cheekbone, and another at the base of his ear.

'You were quick,' I said, aware that my voice was too loud.

'I was allowed to land at the City airport. Then I jumped on a tube train.'

'You've been hurt. Your cheek . . . ?'

He touched it. 'Nothing much. I had to put down in rough country and make myself scarce in a hurry.'

We both heard Leon's voice on the telephone.

'You look pale,' Scott said. 'Is something wrong? I thought you sounded strange on the telephone.'

I took his hand and dragged him with me into the dining-room.

'I think I may have mentioned Leon to you?' I said, facing him. 'We lived together for a time.'

'Yes, you mentioned him,' he replied, unsmiling. 'He sounded a real crook.'

**Philippa Todd**

'He was released from gaol today and he's called in,' I said, speaking hurriedly. 'Right now he's telephoning his mother hoping for a bed.'

Scott's face revealed nothing. 'Had you invited him to eat dinner?' he asked, glancing at the table set only for two.

'No, of course not.'

'Do you want him to go?'

'Well, yes, and he will. I don't want to be unkind.'

He placed his hands on my shoulders. 'Who's going to be unkind? Don't you think that you should introduce me?'

We made our way to the kitchen, and arrived as Leon was replacing the receiver. With his other hand he was stroking the dog's head, but she got up at the sight of Scott and began wagging her tail.

Leon stood up, and I had the distinct impression that for the first time he realized that the visitor who rang the doorbell was a man. He felt in his breast pocket and pulled out a pair of spectacles, which he promptly put on. He used to boast to me that it was what he did if he felt physically threatened.

'Leon, this is Scott,' I said.

Scott put out a hand with ease of style, his face revealing nothing, his eyes on Leon's face. 'Hello, Leon.'

Leon took a spiritless and unusually cautious step forward. I wondered if he would ever return to the spontaneous flashing smile, the brash approach that I'd learned often heralded nervousness. Or was that gone for ever?

He nodded, and shook Scott's hand with firmness.

'Can your mother help you?' I asked anxiously.

'Yes, she can,' he answered. 'I must be going, she said to hurry. Thanks for the beer, Cathy.'

'You're welcome,' I replied, aware that my hands were clenched tightly together.

Scott turned towards me. 'I'll see Leon out for you, Cathy,' he said. 'I have to get my bag from the hall.'

Leon turned towards me, false bravado making him attempt to give the old wide smile in farewell. '*Ciao*, Cathy. Thanks again for the beer. I'll see you around.'

'Goodbye, Leon,' I answered. 'Good luck. Be nice to your mother.'

I lit the grill, turned up the gas under the baby potatoes, put plates and dishes in the oven.

Next thing I knew, Scott was turning me around to face him. In his hand he clasped a large bottle of my favourite French perfume.

'Before you ask, I bought it when I landed to refuel. I'm getting to notice you have a suspicious mind. But since meeting Leon I think I know why.'

I thanked him for the perfume and tried to laugh it off. 'I'm sorry about all that. Whatever must you think of me?'

He leaned towards me. 'Want to know something, Cathy? I'm just happy to discover that this sophisticated lady is not perfect, and is just as vulnerable as the rest of us.'

I rubbed my forehead, as I was prone to do when bothered. 'Some sophistication. I feel so ashamed. It was awful for you.'

He took my hand away from my head, and held it. 'Of course it wasn't. I don't think Leon's a bad person, he's just totally without morals. I can understand you finding him – what was it you told me – amusing after Clive, a breath of fresh air.'

I could feel the comforting warmth of his palm through my thin silk sleeve.

'I only went to the party where I met him because I was lonely, and feeling low and insecure after my crushing divorce. He made me laugh, he could be very funny.'

He looked into my eyes. 'You don't owe me an explanation.'

'He always called Clive the Pompous Prat.'

'Did he know him?'

I smiled to myself. 'Leon hated his nose. I had to agree that it was his worst feature. I suggested he went to see Clive. After all, he was the best.'

Scott played with my fingers. 'Was Clive generous in the divorce? I've heard bad stories about English husbands.'

I lowered my eyes away from his. 'Clive could afford meaner-spirited lawyers than I could. The settlement was far from just.'

He leaned over and slowly rubbed his hand along my arm. 'English courts are never generous to jilted wives, are they? Not like back home where they let wives take husbands to the cleaners.'

'And then the press made him sound like God,' I persisted. 'Which I suppose is what he is in the operating theatre.'

Scott kept his hand on my arm, watched me, let me talk.

'Leon sat by me on a sofa all that night at the party. He was nice to me, brought me dessert, refilled my wine glass. He made me laugh a lot, and I'd not laughed in ages.'

I made myself look into Scott's face. 'What did you say to him, at the front door? You didn't threaten him, did you?'

Scott smiled. 'Why would I threaten him? I merely told him that I was your fiancé.'

'You told him that? What else did you tell him?'

'He told me he wished that he could get into America; asked me if I could help him.'

'What did you say to that?'

'I told him I would try. He asked me what I did for a living. I told him I was in law enforcement, working for the US government. I don't think he'll call on you again in a hurry. But I wished him luck.'

I stood up, moved towards the cooker. 'Only ten minutes till eating time,' I said over my shoulder.

He came up behind me. 'Great. I'm pretty darned hungry.'

'That was the best dinner I've eaten in ages,' he said, as I collected our plates.

'I intend to believe you, though I doubt it's true,' I answered.

He poured another glass of wine for me, a small amount for himself. 'I think that we should drink to our relationship. I think it's a pretty nice one, Cathy.'

'I do, too.'

'Let's try to foster it, shall we? Let's face it, you're a workaholic with a business to run. I'm committed to the life I chose. Meeting won't be without its problems.'

'Nothing ever is,' I mused.

We blew out the candles, took the dishes to the kitchen sink. I changed into jeans and a jacket, and we took the dog out.

'I won't be back this way for about a week and a half,' he said, placing an arm around my waist as we walked. 'After that I'll have a few days off. Why don't I hire a helicopter and fly you into the wilds for a romantic weekend?'

# Whispers On A Pillow

'It sounds great to me,' I answered, wondering if he'd remember that he'd made the suggestion, wondering if my workload would allow me to go if he did. 'But won't the flying part feel like a busman's holiday for you?'

'Not at all, I'm an aeronautics junkie. I just thought that it would be nice for you, unless of course you don't like helicopters?'

'I love every kind of flying; it's a wonderful idea.'

'Where shall we go?' he asked. 'Let's make it somewhere where they have exceptional food, log fires and terrific beds.'

'I've often wished that I could go to a place called Llangoed Hall on the River Wye,' I replied. 'But that's in Wales; would it be too far?'

'No way. That's a wonderful idea.'

'I could make a booking if you like?' I added tentatively.

'Wonderful. D'you think your dog has peed enough for tonight? I feel like taking you home to bed.'

'I feel like drinking a mug of hot tea and then going to bed.'

'We'll toss for it,' he answered.

Back at home, I won the toss. Scott put the kettle on.

We sat at the kitchen table, being thoughtful, steaming mugs of tea in front of us.

Scott got up suddenly, walked around the back of me, placed his strong fingers on my neck and began to massage.

'You're so tense,' he said.

'I know. But surely you're not surprised?'

He hesitated. 'Not because of me, I hope? I can sleep in your guest room if you would prefer. Or even beat it round to Fran's place. I carry a key.'

I lowered my head. The pain he was causing to my knotted shoulder muscles was agony and bliss at the same time.

'Of course it's not because of you. But it's because of what happened earlier this evening. I hated you seeing what a fool I've been in the past.'

He went back to his seat. 'We've all been there, Cathy, in different ways,' he answered.

'You too?'

'Me too.'

'What happened to you?'

'Oh, it was when I was sent to Germany for several months before the wall came down. I had a bad experience with a German girl. She made a lot of trouble for me.'

'What did she do?'

'Apart from a touch of whoring you mean? Oh, she tried to get me for breach of promise, reported to the military that I'd promised to marry her.'

'And had you?'

'Of course not. I wasn't even free to marry at the time. And if I had been I wouldn't have chosen her. I realized later that she was looking for an American husband so that she could get to the States.'

He kissed the nape of my neck; I liked the feeling.

'Lean back in your chair for a moment,' he said. 'I'll relieve you of the pain.'

I did so. He placed his hands around my head, waited for a second and then suddenly pulled. My neck cracked. I felt instant relief.

He patted my shoulders. 'You'll feel better now. Let's go up, I need to shower.'

I awoke to the warmth of his hand caressing my naked back, and his lips on my hair as I lay in his arms, my head on his chest.

'I hate disturbing you, Cathy, my love,' he said. 'But it's almost time for us to get up.'

I scarcely moved. 'I don't want to,' I muttered defiantly, trying to open my heavy eyelids. 'I'd rather stay like this.'

He moved my hair from the side of my brow and kissed my temple. 'I'd rather we were making love again.'

'Is there time?' I whispered as my stomach churned in longing.

'We'll make time,' he answered. I could hear the emotion in his voice, feel the object of his desire pressing against me.

I lifted my head from his chest and up towards his face to kiss him.

Later, in the shower, as the water cascaded over our heads and down our bodies, he took me lightly in his arms, kissed me tenderly and traced a line with his finger down to the base of my throat.

'Cathy,' was all he said.

I buried my head in his wet chest hair, licked drops of water from his skin, revelled at our closeness.

'Go ahead and book our weekend,' he said as we towelled each other down.

'If you're sure,' I answered.

'Sure I'm sure. I'll contact you before then, but I'll be here.'

He combed back my wet hair with his fingers.

'I really would appreciate it if you'd help me find an apartment when I return,' he said. 'I do love London, and now that I've met you, and it's your city . . .'

'I've spoken to two agents and they're both sending brochures. I'll get a short list made up for when you're next here.'

He took me in his arms, kissed my lips. 'I shall be thinking a lot about you, Cathy. And I'll miss you.'

I looked into his face. 'I'll miss you too. But let's tread carefully. I would like our affair to last a long time.'

He gently stroked the base of my throat with a finger. 'Don't worry, Cathy. I won't hassle you. We'll take it a step at a time.'

I passed him a bathrobe. 'Let's go down to breakfast,' I said.

Finally, we stood at my closed front door giving in to a last embrace. He held my face tenderly in his hands. 'I've written down my red field number for you to copy and keep somewhere very safe. It's lying on your pillow. Use it only if you absolutely have to.'

I nodded my head.

'For the next few days I'll be on a refresher. I'll be calling you when I can.'

I nodded again, gazing anxiously into his eyes.

'We have a very special relationship, Cathy. Don't you agree?' he asked.

'Yes, I do,' I answered. Then I reached up and kissed his lips.

As I did so, on an impulse, I turned, opened the hall table drawer and took out a spare set of door keys.

'Take these with you,' I said, thrusting them into the palm of his hand.

He stared at them. 'But are you sure, Cathy?'

## Philippa Todd

'Yes,' I said, reaching up to his lips with mine and kissing him again. Then I smiled at him. 'But go now, before I change my mind.'

I looked at the clock; already knowing I'd be late for work.

Someone was coming to have lunch and I couldn't for the life of me recall who it was, thanks to my night of love with Scott. I telephoned Fran to find out.

'It's Lady Trenchard,' she read from the diary. 'Rose, it says, in brackets. And her daughter.'

Ah, yes, Rose Bellamy as she used to be. My old flatmate. 'That's nice. Would you telephone Abi for me? Have her send round something nice for lunch. Rose wants me to alter her wedding dress so that her only daughter can be married in it.'

'But you don't do alterations,' Fran said, sounding shocked.

'For Rose I'd do anything,' I answered. 'She's great. The dress is nice too . . .'

Oh, yes, that dress. In the six weeks that it had taken me to stitch it together by hand all those years ago, fingers shredded and sometimes bleeding from sharp sewing needles, constant tears in my eyes from straining to see, that dress had been let out more times than an incontinent cat, and thirty-two weeks later we all knew why.

Rose had married well. The groom's father had died young from cancer and left him, while he was still at Eton, enormous tracts of land in England, Scotland and Jamaica, and no mean fortune to go with them. Rose had given him two sons and one daughter for his kindness in agreeing to marry her.

We'd kept in touch after a fashion; but as she lived in a Scottish stately pile complete with hunting lodge and was kept busy with county activities and running a huge home, our meetings were rare. She didn't get to London all that often, even though she'd inherited her parents' Belgravia flat.

But her children used it often enough, and more than once it had featured in the national press. Especially when a young man called Blandford had kicked in the door, in order to get to Araminta.

\* \* \*

I ran up the stairs before leaving the house to retrieve Scott's all-important telephone number. There was no point in leaving it lying around for Madge to peruse in my absence.

She would soon enough be getting curious about us: dishes for two in the sink, a dishevelled bed, and a reasonably flooded bathroom.

My heart missed a beat as I saw his handwriting for the first time: large, round, slightly scrawled.

Cathy, he'd written:

Should you need to find me urgently, anywhere, any time, ring this number: ... When the operator answers DO NOT STATE YOUR NAME. Give this code: ... it will be exclusively for you. Then state that you wish to speak to me personally. You will either be connected to me direct, or they will promise to find me and I shall call you back a.s.a.p. Destroy this sheet of paper when you've copied it. Now turn over.

On the other side he had written: 'I shall have to take care not to fall in love with you. Scott.'

If I was to enjoy an affair with Scott, I told myself as I drove through the heavy traffic, there was one thing I had to come to terms with. I could not allow the sexual part of our relationship to interfere with my working day. I had to get the magic of it off my mind when I walked in through the office door.

I'd had many a sexual experience before, and so had he. We had hardly invented the act. But never before in my life had I experienced anything like this.

I really liked this man. If I had the guts to be honest with myself, and face facts, I'd damn nearly fallen in love with him.

But I had a business to run; a business I had worked hard to bring to what it was today. No one really knew what the responsibility was like. And since I'd been alone, it had replaced everything else. My kids were grown, they didn't need me. I had no domestic responsibility beyond my dog. The business had become my *raison d'être*, like it or not.

'Telephone for you,' Fran said, as I breathlessly pushed open the office door, dog at my heels, panting as hard as I was, it having taken fifteen minutes for us to find a parking place.

'Is that Catherine Anthony?' the smooth as silk, plum-in-mouth male voice purred into the receiver.

It was my sponsor for the charity show.

Hastily, I switched to my most professional mode; work for the day had begun.

'Darling,' Rose shouted from the doorway. 'Look at you, I can see you're not going short of what a girl likes most. You look younger than when we last met, by a long way.'

'Thanks a bunch, Rosie, old girl,' I said, going towards her.

'Mummy, for goodness sake,' Araminta interjected, as she followed her mother inside, tottering on four-inch Gucci platforms and showing off her slender black-tighted legs almost to her crotch. 'Roberts will hear you.'

Roberts was the chauffeur who brought up the rear, bearing an enormous Gucci suitcase which undoubtedly housed the bridal gown.

Rose then pointed to a far corner of the reception area without speaking.

Roberts dutifully took the suitcase to the corner, touched the rim of his cap in deference and went back out to the double-parked vintage Bentley to await her ladyship's pleasure.

We proceeded to devour our lunch of capsicums stuffed with minced aubergine and goose livers, followed by lime and mascarpone flan; and Rose entertained me throughout with her hilarious accounts of country living. What an immoral lot those county folk were; they made us townies seem like religious converts.

We were interrupted by a call from the princess's old school friend.

'I would like to make an appointment to see you this week about my outfit. May I call you Catherine?' she said (taking me straight back to the awful gaffe I made with Scott at the launch several months ago), rushing through her words in the same breathy voice as the princess, but with not quite as much style.

'I'd be delighted,' I answered, and Rose silently ridiculed my instant change of tone to my professional voice.

Fran held open my appointments book under my nose for me to point to a suitable slot.

'I haven't a clue what I want,' she trilled. 'But a rich colour would be nice.'

'I'll have sketches waiting for you to see,' I replied, then ventured, tentatively, 'I've some silk grosgrain in the most adorable colour for you to look at.'

'Oh, how wonderful. What colour is it?'

'I call it raspberries-crushed-up-with-cream. It's very rich in colour.'

'Adorable,' she intoned. 'I simply can't wait to see it.'

'You should dress her in chainmail,' Rose said wickedly as I replaced the receiver. 'And metal toecaps on her shoes. Then you'd really get publicity.'

'That's an idea,' I said jokingly. 'I'll start working chainmail into the clothes right away. A few trips around the hardware shops should provide me with some strapping ideas.'

Araminta sighed loudly. 'Can I try on the wedding gown now, please, and start the adjustments? They're going to take ages. I'm much slimmer than Mummy ever was, you know. I'm not even sure why she wants me to wear the thing.'

'What rot,' Rose replied. 'Let's not forget who was the mannequin in our illustrious family. And how do you think Cathy feels at such a wonderful gown being called a *thing*?'

I declined to get involved.

The pinning and tucking was interrupted shortly after we'd begun when Richard telephoned me.

'It's been a long time,' he said softly. 'Can we meet? How about dinner?'

'Only if it's my treat. I've been trying to find time to speak to you, but I've been so busy.'

'Lucky you,' he said. 'Who on earth is that next to you, a lady with an extremely loud voice?'

'Oh, that's only Rose. Remember her? We've been friends for ever. She's Lady Trenchard now, for her sins.'

'Good Lord,' he said. 'Yes, I remember Rose from the Shepherd Market days, and the friend you used to call Charlotte the Harlot. Give her my regards.'

'So how about next Thursday night for dinner?' I suggested. 'My treat, remember, or the deal is off.'

Richard gave his lovely laugh. 'You win. Am I allowed to pick you up?'

'Of course; I'll no doubt be too exhausted to drive by then.'

'What on earth was all that about?' Rose asked. 'Paying the bill to go out with a man to dinner. That's unheard of.'

I laughed. 'Not any more it isn't. It's the share-everything decade; hadn't you heard about it, tucked away in your fifty-bedroomed mansion? You'll have to make more of an effort to move with the times, dear girl.'

Then, of a sudden, my buoyant mood was flattened.

'Talking of doctors reminds me,' Rose said casually, as we walked away from the fitting-room towards my office, having left Araminta in the expert care of the fitter. 'A friend of mine who lives near Clive in Richmond has been dating him recently.'

'I think I've heard of her,' I answered carefully, not showing particular interest. 'Abi mentioned that her father had introduced her to a neighbour he seemed to be on rather friendly terms with.'

'She's jolly attractive,' Rose said, fearing that I was not reacting in the way she certainly would have done.

'She'd have to be,' I retorted. 'The competition's pretty fierce. Did they meet over a face-lift?'

Rose laughed. She was happier now that she felt she had my full attention, and just maybe was whipping me up a bit.

'She thinks that he should have been knighted by now, all those services to reconstructive surgery you know. All those poor people he helped back to face the world again; in more ways than one.'

'Clive probably thinks the same way, especially as many of his lesser colleagues are already sporting their gongs.'

I poured us some coffee as she sat down.

'He blames you,' she said casually, not looking in my direction.

'Me? How on earth did I get into this?'

'Something to do with having a wife who was a dressmaker. And all that publicity over the divorce.'

I felt anger rising from deep down as I handed her the cup and saucer, something that didn't happen to me often.

Rose could see that I was hurt at such an unjust statement. She, more than anyone, knew how hard I'd tried to keep my marriage and subsequent divorce a private matter. She, more than anyone, knew about Clive's unforgivable behaviour.

I had always suspected that she'd once had a fleeting affair with him herself; and it was only fear of the answer that had stopped me from asking her if it was true.

I sat down stiffly behind my desk. 'It could be that Her Majesty did some checking up on his behaviour through the years,' I said, a trifle bitchily.

'What do you mean, Cathy?' Rose asked, no doubt wondering what was coming next.

'Well, you know,' I said, stalling while I found words cutting enough to describe the injustice I felt. 'Women gossip, even to the queen. Maybe someone suggested quietly that behind that facade and unusual talent there lurks a man with a unique policy for living.'

'Such as?' Rose asked.

'Oh, you know, if it's unconscious, revive it, if it moans give it anaesthetic. And if it moves, screw it.'

It was an unkind thing to say, and I was not proud. But it did the trick. It rendered Rose silent.

I languidly strolled in the park in the late afternoon. There was no one nearby; I threw sticks for the dog to tire her out quickly.

I'd been stupid; it wasn't Rose's fault. She meant no harm, she just loved to gossip. I'd spoiled the visit, and it meant that I hadn't been able to tell her about Scott, which I'd wanted to do.

I usually knew how to handle her; and for me to say a thing like that to her about Clive . . .

There was no one I wished to confess to. If Scott had been around, I most probably would have told him. But he wasn't, and I had to climb out of my gloom by my own efforts.

My head still ached, so I went home and took an aspirin. I

didn't feel like eating; I poured a glass of wine, drank it, and shortly after poured another.

I took my sketching block to the dining-table and began to rough out a few designs for the prêt-à-porter range to lighten my mood before working on that all-important wedding outfit.

I found it refreshing to design for the very young and the not-so-well-offs. For those who had to budget so carefully they seldom, if ever, made a wrong purchase.

Not like some of my clueless couture clients who insisted, against my candid advice, on choosing bright pink when they had red hair, or short sleeves when they had arms as wrinkled as prunes. Then they'd send their new purchases unworn around to the specialists in second-hand designer clothes, to be sold for less than half their value before they had even paid my bill.

It was seeing one such gown in a window that caused me to make a tough rule for myself. Even if I lost the client, I would not make up anything for her that was grossly unsuitable.

It only happened once, and I wasn't really sorry because the client in question was overweight, overwrought, overly rich and extremely discontented.

Knowing that I was unlikely to sleep, even though it was now late, I replaced the *vin du pay* with a mug of hot milk and took my sketch pad to bed with me in order to draw just one more style that the friend of the princess might prefer, and to offer the best choice of styling possible.

Suddenly the telephone rang; I snatched it up, hoping that it might be who I wanted most to hear from; yet fearing it might be about bad news in the family.

'Cathy?'

'Yes. Is that you, Scott?'

'Do I have a wrong number?'

'I don't think so. Is that you, Scott?'

It had to be him. No one else could have a voice that was so soft, sexy – and so American.

'It sure is. I've just landed. The line isn't good, is it?'

'I can hear you, Scott, don't worry.'

'Are you still there, Cathy?'

'Yes, Scott, I'm here. Just talk to me.' (Before you drive me crazy.)

'Cathy, I have something I need to tell you.'
I held my breath. Oh, please, God, no bad news. Not tonight.
'Can you hear me, Cathy?'
'Yes, loud and clear. Is something wrong?'
Suddenly all I could hear was atmospheric noise; why couldn't he use a proper telephone? 'I can't hear you any more.'
There was a click. 'Can you hear me now?'
'Yes, that's much better. What is it?'
'I love you, Cathy. I've been thinking about you all the way across the Atlantic. I love you.'

# SEVEN

Not that I'm complaining; but we'd been saddled with the workload from hell. For five mornings on the trot I'd had to set my alarm for six o'clock to ensure a long enough working day.

By six forty-five I'd showered, swallowed a quick cup of coffee, whipped my single-person household into shape if it was not Madge's day, and dealt with my mascara.

I'd scoured the headlines of the morning paper for anything I ought to know, including the obituary page with the not totally unexpected demise of Hugo and any other of my OFs in mind.

I'd trotted the dog to her patch of grass, with shovel and receptacle in hand. I'd checked that answerphone and fax machine were both switched on, with Scott in mind.

By seven, I'd pulled in to an empty parking space outside the deserted Catherine Anthony Emporium, the first of the workers to arrive.

The amount of energy generated through my veins on account of the news from Scott would have powered a trolley bus, and I should be hanging my head in shame that a mere man could do that to me with three short words.

**Philippa Todd**

Whatever happened to those pearls of wisdom I'd tossed around, I asked myself, on those early morning car journeys between home and work? Such as, 'This is my new manless lifestyle now so I may as well enjoy it.' Not to mention, 'I'll never live my life through a man again,' and, 'I don't want to stay the night with a man, I just want to go out to dinner.' Or, the largest pearl of all, 'My career is so demanding I can't even consider having a man in my bed.'

Now here I was, bowled over enough to make me permanently hyperactive, a woman changed by two nights of sex and the donor's voice saying he loved her over the telephone.

The question I asked myself was: Am I a permanent brainless twit, or temporarily barking mad?

Answer: No, I don't think so.

Question: Was I flattered then that a thirty-six-year-old man could fancy me, forty-nine next month?

Answer: Well, no, not by him fancying me so much as actually telling me he'd fallen in love with me. That was quite flattering.

Question: But he didn't actually say he'd fallen in love with you, did he? I mean, you could tell your cat you loved her, but you're not going to fall in love with your cat, are you?

Answer: I don't have a cat.

Don't try to be smart, you know what I mean.

I had the distinct feeling that the dog had never been more pleased to get these early morning journeys over, as she shook herself out on the pavement and trotted to the front door ahead of me. But she did spare me a quizzical look each time, as though to say she'd enjoyed the verbal entertainment.

The days simply flew past. Everyone seemed to have picked up on my new energetic mood, and it's possible that we turned out more work in that one week than ever before.

I hung my new dark brown suit, with its fashionably slit skirt and high revers, behind the door of my office and jumped into it every time the occasion demanded that I should actually look like a dress designer.

I wore it, for example, with a beige mesh-knit tee-shirt to welcome the princess's friend to our establishment when she came to see my sketches and the proposed material for her wedding dress.

Of course, she wants the outfit in a hurry, like everyone else, and has requested a first fitting in forty-eight hours' time. For no pressing or important reason other than that she'll be out of England playing ladies polo in America for those vital weeks before her wedding.

Ah, well, that's what I'm here for, to pamper the rich. It keeps me humble, and it sure as hell keeps me on my toes. So with light hearts and happy faces we charged into the workroom and started to cut practically before she was through the door; and I've great hopes for a quick delivery.

The next few days I was kept busy cutting out cloth and helping with fittings. Fran keeps me up to date with the office work. If I stay late, so does she, and then we usually go for a drink and supper afterwards in the local.

It was during one of those evenings, while we were eating pub grub and drinking vino rosso, that she told me she had met a girl who she's completely dotty about.

'That's good news, Fran, congratulations,' I said. 'Let's see if the bar can raise two glasses of champagne for us, and we'll drink a toast.'

It was the first time in my life I'd had to congratulate one woman for being in love with another woman. It felt a little strange; a sign of the times, and another reminder of my age, I suppose.

Whatever, it affected me enough to cause me that night, in bed, in the dark, to put my hands on my breasts and try to imagine they were the hands of another woman. I moved my fingers gently over them, and I waited for a bit; but nothing happened. I didn't know whether to be disappointed, or out of touch; if you'll pardon the pun.

I am genuinely pleased for Fran though. Now I knew why she had been on such great form all week, the reason no doubt for *her* operating so energetically in the workplace, too.

'She's from Los Angeles and her name's Jenny. She works for a film company over there,' she said, looking into my face for a reaction. 'If anything comes of it, I may want to join her.'

'Ah,' I said, already wondering. 'That's the part I'll be sorry about.'

'I'll give you plenty of warning, you know that, don't you, Cathy?' she answered. 'That's a promise.'

On the strength of her news, I told her mine. I'd been longing to tell her anyway. 'Scott says he's in love with me,' I blurted out.

She looked up from her apple pie and cream. 'Surprise, surprise . . .'

'What's that supposed to mean?'

'I knew that before he did. It showed. Same with you, you ninny.'

'Oh, really. So you think he means it?'

She gave me the sly sideways look she'd perfected long ago. 'I think he's nuts about you. And don't bring up those thirteen years again, it's boring.'

'I wasn't going to.'

'Good. Are you in love with him?'

'Out of my mind. And pretty scared by it too.'

He'd rung off, after his loaded call last week to tell me out of the blue that he loved me. Or maybe he was cut off, I had no way of knowing. But I had not misheard him, of that I was sure. Sometimes his voice seems extremely deep, and doesn't carry well on the telephone.

The voice, the news, had sent my heart racing, and was most unlikely to promote sleep; and an hour later I took a little pink pill to help me out.

I was in love with him, no question, now that I could let myself into my own secret. And if I had the choice, I wouldn't be without him any minute of the day. But I had to try to control my feelings. He was handsome, and young, and exciting. There would be no shortage of women on his horizon. Maybe he had romances like this quite often and announced these feelings at random.

I was right to be cautious. I'd been let down before, and left to wallow in mistakes of my own making.

Clive had said, 'I'm so in love with you Cathy, Catherine, Charlie. I'll never let you down.'

I was rash enough to believe him.

Leon had said, 'I'm so in love with you, Cathy. I'm yours for life. I'll never let you down.'

I was rash enough to believe him, too.

The pink pill had just brought on the first wave of semi-consciousness when the telephone rang again. I snatched at the receiver in the dark, dropped it, retrieved it.

'You mad at me, Cathy?' he was saying as I put it to my ear.

'No, Scott, whatever makes you think that?'

'You didn't ring me back.'

'I didn't think that I could unless it was desperately important.' What was I saying? None of that came out right.

The line went dead. God help me, now he must be mad at me. I replaced the receiver. The telephone rang again. I picked it up.

'Jesus, you must really be angry,' he said. 'I was only changing to a new battery. Let's start over, shall we?'

'Good idea.'

'I'm in love with you, Cathy. Crazy about you. Might you have a problem with that?'

'Not at all. I'm in love with you too. Scary, isn't it?'

'Don't be scared,' he said in a low, reassuring voice. 'What we're sharing here is very special. We'll talk it all out over our weekend in the country.'

'I'll book us a room.'

'I'll hire us a helicopter.'

'I can't wait.'

'Neither can I. I love you, Cathy.'

'I love you, Scott.'

'Do you have a heavy day tomorrow?'

I had to think. That pink pill was playing hell with my train of thought. 'Heavy enough. A special client is coming in early for a first fitting. Then the nice lady who overprints designs for me follows her. Hopefully I'll find time for some pattern-making. How about you?'

'Reasonable. A heavy briefing or two. My dad will be in town; he's attending something at the White House, so I'll meet him for dinner. We don't get to meet up too often.'

**Philippa Todd**

'That'll be nice.'
'I might have to tell him about us. You know, as in might not be able to resist it.'
'He might have a fit.'
'Why would that be?'
'Because of my age.'
'Do you want me to lie and say you're thirty?'
'As long as I'm never going to meet him, sounds like a good idea.'
'Cut it out, Cathy. Love you. Bye.'
'Bye, Scott. Love you too.'

I replaced the receiver, slid down between the sheets, a sleepy smile across my face. My lover and I had just had our first cosy chat.

The you-know-which wedding outfit looks pretty good already, tacked together on the dressmaker's dummy; and when it's finished, we all agree it'll be way out.

Maybe just a few minor adjustments will be in order; and I shall suggest to the client that if she's going to wear her hair up, we can stiffen the collar into position and that way there'll be no fear of it moving.

I'll do the fitting myself, with Mary, my number two fitter, assisting. With the kind of figure the young lady is lucky enough to possess, I cannot believe we'll have many problems. Apart from the ones of personal taste, such as whether the dress should be nipped in more under the behind, or reveal more cleavage. Or whether the jacket should be longer, or, maybe, shorter.

I'm looking forward to seeing her again, she's such a delightful person.

The princess did a naughty move on us and came along too. No detectives, no security, driving her own car with her friend beside her. The responsibility of having her on the premises unattended gave me ulcer pains; and her mere sudden presence transformed the staff into a load of gibbering idiots. They were bumping into things, smiling when they should have looked serious, bobbing curtsies when it wasn't necessary.

**Whispers On A Pillow**

The princess seemed to think that it was all great fun and ended up doubled over with giggling

She'd really taken the opportunity to come in, she told me, so that she could choose the material for her own outfit for the friend's wedding which she would like me to make. She knew just what she wanted, and I could sketch it as she talked. It would be low-key, of course, nothing to detract from the bride.

'I simply adore that colour pink you're using,' she said. 'And your description is spot on. You should patent it, make the name of the colour your very own.'

'You'll never guess who's just walked in,' Fran cried, bursting into my office just before lunch break. 'Your friend, old Hugo, all five feet of him. And he's parked a vintage sports car right outside.'

'Can't be Hugo,' I said. 'He's a Volvo safe-as-houses man.'

'Well, I have news for you . . .'

'Darling girl,' said the man himself, as I walked through reception towards him, reaching up to kiss my cheek, while I lowered my head to accommodate him.

'Hugo, this is a surprise,' I said, feeling bad about looking at my watch as I spoke.

'I had this, well, you know how it is, darling,' he stammered. 'This sudden desire to take you to lunch. What say, old thing, fancy a spot?'

'What on earth is that you're driving?' I couldn't help asking, staring aghast through the window.

He laughed, turning slightly red from the effort. 'Oh, that's my baby, my old Morgan. I'm giving her an outing from the country.'

My God, I thought, was he safe to be driving it on a motorway, an old car like that, and himself a bit frail? How on earth would he get insurance?

Then I remembered: he was on the board of the largest insurance company in the country. No problems there then. But why did he seem so frisky?

'What do you think, Catherine? Do a chap the honour?'

'As long as it isn't Bucks,' I answered. 'I really only have time for the little Italian place around the corner.'

**Philippa Todd**

And besides, no way am I driving out in that open-topped Noddy car with you at the wheel!
'Capital,' he said.
I collected my coat.

After pasta al pesto, followed by veal piccata, he placed his tiny hand over mine. It was obvious he wanted to say something and I hoped he wasn't going to ask for his percentage on Clemmie's dress in advance. A pay-out like that could only happen when I'd received the cheque. Dukes were notorious for paying their bills but once a year.
Maybe he wanted to tell me he'd found a lady of means prepared to marry him, I thought. It was what he wanted most, and I knew that he was lonely.
'Will you marry old Hugo, dear girl?' he asked.
It was a great way for him to get my undivided attention, I can tell you. But what was going on? Was he making a joke and I was supposed to laugh? Was it silly season for widowers? First Richard, now Hugo.
Unusually for me, my tongue refused to function. I could only gaze at him in mute astonishment.
'Seems a bit silly not to ask for your hand,' he said. 'What with the old stately pile nearly always empty, unless I rattle around in it alone ...'
He tailed off for a bit. I took a sip of coffee.
'Oh, Hugo, you're very sweet.' (What else could I say?)
'We could use it, if only at weekends. I could move in with you in London, sell my place. Sounds capital, what?'
Not to me it didn't. For Hugo it might, though; he'd get a better life for less expense. Unless I was mistaken.
'Sophie is off to South Africa, you see. Marrying a charming chap out there, good family. We thought maybe you'd like to get married out there too. Sort of double wedding, I seem to remember Sophie calling it.'
He giggled, as though the idea were quite titillating.
'I told Sophie that I was sure you wouldn't mind chipping in a wedding gown for a newly acquired step-daughter. And you wouldn't, would you, old thing?'
I thought of my mother at that moment, and how she used

to say to me, 'Good manners are essential at all times, Catherine. Never forget.'

I was grateful for the 'never forget' part, for at that moment I came close.

'I can't remember if you've been to my country place, old thing. Have you?'

Well, not remembering, that would figure. For a man who couldn't remember to repeat a lavatory flush for the woman for whose hand he was now asking, how could he be expected to remember if he'd ever invited her to his country seat?

I shook my head.

He found a faded, dog-eared snapshot of the stately pile in his wallet. 'Palladian, you know,' he went on, unabashed. 'Built by my mother's great-great-grandfather. He made his fortune when iron was at its peak. Sophie will get the lot. Bit of an albatross though, poor girl.'

She could try selling it, I wanted to say, but didn't.

Hugo asked for a brandy for himself, and, can you believe, lifted a cigar from his top pocket.

'Of course, you and I will need to spend a bit of money on the roof; pillars are a touch dodgy, too.'

Unable to bear watching him search for matches any longer, I found some for him in my handbag.

'But the place would be good for your business. Ideal for fashion shows, cocktail parties, that sort of thing. And we could do all our private entertaining there. What say, Catherine, dear heart?'

You wouldn't want to hear, Hugo, old buddy, I said. But only to myself.

I patted the hand that wasn't holding the cigar, after he'd pocketed my matches. I looked at the liver spots on the back, not so much to see if they'd joined up and become dangerous, but because his having them at all reminded me that it might not be so very long before he'd need a live-in nurse, rather than a wife.

'It's very sweet of you, Hugo,' I said again. 'And please don't think that the offer isn't appreciated. But I'm not ready to marry again, you see.' Oops, be careful, he may say he'll wait. 'And I doubt I ever will be, ready that is,' I added.

He looked hurt, positively crushed. I glanced at my watch in the hope he'd recover quickly.

'Shall we get the bill?' I said, anxious to bring our meeting to a conclusion. 'I do have clients to see.'

He seemed visibly to shake himself, then languidly raised a finger to the waiter.

'I felt sure you would honour old Hugo with an affirmative,' he sniffed.

I tried to smile. 'Well, you know what they say, Hugo, never pre-empt the answer from a female.'

He picked up the bill from the saucer left prominently beside him.

'Oh, yes, a very good saying. I haven't heard that one before.'

No wonder he hadn't, I'd made it up on the spot in desperation.

'Two into forty-three,' he said, looking at me thoughtfully over the top of his reading glasses. 'That's twenty-one fifty each. Well, let's say just twenty-one for you, and twenty-two for me.'

The pantomime being played out in his purse was in danger of having me burst a blood vessel. Not that I minded paying half, but somewhere along the line I was sure he'd offered to take me out for lunch. And Dutch treat hadn't been mentioned once.

Then I remembered: that was before I'd turned down his romantic proposal.

On a whim, I decided I would like something new to wear for my weekend away with Scott. I discussed it with Suzie, in my office, and confided in her that the weekend was special to me.

'Of course you must have something new,' she said. 'I shall make it for you myself.'

'I was thinking of a dress for dinner on the Saturday night. Something plain that I can wear a dozen times afterwards. We don't have much time. What have we in stock that would be a suitable material?'

'We have that black silk with the drawn-thread look.'

'No, not black, too dressy and I've loads of black in my closet.'

'What about that fine aubergine crushed velvet?'

'That we made into a long dinner dress for the Princess of Oil?'

'That's it. There's a piece left over. I'm sure it would be enough for a knee-length dress.'

'I'd want it narrow, anyhow, maybe just kicking out towards the bottom,' I said. 'And short sleeves while I can.'

That would be fairly quick for me to cut, I thought. And easy too. Not so many hours ago I'd felt that disquieting dragging sensation in my hand again, and my arm seized up slightly. And now that I wasn't seeing Richard till after my special weekend because he had a heavy cold, I couldn't ask his opinion. Still, what the hell, it was nothing much, and if I was having a good time I wouldn't even think about it.

Suzie jumped up, looking pounds slimmer and rather pale after her hysterectomy, but full of enthusiasm.

'That colour will look great on you. I'll go and find it.'

'Do you think a man would like it?' I asked her.

'Oh, yes, no doubt about it. I won't be a minute.' She turned on her way to the door and smiled at me. 'Can I just say, I think he's lovely, your new man. That night at our party, I was thinking how lovely you looked together; when you stood beside him.'

I simply couldn't hold back the smile that creased my face.

It was raining when I arrived home at the end of my working day.

The dog and I ran from the car which I couldn't park closer than six doors away from my own.

I turned the key in the lock. Sacha did the rest, pushed the door with her nose, barged in, shook herself; she simply hates getting wet.

Then she trampled all over the mail on the mat with her wet paws. It didn't seem to matter; all the envelopes looked as though they contained junk mail or bills. Except one. It was buff-coloured, and under a wet paw mark it said something akin to Special Delivery. It had that official friendless look of a summons. I thought it best to have the glass of wine I'd promised myself first.

**Philippa Todd**

As I went into my study to check for messages, wine glass in hand, I saw a faxed letter curled around the back of the machine. I straightened it, tore it off the roll, put on my glasses.

Dearest Cathy,
I'll be with you 5 a.m. on Friday. Good thing you gave me the keys. A special assignment means I can't get there sooner. But four hours' sleep is all I'll need, and then we'll start off on our special weekend. I love you very much, Cathy, and can't wait to be with you.
Scott
PS I hope my card arrived. I sent it out with the official mail.

I tore back to the hall table, extricated the buff envelope from the junk mail, slit it open with my thumb.

On the front was a picture of what looked like a government building. Scott had circled a window on the second floor and drawn an arrow pointing down from the sky, at the top of which was printed, 'This is where my desk stands.'

On the other side it said simply, 'I love you. S. P.'

I put down my glass, read those three words he had written several times more, then hugged myself around the shoulders and did a twirl of sheer delight.

I'd jogged around the park in the early mornings. I'd exercised in my bathroom every night. Talk about getting to the burn, I was so exhausted I was numb.

But as far as being in good shape was concerned, I reckoned I was as close as I'd ever be. And I had the full-length mirror in my bathroom to confirm that it was as far as a woman my age could go. Even if Diana Ross had the figure of a young girl, at fifty.

So now it was the turn of wrinkles and cellulite.

Abigail said I didn't have any cellulite as far as she could see when I asked her to scrutinize.

Fran said I definitely didn't have any cellulite and if her thighs looked like my thighs when she was knocking fifty, she'd be overjoyed.

Me, I was sure I could see cellulite.

The large round pot of cream with the bright blue and gold lid had cost me fifty pounds. I deserved to be struck poor. Did I need counselling, or what? And that's not to mention the anti-wrinkle lotion with vitamin E and a touch of retine A for my face.

Much more of buying treatments like this in the search to lose thirteen years and I'd need an extended overdraft.

'Just tell me again, Mrs Anthony, why did you say you needed to extend your overdraft, exactly?'

'Well, it's like this, Mr Manager. I'm older than my lover, and, um . . .'

'They're not wrinkles, they're crow's feet,' Abi said, the Sunday before Scott was due to arrive when she, her brothers, and her intended had taken me out to lunch.

'What's the difference?'

'Wrinkles start around your neck,' Charles said knowledgeably. 'We'll let you know when those arrive.'

'Crow's feet are caused from laughing, like those vertical lines around the mouth,' Todd said. 'When we're filming and the subject has to look younger, they're filled in with wax.'

From laughing? My mother should have stopped me from doing it. No wonder she didn't have any wrinkles.

'Scott doesn't have any wrinkles,' I moaned.

'He's too young,' the intended said, reminding me what it was I had reservations about in his personality. It was his insensitivity.

'Maybe not,' Abi said. 'But he does have bags under his eyes. And you do not, mother of mine.'

Hallelujah! There was a God somewhere.

But how dare she say the man in my life had bags under his eyes.

I was exhausted. Taking a few days off from the sweatshop was not easy.

My holdall stood packed and ready in the hall, and my new dress hung in a linen bag near the door. I'd never been so ready in my life, and I was no less excited than the night we had had our first date.

In the interests of the nice clean sheets, after creaming my body and masking my face to within an inch of its life, I went to bed in old pyjamas.

It didn't seem to matter because they wouldn't be seen by Scott. I planned to be awake and at the door to greet him in my new pale blue silk Chanel robe (half price to the trade) before he'd even located the keyhole. It simply seemed a good idea to grab a few hours' sleep before he arrived. That way, he could have the bed to himself for his necessary four hours' sleep during the morning.

Either I was dreaming, or it was actually happening and penetrating my slumbers: someone was touching my hair, and a deep familiar voice was saying in a whisper, 'Hello, Cathy, I'm here.'

A pleasurable male smell was tweaking at my nostrils.

I opened my eyes and blearily focused on his face in disbelief. It simply was not possible that I hadn't heard him put a key in my door, let alone close it behind him; nor hear the dog bark in greeting.

But there he was, smiling down at me, eyes creased in amusement, letting a hand run through my hair the way he did.

'You really must have been tired,' he said. 'Don't move, I'm coming in beside you.'

So that was it, he was early. I immediately felt better.

'What time is it?' I asked, stroking his face, savouring the familiar churning in the pit of my stomach.

'Five o'clock,' he said. 'I managed to get here on time. You don't have to get up yet.'

Then he slipped his arm beneath my shoulders, lifted me towards him and covered my lips with his. He pulled away, looked into my eyes, and kissed me again before returning me to the pillow. I was dazed with sexual emotion.

'We should get you out of these pyjamas,' he murmured, tracing a line with his fingertip from my lips, over my chin and down the length of my neck and on as far as the top button. Then he opened up the jacket, bent over and kissed my nipples.

I closed my eyes in ecstasy as his warm hands slid the trousers down over my raised hips.

It was such an exciting journey. First we drove in my car to an airfield in Surrey called Fairoaks that Scott seemed to know, where a cluster of small private aircraft were housed in one corner of the field, and camouflaged craft and helicopters were lined up in another.

Scott pointed out the pristine white helicopter we would be travelling in and told me that it was a Bell Jet Ranger.

'It must be costing you an arm and a leg to hire. I feel so guilty,' I said to him.

He smiled at me. 'I have special rates. No need to feel guilty.'

Everyone we encountered seemed to know and like him, shaking him by the hand, asking him how he was, smiling, laughing, slapping him on the back.

Preparing to leave seemed to be a serious business, and more than half an hour went by before our baggage was stowed, I was strapped into my seat, and Scott had closed and tested the door beside me. Then he climbed in on my right, housed his map and flight plan where he could see them at a glance, and checked to see if I had my headset in position correctly for us to talk to each other above the noise of the engine when we were in flight.

Scott explained that he wouldn't be conversing with me until he had completed the detour he was required to make to get out of the flight path for Heathrow.

'When we rise up,' he said, 'look to your left at the far line of four camouflaged helicopters. The last one on the right is the one I fly on surveillance missions in Europe.'

He started the engine. The rotor blades began to move and steadily reached a speed at which they could no longer be seen as blades; merely a cobweb circle. At which point the noise became intense.

Scott watched the dials and made adjustments, talking into his microphone to the control tower as he did so.

Then he pulled a lever up with his left hand and elevated us vertically. It felt as though some hidden power was pulling us into the sky. Then we hovered steadily, before swinging away to our right, over the airfield, above surrounding trees, over mansions with spectacular gardens, then a busy motorway. The sky was blue, the weather was perfect and visibility was good. Scott never seemed to stop looking around him.

I stayed silent and enjoyed the excitement of being airborne and watching the countryside beneath, while being in the safe hands of the man I loved.

We flew over a densely wooded area and my thoughts were dwelling on the marvellous spectacle of the multi-coloured trees and landscape, when Scott placed a hand on my trousered thigh and gently squeezed it.

'You can talk if you want to,' he said into his microphone.

I smiled at him.

'Are you happy, darling?' he asked.

'Do you need to ask? I'd like this to go on for ever.'

He laughed.

'How long will it take us to get there?'

He looked at the clock on the control panel. 'About an hour.'

'Do we have to refuel?'

'I think we'll put down at an airfield near our destination and refuel for the return trip. Just in case visibility is not as perfect as it is today.'

'Did you get permission for us to land at the hotel? I didn't think about that.'

'You bet. Their helipad awaits us.'

I fed him on chocolate bars. We shared a Coca-Cola from the bottle. I managed to pour some down my jeans, not being very good at drinking straight from bottles; an exercise that used to crease up my children when they were small, I told Scott.

I had never been more content. These happy times with Scott could become habit-forming . . .

We were walking from the helicopter, having left our luggage beside it to await collection, when he placed his arm around my waist, leaned close, and put his lips to my ear. 'Guess what I want to do to you right now, Ms Cathy.'

'Is it illegal?' I asked, looking into his smiling face.

'Only slightly.'

'Will it over-excite me?'

'Only temporarily.'

'Bet then I'll be the first one to undress when we get to our room.'

There was no reception desk in the entrance hall; just antique furniture, a lovely old floor, and a charming life-size full-length painting of an elegant Edwardian lady presiding hospitably over the visitors' book placed open on a side table.

We were greeted with casual charm by a tall, handsome chap who invited us to call him Harry and said that he was the manager.

He left us for a moment before taking us up the rather grand staircase, in order to send a young man in a short dark green apron to collect our luggage from the helicopter.

We strolled for a few paces to look down an inner hall that was lined with paintings; and as we did so we saw a large man with white hair approaching in our direction. Scott was holding my arm and I felt, rather than saw, him stiffen as he brought us to an abrupt stop. At the same time the man half turned to his right, looked back over his shoulder and called the name 'Regine' rather crossly to a woman dragging behind him.

Scott immediately pulled me around and headed for the nearest door, which turned out to be the library, with book-lined walls and a billiard table in the centre.

He relaxed once we were inside, smiled at me and said, 'Don't worry, I'll explain in a moment.'

We heard them go past, the man, speaking English with a foreign accent, reprimanding the woman for keeping him waiting, saying that the chauffeur would have to drive fast if they were not to lose their plane departure slot for take-off at Cardiff airport.

Scott touched my shoulder. 'Would you object to strolling out into the hall and making sure that they leave? I feel sure that he didn't see us.'

I felt my heart fluttering as I walked out into that entrance hall and assumed mock attention at the porter collecting our luggage. But the dark green Rolls-Royce sped away with its two passengers, and neither gave a backward glance.

When I returned to the library, Scott was viewing a large and rather wonderful scale-model of an old steam engine, in earnest conversation with Harry, who presumably had come to find us.

'Darling,' he said, 'I wondered where you were. Harry would like to accompany us to our room. Isn't this the most divine model of a railway engine? In perfect condition too.'

It was agony for me having to wait for Harry to quit engaging us in conversation in our rather lovely bedroom; asking Scott about the helicopter, saying what wonderful weather Wales had been enjoying by way of a change. Then our luggage arrived, and the boy meticulously explained where all the light switches were, how the TV remote control worked, and would we like to tell him what time we wished to have dinner, so that he could tell the maître d'.

Eventually we were alone. I kicked off my shoes. Scott poured us both a sherry, his smaller than mine, from the decanter nestling with a bowl of fruit on a round table set in a bay window.

We reclined among the pillows on the large four-poster bed. Scott took my hand.

'That man was a banker from Bogotá,' he said without preamble. 'When I was in alias I had to meet with him many times. He knew me as Scott Lyons—'

'So you used your own first name?' I cut in.

'We almost always do. Your own first name is deeply engraved on your brain, and you respond more naturally if it is called out.'

I nodded my head thoughtfully. 'What would he be doing here?'

'Most likely just vacationing. But if he had recognized me and used my alias in greeting, it would have confused you, and, more to the point, it would have confused the hotel staff and caused a lot of unnecessary grief.'

'But who is he exactly?'

'He's the chief drug-money launderer with the Medellin Cartel. If my cover had been blown it could be dangerous for me.'

We quietly sipped our drinks; Scott was deep in thought.

'How did you meet him?' I asked eventually.

'He would tell you that we met by accident in a restaurant bar in Bogotá. He commented that I spoke good Spanish and asked me where I had learned it. I told him at school in Los Angeles.'

'But he didn't know that you were a spy?'

Scott laughed. 'Hell, no. The sonofabitch thought that I was a corporate pilot. I cultivated his friendship.'

'Is he dangerous?' I asked, not particularly liking what I was hearing.

'Not in himself. He's most likely life's greatest coward. He'll no doubt get erased before long. But he could have caused me to have problems today. One word from him to certain interested parties and I'd be dead before the week is out.'

We lay in bed next morning, heads filled with thoughts of love, bodies aching with the night's activity, breakfast tray between us. Scott read to me from the Saturday paper without either of us really taking any of it in.

I felt, well, incredible, as only a woman can, when she's spent the night in the arms of the man she loves.

I turned to gaze at him, propped against his pillows, naked, sheets tucked around his waist.

'Okay, what is it?' he asked, putting the paper down.

'Nothing. Only that I love you,' I whispered from my pillow close beside his.

He closed his eyes. 'I love the way you say that.'

A fear gripped me then as I watched him. He was just so handsome. There must have been plenty of women longing to share his bed; he must have had lots of affairs, lots of opportunities. I wasn't going to ask him, I couldn't bring myself to do that.

'What's bothering you, Cathy?' he asked, without opening his eyes.

'Nothing really,' I answered, picking at the sheet.

He turned his head towards me. 'Not the banker from Bogotá, I hope? That was nothing to worry your lovely head about, I promise.'

'No, it's nothing.'

He ran a finger along my forehead. 'I think it is. And if it's all those nubile women you imagine you see queueing for my favours, forget it.'

'I wasn't thinking anything like that.'

'I think that maybe you were.'

'But there must have been many women wanting to know you?'

He picked up my hand. 'Sure, there were some, it goes with the territory. There's nothing like a dangerous job to excite a female. Except you, that is, that's why I love you.'

'I don't like you having a dangerous job. It's stupid.'

'That's what I mean. And you're right.'

'So why did you get into it, Scott?'

He leaned towards me, stroked my face. 'Oh, I don't know. A few years ago I suppose I liked the thought of danger. I had nothing to lose, death didn't bother me.'

'So how did it begin?'

He sighed. 'As a commissioned officer in the army I was assigned to the National Security Agency at Patuxant Naval Air Station, to train as a covert mission pilot.'

'That's spying.'

'Well, yeah. It's certainly undercover. And I don't go around talking about it too much.'

I reached out and placed my other hand in his for reassurance. 'And you fly jets as well as helicopters?' I said, trying to understand, wanting to get it out of the way.

'Sometimes, if I'm working alone, I cross the Atlantic commercial. Other times, if we're working in a group, we fly as businessmen who are chartering a private jet.'

'Do you keep the jets at Fairoaks?'

'No, it isn't big enough to take a 727. Goodness, Cathy, I hope I'm not being interrogated at this moment and it's hot pokers you-know-where if I don't tell the truth?'

I pulled his head towards me, kissed his lips. 'Not hot pokers, just my fingers stroking you,' I said, finding my way under the sheet . . .

The weather stayed fine. We stayed in bed a lot, went for

walks, hired a car, went for country drives among the mountains.

Saturday night was especially wonderful. We sat in deep chairs in the Great Hall before dinner, drank champagne and ate canapés while we read the menu, a lovely summer breeze wafting through the French windows that were thrown open to the terracing and the emerald green lawns.

'You look absolutely stunning,' Scott said to me. 'And I love that dress.'

'I'm glad you do. We made it up in the workrooms specially.'

'You must wear it for me often.'

'I would like to,' I said, and touched his arm. I could not believe how happy he made me, and how lucky I was to have found such a man.

The food we ate was delicious: iced creamy soup made from baby courgettes and mint from the gardens, roasted duck from the farm, and seven tiny scoops of differing flavours of home-made ice-cream served on tiny trays made from biscuit.

Later we drank more champagne in bed; and watched a late film from the comfort of our pillows before making love and going to sleep wrapped in each other's arms.

We ate everything put in front of us the whole weekend, made love frequently, splashed around together in a bath easily big enough for two, where I lay behind him nursing his head on my chest as we talked, and he operated the hot tap with his toes as the bath cooled.

Much too soon though, following afternoon tea on Sunday, we had to fly back to Fairoaks while the light was still good. It was a peaceful and romantic journey.

I loved him so much I found it impossible to sit beside him without keeping my hand on his thigh. It was as though without physical contact I was afraid he might disappear, and I could wake with a start to find that I'd been dreaming; and there never had been a helicopter ride, or a bath made for two, or a man called Scott . . .

# EIGHT

The following week I was kept as busy as ever at the workplace; and the most exciting event was when I received a call from a film company's wardrobe agent to ask if I would be interested in making the clothes for a forthcoming film. It's to be called *Wait For Me, Darling* and is a thriller about a beautiful Sudanese model who marries an English pop star who turns out to be a control freak.

Strange material, but there's American money in it, and the clothes budget is good, and of course I'd love to do it. The publicity would be invaluable. Paris and Milan dress shows are to figure in it, which will give me plenty of scope to show off my range on celluloid.

The senior staff think that we could cope, although, of course, we'll need to hire more skilled seamstresses, on a temporary basis.

I had scarcely recovered from that excitement when Scott telephoned me. I'd been thinking of him seconds before, hoping that he would call me soon; mainly because I miss him badly.

I knew he'd gone off on something big when he left, and my imagination was running riot.

'Hello, Charlie Girl, my love.'

He'd decided that was to be my name on the telephone in future when he was operational, for safety's sake.

The line was not clear but my heart leaped, same as always. 'Hello, yourself. Where are you?' I still asked the question, even though he had suggested I didn't. He'd assured me that he would tell me, if he could, without my asking.

'Where I told you I was going to be,' he answered patiently.

It was not news I really wanted to hear.

He'd explained to me earlier, in the utmost confidence, that he'd be heading for North Africa, and I didn't like the sound of the operation.

They would be taking the Boeing 727, he'd said, to observe a radical Algerian terrorist group, and they'd be eavesdropping from the 727 before landing and disbanding. They would regroup some time later at a safe house, but he wouldn't tell me where or when. I would hear from him just once, he'd said; and only then if he felt that it was safe.

'What are you doing today, Charlie? I like to get a mental picture of you,' he said.

'Oh, I'm having quite an exciting morning,' I answered, and I told him about the enquiry from the film company.

'Don't mention names,' he said quickly. 'You'll give me details when I return. But I'm thrilled for you.'

'How are things with you, Scott?' My heart missed a beat when I said his real name instead of the code name we'd agreed, 'Johnny'.

He made no comment. 'Going well. The climate's hot, the food's crap, the waiters are ugly; I'm sure you get the picture.'

'I think I do. When shall I see you?'

'Same as I told you, darling. Nothing's changed. I must go now.'

'I know. I love you.'

'I love you too,' he whispered. 'More than you know.'

'More than all the world?'

'Much more.'

I waited while he replaced his receiver long enough to hear if someone else replaced theirs too. I never did experience that happening, and I often wondered what on earth I would have done if I had. But it reassured me to know that no one had been listening in to our conversation then.

Shortly afterwards, Fran and I managed to find the time to look at three flats on Scott's behalf, overlooking the river. One was at Chelsea Harbour and was much too expensive and small. One was at Butler's Wharf, and had a divine terrace; and one was at Wapping, on the fourth floor of a converted warehouse. It had a large living-room, two nice terraces and was sensibly priced. It was my favourite.

As we ate a quick toasted sandwich in a snack bar on the water, Fran entertained me with anecdotes about her weekend with my dog. We'd scarcely had time to chat since then. She'd taken her in for me when I flew off with Scott to Wales; and she and her new girlfriend had taken her daily into the country for long walks. Without doubt Sacha had had a whale of a time, for which I was extremely grateful.

I told her more about how Scott and I had spent our weekend, describing the helicopter ride, the gorgeous food, and our divine bedroom with the huge four-poster bed.

'But for you, Fran, I would have gone through my entire life without knowing him,' I said, as I watched a large barge navigate a bend in the river.

She smiled at me. 'Well, you never know. You might have bumped into each other around a street corner.'

'I could never have imagined in my deepest reveries such a wonderful turn of events as this; just as I was thinking that everything romantic and wonderful had passed me by.'

'Yes,' she said thoughtfully, staring out across the grey water. 'It is wonderful when it happens, isn't it?'

Remember Clara Holiday? The lottery winner from Essex?

She was waiting for me impatiently when I returned. Clara seems not to have learned yet that it's a good idea to make an appointment when you wish to see someone.

It seems she's about to do a 'Shirley Valentine' and run off; only Clara's Greek, Nico Popalopodous by name, is the chap she met on the cruise ship, not a poor fisherman like Shirley's *amour*. He has his own fishing fleet, and is paying Fred handsomely to give Clara a quickie divorce.

'I told my Nico I wouldn't pay that bastard a penny, but he says he wants me as his wife, and my husband deserves to be paid. Sounds bloody daft to me.'

'But honourable, Clara, you must admit.' I felt she expected me to say something profound; but that was the best I could do.

'I told him, he doesn't need to marry me. But as he says, he's already got a mistress. All the men have them, you know, in those sort of countries. It must be something to do with the hot summers.'

She isn't exactly over the moon about the mistress, I gather, but she is over the moon about Nico, totally gone, out of it.

'He's something in the government,' she said importantly. 'And I need a special wardrobe for official functions in Athens. That's why I waited such a long time for you to come back.'

She'd been to Athens, I learned, seen his house, met his friends, and actually been interviewed and photographed, with Nico, by *Hello!* magazine.

I couldn't tell her of my firm opinion that that modern Doomsday Book of shiny pictures and sycophantic writers should put a witch's spell on the romance, if anything does.

In the meantime she's given me an order for still more outfits, and wants me to have sketches ready within a week, if you don't mind.

Clara, soon to be Mrs Popalopodous, bless her, is learning fast how the backing of wealth enables one to order folk around; and the drawing block, and those crayons, will have to go everywhere with me, day and night, or I'll never find the time to complete them.

It was a really busy evening for me the night before Scott arrived back in London: shampooing my hair, fixing my fingernails, varnishing my toenails.

He was due to arrive around four in the morning, and as he'd absolutely refused to take the door keys with him on his mission, I'd arranged to leave them behind the stone pot that holds the clematis that climbs up the house, because he didn't want to wake or scare me by ringing the doorbell.

And so it was that once more he crept up on me and found me asleep. Only this time I wasn't wearing old pyjamas . . .

For the rest of my life, and especially when we are apart, what I'll remember most about Scott is waking up with him. There will always be much to occupy my mind where he is concerned, even when he is right beside me, but waking with him next to me is the greatest of adventures.

I don't know why, but he wakes first no matter what the time, and when I wake, our naked bodies still wrapped around each other, he is always looking at me, a smile on his face and his eyes upon me full of kindness. When I look up from the crook of his arm, it's the most pleasurable sensation I've yet encountered.

'Cathy, are you listening?' I heard him whisper.

'Trying to,' I muttered drowsily.

'You have your eyes closed.'

'Only to hear you better,' I said, curling a leg over his naked body, putting my head on his chest and running my hand lovingly along his torso.

He grabbed it, put it to his lips and kissed it, laid it flat upon his chest and placed his own hand on top in the form of an anchor.

'Darling, I have to leave you today,' he said.

I snuggled closer. 'You're always leaving me.'

'I know, and I have to make sure that you're going to be in a happy frame of mind until I come back.'

'Where will you be?'

'In the Americas, on a mission. I've only just found out.'

I looked up at him, fully awake now. 'When will you be back?'

'It shouldn't be long. Two weeks, outside. But it's important to me to know that you'll be fine, now that we've talked things out and totally understand each other.'

It was true. We had talked over many things during our weekend in the country. He'd told me how sure he was that he loved me, and I confessed to loving him; just how much, he might never know, I'd said. We must share our lives for the moment as best we could, we agreed, with the careers that we both had to run in two different countries.

Oh, yes, I'd said so willingly, we'd manage, we'd holiday

together, swap visits whenever we could, telephone, send cards, write faxes.

He'd apply for the European and African areas exclusively, he'd said. He couldn't live without me, he'd never wanted anything as badly as he wanted me, and we both agreed that everything that had happened to us previously had been directed towards us meeting each other, eventually, the way we did.

He kissed the hand he was holding to his chest. 'I'll not stop thinking about you for a moment till I return,' he said, 'but right now this hand that I'm holding so securely has distracted me into believing that it's time we made love again.'

'Will you be all right in what you term as the Americas?'

He moved my hand down his torso, and refrained from answering.

'Is it dangerous?' I asked.

'What, making love? Not unless I crush you to death in my urgent desire,' he said, in that special voice he used, with humour spilling out of it.

'Oh, my darling, darling Cathy,' he breathed into my ear as we recovered and lay there spent and breathing heavily. 'How am I ever going to tear myself away?'

'I shall worry about you,' I said. 'Being in love is a terrible responsibility.'

'But better than never knowing what love is,' he whispered.

'Oh, yes,' I whispered back. 'But you will be careful?'

He kissed my lips. 'I've told you before, my darling, I'm always careful.'

He rolled away from me as reluctantly as a man would who was forced to leave a warm and sex-drenched bed.

'I'll telephone you whenever I can, and I'll be back before you know it. Soon you'll be wishing that I was away for longer periods.'

'How can you talk like that?' I replied, easing myself up beside him, locking him into my arms, kissing his lips, running my fingers up his spine.

We engaged in one last lingering kiss, held each other with our eyes in veiled desperation, pulled reluctantly away, and parted.

\*　　\*　　\*

I was a woman in love, and it was difficult to hide.

Age, I'd discovered, made no difference to the inner excitement, the urgent wish to share the joy of love, the spring in the step, the smile always hovering.

I was a woman consumed by her man. Nothing quite like this had happened to me before. I'd had two husbands, three children, one live-in lover, and a few casual affairs, and nothing, absolutely nothing had prepared me for an event in my life such as this. And my mind ran riot at every turn.

After we had eaten, Richard and I, and the effect of the ambiance, red wine and nicely cooked food had settled on me, I was reluctant to bring up the subject of my health.

Instead, I wanted to tell him about Scott, rather in the way I wanted to tell everyone about Scott. But I couldn't. I felt that even though I had never made him any promises, he would be upset by the news; and this was not the moment to deliver it.

'I don't really want to bring this up, Richard, but I'm a little worried about a strange sensation in my left arm, and I wondered if you could tell me what to do about it.'

'Which arm?' he asked simply.

I held out my left one towards him.

He immediately took my hand in his. 'How do you mean, Cathy?'

'It seems to drag sometimes, especially when I'm at the cutting-table, using it to anchor material. And then sometimes my hand jerks around with a life of its own.' I laughed then; it seemed the only thing to do to disguise my embarrassment and reluctance to talk about it.

'How long has it been going on?' he asked, an extremely concerned doctor-of-medicine expression on his face.

'A few weeks now, but I'm sure it's nothing serious, and there's no pain involved.'

'Adverse symptoms are seldom nothing, Cathy, you know that.'

'Yes, I'm sure you're right,' I answered, looking down.

'When I take you home, you must show me exactly what happens.'

I really didn't want him to take me home. I wasn't planning

to ask him in. And I certainly didn't want him fussing over me, unkind as it sounds.

I need not have worried, he was in doctor mode. We stood at my dining-table. 'Show me the movement you are doing when you notice it most.'

I showed him, demonstrating smoothing out imaginary silk, and as I did so, it happened. The hand doubled over, the arm was slow responding.

He led me from the table and ushered me to my sitting-room.

'Would you like a brandy?' I said as we went, trying at least to be a good hostess, the dog trailing behind us, watching our every move.

'No, thank you, Cathy, let's just sit down.' He led me to the sofa, and waited formally till I was seated.

'I want you to see a neurologist,' he said, without preamble.

I felt panic quicken my heartbeat. 'Whatever for? Surely, this is not that serious. I thought it might be fatigue, or a touch of rheumatism, something like that. Are you sure that you wouldn't like a brandy?'

'Quite sure, Cathy, thank you,' he said, getting up. 'I'm going to leave you now, and I think that you should get to bed; plenty of rest might help. Would you like me to come with you to the neurologist, or d'you prefer to go it alone?'

'Oh, no, please, if I agree to go, you must come with me,' I said quickly.

'You have to go. I know a good chap. I'll arrange an appointment for us as soon as possible.'

'Not tomorrow or the next day,' I said. 'My workload simply won't allow it.'

He looked at me sternly over the top of his thick-rimmed glasses and shook his head without speaking.

As I opened the front door to let him out he kissed me on the cheek.

'Maybe the neurologist's workload won't allow for tomorrow or the next day either, so I'm not going to argue,' he said, looking at me resignedly.

A few days later we sat in the neurologist's waiting-room nervously making small talk when the receptionist left her desk in the rather grand hall, smiled from the open doorway, and announced my name. Richard patted my shoulder in a stay-put fashion as he stood up.

'I'll pop in first and have a word,' he said to the receptionist. 'As I'm her referring doctor . . .'

He was probably only gone for a few minutes, but it seemed like an age, and I was beginning to get nervous.

I tried to stay calm by thinking of Scott. He'd phoned me from the States just before I left the salon. When he'd asked, conversationally, what I was doing, I'd lied and said that I would be in the cutting-room all day. I didn't like telling lies to Scott. But neither did I want him to know that I was going to see a doctor.

The white-coated nurse came for me at last, with her cool professional smile, and took me slowly down a long corridor as though I were already an invalid, and showed me into the consulting-room.

'So you're Catherine Anthony,' the smartly dressed young man with the head-boy looks said, coming forward with outstretched hand and smiling broadly.

I smiled back, wondering why we were all smiling, and nervously placed my hand in his. He looked so darned young, I found myself hoping that he was old enough to do his job.

'We met once, at a party, do you remember?' he said briskly. 'And I've been reading things about you in the press.'

He most likely hadn't read anything at all, I thought; more likely Richard had told him a few things about me to use as a softener.

He led me to a chair beside Richard, sat down himself behind a very large and impressive mahogany desk and began writing up a file on me: full name, age, family history, childhood ailments.

He looked up and used the professional reassuring smile again. 'Having a little difficulty, are we, Catherine? Why don't you tell me how it troubles you, exactly.'

Suddenly I was talking fast, saying silly things about being sure that it was nothing, a lot of fuss, not of real importance.

He continued to write. 'And your general health, is that good?'

'Oh, yes,' I said, thinking how Scott had told me that I looked ten years younger than I'd told him I was, and laughingly saying that maybe he should see my birth certificate for verification.'

'Anyone in your family had a similar problem, at any time?'

I shook my head, wishing that I could leave, wanting to get back to the familiarity of the workplace, wanting to contact Scott because I needed him.

He stood up. 'Catherine, I would like to examine you,' he said.

He helped me up as though I were an old lady and led me to an examination couch in an alcove behind a Chinese screen.

'Just take off your clothes, put on the robe, and lie down on the couch.' Then, as he turned discreetly away, he said over his shoulder, 'It won't take long.'

As I undressed I could hear him talking quietly to Richard who did not seem to be replying.

'I'm ready,' I called as I tied the cord on the gown, not wanting to be kept waiting with my mental agony a moment longer than necessary.

He felt my arm, tested the muscle power of my limbs, used a pin and then the tickling motion of cotton wool to test for any loss of sensitivity, and finally he used a small hammer to test the reflexes of my arms and legs.

He shone a bright light into my eyes and asked me to look at a fixed point, in order to examine, he told me, the optic discs at the back of my eyes.

'Something's wrong with me, isn't it?' I asked, suddenly panic-stricken, feeling a burn behind my eyes that had nothing to do with the bright light.

He sat me up with a hand behind my head as though I couldn't do it without him, helped me from the couch, then looked away.

'No hurry,' he said. 'When you're dressed come and sit down with us.'

For an agonizing few moments, after I returned to my chair, he steadily wrote up his notes, the same bland expression on his face that Richard had on his.

I tried to will Richard to look at me, but he stared out of the elegant open French windows that led to a small paved courtyard filled with potted ferns and an overhanging willow, and simply wouldn't meet my anxious gaze.

At last the neurologist put down his pen and leaned back in his chair, very much the confident Harley Street specialist.

'Well now, Catherine,' he said. 'I'm not absolutely sure what the problem is, but I do think that you should have a brain scan.'

Both Richard and the neurologist may have thought that I was being extremely brave, or very sensible, or perhaps even both, as, with an air of distinction I played along.

I shook the hand of the professor of doom, and even thanked him for seeing me, and, with head held high, let Richard lead me out of the consulting-room.

After all, wasn't I, perhaps, their idea of a sophisticated, intelligent, well-dressed lady, with obvious business ability, and an up-front approach to life, who could handle any situation?

Actually, both of them would have been hopelessly wrong to think that. I was rendered numb with shock the moment the vague prognosis was made. A scanning of the brain, I was sure, could only mean one thing, and that was to help the experts in their field to find a connected reason for the problem with my arm. I found it all unbelievably frightening.

Richard took me home in silence, though I seem to remember we discussed the weather, and he stayed on for a glass of wine; his idea, not mine. I doubt that I would have noticed if he had left me on the doorstep.

I know that I drank some wine with him, because there were two empty glasses left on the low coffee-table next morning, though I don't remember drinking it. I do remember, though, that Richard seemed to talk a lot.

But of what he said to me, or what my responses were, I can remember little. I'm sure that I was of no help to him in his thankless quest to force me to think positively, and I picked away at his gentle and sensible choice of words; as if relentlessly, almost deliberately, trying to engineer a quarrel.

'You still haven't told me what it is exactly that they'll be looking for,' I said accusingly, trying to make him give it a name, and fixing his eyes firmly and unflinchingly with my own.

'Most likely a meningioma, a benign tumour,' he answered carefully, longing to take his eyes away from mine but unable to do so.

## Philippa Todd

I felt instant, hot, and serious anger rise up from the very core of my being, and I wanted to hurt, humiliate and injure. No, not him, not Richard; what fault was it of his? I mean the whole world, the universe, the planet Earth. What right had it to pick on me all over again. Hadn't I served my time? Jesus, I'd tried hard enough.

'Or a bloody great malignant one intent on killing me,' I said dramatically, with an ugly inflection to my voice and furrows creasing my brow as I stood up and refilled his glass with wine, slopping some of it on to the table, which he promptly mopped up with his pocket handkerchief. Then he looked up at me as I loomed over him, and patted the place next to him on the sofa.

'Come and sit beside me, Cathy,' he said, kindness mixed with despair oozing from him at the sight of my misery.

I sat down to please him, but the anger remained. 'I'm not ready to die, Richard,' I said, with a fierce passion that hurt my chest.

He took my hand in his. 'You mustn't talk this way. Getting upset will make things worse.'

I tore my hand away. 'Oh, come on, Richard, how much worse can it be?'

'I understand how you're feeling,' he said unhappily, trying to retain his professional tone of voice, and failing.

I jumped up from the sofa and marched over to the window.

'Oh, no, you don't,' I said emphatically. 'You haven't the faintest idea how I'm feeling.'

I stared out into my tiny garden, half in shadow now in the late afternoon. There'd been no rain for several days, and I was reminded that I must water the pots or the geraniums would die.

I turned back towards the room and looked at him. 'I've met someone,' I said, trying hard to quieten my voice and find a softer tone. 'Someone very special to me, someone I had stupid hopes of spending the rest of my life with. And no one, not even you, Richard, can possibly know how I feel about the possibility of losing that.'

I distinctly saw a shadow cross his eyes as he mentally winced, but to his credit he said nothing to show shock or disappointment at hearing that his hopes of marrying me had been dashed without his knowledge.

'You mustn't despair this way, Cathy,' he said, a look of utter misery on his face. 'No one has said that your case is hopeless, and I'm sure that it is not.'

'No, Richard, you're not sure at all,' I said, moving towards the door. 'And, I hope you won't mind, but I'd like to be alone now.' I was damned if I would cry in front of him, and I was in danger of it.

He stood up slowly. 'I don't think that I should leave you all alone,' he said. 'Let me ask one of the children to come over, Abigail perhaps, just to be company for you.'

'No.' I shook my head.

'Your secretary then?' he persisted.

'Absolutely not. I don't want anyone to know about this. I must be in my workroom in the morning as though I'm in fine fettle. I've a very important fitting to do.'

'You should rest,' he said helplessly. 'At least take it easy until after the scan.'

'That's all right for you to say,' I answered, glaring at him, tears beginning to form. 'I have a business to run. I'm not dead yet, you know.'

I took some sleeping pills, I'm ashamed to say. Not too many, four I think it was, just enough to cry for help, though who I thought would hear me I cannot imagine. I drank some brandy too, though I don't very much like it, and, mercifully, the combination made me sick as a parrot.

It must have been around two in the morning when the telephone rang.

I staggered from my perch on the edge of the bath, hand-towel clutched ready, to the telephone beside my bed, not at all sure that I wasn't about to vomit once more.

'How are you tonight, my Cathy?'

'Scott, is that you?'

'Of course. Darling, you're not crying, are you? Is something wrong?'

I would have given anything for him not to have asked that, because my eyes began to burn and tears of self-pity welled up. I longed to tell him. 'No, of course not, I was asleep,' I lied.

'Oh, I'm so sorry, that was thoughtless of me.'

'It was a long day, I took a sleeping pill. I have the princess's fitting to do tomorrow.'

'Go back to sleep, now that I know you're all right. You must have been soundly away; I telephoned twice before. You'll find a couple of messages from me on your machine if you haven't already.'

'Scott,' I whispered, fearful of throwing up as my chest heaved.

'Goodnight, darling, I'll telephone you around noon tomorrow, your time. Sweet dreams. I love you.'

'Scott, wait . . .'

He was gone, and I barely made it to the bathroom.

'You look pale, Cathy,' the princess said.

'I can't think why,' I replied, trying to smile as I took another pin from the girl at my elbow and nipped a half-inch from the back of the sleeveless dress that matched the coat the princess was about to be helped into.

'This outfit's going to be such a success,' she said, turning to the side mirrors to get an all-round view of herself. 'Let's risk another inch off the hem, shall we?'

'I was about to suggest it,' I answered, wishing that I could have a whole glass of fizzy water to drink right off, with lemon juice, and a cube of ice.

'I shall only wear a pill-box on the old head. I hate hats, as you know.'

'So do I,' I answered. I felt extremely faint, longed to feel a cool breeze on my face.

'Would you send enough matching material round to my milliner, and tell him that I want a "Jackie Kennedy".'

She held her fingers to her mouth and giggled. The sound was pure delight.

Fran could not understand why I insisted on examining the order book, the day book, the diary, the prêt-à-porter samples. I could tell that my mood puzzled her.

'Are you perhaps planning to run away with Scott and hoping

to leave me to look after this place?' she asked, laughing at the probability.

'I wish,' I replied listlessly from behind my desk.

'As you can see from the diary your daughter is coming in this afternoon at four to be measured and to choose her wedding gown material. You haven't forgotten, have you?' she asked. 'Silly question really, you're probably on the telephone to each other every day.'

Had we talked on the phone recently? I wondered. I remember telling Abigail that we must start her wedding dress early as I'd be fitting it in among a stack of work between now and next spring . . .

It was then that Richard telephoned on my personal line.

'Four o'clock this afternoon for the scan,' he said. 'I'll pick you up at the workplace at three thirty, that way I know you won't duck out of it.'

'That's impossible, I can't manage this afternoon,' I answered, panic at the thought enveloping me yet again.

'Cathy, you must, you have no choice.'

'Of course I have a choice. It's important I'm here at four.'

'Cathy, you don't appear to be hearing me.'

I turned the diary around to face me, and stared into it. 'The day after tomorrow seems to be the best I can do for you. I know that you'll understand.'

Fran was staring at me.

'Understand, my eye. Don't be foolish,' Richard said. 'This won't go away, you simply have to face it.'

'Not today,' I replied, anxious that Fran would get suspicious if the conversation continued. 'Abi's coming in at four. I can't put her off, it's important.'

It was the worst thing I could have said. I'd given him an edge.

'You do now have a choice,' he said, quite sternly. 'Either you promise to come quietly and I keep the secret, or I contact Abigail and tell her the reason why you won't be seeing her this afternoon.'

I paused for only a moment. He had me over a barrel. 'Yes, Richard,' I said in a businesslike way. 'I understand. I'll be ready at three thirty.'

### Philippa Todd

'What's happening?' Fran asked, looking puzzled, as I replaced the receiver.

'There's a funeral taking place I forgot to tell you about,' I said. 'Somebody we know has died.' Well, it felt like a funeral to me, so I wasn't going to worry about lying to her, too.

But Fran did not look convinced. 'Funny, isn't it,' she answered, trying to sound casual. 'People usually have died when they hold a funeral for them.'

At that moment my personal telephone rang again. Fran reached out helpfully but I quickly picked up the receiver ahead of her.

'I hope you managed to get to sleep again after I disturbed you last night,' he said lovingly. 'That was thoughtless of me.'

'Hello, Scott.'

Fran stood up and prepared to leave. 'Say hello from me,' she said.

'I only have a few moments, Cathy, and I wanted to tell you some good news.'

He waited for me to respond, to say something such as how marvellous, I like good news, I can't wait to hear it.

'Darling, are you okay?'

My emotions were running high, it felt as though a salt-water lake was balanced on my lower lids, and if I blinked it would overflow and drown me.

'I'm fine,' I said. 'I'm waiting to hear what your good news is about.'

'Are you getting a cold? You sound nasal.'

'No, no, it's probably hay fever, nothing to worry about. You know what London's like, especially at this time of year. Pollution's hell at the moment. Tell me your news.'

'It looks like I'll get to work in Europe, six months of the year at least.'

'That's nice,' I said lamely, convinced that it would be too late to matter as far as I was concerned.

'Nice,' he repeated. 'My favourite lady only thinks it's nice?'

'No, darling, it's wonderful.'

'So, Cathy, would you tell the agent that I'd like the biggest of those three apartments. Wapping, did you say the district was called?'

## Whispers On A Pillow

'But, Scott, you haven't even seen it,' I said frantically.

'Darling, you showed me pictures. If you like it that's good enough for me. And Cathy, would you consider coming to live there with me? And selling your place perhaps, or renting it out?'

Oh, Scott, do stop tearing my heart out, I said. But only to myself.

# NINE

Fear of the consequences made me flush away my sleeping pills, resulting in my lying awake at night, worrying.

Illness that shows no obvious signs, I have always thought, is isolating. It robs you of the sympathetic word, the small embrace that might make it more bearable.

No one knows what mental agony the sufferer is going through, unless he or she chooses to tell them. As for me, if the worst came to the worst, I didn't even know how I would begin to tell my family about my affliction, or Fran, or the team of people I relied upon for my livelihood. And there was no question about it, I would not tell Scott, ever.

My inability to sleep wasn't because I knew something more dire than previously, but because I did not. I was confused, unable to comprehend the outcome, frightened of the unknown. The dark of the nights piled up on me, and the soul-searching began.

Was life teaching me a lesson? Surely I wouldn't be punished like this unless I had done something terrible to deserve it.

Had I really been such a bad person, such a rotten mate, a terrible mother? Was it no more than I deserved to have to give up Scott?

**Philippa Todd**

Had this man who was so right for me, so perfectly matched to my mind, and to my body, been sent as the ultimate punishment?

Was an illness as serious as a brain tumour settled on me as a warning of my wickedness?

I'd thought bad things with the next person, caused grief to my parents, been stubborn, impulsive, thoughtless; but was it likely I could have forgotten something so monumental as to bring this upon myself?

Was it to do with having had an abortion and killed a foetus? Did that make me a murderer? Oh, God, I remembered all too clearly thinking at the time that it did.

My wretchedness drove me from my bed to pace the house, to sit on the stairs in the dark with my head in my hands, the dog whimpering at my feet.

Richard had accompanied me to the Scanning Services Clinic. He explained in advance that I was to have an MRI scan, which stood for Magnetic Resonance Imaging, and its purpose was to produce an image of the appropriate area by utilizing a magnetic field.

Unfortunately my mind was in such turmoil, and my fear so consuming, I might have understood the details of the splitting of the atom more easily.

Richard offered to gain permission to stay with me throughout, but I declined. It seemed such a weak and wimpish thing to take him up on, so much the little woman. My father had a lot to answer for.

So I left him in the waiting-room and followed a very nice radiographer, who'd introduced herself as Barbara, down a long corridor and into an anteroom, where she attempted to put me at my ease and proficiently explained the procedure.

'There's absolutely nothing to worry about,' she said, smiling at me. 'You're not feeling nervous, are you?'

As a cat at the vet's, I wanted to say. But I shook my head. If I told her about my claustrophobia, I might get sent away. And where would that leave me? It was my illness, no one else's. It was up to me to co-operate.

'A little nervous. And pretty shattered about the whole thing. But I'll be fine.'

'I'll show you to a cubicle where you can undress and climb into a gown. I'd like you to remove all jewellery. Anything metallic may affect the results. I see from your notes that you are not wearing a pacemaker, or have any metal gadgets in your body.'

I shook my head, and smiled thinly.

'And you're not concealing a late pregnancy?'

I shook my head again, and for some reason, laughed.

When I was gowned and slippered I was shown into the scanning-room; and even Barbara, in her dedicated and experienced way, had failed to prepare me for the shock of the layout and the trauma of coming face to face with the scanner; which to me represented a narrow tunnel in which I would be isolated from the rest of the world for as long as it took. Around twenty minutes if nothing had to be repeated, Barbara had said. But supposing she was letting me down lightly, and it would take longer?

When I was led through the door, I actually did consider saying I needed to go to the lavatory urgently, grabbing up my clothes en route, and then running.

I was asked to climb on to a narrow slab with the scanner behind my head, and told to relax, keep my arms, and especially my elbows, tucked closely into my sides. Then my head was rendered immobile and held firmly in position. A thick, padded, protective blanket was placed over me from neck to feet.

'Don't worry about the echoing when you're in there,' Barbara said. 'Or those clicks and bangs; that's just us working behind that dark glass screen.'

Screen, what glass screen? Where was it, why hadn't I noticed it? Did this mean that Barbara, my new friend, was going to leave me?

'You can talk to me, there's a hidden microphone in there,' she added, nodding towards the tunnel. 'Just use a normal voice. And keep very, very still.'

'Yes,' I replied in a small, weak voice, wondering how on earth she expected me to be able to move more than my eyelids anyway.

'I forget how long you said it would take,' I lied, as I sensed that the moment of transportation was nigh.

## Philippa Todd

'Don't you remember? I said twenty minutes. But don't worry, it'll pass quickly,' Barbara replied. 'I'll be asking you if you're okay from time to time.'

I closed my eyes. Already I was as damp and limp as a cod fillet on a fishmonger's slab, and I doubt anyone could have prized my eyes open with a crowbar.

You remember how, in those vintage war films, the German planes on bombing missions over England make a distinctive deep and mournful 'thrumming' beat? That's the noise my slab made as it moved. Controlled panic settled on my chest like a cast-iron weight.

I thought that I could hear distant music, but then I thought that I was wrong.

'You all right?' Barbara's voice enquired, kindly. 'We're giving you some music to listen to.'

I had to cough before my assenting voice was any more than a silent mime.

'Right,' she said. 'Then here we go.'

Her remark was heralded with the clicks and bangs that I was more or less prepared for, only they were louder than I'd been led to believe, and more rapid, and tons more frightening. But even more unnerving for me was the echoing that followed. I wanted to poke out my ears, like the urge one gets when an enthusiastic pilot brings a plane down too steeply, only there was no room for me to move my arms and my elbows were securely wedged. I tried closing my throat and forcing an air-lock out of my ears but the pain was excruciating. And so was, at the same time, the unexpected silence.

'Are you still there?' I called out in panic.

'Right close by,' Barbara's reply came back.

How many magnetic what's-its-names did they need on one female's brain, for goodness sake? Were the images all so bad to see that they needed to double up on the information? And please, Lord, I asked Him, do help them to get it right the first time, because I'll never find the courage to go through this ordeal again. Let's get it sorted now while I'm still relatively sane and calm, even if I am soaking wet with nervous sweat and so very miserable . . .

\* \* \*

## Whispers On A Pillow

It was two days before anyone told me anything. I was just beginning to feel a sense of relief that the doctors had got it wrong, the way you do when the worst is over and yet another false alarm is behind you.

I was working as best I could, attempting to be at the helm of the business ship, hoping I looked the part; smiling, being pleasant.

Then suddenly, it hit; wham, bam, bet you don't get up from this one, ma'am. I plummeted to the depths.

My nemesis came in the shape of Richard, standing uninvited on my doorstep that evening, clutching an overnight bag in one hand.

It had been a busy day for me, my arm was misbehaving and the jerking was worse, and I was tired, but otherwise I was in reasonable shape.

He walked in as soon as I opened the door, kissed my cheek distractedly and said, 'We have to talk, Cathy.'

So we did, seated on the sofa, telephone taken off the hook at Richard's request to enable him to deliver without interruption the dreadful news that I would rather not have heard.

'We have an appointment to see a brain surgeon tomorrow; there's a small problem.'

I went to stand up, perhaps to run out of the room. But I'll never know because he anchored me with his hand.

'You don't need to panic, Cathy. It's going to be all right.'

I pulled my arm from under his. 'Richard, please don't,' I said. 'It obviously is not all right. Tell me, for God's sake, am I about to die or something?'

'No, nothing like that,' he said quickly. 'You'll understand more tomorrow, but we do have a bit of a problem . . .'

He stayed with me. I put him in the traveller's bed. He even went out and bought a Chinese takeaway, a rare event for him, I was sure, and heaven knows why I requested Chinese food that night of all nights.

He called en route into a pharmacy and prescribed a pill or two to help me to sleep.

While he was gone I very nearly telephoned Scott's red number, but I didn't want him to know anything until I knew for sure what was wrong with me.

**Philippa Todd**

I was sure it was no one's fault, but I was being kept in the kind of limbo that is so difficult to bear.

'Well now, Mrs Anthony ... Catherine, I have some images here, and I would like to show you what the problem is.'

Some images, let me tell you, and a big three-dimensional screen for good measure. If only it had not been showing my brain in such detail I could have become fascinated.

The surgeon took his fountain pen from his breast pocket to use as a pointer. 'This is a growth, which I am practically certain is benign.'

He outlined it with his pen, and even I could see that it was a fair-sized tumour.

'It's causing pressure on the brain and a lesion on the right side of the motorcortex, and that is why you have a problem with your left hand and arm.'

He had to get on with it; I didn't need long names that meant nothing to me and diagrams and images. I was beginning to itch. Couldn't he see how upset I was becoming?

'Am I going to die?' I asked, attempting a matter-of-fact tone, my eyes like saucers and my heard hurting like mad now that it could see how sick it was.

'There's every reason to believe that the tumour is benign,' he reiterated in measured tones, still looking at the screen.

'How do you know?'

'The size. The shape.'

I looked helplessly across at Richard, but he was looking fixedly at his shoes.

'There is absolutely no reason why you should not make a full recovery after surgery,' the surgeon continued, nodding his head slightly as he chose his words carefully and delivered them with quiet deliberation.

But it was all too much for my poor wounded brain to absorb. Tumours, lesions, brain surgery, those sort of things only happened to people you didn't know.

'When?' was the only question I could think of to ask, as two tears rolled silently down my cheeks with a will of their own.

He picked up his pen again and rolled it around between his fingers. 'I would suggest right away.'

'The sooner the better, Cathy,' Richard said, taking a folded handkerchief from his jacket pocket and handing it across to me.

I felt suddenly unbelievably low, totally devoid of energy. My skin crawled, my eyes wanted to close, I felt unable even to take another breath I was so tired.

'You'll have to take the top of my skull off,' I said wearily, almost in a whisper.

'Just a small section,' he said. 'Just big enough to get the tumour out.'

'My head will be shaved,' I said, as though to myself, staring into space.

'Yes.'

'But your hair will grow back in no time at all,' Richard intervened.

Yes, I supposed it would, like in a year, or two even, but that was more than no time at all in my book. Still, if I wasn't alive, it wouldn't matter.

'Is there a death rate from the operation?' I asked, slowly moving my tired eyes to focus on his face.

He took his time answering, weighing up how to deal with me. 'There is undoubtedly a small risk to every operation. But you are a healthy woman. I see no reason whatsoever for concern in your case.'

'And if it isn't benign. What then?' I wasn't going to let him off the hook lightly.

'Let's cross that bridge when we get to it, shall we?' he said, twirling the pen a little faster. 'As I've told you, I've every reason to believe that the tumour is benign.'

'I don't want months or years of chemo treatment so that I'm alive but a walking invalid,' I said dejectedly. 'That's out.'

I turned to Richard on the last remark, making sure that he was left in no doubt that he was a witness. He couldn't take my gaze and lowered his eyes.

'When do you want to operate?' I asked the surgeon, searching in my bag with frenzied efficiency for my diary.

'I've reserved a place on my list for you the day after tomorrow. And a hospital room. I understand from Richard that you have private medical insurance.'

Panic made me sit up straight and pay attention. 'That's too soon, I have lots of arranging to do.'

'You must have it done right away,' Richard said. 'Please don't worry about things like that.'

'But if, as you say, it's benign, what's the hurry?'

Suddenly I was crying, not with noise and sobbing, just enough flow of tears streaming down my face and falling into my lap to make me feel at a disadvantage.

'I'm so busy with the business; it won't run itself when I'm not there. And what about my dog?'

Both doctors were wise enough to stay quiet and let me work my way through my personal misery.

'Am I going to be a mindless idiot when I come round from the anaesthetic?' I asked at length.

'Absolutely not,' the surgeon replied. 'You'll be in intensive care for a day or so, and after that you'll have your own room and be able to receive visitors. Your family can come in at any time, of course.'

But not my lover, I thought. Not my Scott. By then I'll have had to find the strength to send him packing for his own good.

I took my notebook from my handbag and a pen, which they must have seen as a welcome positive move.

I headed a clean page with the word URGENT, under which came: alert health insurance, and then the dog.

By the time the day was over there were twenty-two items on the list and the page was full.

For the next thirty-six hours automatism took over, and though all twenty-two items on my list were crossed off at the end of them, I can remember very little of actually carrying anything out, apart, that is, from writing to Scott, telling my children the awful news, making arrangements for my dog, and alerting Fran.

So that I would not change my mind, I wrote to Scott the moment I arrived home from the neurosurgeon's consulting-rooms, having refused to let Richard come in with me.

Dearest Scott,
It is with great sadness that I have decided to bring our

brief but wonderful encounter to an end. I am doing this because it is best for both of us, as one day you will see. It is as painful for me to say these things as I believe it will be for you to read them, and so I shall not prolong our agony. Be assured, my dearest Scott, that no other woman will love you more than I have and it has been a privilege to discover that there is a man such as you on this planet. I shall always think of you as my Renaissance man, and I shall think of you often and with love.
    Cathy

Of course, I was in tears long before I reached the end, and twice I had to begin again.

But there was no way in the world that he would want me as his woman now if he knew the truth. He would try, of course, and he would be as noble as though he were my husband of twenty years, I was sure of that. But we would both know that he'd had the misfortune to walk in on a bum deal, and I knew he deserved better than that.

No sooner was the letter finished, firmly sealed in an envelope and stamped than I literally ran to the letterbox before I changed my mind and did not post it at all.

My despair was now total, and I still had twenty-one items to which I had to attend. My only crumb of comfort was to remind myself of that old saying: It is better to have loved and lost than never to have loved at all. If only I could have believed it, at that moment in time.

Poor Abigail had to take the thankless news all alone and agree to tell her brothers, as I was to discover that both my sons were out of town on different work assignments, and I'd be in hospital before they returned. I forbade her to tell them until they were back in England.

It was probably better that way, and she was brilliant, my girl. No tears, no clinging, no platitudes, just a dead white face and a shaky voice. I was proud of her.

She also agreed to telephone her grandpa with a white lie, saying only that I had gone into hospital for minor investigations after a bump on the head, which we were both sure was nothing at all.

**Philippa Todd**

I was in a quandary about Sacha, who deserved better than kennels for such an unknown length of time. And so I threw myself on the mercy of good friends who have a farm in Yorkshire, a place that the dog knows well because we have been there often, the two of us, for weekend visits.

I know she likes it there by the way she drags her feet when it's time to return to London. One of the reasons for her enthusiasm, apart from the wide open spaces, is that she's in love with their Jack Russell terrier, Bouncer, and it is where she'll miss me least, if they'll agree to take her.

I tried to make light of my plight when I telephoned them, but how light-hearted can you be about a tumour on the brain that needs immediate surgery?

But how about this for friendship: not only did they agree to take her into their home, but to collect her as well, with Bouncer in tow for good measure.

Fran was furious with me when I told her about my letter to Scott, but at least her anger stopped the tears that she was shedding over me.

'You simply can't do that, Cathy,' she said. 'And how do you suppose I'm to deal with it? He's bound to telephone me, even before he gets your letter, when he can't find you and he's going crazy. He'll be calling me.'

'And you won't tell him the truth or I will never forgive you.'

'So what am I supposed to say, for the love of God?'

'You'll say something like you don't know my reason for writing to him, other than you think perhaps I am going to accept Richard's proposal, and I'm out of town.'

'Bullshit,' was all she said in answer.

The staff trooped into my office because I had called a meeting towards the end of my final afternoon so that we could all be emotional at the same time and get it over with.

The end result, bless their hearts, was that they all pledged to work flat out as usual, to hold the fort, to keep me informed, to write me letters, to visit; and to assure me that I did not have a single thing to worry about.

I was able to tell them, and mean it, that they had lightened my load and gladdened my heart, and I would always be grateful to them.

I wouldn't allow anyone to accompany me to the hospital. I could not afford, emotionally, to see any more tears shed on my behalf, and I couldn't run the risk of absconding, through the weakness of being propped up or allowed to lean on others. I know myself, and alone I'm tougher, not weaker.

Or so I thought. But when the taxi drove into the courtyard of the largest hospital in London, and I saw a sign pointing to the private wing, and a porter came to take my bag when I alighted, I definitely considered jumping back into the cab and asking the driver to take me straight to Heathrow airport.

We seemed to follow that yellow directional strip for miles, the porter and I, before we reached my room. It even continued into a lift that was the size of my kitchen, and then crossed, like railway-line junctions, a red strip and a blue strip destined for other mysterious departments.

My first pleasant surprise came in the form of the sister in charge of the private wing.

'Mavis Cartwright,' she said in a friendly sort of way, extending a hand, as I stood forlornly in the middle of my hospital room, my case at my feet as though I'd been abandoned.

Not only was she extremely attractive, with the sort of figure that clothes look good on, and a lovely laugh, but the moment we met she gave me confidence.

'Rotten luck,' she said. 'We just don't know from one day to the next what can befall us, do we?'

'It seems that way,' I said, honestly trying to muster a smile in return for her warmth.

'My sister had the same operation a year ago. The good news is she's absolutely fine now and has never looked better. Her hair's a bit short still, but I like it, it suits her. Honestly, I'm not kidding,' she added, and laughed, when I looked at her slightly sideways.

'Now, we have quite a busy afternoon ahead of us,' she continued briskly. 'But, tell you what, you put all your things away, and undress and get into bed and I'll come back. Do you have much jewellery with you?'

'None,' I said. 'Any that I normally wear I left at home.'

'Hallelujah, someone with some sense at last. You've no idea how many women bring their jewel cases into hospital.'

She pointed out the small chest of drawers and the minute hanging cupboard, as though I may not have noticed them, drew my attention to the bathroom as a way of saying that she would like a urine sample, and left, saying that she would be right back.

I unpacked with dread in my soul, my confidence having departed with Mavis.

It was a strange emotion, the one that had settled that morning. I was dry-eyed, clear-headed, and ready to face whatever was about to be thrown at me; reasonably sure, though not convinced, that I would, in the end, survive.

But it felt unnatural, and unreal, somehow.

I was not particularly into nightdresses. The long ones with the shoestring straps seemed to me to be totally unnecessary. Your shoulders were exposed to night draughts, and the rest of you was wrapped up like a mummy (the entombed variety, that is). Short frilly ones unsettled my stomach at the sight of them, pyjamas were like going to bed having forgotten to take your ski togs off, and second to being naked I preferred to wear loose tee-shirts.

But did one wear a tee-shirt in bed in hospital I had to ask myself? After Mavis's remark about patients bringing their jewellery, I rather doubted it. Not only that, if you were a fashion designer, or the ex-wife of England's leading plastic surgeon, then you were, no doubt, expected to do better than a tee-shirt.

So I rifled through a top cupboard at home where I had kept, for years, a range of nightdresses covering all the 'in case' situations: such as in case of having to share a bed with a maiden aunt, or in case of the unlikely event of being asked to the country for the weekend by the queen, and the most unlikely of all being in case of finding oneself unexpectedly in hospital.

And what a selection they were too, all six of them, all made in Victorian-style fine lawn, and all virginal white. I could scarcely believe I'd chosen them in the first place, no matter how long ago it had been.

Still, I told myself, what did it matter? By the time they'd shaved my head I'd look like a nun doing porridge anyway; or did I mean purgatory? So the white might be rather fitting after all.

Mavis wasn't kidding. I was kept as busy as I usually was at the workplace. They had to weigh me in, take my temperature, feel for my pulse rate. Examine my fingernails for a hint of varnish that might stop them noticing if my nails turned blue, and stick a giant Q-tip up my nose to take a swab. Enquire after my bowels as though I might have mislaid them, my sex life, convinced that I was past having one because didn't all females lose the urge at forty, my sleeping habits, and my drinking habits. By the time we'd reached my smoking habits, they looked pleased on behalf of the anaesthetist, because I assured them I'd dispensed with the killer weed years ago.

Then it was the turn of the cardiographer, who painstakingly stuck patches and paper clips all over my top half, and watched a graph with the unblinking concentration of a football fan watching the World Cup on a television screen.

Every few moments there followed the promise that my anaesthetist would be along shortly to introduce himself, sound my chest, and explain a few details of procedure to me. I looked forward to meeting him as much as a prisoner looks forward to meeting his gaoler before he's locked up.

Actually, when the anaesthetist eventually arrived I felt that my day was looking up. He was extremely handsome, tall, and you can imagine the rest. He wore his stethoscope in his jacket pocket and not around his neck, in a true sense of style, and he'd passed the test as far as I was concerned.

'Catherine Anthony,' he said, offering me his hand. 'I work with your husband sometimes.'

'Ex-husband,' I said.

'Quite. Nice chap. Handful to be married to though, I'll be bound?'

'You could say that,' I replied, non-committally, knowing only too well what gossips they are in the medical profession.

**Philippa Todd**

He sat on the end of my bed and chatted cheerfully to put me at my ease as best he could, and to ascertain what kind of a patient he had on his hands.

To be fair, he explained with great patience what his side of things entailed.

'I hope I won't be sick afterwards,' I said, suddenly panicking. 'I'm not good with anaesthetic.'

He patted my lower leg through the bedclothes. 'I wouldn't dare let that happen; you might report me,' he said, laughing, and standing up.

'I would too,' I said, trying to smile to denote I was joking.

He waved to me at the door, and called, 'Good luck, Catherine. You're going to be fine, we're all pulling for you.'

It was a kind and thoughtful thing to say, and when he'd gone, I shed my first tears of the day.

Everything had been done and the sun was going down, except that my head was still not shaved. This was the part I'd most been dreading, and I agonized over the reason for the delay.

I'd spoken to my son Charles. He'd phoned me as soon as he'd heard the news from Abi, begging me to assure him that I would be all right; and I'd just replaced the receiver when my surgeon blew in.

Believe me, I do not use the word lightly. He came in like a gale-force wind. He was wearing a dinner jacket, and all I could think was, please God, don't let him drink too much tonight.

'Sorry I'm late,' he said, as though I were expecting him. 'Have to go to a wretched hospital dinner so I popped home to jump into the old black tie.'

'You won't drink too much, will you?' I asked, genuinely worried.

'Lord, no. Just been talking to your ex-old man, didn't know you hadn't told him. Pretty upset he was. Says to give you his love and tell you he'll telephone tonight.'

'Thank you,' I replied, not believing it for a moment.

Suddenly, he became sensitive and kind, and he even fondled my covered foot.

'How are you feeling?' he asked softly.

'I've known better days.'

'I'm sure, but try to stay cheerful, it really does help.'

I gave him a thin smile, just to make him feel better and to help him enjoy his dinner.

'We're a good team,' he said. 'The best. You're going to be fine.'

'I believe you, but I'm scared.' I felt my eyes begin to burn.

'Richard's going to scrub up and watch,' he said. 'So he'll be making sure we do all the right things. Nice chap, Richard. You should marry him.'

'I know,' I said. 'But without any hair? I don't think I'll be marrying anyone, do you?'

As though prompted, Mavis knocked and breezed in. 'Oh, sorry, sir, I didn't know that you were in here. I have the barber standing by, bit late, but he's been busy.'

How many shaved heads was my man going to be trepanning tomorrow if the barber was so busy? was my one grizzly thought as the surgeon leaped up, almost guiltily, and made for the door.

'See you tomorrow then, Catherine, bright and early,' he called from the doorway, with unbearable joviality.

Mavis led me to an upright chair and tied a big green cotton cloak on to me that covered me right down to my slippered toes.

'Daniel will be in directly,' she said. 'He's such a nice young man, I know you'll like him.' She patted my shoulder. 'Try to relax if you can. I bet at least once in your life when you were young and a rebel you had your hair cut to within half of an inch of your scalp in defiance. And think positive, yours will grow again and a lot of people do not have that good fortune.'

Her remarks, though kind, were rehearsed, of course; it was all part of standard patient-patter.

But yes, they did help, they gave me something to cling to, something on which to hang my hat.

It reminded me that I did indeed have nearly all my hair cut off once when I was married to Clive, because I'd spotted him in his car with a girl beside him who was sporting the fashionable short back and sides hairstyle of the time, the young-boy look. And I wanted to look like her if that was what turned Clive on. Funnily enough, everyone said that it suited me, except for Clive, that is.

**Philippa Todd**

The barber knocked, then wheeled in a small trolley with a cloth over whatever was on the top shelf, which turned out to be his scissors, razors, a dish for my departing locks, and a few other items.

Our eyes met, we both blinked.

'Daniel, this is Mrs Anthony,' Mavis said.

He didn't speak, he just nodded.

'Hello,' I said, in a flat voice.

'Well,' Mavis went on, 'I'll leave you two alone. Daniel will look after you, won't you, Daniel?'

'Yes, Miss Cartwright,' he replied as she headed for the door.

'Just tell me one thing . . .' I started to say to him as the door closed, in an unbelievably calm voice, all things considered.

But then, I thought, what was a touch of flashing compared to a major operation for a brain tumour. It certainly had helped to bring life into perspective.

'Tell me one thing, did you get treatment after we met?'

He took the small cloth from over his barbering instruments, then walked towards my window, seemingly wrapping it around his hands in a nervous gesture.

I found myself looking apprehensively at his razors and scissors, and stuff.

Then he turned to face me. The concealed lighting above the window made his hair seem even redder and his face even paler than I remembered it from that time on Hampstead Heath when he'd exposed himself to me.

He smiled, just the way he had in the wood, trustingly somehow. 'Yes, I did,' he said quietly. 'I didn't know who you were, but I did it because of what you said. The police told me that you'd asked them to be kind.'

'Your mother must be very relieved, and proud of you too,' I said, because I was a bit stuck for the right words.

He walked back towards his trolley. 'Yes, she is. I still go for counselling twice a week, but I'm better and I'll never do it again. You won't tell people, will you?'

'Of course not,' I said. 'How long have you been working here, at the hospital?'

He selected a pair of hairdresser's scissors and a comb, as though he were about to create a new hairstyle for me. 'Six weeks, and I really like it. I trained as a barber, you see, until I got sick. I'm a theatre porter here as well, and I've always liked looking after people. I shall look after you really specially.'

'I would like that,' I said, feeling better about him. 'I'm scared to death, you know, Daniel.'

'Try not to be, Mrs Anthony,' he said. 'Nobody's ever died in the time I've been here.'

I tried to smile. 'I'm pleased to hear it, Daniel.'

'I shall have a special word about you with God tonight. He'll look after you.'

I envied him his faith.

'I shall have to get on with this now. The quicker we cut it off the better.'

I didn't think, after that experience, I would ever be able to go for a haircut again in my whole life, given the choice, that is. The sound of those scissors as Daniel sliced through whole chunks of my hair echoed in my ears like the clanging of cymbals. I closed my eyes, clasped one hand tightly in the other under my green cotton cloak to keep them from trembling, and tried to listen to Daniel as he hummed quietly to himself while gently removing every last wisp from my skull.

As he reached the soaping and shaving stage, he said to me, 'You've got nice ears, Mrs Anthony. They don't stick out, like mine.'

I couldn't think of an answer and I didn't have the courage required to open my eyes, even though there were no mirrors in the room. And I wondered at that moment how I would manage to clean my teeth without looking at myself in the bathroom mirror that hung over the washbasin.

With perfect timing Mavis Cartwright came in. 'All done, Daniel?' she asked, holding the door open so that he knew she expected him to depart.

'All done, Miss Cartwright,' he answered, carefully covering the cart. As he reached the doorway, he turned towards me. 'Thank you, Mrs Anthony. Good luck for tomorrow,' he said.

# TEN

I solved the mirror business in the bathroom by not putting the light on and only letting in enough glow from my bedroom to stop me falling over things. When I returned to my narrow high bed, however, I did tentatively feel my shaven head, and found it marble smooth and rather cold.

The night sister did not have that certain something that Mavis possessed in abundance. There was no ready smile, no offering of her name. She was heavy-handed, even managing to hurt my toes when she patted my feet in a distracted gesture of friendliness, and said that a nurse would bring me hot milk and two sleeping pills.

Abigail telephoned to say that Todd was back and was staying with her. He was crying about me in their bathroom, she said, but she wasn't supposed to know. He wanted her to ask if I would like him to come and sit with me till I went to sleep.

I declined, reluctantly, because I knew that we would become too emotional. As it was, when she brought him to the telephone and we all wished each other goodnight, I could hardly bear to hear the emotion and misery in their voices.

Fran telephoned too, just minutes before they told me that

they were going to disconnect my telephone so that I would not be disturbed.

Scott had telephoned, she said.

'You didn't tell him anything?' I asked anxiously.

'No, I didn't, and I feel like some low-down rat, I can tell you.'

'He should get my letter tomorrow,' I said. 'I expressed it and sent it to his special address marked urgent.'

'And you think that's going to make him feel better. Announcing you're chucking him without giving a reason?'

'Fran, leave me alone,' I begged her.

'It's unfair to him, Cathy, to treat him like this.'

I wanted the conversation to end. Everything she said grated on my conscience. 'I can't talk any more,' I said. 'I can't take it, I'm sorry.'

The nurse arrived then, bearing two white pills, a small glass of water and a steaming mug of milk. She waited while I swallowed the pills.

All of a sudden, the sister burst in. I was lying back on three pillows, waiting for the pills to take effect, distractedly thumbing through a fashion magazine in the concentrated glow from my bedside light.

I noticed that her cheeks were pink and as she talked she smoothed the front of her dress. She took the magazine from my hands, hauled me forward and plumped my pillows.

'You have a visitor,' she said; and was gone.

I'd spoken to Todd, Charles, Abigail, Fran; it wouldn't be any of them. It couldn't be Scott because he had only recently spoken to Fran on the telephone from overseas, and he had no idea where I was, anyway. I was puzzled.

She put her head around the door, her eyes shining, a smile upon her lips. 'Hello, Cathy. Sorry about the time.'

I cannot tell you how she startled me. How could the most beautiful princess in the world come into a hospital so casually to see one of her dressmakers, and a minor one at that. Even more: how did she know that I was in there?

She closed the door gently, came straight over to me, looking a million dollars in a short black dress I wished that I had designed for her, a pearl choker, and a bracelet to match. She placed her bag on my feet without changing her stride, held out her arms, and took me into them.

She smelled divine, and I don't know for how long she hugged me that way, but it was long enough for tears to fill my eyes and two to fall upon her shoulder.

She released me then and looked at me. Her eyes were watery too, and somehow the light had gone out of them. Her mouth was turned down slightly at the corners, reminiscent of that way she has of suffering with the patient; you've seen it, I'm sure, on your television screen.

She reached out and fondled my head. 'At least you have a nice-shaped head. Imagine what I would look like with a shaven head. An ostrich egg comes to mind.' She began to smile, willing me to do the same.

'You'd look just as lovely as you always do,' I said. 'This is an unbelievable surprise.'

'I didn't want to telephone. I just slipped in through the back door on my way home.'

'How did you know I was here?'

She gave her lovely mischievous smile. 'Ah, well,' she said. 'Funny you should ask that. I'll tell you about it one day.' But she never had the chance.

Her face turned instantly serious. 'But, Cathy, did you not know that anything was wrong?'

I shook my head, and turned to stare at the darkened window. 'Not really. Who would connect a pain in the arm to her head?'

'Poor you; but you're going to be all right. You know that, don't you?'

I nodded. 'Yes, I know that,' I said, wishing that I actually did.

She hugged me again, then pulled away. 'I mustn't stay, you'll be going cross-eyed on me. The sister told me you've been given some sleeping pills.'

'I think they're hoping to knock me out so that I don't give them any trouble before the early start tomorrow,' I said.

'I have to be up early, too. The children and I have a great day planned.'

'That's wonderful.'

**Philippa Todd**

'They go off to Scotland, you see, the day after tomorrow.' A tiny cloud passed over her eyes.

'I used to love it when my children were on school holidays,' I replied.

'We've had the greatest time these hols, the three of us,' she said, preparing to leave. 'Especially our marvellous yachting holiday. Coming back to England again was difficult.'

'Holidays are like that, aren't they?' I said in answer, not knowing if she expected me to comment at all. 'Thank you for coming in. You're so very kind.'

'Nonsense, silly girl.' She moved towards the door, blew me a kiss. 'It's no more than anyone would do for a friend.'

I felt so privileged to have such a wonderful person care about me.

I awoke after each dream, dry-mouthed and anxiously groping for my magnetically anchored light switch on the bedside table. And then, as though by magic, three seconds after the light went on a nurse would glide silently in through the door to see what was happening.

'May I have a drink of water?' I'd ask each time, all trace of drinking glasses, and my fresh-water Thermos jug having been removed from my room and bathroom. There would be a shake of the head, and a do-stop-bothering-us expression, and my light would be extinguished.

But on the last request the nurse looked at the watch on her bosom before she refused me.

'It's five o'clock,' she said, as though I had asked her for the time. 'Much too late. We'll be starting to prepare you in an hour.'

The light went out then again, and I was left to ponder, anxiously, on what preparations she could possibly mean.

As I lay there in the dark, feeling lonely, I fell into a troubled sleep, and began to dream vividly about my childhood.

I was playing football in the garden with my father and I was aged about six. The neighbour's wolfhound was stretched to the limits of its length as it peered over the garden wall and, in the unlikely event of being invited to join in the fun, panted in anticipation.

'Come on, Charlie, give it a good kick,' my father called from the other end of the lawn.

I gave an almighty running right-footed swipe at the ball, and for some reason it made a left turn at a tulip bed and landed smack in the middle.

My mother knocked on the French window as two tulips toppled and the wolfhound gave a sharp deep bark as though he found it funny.

'Bad luck, Charlie, now we'll be in trouble,' my father said.

'Daddy, when can we have a dog?' I asked, more or less as a diversion as I retrieved the ball from the spoiled flowerbed.

'No hope of that,' he replied, as he came towards me. 'You know that Mummy comes out in a rash if a dog goes near her.'

I tucked the ball under my arm and marched in the direction of the house. 'When I'm grown up I shall have my very own dog, and then only you can visit me,' I said over my shoulder, a scowl creasing my face.

'Now then, Charlie, that's enough,' my father said.

It was then that I noticed in the reflection of our greenhouse that I had no hair.

Coming out of the dream, confused and unhappy, I was telling myself that I must never let Scott see a picture of me as a child, or he would find out that I'd always had to wear a wig...

'You really must lie down, Mrs Anthony,' the night nurse said, none too pleased with me.

'I can't sleep.'

'Yes, you can. I'll turn your pillow.'

'Thank you,' I said gratefully, remembering that no one had done that for me since I was a little girl, when my father would do it if I was poorly or upset.

In my next dream I was sitting in Leon's office and I was writing a cheque for twenty thousand pounds which, he was telling me, was a loan to him for three days only, just to keep him popular with his bank manager.

'Top whack, four days,' he said to me, with confidence.

His telephone rang, and it hurt my head.

'Leon Boston,' he said into the receiver, placing his feet up on his glass-topped desk and pushing back his leather-bound office chair. There was lots of forced guffawing, followed by enquiries after the family, which I recognized as signs of the Leon-mind playing for time.

'What's their price?' he said at last, fingering his tie.

'I'd want to go short on them,' he said, after listening for a moment, or something like that.

The voice at the other end became audible to me, in my dream. 'We wouldn't do this for most people, Leon. It's a bit dodgy, but as it's you—'

'Fine,' Leon cut in. 'Sell a hundred thousand shares for me.'

I tore the cheque from my book, and stood up.

Leon said, 'Great, I'll call you back,' and replaced the receiver.

As I staggered towards his office door I knew that I was coming out of my dream. Keep walking, I told myself, and you'll walk away from all the trouble. I felt Leon pluck the cheque from my fingers, and as he did so he gave a yell.

'My God, where's your hair? You had hair when you came in. Now you're bald. You'd better go out at the back of the building so no one will see you.'

When I woke up I discovered that I was calling out, and rocking to and fro with my naked head between my hands. Two nurses had run in and were doing their best to calm me.

'I'll sit with her till she goes off again,' one said to the other.

'No, no,' I said. 'I don't want to go to sleep again, I don't want to dream. I want the light on, I want to be awake.'

They looked at each other. 'What the hell,' one said. 'She's going to get enough sleep in the next three days anyway.'

They gave me an extra pillow on request, and left me alone. I was so thirsty that I seriously thought of going to the bathroom and drinking tap water from the palm of my hand and to hell with the consequences.

Luckily, common sense prevailed, but enough was enough. I wanted it to be time to go to the theatre, I wanted the operation behind me.

If I was lucky enough to come round from the anaesthetic I would not stop drinking water until my thirst was quenched, even if it took several days.

I wished that I could telephone Scott; tell him I was sorry

about the letter, explain what had happened, beg him not to leave me.

I wished that the telephone was still connected in case my children were trying to call me. I wondered if my dog was behaving well, and was happy and content without me. I wished that my ears were not ringing and that I could peacefully fall asleep without suffering from these disturbing dreams.

My eyes kept closing with a will of their own, due to my sedation. Maybe now that I was propped up more I could risk a dreamless nap . . .

Ex-husband Clive was sitting in an armchair opposite mine in his consulting-rooms and I was his patient.

He'd taken my coat and my new 'pudding' hat that hid my bald head, and offered me coffee, which I'd refused.

'You look awful, Cathy,' he said, with his usual blunt veracity. 'I can understand why you want cosmetic surgery. But luckily your hair is starting to grow . . . just a little.'

'I want to look younger, Clive. I want to feel good again.'

'I want both of those things for you too,' he replied, a little more kindly.

'So will you help me, Clive?'

'Of course I will, if you think that I'll do a good job.'

'I know you will,' I said desperately.

He picked up a huge torch, stood over me and shone it down on my face. 'Your skin is in good condition. You know that I'm doing endoscopic surgery now, do you?'

'Endo what?' I wasn't sure what he was talking about.

'Leaves absolutely no visible scars. It'd be perfect for you, just in case it takes for ever for your hair to grow back.'

That was my Clive, keep the patient in her place; especially if she was your ex-wife.

'Is it terribly expensive?' I asked.

'Darling girl, I wouldn't dream of letting you pay,' he replied. 'I'm charging fifteen thousand pounds for this particular op.'

'As much as that?'

'Oh, yes. But tell me, dear, why is your scalp turning green?'

I sat upright, tore off the bedclothes and rushed, staggering and bumping into things, straight into the bathroom, switching on the light in the doorway as I went and running to the mirror.

**Philippa Todd**

Of course, my head was not green, it was pure white, whiter than the rest of me but definitely not even tinged with green. So why had Clive been so unkind in my dream? I wondered.

I looked back towards the mirror. Suddenly, now that my scalp wasn't green, my baldness didn't seem so terrible. And even Clive had admitted that my hair *was* growing again . . .

At six, on the dot, one of the night nurses entered bearing clean sheets and a green theatre gown. Without speaking she placed them on a chair, and retreated. Twenty seconds later she was back to take my temperature and count my pulse rate. The latter must surely have been near to a hundred beats a minute; my heart was thumping like a drum in my chest.

'Take a bath,' she said, as an order not a request. 'And when you get out climb into that theatre gown; it opens up the back. Any false teeth, glass eyes, or anything that isn't your own?'

'No,' I replied, thankful at least for that small mercy.

I was depressed and frightened. I felt lonely and abandoned. There is no place on earth more lonely in my opinion than an operating table. You are the focus of everyone's attention, but you are the only one who is actually facing the ordeal.

'Right, then,' a different nurse wearing squeaky shoes said. 'I want you to take these pre-med tablets. Do you think that you can swallow them without water?'

'I'll try,' I said helpfully, wondering, as I swallowed them, what would happen if they became stuck in my throat and I wasn't allowed any water to help them down. Would I be left to choke to death?

'Good girl,' she said when at last I was successful, as though I were a tiny child. 'Now, I'm only going to leave you with one pillow and I'm putting your bed flat. You'll find you get drowsy in no time, and your mouth will dry out.'

I thought it unlikely that my mouth could possibly feel any drier than it was, but I was to discover that I was wrong.

The nurse placed a cap on my head that resembled a shower hat, drew my curtains, and left. From that moment I knew without doubt that I was totally in the charge of others; it was official, there was no turning back. Battle would commence whether I liked it or not.

## Whispers On A Pillow

Very soon an imaginary bird twittered in my head and static crackled in my ears. I felt giddy, and confused. A row of babies wearing only nappies tottered across the room when I tried to adjust my vision, and I would swear that a helicopter hovered outside my window, and four men wearing black balaclavas were staring in at me.

Two cool soft hands took one of mine. 'Hello there,' Mavis Cartwright said. 'Sorry to hear about your troubled night.'

I tried unsuccessfully to get her into focus while I placed my other hand on hers and squeezed.

'I'm so glad you're here,' I said, slurring my words.

She put her mouth close to my ear and said softly, 'I'm on duty for the next three days. I'll come and see you in intensive care.'

'Oh, no,' I said in panic. 'Does that mean you'll be having time off when I come back?'

She pushed the elastic of the cap from over my ears and tucked it behind them where it was so much more comfortable.

'No, my dear, I'll be here; I'm only off duty for two days.' Then she patted my shoulder. 'I'm going to accompany you to theatre shortly. See you then.'

Almost immediately, or so it seemed to me as I lay in my drugged stupor, another hand came over mine. It was large, warm, and masculine. I thought of Scott. Could it possibly be him?

'Hello, Cathy,' Richard said. 'Bad luck about your lack of sleep.'

'I could have done with a better night,' I replied, opening my eyes and venturing to focus on his face but to no avail.

'After today, everything will improve. You'll only have to concentrate on getting better.'

I tried to nod my head but it made me feel sick in the way that a rough sea might.

'Clive left the children and me waiting at the portside in Greece,' I heard myself saying . . .

It was true, and I'll never forget the relief mixed with anger that I'd felt when I saw his schooner in full sail come round the bay. But why should I have thought of it then, almost thirty years later?

Richard squeezed my hand. 'Try not to worry about it now, Cathy. All that's behind you. I must go and scrub up; I shall stay with you until you are safely back out of the theatre.'

He kissed me on my cheek, then kissed the hand he held. I felt his weight leave the bed.

'He and his friend had girls on board, you know,' I said drunkenly. 'I thought that was pretty mean of them.'

My door opened wide, was secured in position, and things began to happen. I recognized Daniel's voice and as he came near I saw through a fog his pale eyes, and his ginger hair poking out of a small green cap.

'We've come to collect you, Mrs Anthony,' he said, and his voice sounded far away.

He and his colleague then lifted me bodily on to what seemed to be a canvas stretcher, and placed me gently on a trolley, covering me with blankets.

Mavis came in then. She put thick socks on my feet, and checked the blankets. 'Right, boys, let's go,' she said, and patted my leg.

The corridors seemed endless. As I could only look upwards I counted the recessed ceiling lights; it seemed important to know how many there were. Then we were in a large lift and were moving, though I had no idea which way.

Mavis, standing by my head, said, 'Four telephone messages have come in for you this morning. Now let me think: one was from Charles, one from Todd, one from Abigail, all sending love and wishing you luck. And one was from an American.' (My heart missed a beat.) 'She was called Fran, and she said she was sending good-luck wishes from everyone at the workplace, and extra love from her.'

'Thank you,' I muttered.

The lift silently halted.

I was wheeled out, and we were on the move again. I continued to count the ceiling lights, adding them to my list of twenty.

Two sets of double doors flew open at the approach of my trolley, and I knew that we'd arrived at our destination.

## Whispers On A Pillow

'This is the anaesthetic room,' Mavis said in my ear, and then there was lots of muted conversation followed by a sharp rustle as my all-important notes changed hands.

The identification band on my wrist was checked and read out to a witness as I was handed over into the care of the theatre staff.

'Come on, boys,' I heard her say softly. 'Time to go.'

Someone touched my shoulder, gave it a squeeze.

'Hello, Mrs Anthony,' a female voice said loudly, as though I were deaf as well as half asleep. 'I'm the anaesthetist's assistant. Can you open and close this fist for me.'

As I did so someone held my hand up and said, 'Veins are a bit small.'

I heard the double doors burst open again, there was a carbolic smell in the air and two men were peering down at me, who, with my double vision, looked like two sets of identical twins. They turned out to be my surgeon and the anaesthetist, gowned, hatted, and masked.

'Hello, Catherine,' they both said one after the other. I did my best to answer.

'See you in a mo,' the surgeon said cheerfully. 'We'll soon have you well again.' The two of him disappeared from my view.

'Has the lady got some nice veins waiting for me?' I heard the twin anaesthetists say. 'It'll just be a small prick in the back of your hand, and then it's sweet dreams all the way.'

I didn't feel the prick. 'You can start to count, if you like,' he said.

I think that I made some sort of whinney that was meant to be number one, but before I could go any further a rushing noise filled my ears with the force of an express train. It invaded my entire body quickly, stopped for a second, during which period I distinctly heard the anaesthetist say, 'Has she gone?'

Then it started up again, and the noise it made was the last thing I remember.

Day one in Recovery, straight from the operating theatre.

Someone was standing on a mountain across the valley, and he must have had a loud-hailer to his lips because the drawl was extended, and there was an echo to his words.

**Philippa Todd**

'Mrs Anthony . . . Catherine. Wake up now. Catherine, try to open your eyes for me.'

I tried, to please the voice, but something heavy seemed to be holding them shut.

'Wake up, Catherine . . . it's important to wake up.'

I groaned, and hoped that a groan would suffice.

'Good,' he said. 'I'm Roland, your intensive-care technician. Could you say something for me?'

I groaned again, my head was heavy, my mouth was cardboard.

'How are you feeling?' he asked.

'Terrible,' I answered, through lips too dry to part. 'I want to go to sleep.'

There were clicking noises near my head, and I could hear a bleep sounding at regular intervals.

'You can go to sleep again for a little while now that you've woken up.'

I tried to work out without success why I had to wake up before I was allowed to go to sleep.

Roland was repeating his call across the valley. Poor man, I thought, his throat must be hurting by now.

'Catherine, do you feel like opening your eyes now? Be a good girl.'

'No, thank you,' I said dreamily. 'I'd need a drink of water for that.'

'No, you can't have water yet. I'll moisten your lips if you'll promise to open your eyes.'

He gently wiped my lips with delicious ice wrapped in a cloth and even let one drop trickle into my mouth, which was pure heaven.

'Open your eyes now,' he said. 'You promised.'

I quietly begged my eyes to open, and they responded.

Roland wiped them with cool swabs, saying, 'Can you see me now?'

I tried to nod my head but nothing happened. 'Yes,' I croaked.

'Good. What colour are my eyes?'

'Brown.'

He moistened my lips again. 'Good, so are yours.'

He smiled then, and tilted his head, and I decided that he was a very special, caring person, perfect for the job he had been given to do.

The princess would have approved of him.

Day two, first day after the operation, still in Recovery.

'What time is it?'

Roland looked down at me. 'I love it when a patient asks that question, it means the worst is over. It's eight o'clock in the morning and I hear you slept like a baby all night.'

'Can I have a real drink of water now?'

'Would you rather have some tea?'

'Would I ever! Roland, you say the nicest things.'

'I know.'

'Very weak, with lemon please. Can I have a big cup?'

He laughed. 'I'll see what I can do.'

'My throat's terribly sore,' I said, trying to put my hand to it, only to discover that I was attached to a saline drip and lots of wires.

'It's no wonder your throat is sore,' Roland said. 'For a large part of yesterday you had several tubes thrust down it. Be back in a minute, don't go away.'

It wasn't lemon tea that they made for me, it was nectar.

Roland lifted me forward and laughed at the slurping noises I made.

Never had anything tasted so good in my whole life. The cup was huge and someone had had the bright idea to add sugar, which I wouldn't normally like, but that day, I can tell you, it was perfection.

The anaesthetist was the first of my official visitors. He breezed in, listened to my chest much too quickly to have picked up anything, I would have thought; patted my feet, said see you tomorrow, and blew out again.

'Look who's here.' Roland grinned, coming in through the door with Abigail, Todd and Charles behind him.

'Thank goodness, awake at last,' Abi said.

'What do you mean? I was awake early.'

'Not yesterday you weren't,' Todd said. 'We sat watching you all afternoon, but you weren't too keen to face the world.'

'I didn't know,' I answered, feeling mean after they had made the effort to come to see me.

The surgeon arrived later, but I'm not sure how long afterwards. I had no conception of time; everything seemed jumbled and I was not wearing a watch. He was pleased with me, he said.

'The tumour came out neatly, Catherine,' was how he worded it. 'Later today I'll have the path. report. When I do I'll call in. How are you feeling now?'

'Tired,' I said. 'Heavy-headed, a bit like having 'flu.'

'Yes, well, your temperature is rather high, so I'm going to keep you in here over tomorrow. The bandage will be making your head feel heavy, but you can have that off later. You sleep as much as you want to today.'

'Lovely man,' Roland said, as he returned from escorting him to the open doorway.

I was asleep when Richard arrived. Roland told me that he sat watching me for quite some time before I eventually woke up.

He seemed to be fighting back tears, which didn't do much for my confidence, and I wondered if he was the courier of bad news.

'I'm sorry, Cathy,' he said, blowing his nose. 'I'm just so relieved for you that it's over, and I have permission to tell you that the results have come through and the tumour was benign, as we thought.'

Tears welled up in my eyes then too, and I took my first really deep breath since before the operation.

'Do I look a sight, Richard?' I asked hoarsely. 'I haven't had the courage to ask anyone else.'

'Not at all,' he answered. 'You look positively angelic. A little frail, of course.'

'I feel frail,' I said slowly. 'Road-rollered actually. I really must go to sleep again.'

'Oh, thank heaven. I thought you were going to say that you really must go to the beautician.'

When I awoke, the bandage felt much too tight; my head felt as though it were in a vice, and I was wishing that it could at least be loosened.

Then a trolley was wheeled in and the senior registrar whom

my surgeon had introduced me to on operating day came over to me.

'Feel like having these bandages off?' he asked, smiling.

'Desperately,' I answered.

He unbound my head and the relief was overwhelming.

'Nice,' he said, meaning the scar, and the stitching. 'I'll just put on a small dressing. With luck, tomorrow, that can come off too.'

Day three, second day out of the operating theatre, still in Recovery.

The anaesthetist looked down my throat and the spatula made me retch. My vocal chords had all but packed up and my throat was agony.

'There doesn't seem to be any damage,' he said. 'Sometimes the tubes stick as they're pulled out, but we're as careful as we can be. Try not to talk and rest your throat as much as possible. Orange juice might help.'

'I don't feel well,' I croaked, with tears in my eyes.

He took my hands in his. 'It's the dreaded third day, Catherine. You were too perky yesterday.'

Roland followed him from the room. I knew that they were conferring but I couldn't hear what was being said.

Then Roland came sashaying back into the room bearing a syringe in a small dish. 'This will raise your spirits, love,' he said. 'It will also take you to the moon.' Then he smiled down at me. 'Maybe I'll share it with you.'

He groped down the bed, found a fleshy part in my right thigh, and let rip. The pain was so awful I don't think that I'll ever complain in hospital again and run the risk of being given another one of those injections.

Roland massaged the area, saying that he didn't like causing me discomfort (a major understatement), as he watched the unchecked tears of pain and self-pity cascade down my cheeks.

He covered me again, tucked me in affectionately as though I were his child, and checked the monitors on the wall above my head.

'Before you know it, it'll be tomorrow,' he said, 'and you'll be feeling a different person. Ready to go forward, I promise.'

**Philippa Todd**

I don't remember much of what was left of that day, but certainly when I awoke next morning I did feel as though a new stage of recovery had begun. And to prove the progress was genuine, they promised to move me back to my own room.

Mavis Cartwright came by to tell me that she would be waiting, and Roland promised to pay me a visit as Daniel and another young man wheeled me back through the many corridors. It was heady stuff (if you'll pardon the pun), and exciting too, knowing that I would be back in touch with the world.

I gasped when I saw the mountains of flowers that were awaiting me. And a small stack of mail was placed at my bedside waiting to be opened.

Mavis popped her head round the door to tell me that she would be in soon to read the cards that accompanied the flowers, and to slit open my envelopes.

I made the effort to spray some perfume on myself and I touched my lips lightly with lipstick, venturing as I did so to look into my small portable mirror. Apart from looking rather pale, nothing seemed to be the worse for wear on my face; I don't quite know what I was expecting.

Two nurses came in, stripped me of the intensive-care gown and hustled me into a nightdress. Then they walked me around my room twice and put me in a chair. The home stretch of real recovery had begun. Roland was right, I felt ready to go forward.

I asked Mavis if I could have my telephone returned to me as she helped me back into bed. She said no, I'd had enough excitement for one day.

She read out the messages written on the cards attached to the flowers, which ranged from ostentatious displays the size of small cottages to neat tasteful arrangements of posies.

We even played a little game. It was childish, I know, but it involved my guessing at a glance, and before Mavis read out the card, who had sent which floral trophy. Sometimes I managed to get it right, which pleased her, and she would call out 'well done' as encouragement.

As we were playing this game, a posy of blooms arrived, moderate in size, and beautifully arranged in colours of blue and white; they were tied tastefully with a bow of straw instead of the usual shiny ribbon.

**Whispers On A Pillow**

Mavis handed the small envelope pinned to the side over to me to open. The card inside was modest, if gold-edged, and on it in girlish hand was the signature of the princess. 'Get well quickly,' it said. 'I am thinking of you.'

Mavis ran out in a hurry bearing the blooms with the excuse of finding a suitable vase, but we both knew that her real intention was to jungle-drum the news around the wards that at least one inmate had friends in high places.

Lunch arrived then; soup and toast soldiers, followed by red jelly and custard. Mavis said that I was to eat it all up, and she would be back to check that I had done so.

Was she kidding? I was starving; soup and red jelly would suit me fine.

However, when I was halfway through the jelly and custard, major exhaustion overcame me.

A kitchen orderly, arriving to collect my tray, found me slumped over it fast asleep. He quickly reported the fact to a senior nurse; probably as a possible death in the hospital camp; and the next thing I knew, I was roused from slumber by two nurses bent on heroic resuscitation.

'I'm tired,' I remember saying. 'Could I have one pillow taken away?' They were so relieved to find that I was still breathing, if I'd played my cards right I think I might have got away with requesting a large gin and tonic. But be that as it may, I appreciated being allowed to lie down a little flatter, and sleep was instantaneous the moment they closed the curtains against the bright light.

My shallow dreams were filled with thoughts of Scott, as we had been, thankful at having found each other, newly in love, talking all the time, wallowing in our mental jousts, discovering each other in sex. Once, I'm sure that I laughed aloud in my sleep in pure pleasure at how lively we were in each other's company.

In my dream he sat beside me on our bed at home, his strong warm hands placed on mine. He'd just arrived from the States, and his natural male smell seemed to be mixed with leather, and something else I couldn't quite place. He was saying my name, and tracing my face with his finger.

But he wasn't touching my hair, twining it corkscrew fashion

185

around his finger as I'd become accustomed to him doing, or pushing it away from my forehead. Instead he traced a finger lightly down to the base of my throat, then placed his hand back over mine.

'Cathy, darling,' he was saying, 'wake up and talk to me.'

Yes, I will, I thought. But he must have arrived early, it was still dark, and I wouldn't stay in bed if he was expected. That would be unforgivable. What would he think of me?

I tried to stop coming out of my dream. I simply wasn't ready.

My eyes opened of their own accord. His face was still there. I let the lids drift back down; I was confused.

'Cathy, don't go off again,' he said. 'What am I going to do with you?'

I opened my eyes and willed them to stay that way. It was as if he really were in my hospital room, and that wasn't possible because he didn't know that I was there.

I searched for my bell to ring for a nurse.

'What are you doing, darling?' his voice asked softly. 'What's bothering you?'

He pressed then patted my hands, and stood up.

'I'm going to open your curtains a little, so that we can see each other better. Is that okay with you?'

I couldn't find the words to answer. Was I awake or wasn't I? I'd much prefer to know.

I closed my eyes against the light, and I could not so much hear as feel him coming back across the room towards my bed. Then I could smell his maleness again, feel his presence close, his warmth against me as he bent over. He kissed my lips tenderly and I responded.

My eyes burned, my lashes were wet, I couldn't stop the tears escaping down my cheeks.

'Please don't, darling,' he said. 'I can't bear to see you cry.'

# ELEVEN

My hands flew to my shaven head. 'Oh, no,' I cried out. 'You mustn't see me like this, you mustn't look.'

He stood up and cradled me against his chest, tenderly holding the back of my hairless head with the palm of his hand, rocking me, patting my back with his other hand.

Someone opened the door, and quickly closed it again.

Scott was still holding me when it reopened and, out of deference to the person entering, we pulled apart.

It was Daniel carrying a tray. He looked at us shyly. 'I'm helping out,' he volunteered. 'Sister said you should be offering your guest some tea.'

Scott pulled my bedtable across the bed and Daniel placed the tray on it.

'Scott, this is Daniel,' I said, dabbing at my eyes while Scott extended his hand. 'Daniel and I had met before, and then we unexpectedly met again when I came in here. He's been very attentive and kind.'

'That's good of you, Daniel. I appreciate it,' Scott said, as Daniel, grinning from ear to ear, backed out of the room.

'Now let me think,' Scott said, staring down at the tea tray. 'You like your tea not looking like tea at all, way too weak, with lemon, and no sugar.'

**Philippa Todd**

'And you like yours horribly strong with far too much milk and lots too much sugar,' I countered, already starting to smile, even though my hands stayed clasped to my head.

He served the tea, moved a plate of biscuits towards me.

'You're going to be well in no time, you know that, don't you?'

I nodded my head, lowered my chin. It had to be faced. 'You obviously received my letter? It was the hardest thing I've ever had to write.'

Scott pulled up a chair. Then he took my hands from my head, placed them on the counterpane and lifted up my chin. 'Yes, I received it. It came to my office.'

'I had no address,' I answered defensively. 'But on your card you sent me it said the name of the building where you arrowed your window. There was a district postmark in Washington over the stamp. I just hoped.'

'That was clever of you,' he said, smiling. 'All the Urgent and Personal notices caught an agent's eye who was about to relieve me. He brought it with him. But I already knew that you were ill when it reached me. I was in fact just leaving.'

'Fran told you, I suppose. How did you make her do it?'

'I told her I would set the boys on her if she didn't spill the beans.'

I looked up. He was smiling.

'Well, actually, it was pretty obvious that something was terribly wrong. I'd never heard Fran cry before. So I took advantage and told her I would never speak to her again if she held out on me. I was serious, and she knew it.'

'Don't blame her,' I said, looking down. 'I was threatening her too.'

'Yes. She told me you were. Obviously she's more scared of me than she is of you.'

I made myself look at him. 'I didn't know what else to do. I certainly didn't want to hurt you. But it seemed for the best.'

He reached out and stroked my arm. 'Don't ever do anything like that again if you have a personal crisis. I would have been devastated to receive a letter like that cold turkey. How could you possibly think that I'd let an unexpected illness come between us? I like to think that I'm worth a bit more than that.'

# Whispers On A Pillow

I felt so ashamed, and I lowered my eyes again.

'Cathy,' he said, as he took my hand in his, 'I can't live without you, you're the most precious thing in the world to me. I thought you understood that. If you ever don't feel the same way, I implore you, tell me to my face.'

'I was afraid for you,' I said. 'Our love affair's so new, I couldn't bear the thought of you feeling burdened, or wishing that you could bring it to an end but not wanting to hurt me.'

He stood up, moved the bedtable out of the way and held me to him. I locked my arms around him. He kissed the top of my naked head, not once but several times.

'When did you get here?' I asked at length, always obsessed with his movements.

'About an hour before you woke up.'

'No, I mean in this country.'

He looked down at me. 'I mean that too. I landed at the airport and ran. Everyone was very helpful.'

'Did you have to fly the plane yourself?'

'No, I flew commercial,' he answered. 'The firm for once were understanding.'

I looked up at him. 'I'm truly sorry for causing you pain. I just didn't know what to do . . .'

He gently pressed my head to his chest. 'I was so afraid, Cathy. I didn't know what to expect.'

I looked up at him. 'Don't tell me that Fran failed to explain what was wrong with me?'

'Of course she explained. I wrung every last detail out of her. But as she hadn't been allowed to see you, she couldn't tell me what to expect. I thought that you might be unconscious.' He let me go, pulled his chair close and sat holding my hands, rubbing his thumbs over their backs.

'How long will you be in London?' I asked, hoping that he was not rushing away.

'There's a bit of a tricky job on tomorrow,' he said. 'I'll be out of England till the next day, then I'll come straight back to you.'

'Where will you be staying?' I asked, looking startled.

'In a safe house, there's no need to worry.' He turned my hand over in his. 'I'm so in love with you, Cathy. You're on my mind the whole time.'

'I'm so in love with you, too. It broke my heart to write that letter.'

'My God, I've never been so upset as when Fran told me what was wrong,' he said. 'I simply couldn't come to terms with you being so sick.'

'You know that the tumour was benign, don't you?' I asked, fixing him with my eyes to make sure that he was listening to me. 'I'm going to make a complete recovery. But it will take a long time for my hair to grow back properly.'

'So?' he answered, looking directly at my shaven head and shrugging. 'You'll always be beautiful to me.'

It was time for him to go, he said. I must not get overtired. He should perhaps ask Fran out to dinner, if I had no objection.

'Of course not,' I answered him, nevertheless feeling envious at the two of them going out to a restaurant together.

The door opened then, and who should come in, not one of my children, but all three together. Abigail ran to me and threw her arms about my neck. The boys didn't seem to know where to look, maybe on account of my bald head, maybe on account of my entertaining a man; so they rather sheepishly put their bunches of flowers down on the end of the bed, together with a rather bulky plastic bag that weighed heavily on my feet. They then formed a queue to kiss me.

'Hello, Cathy,' Charles whispered into my ear, an emotional expression on his face. 'I'm glad to see that you look so much better today.' He turned to Todd as he moved away. 'She does, doesn't she?'

Todd kissed me, then ran his hand over his own extremely short haircut. 'Much better,' he answered. 'And she couldn't wait to copy my hairstyle, you will have noticed.'

'You better watch out,' I said, as Abigail clipped his ear. 'And of course you all know Scott, don't you? You met at the launch party. He's just flown in from the States.'

All three turned towards him with smiles of greeting.

Charles, ever the suave one, came forward and shook his hand. 'Of course I remember us meeting. Your spine was playing you up. How is it now?'

Scott looked as though he wished the floor would swallow

him up. 'Fine at the moment. I hoped we'd meet again sometime soon. But I really should be going now.'

'Don't go because of us,' Abigail said, up-front as usual. 'We can't stay for very long this time.'

We all made polite conversation. I could feel my cheeks turning pink.

'I'm getting married in early spring,' Abigail said to Scott. 'You must come to my wedding.'

'I would like that very much,' he replied, looking at me. 'And now I'm going to leave you to have some private time with your mother.'

I found it slightly ironic that this man, my lover, who was calling me mother to my children, was only a few years older than they were.

He came over to my bed, knowing that their eyes were upon him. Self-consciously he kissed both my cheeks, discreetly squeezed my hand, said his farewell to the kids, winked at me from the doorway, and was gone.

'What a man,' Abi said almost before the door closed. 'God, you were jammy, being taken on a dirty weekend by private helicopter with him.'

'Yes, wasn't I?' I answered, thinking what a long time back that outing seemed. 'I like him very much,' I added. 'He's a nice man.'

Why didn't I tell them outright that I was crazy about him, that he was a fantastic man not merely a nice one; and that he loved me too?

'You both looked as though there's more to it than that,' Abi said. 'Didn't they, fellas?'

Charles laughed. Todd gave his usual slow smile.

'Well anyway, Mum,' Abi said. 'I'm very pleased for you. Never mind them, what do they know? You need a man in your life, someone to love you as much as we do, only differently.'

I felt a lump form in my throat. 'But what about our age difference?' I asked. 'You must have formed an opinion on that.'

'What age difference?' Charles asked. 'You looked pretty good together to me.'

'A pox on that rubbish,' Abigail said. 'Go for it, our Mum.'

\* \* \*

**Philippa Todd**

The telephone was returned to my bedside, but the incoming calls were vetted at source and I was asked if I wished to receive them. None were put through between two and four in the afternoon, when my nap was compulsory on pain of death to the operator. Or after nine at night when I was supposed to be thinking of sleep again.

As it was, I still received as many calls as I felt able to deal with, and I made a few outgoing ones of my own when I felt up to it. I was amazed and bewildered how quickly I became tired.

Fran came in to see me every day and brought me news of the workplace, the staff and the clients. Once she brought Suzie, our head seamstress with her, and we had a wonderful gossip.

One day I was delighted to receive a large bouquet of flowers from Clara Holiday. They were the cottage-sized variety, and the porter had trouble getting the basket in through the door.

Quite the funniest letter accompanied them: husband Fred, she wrote, on investigation from a hot-shot lawyer, was found to have had a girlfriend for the past ten years. And so Clara was divorcing him and it wasn't going to cost her lover Nico a penny. 'Serves the miserable sod right, doesn't it?' she wrote gleefully.

On her first visit Fran brought me a Hermès silk headscarf as a gift. She also tried to help me tie it around my head and we ended up in fits of laughter as it slipped around on my bald pate like a duck on ice.

Eventually, I got the hang of it by pulling it down lower over my forehead and covering my ears. And by tying it tightly and firmly, and tucking in the end pieces, it really didn't look so bad, even though my reasons for wearing it would not have fooled even the shortsighted.

'You look great, Cathy,' Fran said. 'Just like Caroline of Monaco.'

'Who are you kidding?' I asked her. 'I wouldn't mind being her age though.'

Still, I must admit, that scarf did a lot for my confidence, and as it was only my first attempt at a cover-up, I knew that I would improve with practice.

Richard came in every day, but he always telephoned first to ask if I was alone. News travels fast in hospital; I think he must have heard a whisper or two about Scott, and after a few days he found the courage to broach the subject.

'I'm glad that you've found someone to love, Cathy,' he said, watching my face carefully. 'Is he someone I know?'

'You may have seen him at the launch party,' I said tentatively. 'He's an American.'

I was sitting in an armchair at the time and Richard was sitting opposite. I looked into my lap, avoiding his eyes while he reflected.

'Oh, yes, I remember, your Charles introduced us. Nice chap, I thought; a little young for you, perhaps.'

'I wonder about that myself,' I answered, while feeling that he had no right to say so. 'You know,' I continued, 'I came close to accepting your proposal, and I think that I could have made you happy.'

'I'm sure that you could. But I can see that you're crazy about this man, and I take it that your love is reciprocated?'

I looked over the top of his head and avoided his eyes. 'He says that he's very much in love with me, and I believe him.'

'And you would never have been crazy about me,' he said in a matter-of-fact way.

'My feelings for you are of a special sort of friendship, a fondness,' I said, trying in vain to find the right words. 'I'll always feel a certain kind of love for you.'

'That's nice,' he said, smiling at me rather sadly. 'And I'll always be there for you. I hope you'll remember that.'

He got up then, said that he must go but would return. He kissed my lips and patted my shoulder, told me that I was looking better every day; and that he was sure I had a wonderful and fulfilling life ahead of me.

As he opened the door, he turned towards me, a telling sort of smile on his lips. 'By the way,' he said. 'I don't think that I ever made it clear, but just for the record, I love you very much too . . .'

I longed for Scott to come back, I wished that he would call me.

I'd told them, emotionally, on the telephone control desk that he was a number-one priority, that he would be calling

**Philippa Todd**

long distance, and that I simply must take his call whatever the hour.

Every time my door opened, I hoped it would be him.

When Abigail walked in she said, 'Oh, sorry, Mum, I can tell from the look on your face that you were hoping I was Scott.'

'Don't be silly,' I replied, and settled down as best I could to talk to her without my disappointment showing.

And then, exactly as he said he would, he telephoned. 'I'll have to come over right away, or I won't be let in because it'll be too late,' he said. 'Is that all right, I'm unshaven?'

'Of course, I'll plead with them to let you in. I'll say I shall discharge myself if they don't.'

Abigail stood up as I replaced the receiver. 'I'm off. I can take a hint,' she said.

I could feel my cheeks turning pink and my heart thumping in my chest. 'Don't rush away. He won't be here just yet.'

'You're in love with him in a big way, Mum, aren't you?' she asked.

'Madly,' I replied, looking into her eyes. 'With a passion I don't remember ever feeling before, not even for your father, if you'll forgive me, and I was pretty gone on him.'

She gave me a hug. 'I'm so pleased for you, honestly,' she said, in her generous way. 'Now I'm going. I'll tell them at the front desk to let him in, or you're off home.'

I tired myself out with anticipation, and by the time he arrived my head was heavy as lead and my eyes were closing, no matter how hard I tried to look alert. But I held my arms out and he hurried across the room and locked me to him.

He too was tired, and he looked quite worn down in his crumpled jeans, leather jacket, and dark sweater, his hair falling forward and his stubble thick upon his chin. He looked like a man at the end of an extremely arduous forty-eight hours.

I so wished that we could be at home, in bed together, drifting off into dreamless sleep, safe in each other's arms. We held each other in a lingering embrace, then he kissed me cautiously on account of the stubble.

As he threw off his jacket, he felt in a pocket and produced two of my scarves from home. 'I took them with me yesterday in the helicopter,' he said. 'I really liked the feel of them in my pocket. They smelled faintly of your perfume, and that made you seem very close.'

'How clever you were to choose the cotton ones,' I answered, taking them from him. 'They'll stay in position on my head so much more easily than silk.'

He pulled up an armchair and slumped into it with a sigh.

'Did you have a successful trip?' I asked, not expecting him to tell me anything significant.

'Yes, most interesting. Have they told you when they'll be releasing you?'

'You make it sound as though I'm in gaol and I'm to be allowed out on parole.'

He leaned forward in his chair and took my hands in his. 'I'd like to know,' he said seriously, 'because I want to be the one to take you home, if it's possible. And to stay with you for a day or so. I can take some time off, with a little warning.'

I turned my palms upwards and pressed them against his. 'I'd like that too,' I answered. 'They mentioned my going to a convalescent home in the country for a while, but I can't do that. I'd rather stay in London and be near work and my family, and to make it easy for you to visit me.'

He squeezed my hands, leaned over and kissed my lips. 'You're so right for me, Cathy,' he said. 'No woman has ever fulfilled me like you do. I don't know what I would have done if anything bad had happened to you.'

I tried to push back the lock of hair that was falling over his forehead, but it resisted and fell down again. I looked into his kind blue eyes. 'I love you, Scott Peters, so very much. I don't know how I could ever have contemplated trying to live my life without you.'

He didn't answer. His eyelids seemed to droop.

'I think that you should go home to bed,' I said. 'Are you leaving very early in the morning?'

He ran his hands distractedly through his hair as he stood up. 'Fairly early, but I shall pay you a very quick visit, probably even before your breakfast arrives. If you have any mail at home, I'll bring it over. Is there anything else that you need?'

I shook my head. 'Fran is bringing two big sketching pads and crayons when she comes in during the morning. I feel inspired and I'm aching to set my ideas down on paper before I get idle. I should have brought them in with me, but my mind was much too preoccupied.'

He lifted my chin. 'But you won't overdo it, will you? You've had a major operation, after all.'

'I promise,' I said as he let go of me; and I pulled his head down towards me for a last lingering kiss.

I slept well. But I made sure that I was up early so that Scott could at least see me at my best, bathed, re-gowned, and perfumed. I wrapped my head in one of the cotton scarves that he had brought from home, and decided that I would manicure my nails and colour them with the pale pink varnish that Abigail had given me.

'It'll be good for your morale to polish your nails,' she'd said. 'I'll do your toes for you as well, if you'd like.'

But before I could do so, Scott burst in carrying a huge bunch of white lilies. 'They were being put on show by the flower-seller on the corner,' he said, looking pleased. 'And he'd just come from the flower market, he told me. He was a real Cockney character. I love London, apart from the weather. More rain's just setting in.'

He looked so very wonderful, and I decided then and there that he was the nicest man I'd ever known. I marvelled that, even though it was a fact I was so much older than him, I never noticed the difference in our ages when in his company. I thanked God for sending him into my life when I really had thought I would never love again.

He didn't stay long, and several times he looked at his watch.

When we finally kissed goodbye I clung a little.

'You have the red number with you?' he asked.

I nodded.

'Use it whenever you want to, but I'll be telephoning when I can. You know that, don't you?'

'Do you know when you're coming back?' I asked, suddenly feeling afraid.

He cupped my face in his hands. 'Soon, my Cathy, and I can't wait to take you home. To look after you, and spoil you. Remember that.'

My breakfast tray arrived then. Scott lifted the tiny metal cover hiding something warm. 'Poached egg on toast!' he exclaimed. 'I didn't know that you ate breakfast. You've been holding out on me?'

'Not really,' I answered, laughing. 'But I'm wakened so early in this place it doesn't seem like breakfast, more like a midnight feast. I hope I won't get fat. What are you doing with that pot?'

'Pouring your tea.' He looked at me quizzically.

'You won't get it right, I bet.'

'Yes, I will; I pour half an inch of tea, like so, then fill up the cup with water, and slip this little piece of lemon into it at the end.'

'You even make pouring tea sound sexy.'

He quickly kissed my lips. 'I'm off, you're having too much excitement for one visit.'

I finished my breakfast; they could poach a mean egg in that kitchen, soft yoke, white well cooked, just the way I liked it.

Then I settled down to read my morning paper, noting that it seemed to please everyone that I was taking an interest in the outside world again.

I was interrupted by Mavis, who sidled rather than walked in through my door, a small smile and a furtive expression on her face. It was still incredibly early, and she could only recently have arrived.

She came right up to me and placed her lips near to my ear as though there were other people in the room. 'A huge secret,' she said. 'Even security have not yet been alerted. The princess is coming in to see you at eleven thirty.'

My hand flew to my neck and I gasped. The first thing that came to my mind was, did I have a clean and presentable nightdress back from the laundry? And then, thank heaven, I remembered the silk pyjamas that Fran had brought me in as a gift. I had decided at the time that I would prefer to keep them to wear around the house of an evening, but undoubtedly they would be perfect to wear for entertaining a princess from my bed.

'That's wonderful,' I said, trying to remain calm. 'I must hurry.'

**Philippa Todd**

Mavis patted my shoulder. 'Why don't you disappear into the bathroom while they come to change your bed, and we'll get the room cleaned. Then I'll have someone tidy up the flowers, and bingo, you'll be ready to receive.'

'Thank you, Mavis, you're brilliant,' I answered, pulling back the bedclothes.

'But remember, not a word to anyone. I'm told that if the press are hanging around outside when she arrives, she'll go ballistic.'

'I promise,' I said, tottering towards the bathroom.

At the door Mavis turned. 'When she arrives I'll have your telephone calls diverted, so that you're not disturbed,' she said, talking quietly and mouthing out the words. 'I shall greet her downstairs and accompany her to your room. What do you think, would you like to be in bed or sitting in a chair?'

I thought for a moment. 'In bed, I think, otherwise I'll have to wear a robe and she won't see my lovely new pyjamas.'

Mavis laughed, and flew out of the room.

At first I thought that I had no time at all in which to get ready and I was close to becoming seriously hysterical when I couldn't get the wretched silk scarf to stay on my slippery scalp. Eventually I gave up and used one of my cotton squares, which went on just fine.

Then I lay down on my bed, closed my eyes, and forced myself to calm down with the help of some deep-breathing exercises.

Naturally, I had all the time in the world to prepare myself, and I still had an hour to spare even after varnishing my nails.

So I wrote a letter to Scott, this time to his home address which he had given to me, just to tell him how much I loved him, and appreciated him, and longed to be with him, always. And I couldn't resist adding a postscript about the princess coming to visit.

At that moment Fran walked in. I was startled. How would I tell her she couldn't stay long without saying why?

'Your Housemother informs me I can only stay for a few minutes because you have to go down for special X-rays,' she said, coming over to kiss me. 'My, you look pretty sharply dressed for a trip in a wheelchair.'

'Yes, don't I though,' I replied, thankful for the cover that Mavis had provided.

She walked to a side table, placed the sketching pads and crayons she had brought over carefully on to it. Then she turned to me positively, saying, 'I'm sorry I blew your cover to Scott. It was wrong of me, I know, but . . .'

'Forget it,' I answered. 'I'm actually pleased you did. I don't know how I even thought that I could live without him.' She smiled at me, relieved.

Mavis Cartwright held open the door for her, and in she came, looking like an apparition in her dark brown striped trouser suit, a lighter brown silk chemise beneath the jacket, soft brown leather bag swinging from one shoulder.

'Hello, Cathy,' she said warmly, coming towards me. 'You really are in the best place. It's absolutely chucking it down out there.'

She kissed me on both cheeks, and stood back to look at me.

'You're looking great, much better than I expected you would.'

'Thank you,' I said, as Mavis drew up the best chair for her. 'I'm sure you've been offered refreshments?'

'Oh, yes, but I'm on my way to a lunch date,' she said, 'so I refused.'

Mavis excused herself, and withdrew discreetly.

As the princess took off her jacket and placed it on a spare chair, I noticed that the skin on her arms was taut and shining and golden brown from her previous yachting holidays.

She reached down into her handbag and offered me a soft little package, wrapped in tissue, and tied up with narrow green ribbon.

'It's only a tiny thing, and a bit like taking coals to Newcastle, but you'll need more than one.'

I opened it to discover, beneath several layers of pale pink tissue, the most beautiful fine cotton lawn square headscarf that I had yet seen, patterned in subtle autumn hues with a narrow brown border.

'Oh, how kind of you,' I said, genuinely thrilled. 'And how clever of you not to choose a silk one; they don't stay on easily.'

**Philippa Todd**

'Yes, I know, I have a friend who lost her hair and she told me that. (I knew who she meant.) I was hoping that I wouldn't find you sitting up in bed wearing a ghastly wig. If you were, I'm sure that I would have wanted to laugh.'

'I wouldn't have blamed you,' I said. 'But goodness knows what I'm going to do. I don't think I have the kind of face that can take being framed by a wig.'

'Actually,' she said, a small, slightly wicked smile on her lips, 'my friend did tell me the name of a most wonderful wigmaker here in London that she comes to. Just so that she has a wig to keep by the bed in case there's a fire. I'll ask my secretary to find out his details and phone them through to your secretary.'

She was seated now, her long legs crossed, her narrow trousers accentuating their length, her whole being giving off an air of total relaxation, even if she did have one eye discreetly on her watch.

'I went over to have lunch in Paris with the same friend earlier in the year, and she was wearing one of those soft pull-on hats. It came right down low over the forehead,' she said, describing it with her hands. 'The turn-back brim was lined with fake brown mink and honestly, you just couldn't tell if it was fur or her hair. Perfect for people with dark brown hair, like the two of you. Of course it would make me look a bit of a Charlie,' she added smiling.

'What a wonderful idea.'

'Absolutely brilliant,' she answered, her lovely eyes shining with laughter. 'She designed it herself. You should copy it; just right for you for winter.'

She was quite the most wonderful person to have as a hospital visitor. So uplifting to me, I felt that I was transported out into the middle of London, into the thick of things, leading my usual busy life, and not isolated in a hospital bed at all, impatiently waiting for recovery.

She looked around the room at the displays of flowers and the cards that Mavis had strung around the walls.

'I do that with cards, especially the children's birthday cards. It keeps them tidy, I think. Cards can be such a nuisance. Do they wake you early here like most hospitals?'

'Crack of dawn. I'm dog tired again by nine o'clock.'

# Whispers On A Pillow

'I have to be up very early tomorrow,' she said. 'Earlier even than you perhaps. I'm flying off to spend another short holiday on a friend's yacht.'

'How lovely,' I answered.

We both knew whose yacht she was talking about; but I didn't comment further.

She leaned forward, touched my arm. 'And guess what, I'm taking with me those two sundresses your lovely Suzie ran up for me. I didn't get the chance to wear them last year.' She lowered her eyes. 'But now I'm slipping into them all the time. This summer's different, I'm simply having the loveliest time.'

She raised those clear blue eyes again and fixed them on me like headlights before telling me confidentially where she was going for lunch. 'It's a secret, of course,' she said. 'That's if the photographers don't find me.'

'I shall treat it as such.'

'I know,' she replied. 'So, Cathy,' she continued, giving a sigh and leaning back in her chair. 'Are you having lots of nice men coming round to visit you?'

It was my turn to gaze into my lap. 'One or two.'

'Aha,' she said knowingly, tilting her head to one side. 'That rather sounds like one or two but one in particular?'

I blushed. 'I am rather fond of someone.'

'Do I detect a but in there?' she asked, smilingly intent on drawing me out. 'And for fond, should I read in love?'

'Well, yes. But he's quite a lot younger than I am, which is a bit of a worry. I never do seem to get the age difference quite right.'

'Mmmmm . . . do any of us?' she asked, and then gave her marvellous laugh. 'Is he English? Does he live in London? Come on, tell me.'

'No, he's American. He lives in Washington.'

'Ah, close to the American throne.'

'Sort of,' I said.

She was smiling at me again and looking quizzical. 'Am I allowed to know what he does?'

I wasn't quite sure how to answer that. 'He's a flier,' I said at last. 'He does government work.'

**Philippa Todd**

'Ah, one of those,' she said knowingly. 'Well, tell him he'd better stay out of danger. Seriously though, I'm very happy for you.'

'Thank you,' I replied.

'Oh, look at the time,' she said suddenly, standing up and leaping into her jacket. 'May I take a quick look in your bathroom mirror?'

'Of course,' I replied, smiling at the very thought of a princess asking my permission to do anything at all that she wanted to do.

Quickly – well, quickly for a post-op patient – I got out of bed and was standing beside it when she returned. 'I wanted to show you that I can walk as well as talk,' I said to her jokingly.

'Well done, Cathy,' she said, laughing, hurrying towards me and giving me a goodbye hug.

It was to be a really bad day, the one that followed the princess's visit.

When I was wakened for temperature-taking before dawn, my mood was very black. The night nurse doing the morning thermometer rounds picked up on it right away. By the time Mavis Cartwright came in, every nurse on day duty who had my room on her rota had been alerted.

My head, as I told Mavis, felt so heavy that I had to rest it against the pillow all the time; and she couldn't even tempt me with a soft poached egg for breakfast. I begged her just to leave me alone; I would come out of it soon, I said. But to tell the truth, it did rather frighten me while it lasted.

The surgeon came in later. He sat on the edge of the bed, held my hand, and asked if I had any pains, anywhere at all.

I shook my heavy head and stared into space. He asked me (as a special favour to him, he said), if he could send a counsellor in to talk to me. I consented to please him, as he was the man who had held my life in his hands and dealt with it so successfully. It was the least I could do in return, I told myself.

The counsellor was shown into my room by a nurse I hadn't seen before. I noticed that Mavis and her regular staff were giving my room a wide berth. It was a clever ploy; we all behave better with strangers.

He stuck out his hand enthusiastically. 'I'm Tony,' he said. 'Would you prefer I call you Catherine or Cathy?'

'Cathy's fine,' I said flatly. 'Did you get offered coffee or anything?'

'No,' he replied, 'but it really doesn't matter.'

'Would you like one, a coffee?'

'If you will have one as well.'

I lifted the telephone and pressed number six for the kitchen, ordering coffee for two with milk and a plate of biscuits.

They said they were busy with lunch.

I put up a fight, and won. No reason why, at the prices they charged, I thought, I shouldn't make a special request now and again.

'Feel better now do we?' Tony asked when I'd replaced the receiver and turned back to him.

'How d'you mean?' He had to be getting at something.

'Now that you've shown a bit of aggression, shown that you're not just a pretty face, so to speak? Depression, you see, is only anger turned inwards. Today you woke up angry at what has happened to you.'

'I'm not particularly angry, just miserable,' I replied.

'Then what d'you find?' he asked, ignoring my remarks. 'There's no one to blame. Nobody beat you over the head to cause your tumour, kicked you down the stairs, fired a gun at you. Everyone is showing sympathy, treating you kindly, being charming, bringing you presents. But what the hell, they can afford to be nice, you're thinking, it hasn't happened to them. You, Cathy, are up there all alone, and what all these nice people cannot do is wipe out the last few weeks and tell you it was all a bad dream.'

He scarcely paused for breath.

'Today,' he said, leaning forward, 'you woke up for the first time not feeling sorry for yourself, not particularly intent on getting better, but angry that it had happened at all. Why should it, you don't deserve it?'

I stared at him. 'I hope that your plan is not to make me cry. You'll be very disappointed, I don't feel in the least like crying.'

'Of course you don't,' he said. 'You feel more like kicking the proverbial cat, or throwing one of those many vases of flowers clean through the window.'

The coffee tray arrived, looking very neat with its brightly patterned cloth and tiny napkins.

'Maybe you should pour,' I said to Tony when we were alone again. 'You never know, I may be tempted to chuck it all over the floor.'

He looked at me and smiled. 'That's my girl. See what I mean?'

# TWELVE

The wigmakers of royal approval telephoned, and their head man (no pun intended) made an appointment to come and see me in my hospital room. I asked Fran if she would come round for moral support, and while we waited for him to arrive we talked about the business.

It struck me then, and not without a touch of rancour, that the firm seemed to be managing rather well without me.

She brought in the prototype of a lounging dress that I had designed before entering hospital and for which my new girl had cut a pattern very successfully from my original drawing. My assistant cutter had taken it upon herself to cut it out in a fine, rather softly woven and beautifully patterned material in shades of biscuit, brown and pale blue. Then Suzie had made it up and put it on a dressmaker's dummy where the clients could see it. Fran told me gleefully that everyone who saw it was ordering it like hot cakes in all sorts of different materials and colours.

I decided then and there to keep the prototype and to wear it for the rest of the day in my hospital room. I felt so good in it we ended up telephoning the workplace and asking Suzie to have them run up another one for me to wear when I felt like entertaining my visitors out of bed.

**Philippa Todd**

We went through important mail together, notes of telephone calls, and private messages.

'I've kept all the best things till last,' Fran said, a happy expression on her face. 'Let's start with this one because I know what it is.' She handed me a heavy cream envelope which obviously held an invitation.

'It was delivered by hand yesterday,' she said. And there, inside, was a gold-edged card inviting me to the wedding of the princess's friend. And best of all, it was headed to 'Catherine Anthony and Guest'; and I just knew that the princess had had a hand in the wording.

Of course, I immediately went into a panic about what I would wear and how I would conceal my baldness, and I knew that when Fran left me I would immediately begin sketching what I hoped would be something special.

'I'm sure you'll be pleased to read this too,' she continued, with a huge grin. Then she handed me a newspaper report all about me and my illness.

At first I was rather shocked, but then as I read what was said about me, I rather began to like it. It talked about my own distinctive style as a person as well as a dressmaker, and my flatteringly feminine designs. How brave I had been facing up to my illness (they should only know), not making an issue of it, carrying on with plans for a special charity fashion show, and working right up till the moment I entered hospital. They ended on the happy note that a report from the hospital had said that I would make a full recovery.

'Are you sure that you didn't give them all this information?' I asked Fran.

She raised her hands palms towards me. 'On my honour and hope to die. They telephoned me for approval, and I insisted on vetting the copy. They'd have written the piece anyway, and my being co-operative merely meant that all the right things were said.'

'You sure you didn't insist they omitted to mention that I was the ex-wife of Clive Anthony the oh so very famous plastic surgeon?'

'Promise you,' she said, but I was not convinced.

She then read out a list of telephone messages. A number of

people had called to offer their best wishes after reading the report in the press. 'Everyone was terribly shocked,' she said. 'And they said some lovely things about you.'

'Yes, people always say nice things when they think you might die. Then when you don't, they get back to being themselves again.'

'Now I'm going to make you regret saying that,' Fran replied. 'A daily newspaper *and* a magazine have both been in touch with me to ask if you would be prepared to be interviewed about your brain tumour. The magazine especially said they didn't want to know so much about the fear of possible death, or the horror of chemotherapy. What they really want is an article about facing life with the obvious and unexpected disadvantage of being bald; especially in your case, being in the fashion business.'

'Oh, Fran, really,' I said. 'I don't know if I can.'

She looked me fully in the eye. 'You must think about it,' she said. 'You'll be expected to agree to an interview when you're well enough. I can put them off, say that they must wait till you get home. But the impact of a hospital-room interview would be terrific.'

I thought about it. I was not particularly at ease with the idea of going public. 'But no pictures,' I said.

She sighed. 'They'll want a picture, naturally: a glamorous one, scarf entwined around your head, those silk pyjamas I bought you, fully made up. I'll help you.'

I smiled at her, trying to make light of it. 'Or better still, have them run up similar pyjamas in the workroom, in case I'm asked if they're my own design. We can't have M and S slapping a writ on me.'

'M and S indeed,' she said. 'So you'll do it?'

'Do I have a choice?'

There was a knock on the door, and the wig man was shown in.

His name was Vin, he informed us; short for Vincenti if you don't mind. He was tall, good-looking, comforting as old boots, and very obviously gay; and that was why he had come to the hospital himself, to deal with a very confidence-shaken and shaven-headed patient, who knew the princess personally, and therefore had to be treated carefully.

'My dear, you look wonderful, and I love that scarf,' he said, campily losing control of his wrists.

I introduced him to Fran who seemed completely bewildered by his style.

'Oh, good, you're American,' he said. 'I absolutely adore American women. I've been in love with the late and great Marilyn Monroe, Geena Davies and Liza Minnelli for ever, to name just three.'

'I have to tell you, Vin dear,' I said slowly, getting his attention focused back on to me, 'that I'm anti-wig for starters.'

'Oh, but everyone is,' he replied cleverly. 'Only the people who wear them for kicks think that they're fun. Do you perhaps have a picture of yourself? I need to know the colour of your hair, and how you used to wear it.'

Fran and I looked at each other nonplussed. Well, come on, is it very likely that I would carry a picture of myself around under these conditions?

'Nothing doing, Vin,' I said, 'but I'll do a sketch for you of my former hairstyle, and in that wig box that you are carrying I just know that you have lots of samples. My hair is English silky, by the way, so don't show me Asian thick or we can't do business.'

He looked a touch perplexed, but, professional to the core, he recovered quickly, flapped his hand and said, 'I know exactly what you mean.'

'Well now,' he said, half an hour later over tea and biscuits, while I sketched. 'For a wig to look real you need to have the hair coming forward gently; tiny wisps will do and feathery little pointy bits.'

'Vin,' I cut in, avoiding Fran's eyes because I knew that she was trying to dampen me down like a fire threatening to get out of control. 'I've never worn my hair in tiny wisps and feathery pointy bits in my life. I'm not that sort of person. A wig like that on me would give the show away immediately.'

'She'd sure as hell better start liking pointy bits then, hey, Vin?' Fran cut in, and I could have killed her.

But Vin did not hold down his job for no good reason. 'I'm on your side, Cathy,' he said. 'So here's what we'll do. You and I together will strike a happy medium; I shall design something that you can bear to wear, and something that I'm not ashamed to see you wearing. Know what I mean?'

From that moment on, I knew that Vin and I were somehow going to lick this tricky situation, even if I kept the wig on its stand beside the bed in case of fire as the princess had advised, and tussled away with headscarves for the next two years.

By the time they both left – and can you believe they were planning brunch together for Sunday? – I was so exhausted I lay on my bed in my lounging dress instead of hanging it up, as I should have done to keep it going all week.

But then, I thought, what the hell. Isn't that, by definition, what a lounging dress is all about? For lounging around in? And having removed my scarf for Vin to take measurements of my cranium, I decided not to put it back on again for a spell, as I was not expecting visitors.

I'd fallen asleep; I know because I was dreaming about pink-dyed wigs, when I was startled by an authoritative knock on the door at the same time as the person entered.

And there he stood, Clive, my ex, looking like a film star, handsome as ever, immaculate in a dark Savile Row suit, pale blue shirt and discreet silk tie perfectly knotted. His hair seemed greyer than the last time I'd seen him, but even that served to make him more attractive, dammit.

He ran his eye over me expertly as he always did with a woman. 'So, how's my girl? That's a kinky . . . something . . . you're wearing.'

He strolled over to the bed, squeezed one of my feet sexily as he passed, then lifted my hand and kissed the back of it.

'Quite the little dress designer we look lying there, pretty as a picture; apart from your poorly old head, of course.'

As far as I can remember, I just looked at him. My first thought was thank you, God, for sending me a man like Scott: a man, who, if his life depended on it, would never say a thing like that, not to me, or anyone who was so obviously disadvantaged.

My second thought was surely that was no way for a doctor to speak to a patient? Even if the patient happened to be someone he'd once had sex with every night and twice on Sundays, and called his dearest love more times than I could count. After all, even ex-wives have feelings.

**Philippa Todd**

I resisted the urge to offer to cover my baldness and asked politely if I could send for refreshment.

He collapsed into an armchair before answering, every inch the overworked surgeon, stretching out his long legs and crossing his elegant ankles. 'No thanks, mother of my children. I'm just off to give a talk at the College of Surgeons to visitors from the East. Then on to a reception at Mansion House. Oh, by the way, I've had them put two bottles of champagne in the fridge for you. Laurent Perrier Brut, good stuff. It'll be good for you to entertain a bit.'

'That's generous of you. I'm sure I'll manage to find someone to share a bottle with,' I said, reasonably icily.

If someone right then had asked me what could possibly be worse than an unannounced visit from my ex-husband, I might have answered, 'If Leon walked in.'

And that's what he did. No knock or anything. The door simply slammed open, and there he was. Looking better than the last time I'd seen him, granted, but not too much, clutching a paper sack that oranges and grapes peeked out of, the usual grin on his wide lips.

A grin that slipped slightly, I noticed, when he saw Clive sitting in state, rather looking as though he owned the place.

Poor Leon. But he managed to put a brave face on it. 'Hi,' he said. 'Shit, Cathy, your head looks funny. I hope they gave you back your hair to keep for posterity.'

'Come in,' I said in answer, the shock of it all rather getting to my tongue and stopping me from giving him a more loquacious welcome.

The suave Clive removed himself from the armchair elegantly and moved across the room with his hand extended.

Leon had the expression of a man wondering if he should put up his fists; something to do with his experiences in prison, perhaps? But he didn't need to worry because Clive passed in front of him, and rather pointedly closed the door.

Leon used his most brash gait to avoid his embarrassment and came over to kiss me. He placed the paper sack precariously on the bed and it toppled over, causing two oranges to roll across the floor.

As he chased after them, then straightened up, Clive moved

towards Leon, put on his glasses and gently, by the elbow, propelled him towards the window. It caused the latter total confusion, especially when Clive placed his fingertips on Leon's chin, and moved his head first one way, and then the other.

'Rhinoplasty looks good,' he said, without modesty.

'Yes, doesn't it,' I replied lamely, rather feeling that he'd addressed the remark more to me than to Leon.

'It's good for a chap to see the effects of his work rather later, once in a while, than in the usual follow-up.'

'Quite,' I said.

Leon looked across at me helplessly. I tapped the side of my nose discreetly. But discreet movements had never been easy for Leon to interpret and he frowned. I mouthed the word 'nose' and he physically cheered up.

'Oh, my nose,' he said, and felt it, as though surprised to discover that he had one at all. 'Yes, everybody who knew the old one says it's a hundred per cent improvement. We've got our Cathy to thank for that.'

Clive was not best pleased at Leon's casual use of the term 'our Cathy'.

He looked at his watch at the very moment I knew that he would; isn't it awful how you anticipate little habitual things when you've lived with someone for any length of time?

'Must go, darling,' he said by way of claiming me as his own and putting Leon firmly in his place.

Then he strolled over to the side of the bed and kissed the air, like royalty, on both sides of my face.

'Remember to stay quiet,' he said pointedly. 'I shall look in again.'

Liar, I felt like saying.

'And you mustn't worry your pretty head about the hair. I seem to remember that your hair grows awfully quickly.'

'You must go,' I said, 'or you'll be late for your lecture.'

He executed a languid wave to Leon, threw a kiss from the door to me, and, thank the Lord, left.

I lay my bald head back on the pillow, wondering how long Leon intended to stay because I was drained dry.

'What are you going to do about your bald pate, Cathy?'

I raised my head a fraction. 'Oh, I thought I might take it to

## Philippa Todd

Charing Cross station and sit on the floor with a begging bowl and a mangy old dog.'

'Bit extreme that, isn't it? You could cover it with a scarf or something, or wear a wig.'

'Gee, I never thought of that.'

We looked at each other. 'Old Clive's a pompous prat, isn't he?' he said.

'I seem to remember telling you that the first time we met,' I replied.

Leon looked around, as usual unable to concentrate for long. 'I don't like hospital rooms.'

'Why's that? Remind you of prison cells, do they?'

'They sort of have a peculiar smell.'

'What kind of peculiar smell?' I resisted the urge to sniff the air around me or get out my perfume spray.

'Sort of . . . putrefying flesh.'

'Leon, I hope you're joking, you terrible man.'

I was saved from the overwhelming urge to pelt him with the overripe fruit in the bowl beside my bed by the arrival of my supper tray.

Leon lifted the metal lid on the hospital version of *sole bonne femme*, and smelled it. 'Jesus, Dolly, I hope they're not charging you anything in here. They serve better stuff than that in prison.'

'Well, you can always go back,' I said. 'But thank you for coming to see me, I appreciate it.'

'Any time,' he answered. Then he fished in his pocket. 'Nearly forgot, I brought you some Polo mints as well. How's the lover?'

Like a breath of fresh air, after you, I said to myself, as I sighed. 'Fabulous, thank you. The best lover I ever had.'

I spent most of the next day in bed on hospital orders, drawing and napping a bit, trying not to overtax my brain.

I flitted about with the crayons, sketching and re-sketching an outfit for myself for the big wedding. And then for Abi's spring affair, just for fun. Then I tried out a few ideas for costumes for the forthcoming film.

My head figured large, if you see what I mean, in the wedding sketches, as I was well aware, as any woman would be, that

I would only look as good as my bald head allowed. Still, by spring a little of the brown stuff should've sprung, I told myself. Men grew beards in that length of time, didn't they? Though I had been warned that men's facial hair grew more quickly than hair on a woman's head because it had been stimulated by daily shaving.

The telephone rang. The girl on the switchboard wanted to know if I would like to take a call from a man calling himself Scott Peters from Washington?

Would I ever, I so nearly said.

'How's it going?' he asked, that slow deep drawl driving me wild.

'Yesterday was a bit of a riot,' I replied, and I told him what had happened. 'I was exhausted at the end of it and my temperature was up. Today I'm having a quieter time on orders from above.'

'Goddammit, that Leon. But you sound on good form anyhow.'

'Yes, I am. Apart from being bald, and cut off from everything, and worrying about the workplace, and my dog, and having the man I love three thousand miles away, I suppose I am,' I answered, not letting him off lightly. Well, I was a bit frail, after all. I was having an invalid's day on orders, and I didn't want anyone making me feel like a hotel guest resting up before attending a cocktail party.

'Darling,' he said, 'I would like to take you on a vacation. Would you like that?'

'It sounds wonderful,' I replied, feeling light-headed and excited at the idea, although I knew of course that it couldn't possibly happen.

'You could meet my folks in San Francisco, and then I'd like to take you to Hawaii. October would be a good month.'

'Heavenly,' I answered weakly, wondering what I'd look like on a beach, wondering if I'd have the right clothes. I really couldn't take the girls away from important work just to make me a range of clothes to take to Hawaii.

And speaking of work, how could I possibly afford to take the time off, even in the form of recuperation? Here I was now, lying in bed, when maybe I ought to be trying to get back to the workplace. I wanted to go with Scott, goodness knows, but I really wasn't up to making plans for our future just yet.

'It kept me awake all last night,' he said. 'Once I started to think about it the planning really excited me. I love you so much, Cathy.'

'And I hope you miss me?' I badly needed to feel missed.

He laughed. 'You know I miss you. Can we plan how to decorate the interior of the apartment soon? I want us to be together so badly.'

My heart seemed to miss a beat. I wanted us to be together just as much as he did, but thinking about it as a possibility was one thing, being asked to plan was quite another. When it came to the crunch, my mind seemed to shy away from serious positive thinking, or any sort of planning.

And now I was panicking and I couldn't think straight at all. I didn't even know what the date was, or even the day. Never mind how many weeks it was till October.

'Cathy, are you still on the line?'

'Oh, yes, I hope that I can spare the time.'

'For a vacation? Darling, you've been sick, the weather in the UK will be getting colder, your recovery will benefit from some sunshine. But you don't have to do anything you don't want to.'

'I want to, Scott, I really want to, but somehow I can't think straight.'

'My darling, don't try,' he said very softly. 'We'll talk about it some other time. I don't want you to feel too pressured, or suffer from brain overload. Those of us who haven't just been through a major operation tend to forget.'

'You don't think then, Scott, that I'll always have a woolly brain from now on?'

'I'm sure that you won't,' he answered in a quiet measured voice, 'but since you're not going to believe me, tell them how you're feeling in the hospital, ask to discuss it with an expert in the field.'

'Yes, I will.'

'Promise me? It's important for your peace of mind.'

I promised him; we talked some more. He kept it light, reminded me of our happy times together and how we would repeat them. We exchanged words of love, and I felt calmer.

\* \* \*

## Whispers On A Pillow

As though by magic, or more likely through the network of observant staff, the surgeon came into my room not ten minutes later. I asked him if he had a moment to talk to me.

'Of course,' he said. 'I've just finished a long day in the theatre. I feel like a change.'

He pulled up a chair, stretched out his legs. 'So what's bothering you, Catherine?'

I told him about my panic attacks, my fear of not being able to run a business again, make decisions, plan ahead, all the things necessary to leading a normal life.

'You're expecting too much too soon, Catherine,' he replied. 'I have just removed from your brain a very large tumour. Luckily it was not malignant; if it had been we would not be discussing your future so much as the treatment for, hopefully, keeping you alive. But nevertheless, that tumour caused a great amount of pressure on your brain, hence the seizures in your arm. You've had a major operation and operations of any kind take their toll.'

'But sometimes I can't work things out like I used to,' I said.

'That's only because your brain has been disturbed; it needs to rest. You must let it rest, Catherine, and then you will have a hundred per cent recovery.'

He leaned forward and took hold of my hand. 'Just do as much as you truly feel like doing at this time, and nothing more. Get up for short spells because it's important that you move around, but go back to bed when you feel like it. Rest and sleep as much as you can.'

'I have the chance to go on holiday in October,' I said. 'To Hawaii. It will be a rest cure. What do you think?'

'Wonderful idea,' he replied. Then he smiled. 'With the chap who bumped Richard out of the way?'

It was a back-hander. It stopped me for a moment. 'Yes, sort of, but you know, I'd never considered Richard seriously. I'm sure that I've told you. Though he's a very dear friend.'

He stood up and pushed the chair away. 'I know what you mean, and I'm only teasing. And now you're well and truly in love, is that it?'

'Yes, I am,' I said, trying to conceal a blush.

'And I'm making you blush. The sex is good, and all that? No problems, nothing that you'd like to talk about?'

Not likely. It would all be around every operating theatre in town if I as much as talked about my private life in my sleep.

'No, nothing. But thank you for enquiring.'

'Good, good,' he said, on his way to the door. 'I've never heard of anyone dying from too much sex, but gentle on the activity.'

'When can I go home?' I asked him on a sudden whim, wanting to change the subject, wanting the last word perhaps, surprising us both.

He turned around as he opened the door. 'Ask me again in a couple of days,' he said, and waved his hand at me in goodbye.

The telephone rang. It was security. Hugo, it seemed, was at reception asking if he could see me, and he was accompanied by a lady.

That would be Sophie, I decided, and as I liked her and considered that Hugo was less likely to be a pain in the neck in her company, I consented.

Imagine my horror when a short lady entered my room with Hugo in her wake. And what a strange lady to boot.

She wore her dyed red hair in short bubble curls all over her head, her heavy facial make-up was deathly white, making her rouged cheeks and 1950s bright red lips seem almost gargoylish. Her gold earrings, gold necklace and gold brooch shone garishly against her well-tailored purple suit. She looked like someone who'd just come off the stage having performed a matinee and hadn't had time to cream off her make-up or change her garb.

Hugo looked pleased with himself, if a touch embarrassed, and no wonder. Of all the things I have said about Hugo, I could not say that he didn't dress impeccably and always in the very best of taste. Certainly some of the trousers to his Savile Row suits were a touch frayed around the bottoms, and the velvet collar on his one and only thirty-year-old winter overcoat was wearing a bit thin. But I've known a few 'titles' who looked equally threadbare, and, as with Hugo, it took nothing away from their elegance.

'Darling girl,' he said to me, coming forward and kissing my cheeks as I sat in my armchair doing my out-of-bed duty, wearing my lounging dress, the princess's scarf tied nattily around my head, sketch pad on lap to make me feel busy. 'How absolutely delightful you look, much better than I could have hoped.'

'Hugo, how nice,' I said, looking over his shoulder at madame, giving her my friendliest smile out of deference to Hugo.

He turned to her. 'Didn't I tell you, old thing, that we shouldn't spend money on flowers? I knew she'd have a room full of them.'

'A lady can never have too many flowers, now can she?' she said to me, coming forward in her high-heeled black patent shoes, which meant that she had to be even shorter than Hugo in her bare feet. 'That's like saying she has too much money, or is too thin. I'm Phoebe Peabody. No point in waiting for old Huggie here to introduce us.'

Phoebe Peabody? My God, I thought, she must be on the stage, and if she wasn't she was having me on. And could that South African accent be for real? I mean it's a strange accent at best, but hers sounded as though she'd had elocution lessons that had gone wrong somewhere along the way.

'Darling old things,' Hugo was saying in the background. 'How rude of me. Phoebe, this is Cathy.'

Not so much of the lumping me in with old things, Huggie dear, I thought. She had to be at least sixty-five.

'Well, I know it's Cathy, Huggie dear, or I presume you wouldn't have kissed her,' she answered.

He laughed, and shut up.

'Please, sit down,' I said, and as I was the patient I didn't unseat myself.

Hugo placed an upright wooden chair in position for Phoebe, then took the remaining comfortable armchair for himself, which, knowing him as I did, was the real reason for my staying seated.

'Phoebe's over here from Africa,' he said.

'*South* Africa you should say, dear,' she interjected quickly. 'We don't want Cathy thinking that I'm from somewhere terrible.'

'How nice. On holiday?' I asked.

'Yes,' Hugo said.

'In a manner of speaking,' Phoebe interjected again. 'I'm the mother of the bridegroom. I'm sure that Huggie told you about that dear girl Sophie and my son being betrothed.'

'Oh, yes,' I replied, with genuine fascination. 'Do congratulate your son, Phoebe. Sophie is a lovely girl.'

'Darling, that's generous,' Hugo said, as ever the purveyor of unnecessary words.

'And there is more,' Phoebe said, one red-nailed finger to the fore.

Silence fell. I tried to look agog with curiosity while suddenly remembering who it was she reminded me of: it was a scaled-down version of that Dame Edna person that Barrie Humphries has perfected, but with a South African accent instead of an Aussie one.

'Can't you guess?' she asked.

I was sure that she was looking at me, but her glasses were shining so much that I couldn't see her eyes behind them, so I looked at Hugo instead for confirmation.

'Phoebe would prefer to tell you herself,' he said, and I knew then, that, war-time hero or not, he hadn't the guts to tell me the news himself.

'Huggie and I are getting married,' she said. 'We're having a double wedding with our children in Cape Town in January.'

The sneaky old dog; that was sudden, I thought. She must be seriously loaded for such a drastic step. She was a funny little soul, but there couldn't be an attraction greater for Hugo, nice as I'm sure she was, than the moolah she had in the bank.

They planned to live in Cape Town, they told me. 'In my mansion' was how she worded it. That didn't surprise me. Hugo would never ever be able to show her off in London, not among the sort of people he mixed with. One lunch in the ladies dining-room at Bucks Club, and they'd lock the doors on him for the rest of time.

I turned to Hugo. 'Congratulations,' I said.

He nodded curtly, terrified that I was going to add something else; something like, perhaps, so you've made it into money at last, old chap.

'There is just one thing, Cathy,' Phoebe said, and I primed myself with a ready answer just in case she dropped a bombshell about my relationship with Hugo.

'I would very much like you to make me a special evening dress for a ball we'll be giving the night before the wedding. A dress made in London would top everybody else's. Especially when I tell them that I'm a friend of the designer.'

'Nothing would give me greater pleasure,' I said, wondering what those hips looked like beneath her loose jacket, and how long her legs were when she ditched the high heels.

'Splendid,' she said. 'I rather fancy pink.'

Pink and carrot? Not on your life, not if this London dress designer's making it; it would be the end of the Cape Town connection for me before it even began.

'You know what would look divine on you with your special brand of colouring?' I said, glad that Fran was not around to hear me and pull a hideous face. 'A deep green, the sort of green in Victorian paintings of bowls of roses.'

'Capital,' Hugo said, as even he registered the full force of the horror of carrot and pink.

'Yes, I quite like the idea,' she said. 'Taffeta, perhaps?'

No way, José. 'Well, I thought something in chiffon, all floaty and soft, would be nice, rather Grecian.' (God help us.)

'I must say, you really know your stuff, Cathy,' she said, clapping her little taloned hands together in the kind of girlish gesture that can set your teeth aching.

'Would you like me to sketch you something now?' I asked, feeling benevolent.

'Would you mind if I popped to your loo?' Hugo cut in.

To do what? I longed to ask, retaining as I did the memory of an elephant even while having trouble with the present. But I was saved by his explanation of 'the old bladder, you know'.

Phoebe clapped her hands together again. 'That would be exciting. My, you are so clever.'

It didn't take long. I used a basic drawing and added some floaty bits. But Phoebe found it orgasmic and I asked Hugo to take her into the salon next day for measurements. Fran would bring me round patterns of suitable colours and materials, I assured her, and then we would meet again to finalize everything.

When they left, the first thing I did after getting into bed from sheer exhaustion was to telephone Suzie, giving her the details and telling her to add ten per cent to the cost of the dress at source as that was the discount Hugo would ask for as a special rate for close friends. And to be sure to tell Fran.

\* \* \*

**Philippa Todd**

It could not have been later than five thirty in the morning for him when he telephoned me.

I was immediately fearful that something was wrong.

'First of all, how are you?' he asked.

'Much better, darling,' I replied. 'I've been taking things a lot easier, as the surgeon advised me to do.'

'That's great. I had to tell you before anyone else. I've had notification that I'm to be given the Legion of Merit. It's the highest award you can get, and it's for services to the country.'

'Oh, Scott, how wonderful.'

'Well, you know, it's nice to get recognition,' he said, sounding bashful at being so pleased.

'Well, naturally, and well deserved it is. When do you get it?'

'The invitation says four weeks from now. The President himself pins it on.'

We laughed together. 'At the White House?' I asked.

'Sure,' he said.

'I don't know what to say, I'm so proud of you.'

'One thing you can do for me, please, is tell Fran. I know she'll be pleased for me.'

'I shall phone her right away,' I said. 'We've been talking most of the morning already.'

'Nothing wrong, I hope?'

'Oh, no, quite the contrary.' I told him about Hugo and Phoebe.

'By the way,' I added, 'you've been invited with me to attend that very special wedding I'm making the bride's outfit for.'

'Oh, my God.'

'Do you have a morning suit?'

'Sonofabitch. Is that like tails?'

'No, tails are for evening only over here. This is a morning wedding. You wear a topper with a morning suit.'

'No, I don't have anything like that. Can I get one made in time? Or are you trying to tell me I can't go?'

'Of course not, silly. I'll think of something.'

'It's wonderful to hear you in such good spirits. Your voice does so much for me when you're happy. Have I told you that I love you?'

'Not recently.'

'Well, I do. And I think about you more than you would believe.'

'I think about you all the time,' I said, 'and I miss you. When am I going to see you again?'

'It could be as soon as the day after tomorrow.'

'Oh, I hope so.'

'Don't get excited yet; it's the reason I didn't tell you sooner. The weather forecasts in Europe are God-awful, so my orders may be delayed.'

'When will you know for sure? I simply can't wait for you to come back.'

'I'll know tomorrow. I'll call around this time.'

'Guess what?' I said. 'I've agreed to be interviewed for the press, all about my illness.'

'Do you feel up to it?'

'Yes, I think so,' I said slowly. 'And it would be churlish of me not to do it. A journalist will come to my room tomorrow, a photographer the next day.'

'Well, good luck, darling,' he said. 'When are you going home, do you know yet? I'd like to be there if it's possible.'

'My surgeon will be in later. I intend to ask him then. I feel ready to go home now, I think.'

'Would you like to go home the day after tomorrow?' the surgeon said.

'Oh, so soon,' I answered, feeling suddenly panic-stricken, even though I'd begged the question.

'As long as you have someone there to keep an eye on you,' he said, adding, in deference to Mavis, 'Don't you think so, sister?'

Mavis Cartwright smiled at me from where she was standing at his elbow. 'We'll miss her,' she said. 'It's been quite a busy room.'

'Not too much excitement though, Catherine,' he said. 'And you must take a month off work. Rest up, enjoy a quiet life, look forward to that tropical holiday.'

I begged Fran to come round immediately, and reached for my notepad to make the all-important lists.

The photographer would have to come to the house instead

of the hospital when he came on Friday. I hoped he wouldn't mind.

I'd need to contact Scott on his red number. Abigail must be telephoned and she would alert the boys . . .

Fran of course spread the calm around me that I needed.

'I have to speak to Scott,' I told her. 'He was going to take me home himself, but I doubt he'll be able to at such short notice.'

She found him on his red number, and even spoke to him before I did, making me feel quite jealous as she congratulated him on being awarded his medal, and then laughed at something he said.

'Here's Cathy,' she said at last, 'she has something to tell you.'

Scott said, when he heard my news, that as bad weather persisted in Europe, he was sorry, but he doubted he would make it over here in time. Would I have someone else standing by in case of mishaps? If he couldn't be there to take me home he would be sure to be with me soon afterwards.

Fran said that she would take care of everything. I was not to worry about a thing.

'No point in asking Abigail to take time off when it might give her problems,' she said. 'I'm perfectly capable of dealing with everything, and I'll stay with you till Scott gets here. Stop giving yourself and everyone else a hard time, Cathy. Just relax.'

She was right, and with my copious lists to enable me to check on how well everyone was doing on my behalf, and my deep-breathing exercises, I did my best not to let anxiety get the better of me.

The press interview next day went well; the journalist they sent along was intelligent, warm, sympathetic and helpful, as well as being an absolute dish to look at, and fashionably dressed, too. We hit it off immediately and she had the words tumbling out of me in no time at all.

The big day dawned, and by eight thirty in the morning I was packed and ready to go, which actually was totally unnecessary because I was not scheduled to leave until eleven.

At ten, a milliner I gave a lot of work to sent around to my room, by special delivery, four cloche-type deep pull-on hats for me to choose from. I played around with them in the bathroom for half an hour and then decided to keep them all, even telephoning to ask if I could order a black one as well. I think they thought that I was going to a funeral, and they didn't like to ask whose it might be.

The princess telephoned from her yacht to wish me luck and to say that she'd see me at the wedding, ending charmingly with, 'Stay well, Cathy, I'm pulling for you.'

I'd entered hospital in jeans and tee-shirt, not really interested with how I looked personally. I'd had more important matters on my mind.

And now, here I was on my way home again, demanding that Fran brought me one of my smartest suits to wear, in keeping with my new hat, concerned only with how I looked. I could hardly slouch out of the place in any old thing, I'd told her; it would be disrespectful to the people who'd clubbed together to give me a future.

She arrived in good time, bearing the right clothes. She had also brought the firm's delivery van to take me home in, complete with driver. To avoid parking problems, she said, and then confessed that we were taking with us some of the latest flower arrangements that had been gifts; to arrange around my house, she insisted, for the photo shoot.

And so, eventually, we were ready. I hadn't known what sort of gifts to give to those who had looked after me and taken such willing care, and so I decided to give vouchers to the nurses to spend in the salon on anything they fancied from my prêt-à-porter range, and cash to the chaps. Daniel came in quietly to thank me and to give me his telephone number.

'In case you ever need help or anything. You never know,' he said.

I kissed his cheek. I was truly touched, and I said that I hoped he would never regret making such a generous offer, because I may easily call it in.

To Mavis I gave a fine leather Italian handbag and matching gloves from my stock, to match a new autumn coat that she had shown me one day, to ask if it was the right length for high fashion.

She was beside herself with joy, and even though she thanked

**Philippa Todd**

me profusely at the time, a few days later a formal beautifully written thank-you letter came through the post to my home.

All the staff on our floor wished me goodbye and good luck and kissed me at the lift door, and some of the other patients were waiting there too.

I think that I had become a celebrity by proxy on account of my visit from the princess. I'd heard that by the time she'd left my room that special morning, word had travelled with the speed of light around the hospital, and a few carpet-slippered invalids on our floor clapped from their doorways as she hurried to the lift. And bless her darling heart, she turned at the lift door and waved to them.

Mavis Cartwright saw me into the delivery van, admiring the subtle brown paintwork and my name written on the sides in black capitals. She asked if I'd left the Rolls-Royce at home and sent herself into paroxysms of mirth at her own sharp wit.

I got to sit up with the driver and Fran hung out in the back among the blooms. Mavis fastened my seat-belt, commented on how smart my hat looked and told the driver to take good care of his precious load.

While it had been humid and raining for most of my hospital stay, suddenly the day of my departure was glorious. A cloudless sky and a sunny London, more like the Med than south-east England. Everything and everybody seemed to me to be smiling. I hoped the change in the weather would bring Scott flying in.

I forgot about my hairless head under my linen cloche hat, and about the fading bruises everywhere where various needles and tubes had been stuck into me. I forgot about the tickly cough that hadn't left me since the anaesthetic, the strong smell of lavatory cleaner, and the pungent aroma of the lunchtime chicken and onion soup.

I was alive, I'd been made better.

I'd had a reprieve. And I was going home.

# THIRTEEN

A painted sign pinned to my front door spelled out a large Welcome Home, Cathy. There was a repeat of it on the hall floor.

It was cosily silent in the house, beautifully sunny, and, best of all, it smelled like home.

It crossed my mind, as I made my way slowly over the threshold, with Fran leading the way, that I must be careful not to panic when I found myself alone after being surrounded by so many people in hospital.

Imagine my shock when, as Fran pushed open the sitting-room door the whole room exploded with happy clapping. There were at least fifteen people standing there: my neighbours from each side, my children, Richard, my senior staff, Madge the cleaning lady, my postman and the newspaper boy. I felt like a lost wanderer returning to the fold, as champagne corks popped and bubbles fizzed in glasses.

My hand was shaken and I was kissed by everyone in the room. I was so overcome I could scarcely speak. My jacket was taken from me as though I were an invalid, and even my hat was in danger at one point of disappearing from my head, until Fran intervened and anchored it down properly again.

**Philippa Todd**

I was firmly seated in an armchair beside the tiny Victorian grate, and then stared at by fifteen pairs of eyes as though a miracle had occurred and I'd risen from the dead.

All was revealed as to why Abi was unable to collect me from hospital when she produced mounds of mouth-watering canapés, of which the newspaper boy, the postman and I ate far too many.

I was a star for an hour, until I had to go for a recuperative rest seconds before I fell unconscious with fatigue.

I slept for at least three hours, and I was starving again when I awoke, having become used to such regular meals in hospital.

My own bed seemed like a dream come true, an ocean of comfort, and I wondered why I had not appreciated it more, like many other things that I had taken for granted. It was as though my eyes were opening for the first time to a world much more full of wonders than I had ever given myself the time, or the will, to discover.

Suddenly, I could sniff bacon grilling; it was glorious, even my sense of smell held new magic. I hustled into a robe and made my way down to the kitchen.

'I was going to wake you with a hot bacon sandwich served in bed,' Fran said, looking busy in my red striped apron.

'I'll have it with you, in here, please,' I replied. 'That would be much more of a treat than eating in bed.'

We sat at the kitchen table, we ate, we talked. I thanked her emotionally for all her help, which had gone far beyond the call of duty when I was in hospital.

She brushed it off, saying, 'Don't overdo the catch in the throat, or I might think that you are still sick.'

It was a simple remark, and she obviously didn't mean any harm by it, but it stayed in my mind. Was I learning things about myself that I may never have recognized if I had not been ill? Had I been short on appreciation, on understanding? Had I ridden rough-shod over other people's feelings, not cared as much as I could have?

'There was a phone message from your beloved while you were asleep,' Fran said, watching my face. 'I don't know where he was calling from, but he said he'll be here with you by nine o'clock tonight.'

'Wonderful,' I answered. 'If you're aching to go, I'll be all right till then.'

'Not on your life,' she answered, putting our plates into the dishwasher. 'I'm staying till he rings that doorbell. Besides, I have to find out from him what tomorrow's plans are. You're not to be left on your own, remember?'

'That's silly. You're needed at the workplace. I might come down there too.'

She gave me a look enough to kill. 'I'm not even going to answer that. So belt up and go and start the long process of making yourself beautiful for you know who.'

I left the two of them talking and retired to bed as casually as I possibly could. Scott had arrived looking so weary it made me wonder how he could bear crossing the Atlantic as often as he did.

At last I heard him escort Fran out of the house and put her in a taxi.

It took all the nerve I had to lie in bed and know that shortly he would be looking at me, naked, and bald as I was. I knew that my appearance left a lot to be desired, even if he did love me dearly.

Almost immediately his head appeared around the bedroom door. 'I'll just shower,' he said, 'and then I'll come to bed.'

I made myself turn my head and look at him. With bravado, perhaps. He simply smiled and disappeared into the bathroom.

I wanted him so badly I could scarcely contain myself. But it was all right for me; I couldn't see what I looked like lying there with a naked head.

But I knew I would register with horror the moment, the very second, if he hesitated as he looked at my bald head, or touched it reluctantly. My heart beat fast in my chest, and I was unable to tell if it was in sensual anticipation of him being naked beside me, or in fear of seeing him discover that he could no longer cope with me.

I needed the darkness, longed to turn out the light. But it would have been wrong. I couldn't stay in the dark like a pit pony until I grew hair again. But why couldn't I take it in my stride, like people I'd read about in magazines?

He came around the door, moved close to the bed, stared at my scar. 'Neat,' he said. 'I'd love to know what makes a person want to be a brain surgeon, with all those cells and electrical impulses to worry about.'

'I feel the same about telephone engineers,' I said, trying to sound light-hearted. 'With all those bundles of electric wires to worry about.'

He laughed and went around to his side of the bed, putting out the bedside lamp as he climbed in, the way men do, for some reason.

He turned my face towards him, leaned close and kissed my lips sensuously.

'How about putting your light out and letting my poor sore eyes have some darkness,' he said, running his hand slowly down the front of me, down between my breasts, beyond my waist, bringing it to rest on my mound of Venus. 'God, I love you, Cathy,' he whispered as I reached over for the light switch before stretching out and spreading my legs.

I lay in the bath and inhaled the sweet smell of gardenias from the bath gel, which had been a lovely and unexpected present from my new junior cutter. On an impulse I reached for my cordless phone and telephoned to tell her what pleasure it was giving me.

Fran had thoughtfully placed my portable tape deck on the vanity unit with a Carly Simon tape in position, for the patient to enjoy easy untroubled listening.

I rested my head back on the tiny waterproof pillow, a get-well present from a neighbour, and was thinking about the forthcoming photo shoot when Fran appeared at the door.

'Da-daaa,' she sang out. 'Surprise, surprise, look what I've got.'

She held up a lounging dress made in material of the most fabulous shadow-dyed hues, and a headscarf to match.

'It's a special homecoming present from the staff. They ran it up specially in their own time,' she said. 'She can't keep wearing that same ones, they told me, it'll be bad for business.'

It was difficult for me to keep my mind on anything, as I think Fran guessed; steeped as I was in my night of love, and in my lover . . .

I'd been wakened early by him standing beside the bed looking down at me, and I simply did not want it to be morning. I'd not stirred once since our last session of love-making, and the night had gone so quickly.

'You were smiling in your sleep,' he'd said, stroking my cheek with the backs of two fingers.

I stretched, and smiled again. 'Are you surprised?'

He'd sat down on the edge of the bed, looking serious. 'It was wonderful, but we must be careful. You're supposed to be taking things quietly.'

'It was more than wonderful, it was magical,' I said, keeping my arms raised above my head so that I could shade it a little from his view. 'And you were so gentle no harm could possibly have come to me.'

He'd taken my arms away from my head then and put them at my sides. 'I have to go,' he said. 'Fran has arrived and she'll stay till I return, no matter how late. Then we'll have three whole days together to do as we please.'

'Might we even stay in bed?' I ventured.

He gently pressed the end of my nose, then kissed my lips. 'We'll see,' he said, smiling.

I'd twined my arms around his neck and pulled his head down to return his kiss. 'Be safe today.'

'I will. Bye my love, see you tonight,' he'd whispered.

'My, don't we look gorgeous,' Fran said as she gazed at the apparel I had chosen for the shoot. 'Nice choice.'

I'd decided on a pair of wide-legged stone-coloured pants and a fine loose sweater in thin uneven streaks of stone and white, aubergine and pale blue, and on my feet I wore flat pale calf shoes.

My head, of course, was a major issue, and, knowing that somewhere I had a fine, plain stone-coloured long scarf that, with luck, I could wind around my pate into some semblance of high fashion, I'd gone through all the spare drawers and cupboards with the controlled hysteria of a robber on a time limit until I found it.

Madge was equally hysterical, not so much over the lost scarf as her conviction that I would do irreparable damage to my brain if I didn't slow down. She had then, with great kindness, cleared up in my wake and begged me to remain calm.

It was all right for Madge, as I told her, she'd never been called upon to do a photo shoot; let alone to face both heartless lighting and a close-up camera with a hairless head.

The saga reminded me that Vincenti (call me Vin) the wig man had left a message to say that when I felt up to it he was ready to show me a mock-up of a hairy headpiece; a first step on the rocky road towards that magical wig he was convinced he could persuade me I would look great wearing.

It shows the lengths to which my hysteria over the scarf had taken me when I willingly picked up the phone and returned his call, making an appointment for late that very afternoon.

'Why don't you wear that lovely pearl choker for the shoot?' Fran said, seconds before the crew arrived. 'That would rivet anyone's attention away from your headscarf.'

'In the daytime?' I replied impatiently. 'You don't wear pearl chokers in the daytime, not in England anyway.'

She gave me one of her 'would you like to be put to death slowly' looks, and with controlled patience said, 'Who's gonna know what time of day the pictures were taken?'

She had a point; I fetched the pearl choker. At the very least, I told her as she fastened it on, it would please Clive to see his choker pictured in the press in all its glory, even if it was wrapped around his ex-wife's neck.

It had cost him a hefty sum when he'd bought it at a jewel auction as a softener to my expected rage when he was caught at Heathrow airport by a cameraman for a Sunday rag, furtively on his way with a page-three girl to a dirty weekend in Paris. A weekend, I might add, when he'd told me he was going to a convention, to which spouses had not been invited.

The cameraman and the lighting expert were both young, and very professional. They put me at my ease in no time, accepted coffee and biscuits on the understanding that I had some too.

I was left wondering if it could possibly have been a clever ploy to create amusement and cut through my tension when subsequently my stomach gave a major rumble as it usually does after coffee.

'Yours or mine?' the cameraman asked me.

'Oh, mine, I think.'

'Could have been mine, coffee does that to me.'

'Same here,' the lighting chap interjected.

Somebody's stomach was rumbling throughout, though, I can tell you, during all the Polaroid tests and the changes of positioning. And consequently, the end result was four shots to choose from for publication of a happy, laughing, relaxed me, as we tried to decide whose insides were misbehaving at any one time.

'What are we going to do this afternoon?' I asked Fran after the shoot was wrapped up and the crew of two had gone, and we were sitting at the kitchen table eating yummie American-type sandwiches that she had made for our lunch.

'You must take a nap, and then, I seem to remember, you have the wig man coming over,' she said.

'He's not due till six, and you must go to the office,' I answered, not hiding my devious thoughts well enough. 'We can't afford to let the business suffer.'

'The business isn't going to suffer, Cathy,' she said. 'I'm on the case.'

'I know,' I whinged. 'But I'm not, and it unnerves me.'

'Do not be unnerved, my dear,' she answered pedantically, hiding her head behind the morning paper. 'You just concentrate on getting well.'

'After my rest I would like to go out for a drive,' I persisted. 'We could call in to the workplace just for ten minutes. No more, I promise, and I'll sit down and keep my hands in my pockets.'

'No way,' she answered.

It was almost four o'clock by the time we arrived at the back door of the premises, me having been slow to get my act together post nap, and Fran having fought our way gamely but slowly through the heavy Friday afternoon traffic.

'I want it on record that I do not approve of this, Cathy,' she said.

'I'll record it, I promise,' I replied, trying not to let my excitement show at seeing my workrooms again.

Of course, nothing had changed, everything was chaotically running smoothly as usual.

**Philippa Todd**

I had trouble keeping my promise of remaining uninvolved, and longed to answer telephones, interfere with the cutting of a couture robe, and move a few pins around on a newly tacked outfit on a dressmaker's dummy.

But at least I was able to say hello to everyone, let them know I was still their boss, alive and kicking, here to stay, so to speak.

We arrived back home as Vin was ringing the doorbell, looking attractively guilty because he was twenty minutes late.

I eased his guilt with a glass of champagne; can you believe I received twenty-two bottles of champagne as presents, including a whole case from a millionaire client, and I hope that I won't get too used to drinking the stuff.

But honestly, when I saw the prototype of what was laughingly called a wig, I was pleased to be the tiniest bit tiddly.

'Remember,' Vin said deliberately, as a precursor to trouble when he prepared to lift the lid on the box, 'this is only to see how you feel wearing false hair and to establish that the colour is correct.'

He was wise to have spoken such words, because when the object emerged, if he had not been holding it between thumb and finger, I would have sworn that it was a grizzly bear cub looking for its mother.

'Vin,' I screeched from the chair in front of my dressing-table mirror. 'I wouldn't wear that thing if the Pope himself ordained it.'

'Of course you wouldn't, dear,' he replied, placing it on my unsuspecting head and standing back to admire his handiwork.

'Oh, my God,' Fran said from the doorway as she appeared, thankfully, with champagne bottle in hand, her controlled expression showing that she knew if she laughed she did so at her peril. Though I was pleased to note that I wasn't the only one to find the apparition pretty frightening.

I tore it from my head. 'I want a sweet tiny little wig that looks real, not a thumping great guardsman's bearskin,' I said to Vin, as Fran silently refilled my glass. 'Did you bring some scissors with you?'

'Well, yes. Why?' he answered. 'You can't cut it down.'

He looked helplessly across at Fran who wisely fixed her gaze elsewhere.

I stared at him. 'Don't tell me that I can't cut it down. How else will you know what it is I want?'

'Well, I'll have to ring the boss.'

I jumped up truculently and bundled the wig back into its nest. Then I grabbed a picture of myself taken by Abi on holiday the previous year, yanked it out of its frame and handed it to Vin.

'That was me with hair. I'll only wear an exact copy of that. Take it back to your workshop with you. I'm sorry, Vin.'

I knew that I was getting out of control, and it was all because of a stupid wig that I didn't want. This nonsense had to stop; it was only a bald head, after all. Was I losing my senses?

'Oh, but look, Cathy, how wonderful,' Vin said, camping it up like mad as a defence against my anguish. 'The colour at least is perfect.'

Next morning, Saturday, Scott and I lay in bed till gone eleven. Well, that is, apart from Scott making a few sorties down the stairs for coffee and juice for me, tea for him, the morning paper, the mail and then the toast, which he'd forgotten to make in time for the first trip.

He read to me from the newspaper while I buttered and honeyed our toast and fed him from my plate.

'I'd like to do some shopping today,' I said.

He put down the paper. 'Are you trying to get me extradited? Agreeing to a thing like that is a hanging offence.'

'Oh, please,' I begged. 'No one will know, just half an hour in Harrods. I've made a list.'

He leaned over and kissed me. 'Not a word to anyone then, and only if there's something for me on that list.'

I threw my arms around his neck. 'My lips are sealed and you are top of the list, I promise. You'll just have to wander off while I'm buying it.'

'What's the it?'

'Not telling.'

'Then you'd better remove those arms,' he said. 'I'm starting to remember something else I would rather do.'

My knees felt weak, my face was pale and I trembled slightly. The shopping had indeed taken its toll. Scott became alarmed as

**Philippa Todd**

I lay on the sofa without so much as changing my clothes, and he insisted on telephoning Richard for advice.

I let him do whatever he wanted without interfering, smiled at the thought of the outcome, and wished that I could have listened in to the conversation.

'He's coming round,' Scott said, having made the call from the kitchen.

'Whatever for?' I asked, slightly startled.

'He asked me if I'd like him to, and I said sure,' was his short answer.

That was a bore. Now I would have to change and Scott would have to open a bottle of wine. Still and all, it could make for an interesting evening.

Fortunately, by the time Richard rang the bell, and the men met at the door, I felt much better. I imagined them shaking hands firmly while sizing each other up, mentally circling one another as in the jungle.

Richard felt my pulse and declared it too rapid; Scott brought in the wine bottle and the glasses. Richard said that I was foolish to have gone shopping on my third day home and Scott lied and said that it was all his fault, which it wasn't.

Richard mellowed with the wine and didn't show any signs of moving. I declared that I was starving and Scott decided to go out and buy Chinese food.

'Nice chap,' Richard said when he was gone. 'Is he here for long?'

'Only two more days,' I said sadly.

'But you won't be on your own afterwards?'

'No, only in the daytime,' I replied. 'I think that Abi is coming round to sleep, and I'm sure that Fran will look in on me if I need her.'

'You know that you can always call on me,' he said. 'I could sleep in your guest room.'

'Thank you,' I answered non-committally.

'I might like to ask you out to lunch one day,' he said. 'D'you think he'd mind?'

'Who? Scott? I'm sure that he wouldn't; why don't you ask him?'

'Wednesday then?'

# Whispers On A Pillow

'I would like that very much, I've really missed going out.'

I heard the key in the door, and knew that dinner had thankfully arrived.

Scott and I were deprived of talking about our pending vacation, which was only four weeks away, as we had planned to do, by Richard's visit. Scott had organized the trip down to the last detail, and intended to give me a full rundown.

So we talked about it later, atlas between us, in bed. Truth to tell, I was happy to leave the finer points to Scott and to enjoy the surprise when the time came.

I must have fallen asleep while he was still talking, because when I awoke we were wrapped around each other and Scott was breathing deeply. For me, there was something magical about waking in the middle of the night to find him beside me that way, our legs entwined and my head on his chest.

He moved, and said my name as though in his sleep. I leaned over and kissed his lips, he moaned, and I felt a stirring in his groin.

I slowly ran my hand over him, and touched him with light feathery strokes.

'Cathy,' he said huskily.

I eased myself over him and he held me against him closely. I took him into me, and his warm hands slid down and began to do the most wonderful things to me . . .

After love-making we were too aware of each other for sleep; and besides, there was something I wanted to say to him. He was exchanging contracts on Monday on the new apartment.

'You haven't told me yet if you'll come and live with me beside the river, Cathy,' he said, as though once more he was reading my mind.

I hesitated.

'But only if you truly want to,' he added. 'And if you want a commitment, I would like to marry you, you know that.'

I sighed. 'It isn't that. It's the dog. Supposing she were unhappy cooped up in a flat? At least here she has a tiny garden, even if it doesn't compare to the park.'

He leaned over and kissed me. 'Does that mean she has to give her approval for you to marry me?'

I took his hand and kissed his fingers. 'Of course not, silly. And

235

**Philippa Todd**

I haven't said that I won't marry you one day. But I'm not ready yet; my track record at marriage, as you know, is not good.'

He was silent. It was time to say what I wanted to say.

'A thought occurred to me when I was in hospital. If I come to live with you, maybe I could sell this house and buy a weekend cottage in the country.'

He threw back his head and laughed. 'A country cottage for a dog. That's rich.'

'Not for the dog, for us. But she would like it too. Wouldn't you like that? When I first met you I remember you said that you longed to have an English country cottage.'

He stroked my head with his warm hand. 'I'll be darned if you don't have a memory like an elephant. But yes, you're right, it makes a lot of sense.'

I leaned towards him. 'But only if you're going to be here to share both flat and cottage with me.'

'I intend to be here much more, as I told you,' he said in answer. 'If I fail to make that happen I shall retire and start my own worldwide consultancy. Then I'll keep the house in Washington for when we visit together, or for when I need to be there on business.'

We hugged, we kissed in sheer excitement at the thought of being able to spend more time together. For me it was the dawning of a new future. It had been proved to me during my illness that my business was established enough for me not to feel that I had to hold the reins on a daily basis.

Like it or not, it could exist without me being there all the time; and now that I had Scott, I was beginning to like the idea of being able to take more time off.

But the thrill of it all meant that we were now wide awake.

Scott volunteered to go down and make some tea. I turned on the TV while I waited for his return.

There was a 1930s American gangster film on Channel Four. I watched mindlessly for a few minutes, then I switched channels to BBC1, just in time to catch the end of a special news bulletin.

The princess's companion for a weekend in Paris was dead, the newscaster said, and she was injured and in hospital.

I felt sure that someone must have fired a gun at them, and was at least relieved that our lovely princess had not been killed.

On Scott's return we sipped our tea and remained glued to the television set to await a further newsflash.

There had been a car crash, we learned. The driver of the vehicle and the princess's companion were dead; the princess and the bodyguard were alive and had been taken to hospital.

I went to sleep relieved and left Scott to see the end of the gangster movie.

It was only eight thirty, it was Sunday, and the telephone was ringing. I snatched it up before it disturbed Scott.

It was Abigail, and she seemed to be crying. 'I have some terrible news you have to be told about,' she said.

My heart lurched. It must be something to do with the family.

Then I remembered. 'Yes, it's sad,' I said. 'That poor girl never seems to have real joy with a man. But thank heaven she'll be all right—'

'Mum,' Abi said. 'She's dead.'

'No, darling. You're wrong. You mustn't upset yourself like this.'

'You're not hearing me,' Abi said, more loudly, frustration at my lack of reaction making her agitated. 'She's died from her injuries. Turn your TV set on.'

Like everyone else around the world, I grieved. Like everyone who knew her personally, I was distraught.

Scott tried every means he knew to console me. God knows, I didn't wish to be a problem, and maybe it was because I was not properly well, but I felt totally unable to control my emotions. If he tried to turn the television set off, I accused him of not caring. If he spoke, I truly did not listen to the words he had uttered.

In desperation, though I didn't know it, he telephoned the hospital and spoke to Mavis Cartwright. She was about to come off duty, and within forty minutes she was bustling through the front door, bearing several bunches of flowers.

'Those are for you,' she said, after kissing me, and handing over a bunch of spray carnations. 'These lilies are for the princess. I suggest you go and leave them outside Kensington Palace; it will be good therapy for you. Oh, and this posy is from Daniel. For you, with his love, he said I was to tell you.'

237

She took my temperature, which was normal. She felt my pulse, which was rapid.

'My head itches like mad,' I said to her through my tears. 'I could tear my scalp apart.'

'No wonder, Cathy, the way you are getting so upset. You must try to get a grip on things. And your scalp will start to itch for a short time now, it's the new hair breaking the surface.'

I felt, from the look on her face, that she was making it up. But no matter; she cared. I truly broke down then, and cried on her shoulder.

She glanced up at Scott as he stood in the middle of the room, looking helpless.

'I've never seen such a decline in the wellbeing of hospital patients since this death,' she said. 'I simply would not have believed it. Cathy will be fine now though, won't you dear?'

Next day I insisted on going to the workplace. A few clients who knew full well that they would be invited to the funeral whenever it was held tried to cajole us into making them something new in black.

Apart from the very important clients who really sounded desperate, we had to refuse. The staff were beside themselves with grief, and I simply couldn't face getting extra trade from such a tragedy.

By Tuesday the funeral date was given.

Scott had had to leave me again and Fran took me to look over his apartment. I know I'd seen it before, but what a heavenly place, situated as it is on the most interesting bend of the Thames, where all the river craft hoot as they pass each other with dignity and assume a waterway bustle all their own.

Scott says that he doesn't think he'll ever be able to tear himself away from the windows.

Fran telephoned a few estate agents for me who handled country cottages to start that ball rolling. She was right, why delay? Life goes on.

On Wednesday I received an invitation to attend the funeral in Westminster Abbey. At first I said that I simply would not be able to go.

But Fran must have contacted Scott and he told me on the

## Whispers On A Pillow

telephone that I must attend. I would never forgive myself if I didn't, he said. He would be back by then, and would drive me to the abbey and pick me up again. I was persuaded that he was right.

On Thursday I tore one of my special cloches apart, and Suzie and I decided that we could copy it in a fine black silk. There was not one milliner in London who could fit in a single extra client, and my head had to be covered for the funeral come what may.

On Friday, the princess's friend of the crushed-up-raspberries-mixed-with-cream wedding dress telephoned to say that she had returned to London for the funeral, and her wedding would be held as planned in three weeks' time, because she knew that it was what the princess would have wanted.

Of course, I was sure that she was right; and I assured her that everything from my end would be perfect, including a tiny outfit in matching material that we had been asked to make for a small bridesmaid.

On Saturday Scott arrived at five in the morning. We made love. I cried. I was so nervous I was up and making tea by seven.

It was a beautiful late summer's day as everyone knows, and somehow that added to the nostalgia and grief.

Scott let me off as near to the entrance to the abbey as was allowed and it took all my self-control and energy to walk the distance, and find my seat. It was a very long journey.

I cannot describe to you how moving that ceremony was inside the abbey to someone seated there in the midst of it. But I've since seen it all on video, and it was equally moving wherever you were.

For me, I lost it when those two boys walked down the aisle with such dignity; and I saw those small fists clenched so tight on the younger one. I tried not to cry, but I lost the battle.

Scott picked me up when it was over and took me for a quiet lunch at a corner table in the Ritz.

It was noble of him; I was not good company.

# FOURTEEN

Fran spent her days with me at home. London was gloomy after the funeral, especially for the first week. We had no new clients. The telephones scarcely rang, and if they did it was usually a client due for a fitting ringing to cancel.

To cheer me up in Scott's absence, Fran drove me into the country several times to view cottages. I'm not allowed to drive, you see, for a year to the day after my operation, and it means that I've lost my independence. I think that the disturbing of my brain during the operation has left me temporarily with even greater feelings of claustrophobia, and this in turn means that I cannot face using the Underground trains without company.

I missed Scott most horribly, and simply could not wait until we could be together again. He telephoned me whenever he could, practically every day; and I loved him more than I ever thought possible.

On his return, we planned to spend two days in Yorkshire visiting my friends and my dog. We had arranged for Sacha to stay on the farm till after my holiday.

I ache to have my family life returned to normality.

It didn't happen quite that way, about the dog, that is.

On our first morning in Yorkshire I awoke with a start to the echo of strange noises coming in through the open window:

sheep baaing, dogs barking in the distance, cows lowing nearby, someone calling across the fields, a horse neighing in answer. It was much noisier than it seemed to be in London.

'Good morning,' Scott murmured from the depths of his pillow. 'Welcome to the sounds of the country.'

'Everything smells so different,' I said in answer.

'You and your nose. What did you expect in the middle of the Yorkshire moors: the smell of exhaust fumes?'

First I kissed him. Then I did what until that morning I had scarcely dared to do: I furtively felt my bald head. I froze. I could feel bristles, stubble, like on a man's face when he needs a shave. Mavis had told me how it would be, and said it would take a time to smooth off, to become soft and downy, the way short hair should be.

'You've tensed up. What's wrong?' Scott asked.

'It's my hair. It's starting to come through.'

'Congratulations.'

'No, it isn't like that. It's bristly. I don't want you to put your hand on it, you'll think you're in bed with a hedgehog.'

'Shucks, girl, you mean I'm not in bed with a hedgehog? There I go, wrong again, as always.'

I went to hit him for fun, but he caught my wrist accurately, even in the gloom caused by the thick, drawn curtains.

We laughed, and we kissed. I told him that I would never sleep with him again if he as much as touched my bristly head, even with one finger, until the slow growth turned silky. He immediately touched it, smothered it in kisses, in fact.

Then we became serious in our intentions, and we made love.

Sacha, of course, became frantic with excitement when she first saw me. But then so did Bouncer, and there was no way of knowing who was leading who on.

It was, however, obvious how much healthier she looked than she ever did in London. Her coat was thick and gleaming from her outdoor life, her eyes shone like stars. And when we played football with the two of them later, it was touching to see how she hung back and let Bouncer chase the ball into goal, even standing aside and encouraging him. I realized then that theirs was a serious love affair.

## Whispers On A Pillow

It wasn't long before Mark and Celia, our hosts, sat me quietly down at the big kitchen table and asked if I would possibly consider letting her live with them indefinitely.

She was so happy, they said, she loved Bouncer, and they feared he might pine if I took her away because he loved her too. And besides, just look how healthy she was . . .

I had the distinct feeling that they had talked to Scott first because he held my hand and fondled it as talks began, in a rare show of public affection.

I felt pretty gutted at the thought of life without her.

'She still sleeps on your old sweater,' Celia said, noticing my inner turmoil. 'And she makes an awful fuss if she mislays it.'

'I have an idea,' Scott said, holding on to my hand tightly. 'It's just a small suggestion. If, when we're ready to leave, she wants to come with us, doesn't want to be left behind, or shows any signs of distress, then we take her back to London and Bouncer must settle down to life without her.

'If the reverse happens, and she's stressed out at leaving Bouncer and doesn't want to get into the car, we could make that the answer to the dilemma.'

'You know that you can come and see her whenever you want to, Cathy,' Mark said. 'And she'd love that as much as we would.'

'No need to worry about the long drive,' Celia said. 'Come on the train, fast as all hell. I'll pick you up at the station.'

'Something to look forward to when I'm not around,' Scott said.

'Ah, yes,' Celia answered him. 'But we'd like to see you too.'

I wanted to run out of the room.

It all made good sense, of course, and I would go along with it. But I found myself childishly hoping that the dog would want to come back to London when the time came for us to leave.

She didn't. Bouncer bounced around. Sacha lay down and watched him avidly, as though to prove to me that she was staying. She even got up at one point and lay down again further away from the car as we packed it, even calling to Bouncer to join her.

To her credit, as I moved towards her to say goodbye she kept her head high and allowed me to give her a huge hug. I whispered

## Philippa Todd

to her that everything was all right, and that I would see her soon. When I kissed her head she wagged her tail and visibly relaxed. She even licked the backs of my hands.

When we had begun our journey and were out of sight of the farm, I cried a bit. She had been my best friend for such a long time, and I loved her so.

But love and passion for your own kind, as with humans, supersedes all else, doesn't it?

The weather on the way home was foul and blinding torrential rain rendered the headlights and windscreen wipers ineffectual. Eventually we decided to pack it in and we checked into a homely looking small country house hotel for the night.

When I was returning to the dining area from our bedroom after once more securing my scarf, which had been slipping, the proprietor's wife was waiting for me outside the door.

She hoped that I wouldn't take offence, she said, but wasn't I the dress designer Catherine Anthony whose picture was in the papers that morning?

I'd not been informed when the article about me was to be published. I was taken by surprise, and the trouble with the Yorkshire moors is, no one delivers the morning papers.

Of course. Scott had signed us in as man and wife and our cover was blown; but what the hell. I mumbled something incoherent in the way of an explanation.

She brushed it aside, and we ended up with her husband opening a bottle of champagne, and the other guests congratulating me. For what? Well, being alive, I reckon.

I telephoned Abigail, who had already seen the paper and had tried unsuccessfully to contact us earlier. Likewise with Fran, who had bought six copies for me, and said she hoped I realized how clever she'd been to make me wear the pearl choker.

It just goes to show what can happen, Scott said, when you make a forced pit stop in blinding rain, and hope that you look like a cosy married couple.

On our fourth sortie we found it, Fran and I, the cottage of my dreams, in the village of Clifton Hampden in Oxfordshire. It was thatched, not too much land, large fireplaces, lavender hedges bordering the footpath.

All it needed was a few coats of paint inside and out and the two bathrooms improved upon. And guess what? There are roses round the front door, and it's called Rose Cottage. I shall put my London house on the market now, before I go on holiday.

Scott has not seen it yet of course; but he suggests I exchange contracts and show it to him when we return from Hawaii. He has so much blind faith in me, that man; it really keeps me humble.

Soon after I returned from Yorkshire my wig was delivered, and the best part was the attractive blue box containing it. Well, it's not so bad really, I suppose. The wig I mean, not the box.

At least it's sleek, short, and shiny; and there's a chance that when I wear it, from a distance, on a dark night and to someone with impaired vision, it could almost look as though I had my own head of hair.

Not that I shall ever wear it; not unless it's to have it peek out coyly from under a hat. Or when I've had too much wine to care.

It really was the most wonderful wedding, and the princess would have loved it.

The guests were unreal in both lineage and looks; and the bride was a dream come true in the outfit that had so pleased her friend; and it made me feel proud to have produced it.

The groom could not keep his adoring eyes off his bride. But then, I think she felt the same way about him; and no wonder, he was one of the most handsome young men I had ever seen. Talk about good looks.

It was the most wonderful Indian summer's day, the only cloud being, for everyone present, the absence of the princess.

I remembered how she had told me that she would arrive early and slip into the second pew on the groom's side of the church, thus ensuring that at least half the congregation would not know that she was there; and no rubber-necking would take place or turning around by the blatantly curious expecting her to slip into a seat at the back seconds before the bride arrived.

It made me sad to think about her. I truly loved that young woman; she was so full of empathy and understanding, wit and quiet wisdom. Still, her beauty would now never fade, her pedestal never crumble beneath her. She'd be an icon for ever.

For what it's worth, I felt that I didn't look too bad that day; no mean feat for a woman with no hair to speak of.

I wore an olive green silk fitted coat over a matching sleeveless dress, designed by myself and made by Suzie. My milliner friend had made me a deep-brimmed squashy hat to match, from under which I peered as mysteriously as I was able. Scott said, though I'm sure not accurately, that no one on earth would have been able to tell that under that hat nestled a hairless head.

Not entirely hairless, I told him in answer. Mavis had been right, the stubble was becoming soft at the ends.

But never mind me, you should have just seen my man. He looked so handsome in his morning coat, his cravat, his top hat; and I could have burst with pride. He looked the epitome of the English gentleman; his forebears would have been as proud of him as I was.

The happy couple had been loaned a stately home in which to have their reception; and Scott spent most of his time studying the art collection, being as he was himself no mean artist and a great appreciator of the Old Masters.

My darling daughter had held out on me. She was one of four chefs who'd been given the joint catering contract, and she hadn't even told her mother until the day of the wedding.

'You'd have planned to dish out my business cards in the church,' she said.

'No, I wouldn't, don't be mean,' I answered. 'Anyway, what are we eating?'

'Not telling. But ask me to make one more batch of lemon tarragon sauce for those poor bloody chickens, and I might tear my clothes off and run screaming through those hallowed halls naked,' she said, with her usual brand of caustic humour.

Probably the nicest thing that happened to me that day was meeting up with Charlotte the Harlot, my old friend from the Shepherd Market days, for the first time in years.

She'd come to me now and then as a client, though not too often. Mainly because she didn't care much how she looked since she'd put on weight. So imagine my delight when I saw her looking slim, attractive and extremely happy.

'It's the sex I'm getting, darling,' she said to me, causing Scott to turn to look at yet another Old Master. 'I have the most wonderful young stud as a lover.'

Boy, was I ever grateful to Van Dyke, or whoever it was who'd painted the particular nobleman hanging in the spotlight whom Scott had found so intriguing.

'We're at it night and day. It's sheer heaven,' Charlotte expounded.

'Just like old times, dear,' I answered.

She sighed, nostalgically, and pressed my arm intimately. 'God, you're right. Remember what I was like in those days?'

'As though it were yesterday,' I replied as I beckoned to Scott to come back and claim me.

'Incidentally,' she said, as he came towards us, 'I must come and see you. I need some new clothes for when I take the stud to the West Indies in March.'

'Love to help. Come and have lunch,' I answered.

'Have you seen my husband anywhere?' she asked, looking around. 'He's the horse-faced one with the florid complexion and the vanished waistline.'

I looked around too. 'But he used to be so handsome, surely?'

'Darling,' she retorted. 'Are you sure they put your brain back after that operation? He's simply dreadful. If he wasn't so fucking rich I'd leave him.'

Scott came through from the flight deck where he had been talking to the captain. He looked so attractive with his prematurely greying temples and his Pacific tan, and I wanted only to feast my eyes on him.

He slipped into his seat and leaned over to kiss me. 'It's a real pleasure for me to see you looking so well, Cathy.'

I smiled at him. 'I like it too. And you don't look so bad yourself.'

We were returning to London from the Hawaiian Islands, after what was, for me, the holiday of a lifetime, and truly one that I would never forget.

I had snapshots scattered around on my seat table, every one of them a memory of happiness. There was Scott sitting on a rock, Scott astride the Harley motorcycle he had rented in Lahaina to take me on an island tour; me in a sarong sitting by a rock pool, another of me in flippers and mask pushed up on my head, coming out of a lagoon. Then the two of us sitting together on the beach when he'd finally got the hang of the delayed-action shot, and no one could have looked more surprised than we did.

'Some of those are for the trash can,' Scott said laughingly, looking over my shoulder.

'No way,' I answered. 'I shall treasure every single one of them.'

He tried to reach over. 'No, please, Cathy, trash that one of me sitting on a stupid rock. I look ugly and gross, and so does the rock.'

Never had I looked healthier than in those pictures, I thought; and never had my skin been more radiant or tanned. I would be the envy of everyone; except maybe, that is, of those lucky creatures with thick long shining tresses.

On quiet beaches and in remote areas Scott had persuaded me to uncover my head and to let the air and the sun get to it. The sun bleached the thin fine hair coming through and my skull soon matched the tan colour of my shining face. It was at least beginning to be bearable; perhaps I was just getting used to it.

On the first leg of the journey going out we had flown to San Francisco specially for me to meet Scott's parents, who had greeted me with warmth and charm, and made me feel instantly at home. It was obvious that they adored their son and were excited to see him, but they shared him graciously with me for two days.

When I questioned him later, Scott told me that his father had taken him aside and asked him what was wrong with my head. Was I terminally ill, he wanted to know? Was Scott merely being heroic? Just how much older than him was I?

At first I felt put out. But then I told myself it was exactly what I would have done if one of my sons had turned up with a female looking like me. I had to keep my feet on the ground, and I couldn't have faulted Mr and Mrs Peters for their unbiased hospitality during my stay.

We motored then, Scott and I, to the Napa Valley, a most

beautiful area where California wine comes from; and we stayed in a lovely small hotel and sampled good wines and ate great food. The weather was perfection, always sunny and warm. I felt like a pig in clover, and slept like a baby in Scott's arms every night.

We flew on then to the Hawaiian island of Maui, where so many wonderful things happened and I saw so much beauty that I have to look at my collection of brochures and pictures to remember it all.

'I simply loved that week we spent in Hana,' I said to Scott as we were settling down for the night in our jumbo jet reclining seats.

He turned his head towards me, a smile on his face. 'I thought that you were sleeping. You specially liked it there, didn't you?'

'Oh, yes,' I replied, thinking of the wildness and the inner peace that I had felt. 'We must go back again, one day.'

'We will. If you'll marry me we'll go back there for our honeymoon,' he said simply.

'I won't need another one,' I said dreamily. 'That one felt like my honeymoon.'

'We'll go back anyway, and to lots of other places too, I promise you,' he said quietly. 'Now go to sleep.'

I closed my eyes to please him, but the vivid colourful pictures of the island of Maui danced before my eyes and my mind was whirling with all our adventures. With his gift for planning, Scott really had made it all so exciting for me.

'Will it be a bumpy flight?' I asked, shaking his arm as I felt a small tremor.

He turned his head towards me sleepily. 'I have it on the captain's good authority that nothing too bad is expected, but you don't need to worry about turbulence, my darling.'

He took my hand into his, kissed it and held on to it. 'I'm a lucky flier, you'll always be safe with me in the air, even when I'm not at the controls.'

Yes, I was sure of it; that was how I'd felt when he chartered a Cessna to fly us to Hana.

I'd been hoping ever since I'd flown in a helicopter with him that one day I would be able to fly in a fixed-wing plane with him at the controls. It had been a great joy for me. I even took a picture, much to his amusement, of him in the cockpit, and then another one after we'd landed of him standing beside the plane. He said that he felt like a real prat.

I really don't know what the family will say when I tell them about my new-found prowess with a camera. They regard me as a camera-wielding idiot, which up until now I have been.

Once on holiday I took thirty-six exposures before asking the man in the camera shop if he would remove the film for me for processing as I was not very clever at it.

He would have, he said, with pleasure, if only I'd fitted a film in the camera to begin with.

We had been able, on vacation, Scott and I, truly to get to know one another; all our little whims, our foibles, and our likes and dislikes had been aired, sometimes to fits of laughter. We lay on a beach one day and merrily made lists.

'You don't like shrimp, do you, Cathy?'

'Only if you peel them for me. And it's shrimps, plural.'

'Not to me it isn't. We say shrimp for plural too. Jesus, you speak a funny language.'

'You don't like liver, do you?' I said.

'Hate it, don't even want to see it on anyone else's plate. I could throw up at the thought.'

'I get your point. And you don't like marmalade, or coffee, or dancing.'

'You don't like hamburgers.'

'I don't mind them if they're not overcooked and don't have buns shrouding them,' I said. 'But I hate all that other garbage that goes with them, ketchup, and onions and stuff. And especially when you have Coca-Cola in a bottle on the side and no glass to pour it into.'

'But that's part of the fun.'

'The yuck part.'

'You sure you're done griping?'

'You Americans, really . . .'

'Let's run down the beach and dash into the sea and dive into the waves, shall we?' he asked, getting ready to leap up and sprint off. It was the way he did things, always in a hurry.

'I hate big waves, they scare me,' I answered.

He leaned over me, placing a handful of sand in a small pile on my navel. 'You know something? We just might be incompatible. Have you thought about that?'

I chased him into the sea after that remark, big waves or no big waves to frighten me.

He had to rescue me when I panicked, though, and wrap me in a towel, and thump my back because I'd swallowed sea water and was choking. And I never did get around to telling him that I'd once nearly drowned in large waves in the Seychelles, caught in a mighty undertow; and the memory of it was not likely ever to fade.

The clouds were so low on our approach into London that the ground could not be seen.

It was raining, and unseasonably cold, the co-pilot announced almost cheerfully. I felt he didn't much care because he was going home to bed.

Never mind the weather, feller, I wanted to retort, just don't be so hearty. It was much too early in the morning to be awake for my liking. Breakfast hadn't appealed to me and I was not in the best of moods.

We circled for half an hour, which made Scott restive, as, with other trans-oceanic aircraft, we waited in holding pattern for permission to land, and the smiles, understandably, began to slip from the faces of weary cabin staff.

Then suddenly, there it was, the city I called home, rain-lashed, miles of traffic on a visible motorway, shining wet roofs on buildings; and all coming up much too fast for my liking.

I grabbed Scott's hand, closed my eyes in case of trouble, and waited for . . . much to my surprise and relief, the most perfect landing one could wish for.

It was cold and draughty in the baggage-claim hall. Scott took me with him to a telephone and hugged me tight to keep me warm in my thin clothes while he made what seemed to be an important call.

'Just a quick call to confirm my return,' he said to me simply, before announcing himself in a series of numbers and passwords which he followed only with a yes or a no.

He replaced the receiver and patted my hatted head. 'Well, at least we have the rest of the day together.'

'Meaning?' I asked.

'There's a mission on tomorrow,' he said calmly, as we collected two empty luggage carts.

'You should have told me. I didn't know you had to work,' I answered, trying to keep up with his fast pace while feeling uncommonly low after such a long journey.

And truth to tell, I'd successfully wiped from my mind what he'd confidentially told me about his next mission because it sounded particularly dangerous.

'Darling, you did know, I told you,' he answered patiently, but in a tone that told me he had already leaped into work mode. 'Now let's hunt our bags down, shall we, and say no more about it.'

I had risen at six to see Scott off at the door.

All physical signs of our vacation had disappeared, cases had been unpacked and put out of sight, pressing, dry-cleaning and laundry had been collected.

A new day had dawned. I was energized, relaxed, tanned, and relatively happy.

Scott had talked to me long into the night, in our own bed, and begged me, for his sake, not to live in fear of what he did for a living.

'I'm sorry,' I said. 'It's because I've been ill, I think. But I'm better now, and I'll be sensible.'

I gathered my thoughts as we kissed goodbye at the open door. He was right, he needed a clear conscience and an uncluttered head, and if I was to be his partner it was important that I provided a calm life for him.

I put my arms around his waist. 'I'll get back to work tomorrow,' I said. 'Get stuck in and take up the threads again. You'll be proud of how supportive and sensible I'll be, you wait and see.'

'Good girl, I love you,' he said, and kissed me. 'But don't try to do too much.'

'I won't. I promise.'

* * *

## Whispers On A Pillow

I gave tiny touristy presents from Hawaii to the girls in the workplace, and a genuine fine lawn sarong to Fran.

'You look incredibly healthy, Cathy,' she said. 'As for that tan, I'm just so jealous. And I can tell from your face that you're still in love.'

More than she could even believe, I told her, more even than I could find the words to explain.

'That's just what he says,' she quipped. 'You two really are something.'

'So tell me what's cooking,' I asked as we sat in my office sipping coffee and munching croissants.

'A lot,' she said. 'But when do you have your final check-up? I would like to be reassured that you're up to life as it used to be lived before the dreaded tumour got you.'

'Tomorrow,' I replied, 'or maybe the day after. And then, dear girl, I'll be in charge of my own life.' I smiled sweetly. 'So tell me all now, and don't shimmy around.'

'Okay, boss,' she said. 'But Scott says I'm to keep an eye on you and not let you overdo things; so that's what I'll be doing.'

'He's gone on a mission today that I don't like the sound of. He will be all right, won't he?' I blurted out, as though she would know the answer.

She looked at me unblinkingly. 'I'm sure that he will be fine; he's the most sensible man I've ever known. Try not to let your worry show, Cathy, or it could rub off on him.'

'I do try not to, I know that it's wrong of me. So spill the beans, let's hear all the news about my business.'

There were reams of it. Business was booming again, the final months of the year were shaping up to be fantastic. We had a slot in the prêt-à-porter spring shows in Paris and Milan as well as in London. The haute couture side was going to be as much as we could handle, with three spring weddings and a semi-royal christening in May to cater for.

I of course noticed that she had removed the pages from my loose-leaf diary that had included the princess's next year's engagements that we were involved in.

But she need not have been so careful, I could remember most of the commissions. There was the opening of a new public

## Philippa Todd

library in the East End of London for which she'd ordered a suit, a charity ball in Washington for which she needed a dress for a breakfast meeting the following morning. A cruise on an American billionaire's yacht with her children, more sundresses. And for two more visits to Third World countries to bring home the perils of anti-personnel land-mines, she'd requested two pairs of my special stretch pants.

'One more thing,' Fran said, 'and it's a bit of an honour, in my opinion.'

I waited while she sat there smiling. 'Okay, tell me; enough of the silent treatment.'

'You've been asked to present one of the prizes for the *Interiors and Gardens Magazine* designers awards in December.'

'You're kidding?'

'No, I'm not, the editor telephoned me herself.'

'My God, imagine, and I won't have enough hair. Is it an evening do?'

'Yes, Grosvenor House, televised too. And you will still have a tan enough to drive everybody wild, especially if you cheat and top it up once a week in a cubicle.'

'I can wear that red silk dress I wore on launch night,' I said. 'It'll look good with a tan and a matching scarf wound round my head. I'm sure we still have some of that material in stock.'

'And Clive's pearl choker round your neck,' Fran added.

'Thank the good Lord for Clive's pearls,' I said. 'Any other shocks?'

'They want you to say a few words.'

'Oh, my God, it gets worse.'

I spent the evening, apart from waiting anxiously for Scott to return (he'd told me he'd be late), making a list of what furniture would be needed to fill both a cottage and a flat. Most of mine from the house, but not all, would be needed to furnish a two-bedroomed cottage, and rather than part with any, it could go towards filling up the apartment.

Scott likes ultra-modern furniture, and I'd like to change his mind a little. But the main thing is that he should be happy with what he buys.

At ten o'clock he announced his arrival by putting his own key into the front door lock and letting himself in: I had given him his own newly cut set of keys on a silver ring, in a gift box prettily wrapped, as a modest present for taking me to Hawaii.

He looked more exhausted than I had ever seen him, and he was not at all talkative. He was, however, pleased to listen, and I had plenty to tell him.

'Was it a bad day?' I ventured to ask later, when we were in bed.

'Bad enough,' he replied. 'But we'll have cracked it by next week. The trouble is, they know we're getting close.'

I held him tightly to me. 'I'm beginning to wish that you would make the decision to go into consultancy; it would be less hair-raising.'

He relaxed in my arms. 'I promise you I've already made the decision. Now that I've met you I have too much to lose.'

I kissed him. 'Is it an early flight tomorrow?'

'Fairly. I have to pilot a small plane to Hamburg and then I'll go commercial to Washington. You know that I have to be there for a week, don't you?'

'Yes, and you get your medal while you're there.'

He felt for my head in the dark and caressed it. 'This stuff called hair is feeling nice and silky now; you may soon be tying it back.'

'I should live that long,' I said. 'Are you getting excited about receiving your medal?'

'Well, yes, just a little.'

'You said you would tell me what it was you did to deserve it.'

He stroked my shoulder. 'And I will one day, I promise. Tonight I'm much too tired for blowing my own trumpet. Goodnight, my darling.'

'Goodnight, Mr Scott.'

He had a restless night, twitched, tossed around and said unintelligible things.

I was surprised next morning to find him dressed in dark suit and tasteful tie. 'You look more like a businessman than a chap about to fly a plane,' I said, as I brushed a speck of dust from his shoulder.

'I'll be a businessman in Hamburg for a few hours,' was all that he said in answer.

\* \* \*

**Philippa Todd**

Three nice couples came to look over my house in answer to the agent's adverts, and I'm about to receive a firm offer from one of them, I'm told. I'm so excited about it all, and I only wish that Scott was here to share it with me.

He telephoned me when his award ceremony was over. 'I'm about to fax the citation for you to read to Fran,' he said. 'I'll bring the medal for you to see when I come back.'

'I'm so proud of you,' was all that I could think to say, and even those few words caught in my throat.

I'd been about to leave my office and find a cab when the fax came through. So instead of going home I raided the office fridge and opened a bottle of champagne. Well, it was better than going to an empty house, with no one there to boast to about the honouring of my Action Man.

'You read it?' I asked Fran, as we settled down in my office.

'No, you must read it first.'

'Oh, look at this,' I said as I took my first sip and held the fax in front of me: '"For distinguishing himself by exemplary meritorious service . . . performance of outstanding duty . . . as Special Operations Mission Pilot-in-Command, Aviation Troop Signals Intelligence Squadron of a special mission unit . . ."'

'Sonofabitch,' Fran said.

I took another sip. 'And listen to this. "His extraordinary performance in support of sensitive . . . something . . . level . . . overseas operations, outstanding . . ." and some more that hasn't come out. We'll have to wait till he brings the original.'

Fran blew her nose rather tellingly. 'Did he tell you if it took place in the Oval Office?' she asked, sounding emotional.

'Yes, it did. A very private ceremony, he said, just the President, and the heads of NSA and the CIA and two generals, no one else.'

She dabbed at her eyes. 'Oh, my God, it's all too much.'

I was half expecting her to stand up, put her hand over her heart and launch out with a rendering of the Star-Spangled Banner.

Luckily, she managed to control herself.

I spent nearly every afternoon in the workplace, and some mornings shopping for the apartment. I'd accepted the offer on my house, and I had to be a jump ahead and have the other place ready in the hope that the contract went through without a hitch.

If the cottage wasn't ready in time that wouldn't matter because the furniture going there could be stored, and we would have another London home ready and waiting for us to move into. Well, almost.

My check-up, too, went through without a hitch. The surgeon and I sat and talked in his consulting-room for twenty minutes about Hawaii before he even mentioned my head or my operation. He made notes, on Hawaii that is, and I promised to send him a brochure about Maui.

'You certainly look well and happy, Catherine,' he said at length. 'No especial problems I presume?'

'No problems, plenty of pressures, but no problems,' I answered.

He raised his eyebrows questioningly.

'We're rushed off our feet in the business, I'm moving house, I've bought a weekend cottage in the country.'

'And you're still in love.' He said it as a statement not a question.

'Very much,' I said. 'We're moving in together.'

'Not marrying?'

'Not at the moment, but I think I may be weakening.'

'Ever asked him how he feels about not having children by you? Does he have any already?'

I felt startled at the directness of the question. 'No, he doesn't have children, and yes, we have discussed it.'

The surgeon remained silent, watching my face, waiting for me to continue.

'I think he's seen too much, it's given him a jaundiced view of the world. The future scares him. He said that to bring children into it, you must face up to doing so for your own pleasure . . .'

We were walking, arm in arm, in the Welsh hillside when I found the courage to bring up the subject again.

'I still think that you should be thinking of marrying someone who can give you children,' I blurted out. 'Technically I could probably get pregnant again, as I've told you, which is why I'm still on the pill. But I wouldn't be able to deal with it.'

He'd turned me towards him on the narrow path, and, looking down into my face, told me, again, his feelings.

I felt that it threw light on his preference for older women; it did away with the conflict. I told him so.

He smiled, slowly. 'You could be right. But I don't have a problem with it.'

'Having children is so fulfilling,' I persisted.

'There are enough children in my extended family around the world for me to indulge. And before we know it your children will be producing sprats. I can thoroughly ruin them, buy them too many presents, feed them up on forbidden candy. Don't you worry about it any more. I'm comfortable with my decision. It has nothing to do with wanting to marry you.'

He kissed me, then took my arm again, and we walked on . . .

The surgeon pushed back his chair, stood up, held an arm out towards me. 'Well, that's all right then. Let's take a look at you on the couch, shall we?'

I met Richard for lunch afterwards. He couldn't believe how well I looked, he said.

'And happy too, Cathy,' he added when we were seated in the restaurant. 'Being in love suits you.'

I smiled at him. 'Yes, I think it does too.'

Because he was such a true friend I told him about Scott being awarded the Legion of Merit. He listened smilingly to my enthusiasm, then he placed his hand on mine.

'That's wonderful, Cathy,' he said, 'and it doesn't surprise me. I've decided that he's a rather special person, and I can see how you came to fall in love with him. I hope you have a long and happy life together.'

Most evenings when the salon was closed I went to the new apartment. Twice Fran joined me and helped me to unpack the boxes of items that had been delivered from the stores: cutlery, china, kitchenwear, bed-linen. It was all so exciting, and there were moments when I felt like a young bride delving into her hope-chest.

It was early on a very wet morning when he came back to me.

But I was waiting for him, and the sound of his key turning in the lock sent me into a welter of joy.

Hardly had he set down his bag and an extra case before I flew into his arms, to be lifted up, spun around, kissed and set down again. My man had returned, the longest week in living memory was over.

'I've missed you,' he said, as he led me to the stairs.

'And I've been longing for you to come back,' I added, turning to kiss him.

At the top of the stairs he stopped, placed his hands over my shoulders and whispered into my ear, 'I've been longing for you too. Come to the bath with me, I don't want to be away from you for a second.'

I made him move forward along the bath. I settled down behind him, and the water rose to within an inch of the rim.

I entwined my legs around him and quietly lay back. He lay against me, his head beside my chin, my arms embracing his chest. We were silent, neither of us spoke; words would have broken the spell.

Our love-making that followed was somehow different from usual. Silence rather than sighs engulfed us. The magic, however, was still intense. We coupled, it seemed, with a compelling desire to own each other's bodies, torn between wishing to prolong the act for ever while intent on an urgent journey.

Scott, when he climaxed, did so, I thought, with a wish to leave the very core of his life within me.

Later, he said to me, 'Did you notice that I brought my guitar with me this time?'

'Yes, I'm glad you have. I'm longing to hear you play it.'

'I shall leave it with you. Maybe tonight you'll let me serenade you.'

'I'll insist on it,' I answered. 'Fran says you play a mean guitar. It's always bugged me that she knew something about you I didn't know.'

We went to the apartment, and for me it was worth every moment of the work I'd put into it just to see the pleasure on Scott's face.

We stood in the drizzle on the terrace, and through the mist

## Philippa Todd

watched the river traffic cautiously ploughing its way through the murky waters, and the urban seagulls swooping hopefully and keeping pace with the boats and barges. One landed on our low terrace wall, eyed us with distaste and flew off again.

I'd waited for Scott to arrive to help me choose our bed, and having seriously discussed the joys and the doubts of the size and type of bed we preferred, we finally settled on a seven-foot, deep-mattressed beauty.

'I'll never find you in that,' Scott said.

I rubbed my hand along his back. 'Don't worry, I'll find you,' I whispered.

We decided, for dinner, to go down south-west in casual jeans and sweaters to eat a simple Italian meal.

The night traffic moved slowly on account of the weather. Scott drove and I huddled into my leather jacket in the passenger seat. Halfway there he said suddenly, while executing an illegal U-turn, 'We'll have to go back, I've forgotten my wallet.'

There was nothing I could do; I had not brought any money with me.

The parking space we had vacated outside my house had been filled. I noticed two men at my door as we cruised by slowly, apparently ringing the bell.

Scott saw them too and stopped in the middle of the road, pulled on the handbrake, and told me in a controlled voice not to get out of the car. Then, with unbelievable speed, he was out of the door, across the pavement, up the five steps leading to the front door and instantly embroiled in unarmed combat. One of the men went down like a rag doll after he was hit with Scott's flattened palm on the side of the head, and ended up at the foot of the steps, while the other pulled from somewhere a short-bladed knife.

It took me till then to realize that the men were trying to break in and were not ringing my doorbell as I'd thought, and I was out of the car as quickly as I could, my shoes slipping on the wet road as I hurried over to help.

I heard the sound of the knife hitting the pavement. Scott must have either grappled it or kicked it from the assailant's grasp. Seeing that the first man was stirring and stretching out his arm

## Whispers On A Pillow

towards the knife I quickly grabbed it and stood on his arm. Or rather I tried to stand on his arm but he was already getting to his knees as his companion, avoiding the karate blow that Scott was aiming to his neck, dashed down the steps and pulled the other man up by the shoulders.

'Move away, Cathy,' Scott shouted, and I jumped back.

'Come on, run,' I heard a voice say as they made off through the rain, the one who'd been felled limping and holding the side of his head.

Scott unlocked the door while watching them go, then he pushed me inside and followed.

'Put the bolts on, they might come back,' I said with a definite tremor in my unsteady voice.

'They won't come back,' he said quietly, pulling the bolts across anyway.

'We must call the police,' I said, going towards the sitting-room, or maybe the kitchen; I didn't quite know where.

Scott followed me. 'Why, Cathy?' he asked.

I turned to face him. 'Because they were trying to rob me, they were breaking into my house.'

He pushed back his hair. 'And now they've gone. They were in dark clothes, they had dark hair, it's a dark night, could you possibly give an accurate account of them? I couldn't, and I was nearer to them than you were.'

'But they had a knife,' I said.

'What knife?'

It was still in my palm, I realized and I held it out towards him.

'Oh, that,' he said vaguely, folding the small blade into the handle and putting it in his pocket. 'Believe me, darling, nothing can be gained by calling the police, and they'll mess us around all night long.'

'But they may be the same criminals who tried to break into my salon last year. They may think that I have money, or valuables, or something. I'm frightened, Scott.'

He came close, placed his arms on my shoulders and said, 'I can understand you being concerned, my love, but they're not the same men.'

'How do you know?'

He stroked my face. 'I know.'

'I don't feel like going out now,' I said as a way of letting him know that I did not intend to push the point, even though his facial expression seemed different, and, despite his tan, I would swear he looked paler.

'Neither do I,' he replied. 'I'll make us scrambled eggs and bacon.'

'No,' I said quickly, moving towards the kitchen, 'you do the bacon, I'll cook the eggs. Your scrambled egg tastes like chopped-up bits of rubber.'

'Flatterer,' he replied. 'But first, I must make a quick phone call.'

He made for the stairs. 'Why not use the sitting-room telephone and sit comfortably?' I said to his back.

He hesitated. 'No, better I use my own mobile, I think,' he answered.

Again, I didn't push the point.

Later, we watched TV in bed; there wasn't much hope of us sleeping.

We lay there on raised pillows, holding hands, staring at a film on the screen on which neither of us was concentrating.

Eventually, without speaking much, we put out the lights. Scott took me into the crook of his arm for my favourite position with my head buried in his chest. He stroked the arm I'd spread across him, and kissed the top of my head.

'I owe it to you, Cathy,' he said in a low voice, 'to tell you that I think those men were looking for me. I'm only telling you this because I don't want you to be frightened, and for your own peace of mind when I'm not here to protect you.'

'But why?' I asked, lifting my head and feeling my heart begin to beat faster.

'Just my job; we're getting close to a bust. But I'll be okay, it'll soon be over. Please don't mention anything to anyone, not even Fran.'

I sat up in the dark, and took a deeper breath as he pulled me gently down again. 'Let's just whisper, shall we,' he said tenderly. 'Besides, I like to have you pressed against me.'

I placed my head close to his. 'When you go, the day after tomorrow, how long will you be gone?'

He thought for a moment. 'Difficult to say; three days, four at the most.'

'I wish I had the dog for company.'

He kissed my head. 'I'll be back in no time.'

'If the bed's delivered in time I may sleep at the apartment,' I said.

He placed his warm hand on my head, stroking my ear with his thumb. 'If that's what you want, but I honestly am certain that you have nothing to worry about.'

'It isn't that,' I whispered. 'I'll feel extra close to you there.'

# FIFTEEN

He was ready to leave; we ran through the plan once more. Unless I received a message to the contrary we would meet at Paddington station at five thirty on Friday afternoon. He would come up from the Underground opposite the large information board and walk across the concourse towards it. I would wait underneath it, as near to centre as possible.

We were going to spend the weekend in the country, near the village where our new country home was to be, so that Scott could see it and we could meet a builder.

We would both be bushed; it made sense to board a train instead of battling through the traffic jams out of central London at that time of day.

The plans were set; if I did not get a further message, that was where he'd find me. I would not board without him. We would catch a later train.

We clung together in the hall, expressing love, exchanging kisses.

'I'll miss you,' I said, averting my eyes from his gaze, not daring to let him see how worried I was.

Then he stroked my face. 'I'll miss you too. And I'll be back safely, you'll see.'

## Philippa Todd

'I know, I'll be waiting,' I answered.

Then he seemed to hesitate; he looked at his watch. 'Cathy...'

'What is it?'

He took my arm, rapidly ushering me towards the kitchen.

He sat me down at the wooden table, dragged a chair out for himself and faced me. I held my breath.

'I have a few moments,' he said, talking fast. 'In the unlikely event of my not returning on time, don't panic. After a reasonable space of time go back to my apartment, and wait. I'm on active service and the agencies have been asked to inform you of any problem or delay, just as they would if you were already my wife.'

There seemed to be a shortage of air in the kitchen. I couldn't breathe properly. I could feel my heart thumping.

'So why are you telling me now, at this moment? You don't have a feeling that you're not coming back, do you?'

He shook his head and held my hands. 'Nothing like that. Sure, it's a big mission, but I'm used to that.'

My eyes were beginning to burn. 'Can I know where you're going if I promise on my honour not to tell a living soul? You know that I would never go back on my word.'

'I know that you wouldn't. I'm going to South Africa.'

I looked searchingly into his face. 'Were you not telling me the truth about starting up in business?' I asked. 'Giving all this up. Was that a cover?'

'No, no, of course it wasn't.'

'You can tell me, Scott. I'd be incapable of falling out of love with you now.'

He pushed back a stray lock of his hair that had fallen forward. 'No, I wasn't lying, believe me, Cathy. I've had enough. We'll talk more about all of that when I get back.'

He stood up, placed a hand on my shoulder.

'I must go now, Cathy. Come to the door with me.'

We went silently down the hall.

I lifted my face to him in the doorway. 'Be safe; take good care.'

He kissed my lips. 'I will. I'm coming back to you, remember that.' He kissed me again. 'I love you, Cathy.'

'I love you, Scott.'

\* \* \*

It was a week to be reckoned with.

I bought our tickets in advance, booked for dinner on the train, found a country-house hotel near the village of Clifton Hampden and made a reservation.

Fran went down with flu.

Freda telephoned to say that her husband had been rushed to hospital with a bleeding ulcer, and she'd need at least two days off work.

My assistant cutter managed to cut the tip off her middle finger and could only work with one hand; which was rather the same as not working at all.

At one point I found myself working a sewing machine in between cutting an important dress for a difficult client, putting the finishing touches to an urgent order, then doing a fitting without an assistant at hand; which didn't matter to me, but was not too impressive for the client.

I was forced to postpone a meeting with the film people because I needed both Fran and Suzie there too.

I had to cancel a dinner date with Richard because I lacked the strength to go out again after working so late.

All in all, if I had not been so worried about Scott, I think that I would have enjoyed the responsibility of being in the driving seat again, so to speak.

Paddington station was crowded with damp, winter-weary, anxious travellers intent on getting to their destinations with a minimum of hassle. Trains were running late, ticket queues were long, and unintelligible announcements crackled and blared above the echoing din of the usual travel-crowd noises.

Half the travellers, it seemed, either stood around with pale anxious faces raised to stare up at the information board, or walked around in a daze causing collisions and chaos on the overpopulated concourse, while the other half rushed around like laden ants, without any apparent direction.

Bags, briefcases and boxes thumped against me as I eased my way to the rendezvous point by the information board where Scott would find me.

I dropped the weighty overnight bag to the ground, pulled my tea-cosy hat further over my ears and turned my head like everyone else around me towards the all-important information board.

The ever-clicking, ever-changing names of destinations and times of departure told me that our train would leave from platform twelve and would be half an hour later than the scheduled time.

I decided to buy a local evening paper and a magazine for the journey, and I transferred, at that point, our tickets from my shoulder-bag to my cavernous raincoat pocket for easy access.

Only two minutes before the scheduled departure time, I glimpsed Scott through the milling crowd as he stepped through the Underground exit. My relief knew no bounds.

He carried nothing and his hands were thrust deep into a black belted raincoat, collar turned up around his ears, that I had not seen before.

Expecting him to move ahead towards the information board, and to me, I ineffectually raised my arm and waved. It was instantly obvious that he would not see me through the crowd of ever-moving travellers and I brought it down to my side again.

For a moment I lost him, and a panic overcame me as I wondered if it had not been him at all, the man who looked like him blending well into the crowd by way of the dark clothes he wore.

Then I glimpsed him again and I knew for certain that it was Scott; and that this time he was turning left and urgently easing his way, moving sideways, using his shoulders, using any method necessary to speed his progress as he went towards the men's lavatories.

From his anxious expression I registered that he knew he was short of time (in fact, he was not but he didn't know that) but needed to pay an urgent visit to the men's room.

I settled down again, my eyes directed unblinkingly on the entrance to the men's facilities to ensure that I did not lose him again when he exited. Then another small panic set in as I wondered if there might be more than one exit.

I was, therefore, taken by surprise when he came out almost immediately, and without a glance in either direction literally fought his way across the concourse to the other male facility on the opposite side of the station. I couldn't believe that the lavatories had been so crowded as to make him leave that rapidly, but there he was, successfully fighting his way through to the other conveniences. I waited anxiously, intent only on ensuring that I didn't lose sight of him because he now had to cross the concourse diagonally to find me, and the crowd was getting thicker.

Time was also moving on, and the information high on the board told me that our train had arrived in the station earlier than previously announced, and was currently being boarded.

He exited again as quickly as he had done previously. He certainly couldn't have had enough time to relieve himself.

I was puzzled and uneasy without quite knowing why, for now, as he came in my direction, he looked around him as he pushed forward, as though he were searching for someone.

And that someone was not me . . .

Events, after that, happened fast. He was not so very far from me and moving positively towards the kiosk. In another moment he'd be taking my arm, picking up our bag, asking if I thought we'd make the train.

And then it happened.

I clearly saw a nondescript-looking man with light brown hair, shorter in stature than Scott, rush up behind him, strike him with something small on the back of his neck and disappear into the crowd.

Scott's hands left his pockets. One grabbed his neck, reflex-fashion, the other, which seemed to be clutching something, moved to his chest.

His head went back as his face distorted in agony, then it came forward again; and it was as though his eyes focused for a second on mine, though I couldn't be sure, before his knees buckled, his shoulders hunched, and he went down.

I screamed his name and fought my way towards him.

People carried on walking, even stepping over him without a glance as he lay, unmoving, in a tight foetal position on the cold damp stone, his hands bunched into fists across his chest.

I pushed complaining travellers out of the way, my shoulder-bag swinging in all directions, my travel bag left where it was. I fought off those who tried to impede my progress and stumbled round others who were in my way as they stopped to turn in the direction I was headed to see what my problem was.

We seemed to arrive at his crumpled form together, the tall unknown man and I. We dropped to our knees at the same time, then we turned and looked at each other.

'He's had a heart attack, help me,' I cried out to him in obvious distress.

He pressed his fingers to Scott's neck above the carotid artery, his face expressionless. Then after a few seconds he turned him on to his back, tore at the belt of the raincoat he was wearing and opened it up.

One limp arm fell to Scott's side, the fist remaining closed.

'We must thump his chest,' I cried out. 'Oh, my God, Scott my darling, please don't die.'

To my horror the man stooping beside me snatched a black leather wallet from the inside pocket of the raincoat, and there, suddenly, in his other hand was a near-identical wallet I recognized as Scott's. He pushed the latter into the same inside pocket from which he'd retrieved the first wallet, then turned to look at me, fleetingly touching my hand.

'I'll see you later,' he said quietly, or something like that, then leaped to his feet, and ran.

A few yards away, as I watched in disbelief, I saw what seemed to be a small computer disc wrapped in plastic slip from the wallet. The man stumbled as it happened, then caught it adroitly as it almost hit the ground, and ran on.

Part of me died at that moment as I faced the fact that the one person who I thought had come to help us, the one and only human being in that God-forsaken station who had seemed to want to help, had run away.

'Stop him,' I screamed.

No one appeared to hear me in that crowded place, no one listened.

I blindly leaned over my man and began to pump his chest the way I had seen it done. Hot, salty tears cascaded down my cheeks.

The arm that lay across Scott's chest was in the way and I took his fist into both my palms and gently moved it to his side.

It was then that I noticed what he'd been holding when he went down.

I prized open his fist and in the centre was a tiny brown box, no more than two inches square, fastened with a single binding of shiny brown parcel tape, on to which a small white paper label had been fixed, and written on it in black ink, in Scott's scrawled handwriting, was the one word: Cathy.

Seeing his writing, seeing my name, made it even more unbearable.

I slipped the box quickly into my pocket and began pumping his chest again. I was sobbing hysterically. Tears from my eyes and mucus from my nose began to drip on to the front of his raincoat.

'Speak to me, Scott, please speak to me,' I heard myself calling out to him as I pumped. 'Oh, God, please don't let him be dead. I'll do anything, anything at all if you'll just not let him be dead . . .'

'Stand back, make room,' I heard a female voice saying with authority. 'I'm a nurse, let me come through.'

I looked up through my tears and saw a rather plain thin woman in coat and rain-hat looking down on me.

She dropped down beside me, and slipped a red rough hand over Scott's heart inside the raincoat and his jacket. I thought she was an angel sent by God.

'He is alive, isn't he?' I sobbed. 'What can we do?'

'Has anyone sent for an ambulance?' she asked, looking all around.

'I don't know,' I said weakly, wiping my top lip with my fingers, wishing that the pain in my aching arms would go away, wishing that Scott would speak to me, open his eyes, anything at all to signal that he was still alive.

The nurse stood up. 'Somebody get an ambulance fast,' she shouted. 'Hey, you over there with the mobile phone, yes you, do us a favour, dial 999, heart attack, it's bad.'

'You've got it,' I heard a young man's voice call back in answer, not wavering in his stride as he punched out the three digits.

'Okay, stop what you're doing,' she said to me. 'Stand up, take your coat off, put it round him.'

While I was doing that she took off her own coat, folded it

carefully and placed it under Scott's head. Then she dropped back down on to her knees, pushing up the sleeves of her yellow cardigan as she did so.

'Okay, what's your name?'

'Cathy.'

'Okay, Cathy, now you kneel at his head, have one hand ready to pinch the end of his nose when I tell you, and open his mouth with the other. Make sure his tongue is in the bottom of his mouth and keep it there with two fingers. When I say "ready" you take a deep breath, pinch his nose shut, and blow into his mouth as long as you can to fill his lungs with air.'

She pumped his chest and on every fifth thump she called out, 'Ready.'

I emptied my lungs into Scott's at every command.

She pumped, I blew, she pumped, I blew, she pumped . . .

At one point, as I emptied my lungs into him I could have sworn that he gave a small sigh. I cried out in thankfulness.

At another, as I blew, the world went black and I keeled over. It was momentary, but as a result my hat fell off. As I straightened up I heard someone say, 'Look, she's bald.'

I looked across at the nurse in desperation, to find her staring at me.

'You'd better take it easy,' she said. 'Besides, he's not responding. And put your hat on before somebody makes off with it.'

First came the wailing of sirens, and then the ambulance and two police cars came on to the concourse.

I didn't want to leave Scott lying where he was, but the paramedics made me. I tried to fight them off, but someone lifted me up, a policeman I think, and placed my bag back on my shoulder.

'You his wife?' somebody else asked.

I was about to answer truthfully that I was not his wife when I remembered something I had once heard Clive say while answering a message from a hospital. 'Send her away,' he'd said down the telephone. 'Wives only allowed in on this sort of emergency.'

'Yes, I'm his wife,' I said, in a low voice.

I was led to the ambulance, helped up the steps, told kindly but forcefully to sit down. I was numb and cold. There were no more tears to shed, my brain had reached cut-off point.

## Whispers On A Pillow

I knew what they were thinking, all of them out there with Scott, uniformed policemen, green-overalled paramedics, the nurse in the yellow cardigan. They thought that he was dead.

I could see them, shaking their heads, getting him on to a stretcher, covering him with a blanket right up over his head to hide his face.

I wanted to tell them that they had no right to remove my raincoat from around him. It would be giving him comfort as well as keeping him warm. He'd smell the familiar aroma of my perfume and he'd know that the woman who loved him was there. And how could he breathe if they covered his face?

If only they'd asked me, I could have told them that he wasn't dead at all. He'd sighed, I swear he'd said my name, whispered that he loved me, asked me to stay with him.

It was the truth . . . it was the truth . . . it was.

I had started to shiver and my teeth were chattering. Someone came up the ambulance steps and brought my raincoat to me. 'Let's put this on, shall we?' he said.

I couldn't fight them, I had no strength left. My knees would barely hold my weight, my voice refused to work, my nose and my ears were blocked. I was as useless as a rag doll, and worst of all, when Scott had needed me most, I'd failed him, hadn't I?

I could have run to him faster, called to him not to rush; it didn't matter if we missed the train; we'd catch the next one. If I'd tried more I could have pumped his chest harder, breathed more air into him, held him in my arms for comfort.

'Mrs Peters,' someone suddenly said, 'you'd best come with us now.'

I looked up. He was holding Scott's wallet in one hand, and holding his other hand out to me to help me along.

'Can I hold that, please?' I asked as I was escorted to a police car.

'Don't see why not,' he said, shielding my view from the stretcher procession as it made its way to the waiting ambulance.

'Why can't I go with . . . my husband?' I asked as the car started up.

**Philippa Todd**

The man beside me said nothing and looked out of the far window.

The man in the front passenger seat turned round and said, 'You can see him later, love, don't worry.'

I recognized the police station: Paddington Green, but why were we going in through the back entrance? I opened my mouth to ask, but closed it again in the certain knowledge that, whatever the reason, I would not be told.

I was shown, with deference, into a back room, a rather large one with a boardroom-type table at one end, several chairs drawn up to it, two small desks against a wall and a group of four armchairs and a low table taking up a corner.

There were several men standing around, talking in small groups, all in suits, rather than uniforms, all turning towards me as I was shown in, my escort backing off without a word and closing the door behind him.

Then there he was, coming towards me, the tall man who'd switched the wallets on the station concourse. His eyes locked on to mine unwaveringly the way Scott's did. 'I'm Spencer,' he said with an American accent.

Was that his first name or his surname? I wondered.

He put his hand into the inside pocket of his jacket and pulled out a white envelope, holding it out towards me.

'This belongs to you, Cathy,' he said simply. 'It was in the wallet.'

I took it from him, and saw my name written on the front in exactly the same way as it was on the tiny box, the one that lay forgotten in my raincoat.

I felt in my pocket and brought it out. 'There was this, too,' I said in a flat voice. 'Scott was holding it in his fist.'

He glanced at it and said, 'Put them both away, Cathy, they belong to you.'

I noticed then that the envelope had not been opened. 'Where is he?' I asked, feeling hot tears forming in my eyes.

'Try not to cry,' he said. 'You do know, don't you, Cathy, that Scott is dead?'

'He might not be. I'm not sure,' I persisted.

He placed a hand on my arm. 'It's official, my dear. I hear he was found to be dead on arrival. I think that I can take you to say goodbye, if that's what you want. He was my friend too, you know.'

I stared into his eyes. 'He was more than a friend to me,' I said. 'We loved each other. We were going to spend the rest of our lives together.'

'I know,' he answered, looking utterly miserable. 'He told me.'

Two other men joined us, the taller one dressed in casual clothes, the other in a shirt with a stiff collar, and a sober conventional tie.

'You're Cathy,' the taller one said in an American-accented voice, not offering to give himself a name. 'We'll be moving Scott back to the States for burial.'

I felt a knot of anger rising up within me. 'I want to know what happened,' I said. 'And his body belongs to me, not to you.'

'What happened?' he echoed, ignoring the rest.

I noticed Scott's friend Spencer take a pace back as I looked at him.

His eyes held mine with a steady severity. Nothing about him moved, his face seemed etched in stone. Yet I knew, somehow, that he was telling me to let it go, leave it alone, try not to get involved.

I'd never been to a mortuary before, and I hope that I won't be called on to do so again. It was a mistake, and I'll never be able to talk about it.

The worst part was when we were leaving and I'd said goodbye. I thrust my hands deep into my pockets because mortuaries are cold. The left pocket contained the little box and the as yet unread letter. The right-hand one held things strange to my touch, cards, paper.

I brought them out to find in my hand two rail tickets and two dinner vouchers for the five forty-five train out of Paddington to Reading and the West Country.

And I remembered, for some reason, that the train left from platform twelve.

Fran let us into the apartment before I had a chance to put the key in the door. Wisely, she didn't try to offer words of comfort, she merely quietly closed the door behind us, nodding her head to Spencer.

'You know, of course,' I said flatly.

'I heard,' she replied. I could see then that she'd been crying.

'I want to be on my own,' I uttered, almost inaudibly. I turned to look at Scott's friend. 'No offence; Fran will give you a drink, won't you, Fran?'

She put out a hand and removed my hat, unbuttoning my raincoat as though she were my mother. 'Okay, but call us if you want us.'

I went to our bedroom, Scott's and mine. The first thing I saw was the guitar in the grey leather case. I'd never heard him play. And now I never would.

I opened the French windows that led out on to a small balcony and went out into the autumn night. The air was damp; I felt chilled from the core of my bones. It was a strange sensation.

There was almost no river traffic that night, just one pleasure steamer moving slowly, on which a party was in progress. I could hear disco music throbbing from the loudspeakers below deck. It seemed to me to be a bad night for a river party, and I hoped that it was warm inside the craft.

Lights on the quay across the water winked in the wind; more music, from a bar this time, carried across to me.

I took the train tickets from my pocket, slowly and methodically tearing them into minute pieces before holding them high and throwing them into the wind.

Back inside, I placed the envelope and the little box on our bed, hung up my raincoat in the closet between Scott's leather jacket and his only remaining dark suit; the one he called his 'serious suit'.

I had trouble removing the sticky tape from around the box and had to enlist the help of my nail scissors. They stuck into the end of my thumb as they slipped and made it bleed. I felt no pain as I licked the blood away.

Eventually the lid came away, and there inside, tightly secured between two layers of cotton wool was a large magnificent oval diamond. It picked up the light from the bedside lamp and played

# Whispers On A Pillow

with the colours in the room as I moved it between my thumb and finger and balanced it in my palm.

Then I slowly opened the envelope. Slowly because I hadn't yet made up my mind if I wanted to read the contents immediately, or savour the mystery till another time.

The latter seemed cowardly, and I hesitatingly began to unfold the paper. It was just one sheet, white, no markings, no address of any kind, no date even. It was merely headed Cape Town, in black ink, in Scott's scrawled handwriting.

'My Darling Cathy,' he wrote, and in my mind I could hear his voice clearly saying the words.

> If I come back safely, and I'm doing my damnedest to make that happen, you will not be reading this, or indeed taking your diamond from its box yourself. That would be for me to do, and then, dearest love, I would place it in your palm, look into your eyes and ask you, very sincerely, to marry me. If you are reading this, therefore, it will be because I am seriously disadvantaged and you will have to design the gold ring and have the diamond set into it yourself. But please do it, and wear it for me. I have fantasized about you wearing my ring on one of your lovely fingers for a long time.
>
> You already know that I love you. You were, and always will be, my soulmate. Don't grieve for me, Cathy, my darling, we knew too much happiness for that.
>
> Stay well, be successful, think of me with love, and remember me as the man who adored you from the moment he set eyes on you.
>
> Scott.

I was crying of course long before I had finished reading.

My heart broke that night. I knew that if I was ever to recover I had to give in to my grief, let it wash over me, plough my way through it.

Was it another test? I asked myself. I hoped not; I hadn't done well with tests. Better that it was a glimpse at a love story too perfect to last, brimming over as it had been with passion and laughter and love.

\* \* \*

**277**

'Do you know what went wrong?' I asked them later, when they crept in to ask if I was all right, and I invited them to sit with me while I showed them my diamond.

'Scott went to South Africa in alias to set up a long-term spying operation. He himself was to come back here with critical information after three days,' Spencer said, sitting down with his hands between his knees, looking down at them. He raised his head and his eyes were full of sadness. 'He'd found a safe house for the operators, everything was set.'

'But why him?' I asked.

'American government money invested in a very large company was being syphoned off for corrupt use. Drugs, terrorism. Infiltration was a dangerous mission.

'The embassy knew that a top agent was coming over. They gave him a house in Constantia and a car and driver while he operated as an important businessman. It seems the driver and Scott recognized each other from a year or so back when Scott was down there using his own name. The man was a weak link. Scott's cover would have been exposed quickly.'

'But he was expecting the mission to be successful. He told me so.'

'He was successful, he'd set up a big team,' Spencer said. 'That's why he had to die.'

My heart ached so much I could barely speak. 'But the railway station. Surely he should have been safe back in England?'

'Scott would have known he was being tailed all the way from SA. And where better to strike than in a crowded station, using a spring-loaded syringe. It isn't that difficult to induce a heart attack.'

I raised my knees, leaned towards him. 'And what about the switching of wallets; you had Scott's wallet.'

Both he and Fran sat very still.

'I was his contact,' Spencer said. 'We had intended to do the switch in the lavatories.'

'So why didn't you?'

'We both knew that the enemy was out there on the concourse. I, as his contact, had to change our plans. I had to try to work out a different way to give Scott his own identity back, and get the computer disc before someone else did.'

My head felt heavy. I rested it between my knees. 'It was awful, Fran,' I said. 'I've never seen someone killed before.'

She came over to me, rubbed my back with her palm. 'He was a brave man, Cathy, the bravest. He'll be missed.'

I lifted my head and looked across the room to where stood an enlarged photograph of him. Only two days previously I'd bought a frame in which to put it.

I'd taken the snap in Maui as he sat on a bench. He was laughing and looking directly at me, his intense blue eyes crinkling at the corners against the sun.

'That's a good one,' I'd said, looking down at the camera. 'It's the last on the roll. Could you change to a new film for me, please?'

I can hear him laughing now. 'It probably won't come out. The last film on the roll often doesn't.'

'Oh, it will,' I'd insisted. 'It's going to be my favourite, I just know.'

'Quite the photographer you're becoming.'

I laughed, just because he was, and his laugh was infectious.

'I loved him,' I said, unable to hold back my tears.

'I know you did,' Fran answered, 'and God knows he felt the same way about you. I think he discovered love in you.'

'He was so right for me. He made me feel . . . well . . . a woman.'

'He told me that he'd never loved another woman the way he loved you,' Spencer said quietly.

'I must give you his medal and the citation. Will you make sure that his parents get them?'

'Of course. I'm flying directly to California to see them personally after the final debriefing tomorrow.'

'Could you get me a copy of the citation?'

'Sure I can.'

'Promise?'

'I promise you, Cathy. It's the least I can do.'

I stared out across the river. 'There'll never be another one for me,' I said.

Fran began to cry.

A lone barge hooted.

**Philippa Todd**

'It was such a brief encounter. I'd hoped it would last for ever.'

'Oh, Cathy . . .'

I looked at her through a mist.

'I'll never forget him. Never. He was my Renaissance man.'